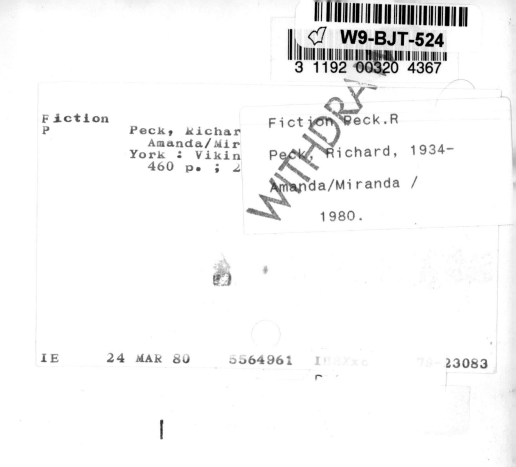

Fiction
P
Peck, Richard
        Amanda/Mir
York : Vikin
    460 p. ; 2

Fiction Peck.R

Peck, Richard, 1934-

Amanda/Miranda /

1980.

IE   24 MAR 80   5564961   I   Xxc   79-23083

MAR 2 0 1980

Amanda/Miranda

Richard Peck

Amanda/ Miranda

The Viking Press / New York

Copyright © Richard Peck, 1980
All rights reserved

First published in 1980 by The Viking Press
625 Madison Avenue, New York, N.Y. 10022
Published simultaneously in Canada by
Penguin Books Canada Limited

Library of Congress Cataloging in Publication Data

Peck, Richard.
Amanda/Miranda.
I. Title.
PZ4.P3672AM[PS3566.E2526]813'.54 79-23083
ISBN 0-670-11530-4

Printed in the United States of America
Set in CRT Compano

Illustration on page 335 reprinted through the courtesy of
Mr. Barrie Roger Davis

Amanda/Miranda

Prologue

―――――∞―――――

The Wisewoman lived in the last soft fold of earth before the sea. Some said her rude cottage was built from the stones of the Ancients. Stones that once lay on Ashey Down in obscene patterns decipherable only by the prehistoric priests.

But the folklore was false. The rough rock walls of the Wisewoman's house had never been the altars for the Druids' ancestors, though they glowed with mystery in the hill twilights, a bruised gray, like drowned flesh.

A century earlier the Wisewoman would surely have burned as a witch, with the local louts wielding the torch. The local gentry, in pursuit of blood sports of their own, would have averted their eyes from the spectacle.

But the new age had dawned, the twentieth century in its infancy, which brought a fugitive breath of change even to the backwaters of the Isle of Wight, where once the old Queen Victoria had been happiest. The small woman who had ruled an empire and populated the royal families of a dozen more was gone. Her aging son had sealed the gates of her royal residence, Osborne House, not ten miles from the Wisewoman's garden gate. And the orderly universe Victoria Regina had shaped and ruled was already slipping into history.

Smoke from the long liners to America blackened the horizon. On clear days their proud prows knifed from Southampton port across The Solent to conquer the ice-strewn Atlantic. The world beyond this craggy corner of the tiny island that clung to the underside of England seemed to stir and rise, sending a faint ripple of anticipation back across the crouching velvet hills.

And thus the Wisewoman was not burned or ducked or hounded from her native neighborhood. She was allowed to live, though not entirely in peace.

She figured in the nightmares of half a hundred small local urchins. And they in hers. By day they dared one another with extravagant taunts to advance on her cottage by elaborate stealth. Like their idols, the Indian braves of remote North America, they crept through the Wisewoman's tangled garden, promising one another that discovery meant death. Often enough she spied them from a crooked window. A dozen urchin faces, like pale cabbages, sprouting down her garden rows.

When they fancied that dusk shrouded them, the bolder ones cast small stones at the Wisewoman's roof, dislodging the lichened slates with a sound like sudden thunder. Distracted by her thoughts, she would hardly have noticed if her cats had not jerked sleepily at the noise, pulled the kinks from their furry shoulders, and resettled on their hearthstones.

Once the urchins' arching stones dislodged a field mouse descending the Wisewoman's flue under the impression that it was a particularly warm and spacious burrow—a rabbit hole, perhaps, that poachers had failed to stop. The horrified rodent fell directly into a pot of soup she had just swung over the fire.

She ladled the creature out with her stirring spoon and flung it to the nearest cat. For the Wisewoman possessed a soul that was all but French in its intense practicality. She refused to regard a suddenly airborne field mouse as either a supernatural sign or the ruination of her supper.

First and last, she was a businesswoman. And the least superstitious inhabitant of the Isle of Wight. She turned a handy profit in the herbs and root mixtures that any cottager might raise in a shady dooryard garden. And she harvested her crops and dug her tubers by moonlight only because her clients expected it of her. One of her infusions of common bugloss and eglantine gall was a passable headache remedy and reducer of fever. She took it herself on occasion. The rest of her prescriptions were less effective, but her reputation augmented their potency.

As an organic pharmacist, the Wisewoman was neither remarkable nor very near the top of her profession. What she could do really well was to foretell the future.

Not her own, for she had no curiosity about the years left to her. But more than once she could foresee in a lovesick lad creeping to her door in desperate need of a love philter the precise moment of his death, be it forty years in his future.

Once a gaggle of young girls no more than children were emboldened to nudge one another up the Wisewoman's flags, intent on having their fortunes told. She received them with more kindness and less mystery than they had anticipated. Instead of being assailed by the fumes of witch's brew, the small girls, still in ragged skirts above their boot tops, were offered tea in thin china cups and settled in a row on a bench. Chastened by this rather stiff hospitality, they went their way in a quarter of an hour, none the wiser about their futures. It was the Wisewoman's plan, for she saw early death clinging to the oldest child and would neither lie to her nor frighten her.

There was, the Wisewoman persuaded herself, no market for this sort of knowledge. Therefore, she never turned a profit from prophecy. The futures of most of her neighbors were as humdrum as their pasts, too predictable to astonish. The wars to be in the twentieth century, flashing on her mind's horizon like sheet lightning, seemed remote even to her.

And her vision of more private moments yet to come were too frequently beclouded by a kind of windswept poetry, vague as organ music distorted by distance. Only once, startled by a stranger at her door, did the Wisewoman break silence and speak in the baffling language of the young woman's future.

One

Rattling down Nansen Hill, the wagon driven by Josiah Cooke grazed a jutting strap of iron railing on Dunnose Bridge. The old plow horse staggered but strained on, over the hump of the bridge and into the easier dust of the roadway. But the rusting pin on the rear wheel was loosened. Twenty paces farther along it fell free. The wheel described a drunken revolution, then abruptly collapsed, shearing off the tip of the axle.

The reins never left Josiah's hands, though he pitched out of his high perch and went sprawling across the horse's broad rump. His wife shrieked once and slipped sideways into a hummock of bright wild flowers. Her decent black bombazine petaled open. Two shapeless legs in much-mended black stockings flailed the air. Mary Cooke, wedged between her parents, slid more slowly to earth. With one quick glimpse of deep blue sky, she joined her mother deep in the wild flowers.

They were a hardy trio, no strangers to adversity. Mrs. Cooke leaped to her feet at once, adjusting her skirts—and Mary's—before she examined her person and her family for broken bones. Josiah untangled himself from the hind legs of the horse and gazed without hope at the wagon, the only possession he owned outright in the world. It sagged half in the ditch.

The only luck of the day was that the accident took place within sight of Old Church tower at Bonchurch. With a minimum of words,

Josiah Cooke trudged off toward the straggling village in search of a wagonman who might spare him a mallet and a linchpin.

Mrs. Cooke settled back against the flowery bank and gave way to her customary laments. There was hardly a hint of autumn in the breeze blowing up the Undercliff from the English Channel. Still, she pulled her snagged shawl almost up to her eyes.

"Stand back from the road where you won't be seen, Mary!" she barked. "Then tuck up your skirts, you simple baggage! How will it look to arrive at your first place grass-stained? Though at this rate we'll never in this world see Nettlecombe this day, and then where will you be, I should only like to know. The fates are against us." With that, she dipped her narrow chin into the shawl and complained bitterly of the damp seeping from the perfectly dry bank.

Mary Cooke gladly withdrew from her mother and strolled back into the field, her skirts held obediently above her shoe tops. Because she never answered back, she did not mention to her mother that even on foot they could reach Nettlecombe an hour before darkness. And then Mary would have the opportunity of exchanging one bondage for another.

She was happy enough to be ordered to stand farther off, though no strangers were passing on the roadway to be inflamed by her beauty. She walked with quickening, silent steps across the billowing cushions of unmown grass until her mother's whining voice was lost in the wind sounds from the Channel. A sudden mischievous gust tugged at Mary's black hair, anchored in the same austere knot that her mother wore and decreed.

Determined to enjoy the silence and the short reprieve, she wandered with her thoughts. Had she dared, she would have unbuttoned her shoes and kicked them aside. Then she might have raced against the wind until she was in sight of the sea.

Mary Cooke had lived all her eighteen years at Whitely Bank, the farmers' hamlet that stands where the roads to Shanklin and Ventnor jog in crossing. Both these rough roads lead finally to the sea, and she had forever felt stirring inside herself the restless turning of its tides. But she had never more than glimpsed the green-gold waves scalloping the beaches of the seaside towns. The boardinghouses there, packed with London trippers, were vulgar. And sea bathing was dangerous and an offense against modesty and God. Her mother had told her so.

It was never the rough carnival atmosphere of Ventnor or Shanklin or Ryde, where the steamboats from Southampton docked, that Mary dreamed of. She had been reared to shun pleasure. It was the restless, rolling sea itself that inundated her dreams, waking or sleeping. Sometimes the waves seemed to beckon her to destruction, sometimes to life. But always faraway. Always.

She wandered on over the fields, savoring the September stillness. For when her mother and father delivered her to Nettlecombe, these drifting moments would surely end.

To fulfill her mother's plan, Mary Cooke was to go into service for the Whitwell family, whose estate stretched from Nettlecombe village as far west as the town that bore their name. Mrs. Cooke had trained Mary for her years—her lifetime—of service as other girls were prepared for their wedding day.

Her earliest memories were of her mother's tireless planning. "Someday," she would say in a voice grown strangely soft, "someday you will serve a great family in a fine house. You will anticipate their every need, for you will be taught to serve before you are hired to do so." Those were the tenderest words Mary ever heard her mother speak, for they lacked the snap of her commands.

And so Mary was taught to serve, if only in the cramped, stone-floored house where Josiah Cooke sheltered his small family. When she was barely tall enough to stand on a chair, she had learned to set a proper table. No matter that the teacloth was laundered to a rag and the bent spoons were pewter with an acrid taste of their own.

Later she could carry a laden tray and open a heavy door with her free hand at an age when other girls were too awkward to cross a threshold without sprawling.

And silence. To speak of the rebellion that often welled and broke in her throat was as unthinkable as flight itself. Mary was taught the necessity of silence. Silence was golden. Golden as the worn band that rode loosely on her mother's finger. The only gold Mary ever expected to see.

There was little silence in the Cooke household, no matter how quiet Josiah and Mary had learned to be. Mrs. Cooke filled the empty evenings with her inexhaustible memories. For she had been in service herself, across the water in Hampshire, before marrying a penniless farmer, a bumpkin, who buried her at Whitely Bank.

She'd been driven from the proud panorama of a great country house where she was trusted everywhere, from drawing room to attic airing cupboard. She took her tea not in servants' hall, but with the governess and the housekeeper themselves. Often enough a *foreign* governess, French or German, who remembered the war of '71 and who knew the world.

She had left the starched rustle of impeccable gray faille for the manure-stained tatters of a farmer's wife. She had left a lady dependent upon her for every one of life's necessities, a lady who called her "my treasure" as she turned back silken sheets.

The single compensation for her fall from this grace was to create in Mary a servant who might nearly rival herself. There was justice in this, Mrs. Cooke was certain. For Mary was the unwanted child whose birth had forced her to leave her lady's house in hasty disgrace. A wound never healed, for was she not imprisoned with that child and its father, the two sources of her shame?

"Never," Mrs. Cooke would say at the end of an evening, half-sleeping beside the only fire, "never turn your back on your betters . . . keep your eyes down . . . speak clearly when they find it necessary to speak to you . . . learn your chimneys, how they draw. A smoking chimney will yellow your lady's complexion, taint the food . . . quality, persons of quality are more sensitive than you can hope to be, my girl . . . learn . . . to respond to a sensitivity that you can never have . . . learn. . . ."

Mary was allowed a little schooling, for her mother knew the value of a well-spoken servant. She feared her daughter might mimic the cloddish accents of her father, although he was rarely given to speak. And so Mary spent four years under the tutelage of an educated spinster who kept school in the chilly rented parlor of the only house in Whitely Bank that took paying guests.

Under an easier tutor than her mother, Mary learned to read, to write a plain, serviceable hand, and to add the figures of a household account. She heard poetry for the first time in her life and was haunted by the spinster's mournful intoning from Coleridge:

> *Alone, alone, all, all alone;*
> *Alone on a wide wide sea!*

And she learned to speak in a tone respectful enough never to echo the fashionably whinnying drawl of the upper classes—the persons of sensitivity and quality, the gods and goddesses whose pantheon she was being shaped to serve.

Kept home not so much to be perfected as to attend her mother, who had belatedly learned the pleasures of being served, Mary was at last placed in a suitable position. The Whitwells of Nettlecombe were to receive a new servant. And whether she was to find her place scouring the roasting pans and sleeping among the poultry or dressing the young lady of that house depended very much on the impression she made at the outset. Even Mrs. Cooke was half-satisfied that Mary would not wholly betray her training.

Overconfident, her mother thought she had driven even the possibility of rebellion from Mary's mind.

As she drifted farther from the broken wagon, Mary seemed to slip free of all her hard-learned lessons. She climbed a stile and started up a fold of earth where the tang of salt air grew sharper, mingling with the delicate scent of a verbena set somewhere in this rolling landscape. She might have appeared to be running away. But of course there was no place to run to, for the circling sea formed a final wall.

She was at the Wisewoman's cottage before she knew the shallow dip in the land was inhabited. The little stone house seemed to rise half out of the earth before her eyes. And as she noticed the door, it opened.

Though strangers were sometimes sent to her, the Wisewoman knew she was not being visited by a client. She knew, of course, much more at the first glimpse of the young girl, whose shapeless brown dress was tucked up above her broken shoes. And she favored her with the sort of formal nod none of her adult clients had ever received from her.

"I meant no harm. I was only passing," Mary stammered from the front gate. But the quiet tones in which she'd been schooled were lost in the singing sea wind.

The Wisewoman nevertheless nodded again and swept her hand back to the open doorway in invitation. Uncertainly Mary advanced up the steppingstones of a dooryard overgrown with purple betony and red chickweed.

"You have lost your way, perhaps," said her hostess politely. Confused by kindness, Mary only stared at the old woman, whose neck was webbed with wrinkles as fine as ivory lace. The very old woman and the very young one found each other beautiful in a wordless moment. "Lost or certain of your course," the Wisewoman said at last, "come and rest yourself. I take only tea at midday, and there is a cup to spare."

She gestured twice before Mary would sit in her presence. And when she finally settled beside the low embers, the cats that had been impersonating hearthstones stirred and examined her with agate eyes. Above, the rafters were festooned with bunches of drying herbs and heather, pale silver and paler lavender. Mary wondered at their uses until the Wisewoman placed a gold-rimmed cup of black tea in her hand.

More like a cool cave than a parlor, the cottage's only room served as the Wisewoman's kitchen and dispensary. When Mary left off staring shyly into her lap, her eyes roamed among the apothecary bottles lining the walls. A hundred curving, murky rooms were reflected in the pale cylinders.

To be received into a drawing room of any sort was beyond Mary's experience. And the only conversations she had ever held were with herself. The Wisewoman divined this and allowed the silence to lengthen while astonishing images of the strange girl's future played in random patterns across her inner eye.

Bested by curiosity at last, Mary asked, "Is this a chemist shop, my lady?"

The question brought the old woman firmly back to earth. She paused a moment, selecting the words to describe her livelihood. "In a manner of speaking. Here there is folk medicine for those who mistrust doctors even more than they mistrust me. Why do you call me 'my lady'?"

Mary went pale with shame. "I—I was taught that it was proper."

"You are a servant?" The Wisewoman was almost amazed, for her visions of the girl's future suggested—even foretold—otherwise.

"By nightfall I shall be," Mary said softly. "At Nettlecombe, for the Whitwells."

"A servant speaks as you have done only where she is employed. You are not servant to all the world."

The idea was strange to Mary, nearly meaningless. But she saw it was meant kindly.

"And you will serve the Whitwells until you marry?"

"I—I think I shall never marry, for my mother said—"

"Oh, yes! You shall marry twice," said the Wisewoman emphatically. She had been startled into the truth she'd foreseen in the first moments. She sat back suddenly in her wooden chair, shocked by her rare indiscretion.

Mary might have thought the old woman crazed by loneliness or by the strange potions in the jars that ringed the room. But she only thought her mistaken, even though the woman's limitless knowledge hung heavily about them in that place.

"I can divine the future," the woman explained, "though it is an uncertain gift, perhaps useless. I take no credit for it, nor any pay." She dismissed her talents with an idle gesture.

"And can you see more?" asked Mary, meeting the woman's steady gaze, though it cost her an effort. "More about my future?"

After a silence an answer of sorts came. "I am addled by it— and by you. Your future lies farther off than Nettlecombe. A great deal farther off. It lies beyond a mountain of ice where you will die and live again. I see you in a world so strange and distant that the images seem the trickery of a gypsy's false promises, even to me."

She broke off then, and the two sat motionless until the mantel clock struck noon. If it had been midnight, Mary would not have been surprised. But as if she'd heard her mother's far-off cry, she rose to obey it.

At the cottage door the Wisewoman motioned her to wait while she disappeared back into the gloom. Returning, she pressed a cold disk into her hand. "It is for you," said the woman who had never given a gift. "Though it has no talisman powers, I believe it should belong to you. It is of no value to me."

Mary stared down at the object pressed into her hand. It was a coin, foreign but not old. There was the face of some copper savage in worn relief on its surface. "I found it on the beach one day," the Wisewoman said. "There were other things scattered in the sand, perhaps from a shipwreck. An American ship, I shouldn't wonder, for it's an American coin. Take it back."

The gift meant nothing to Mary, but she accepted it out of politeness and the knowledge that it could be concealed from her mother's prying eye. She was out in the sunshine when she turned back one last time just as the Wisewoman was closing her door.

"When shall I meet the men I shall marry?" she asked, too shamed at her own boldness to look up.

"Why, tonight, of course. Both of them."

Mary looked up suddenly. "Surely not both," she whispered.

"I would not try to convince you against your will," the Wise-woman said in a neutral voice. And then as she watched Mary moving quickly away across the flagstones, almost in flight, she said, "Good-bye . . . Amanda."

But the Channel winds swept the name far out to sea.

Two

———⌒∞⌒———

A double row of black Italian pines threw long afternoon shadows across the lengthy approach to Whitwell Hall. In the great square salon with the painted ceiling where Lady Eleanor sat with the female members of her house party, the rosy-shaded lamps were already lit, throwing rainbows across the shawls that clothed the small tea tables. The lamps cast squares of pale light across the dahlia borders of the gravel circle before the house.

The ladies lingered over the remnants of their tea, still balancing the cups on silken knees, brushing a crumb of tea cake from the folds of their afternoon dresses. Tasseled pillows were idly plumped. Conversation was allowed to drift aimlessly as the ladies savored the final languorous moments before the taxing regimen of dressing for dinner.

It was that lulling moment of the rather pointless day, perhaps the only moment, when every reputation was safe from assault. Everyone was present, and so no one could rise to the witty remark at the expense of the absent.

If any of these ladies had summoned the energy to rise from her chair to glance down from the long front windows, she might have noted far along the drive the Cookes' crippled wagon dragging over the crushed rock behind the ponderous horse.

The house glowing at the top of a slight rise seemed vast to Mary, as if an entire village had been gathered neatly under a single roof

—a village like Nettlecombe that nestled to serve the Hall far down beyond its gates. Even Mrs. Cooke caught her breath at its magnificence.

To cover her awe, she barked at her husband, "Look sharp for a turning to the back of the house, Josiah! Have you no more sense than to fetch up at the front door? They'd set the dogs on you, and quite right, too!"

To Mary she said nothing. She'd left the red marks of her fingers across her daughter's cheek when the shiftless girl had finally returned from her noontime wandering. Josiah had come back before her to repair the wagon, lifting its bed on his own muscular back while his wife, grumbling, guided the wheel back on the sprung axle.

The tall columns of the front portico already loomed above them before Josiah found the tradesmen's lane forking to one side. It was hardly more than a slit in the high boxwood, trimmed to an unnatural smoothness. At once they were enveloped in the near-night of the hedgerows screening lane from house. At the end the narrow way widened to a paved yard between the kitchen wing and an apparently endless jumble of outbuildings.

If Josiah's ancient, nameless horse had been more alert and less than half blind, it would have shied at a motionless figure standing just off the lane in a gap between hedge and stables. The man immobile there might have been a statue implanted in that unlikely spot.

John Thorne had stood the better part of an hour while the shadows crept over him, swallowing him whole at last except for the glints in his straw-blond hair. Only his hands moved, rhythmically over each other, working the knuckles into hard bunches. With a filthy rag he rubbed at the grease embedded in the lines of his palms, only to grind it deeper into calloused flesh.

There was little point in cleaning leathery hands that tomorrow's labor would only blacken again. But his mind was elsewhere, in a world above grime and stench. He stared up at a pair of windows in the great house far above the servants' domain. He'd watched reflected sunset wash them red, then purple. And still he stood until another servant of the staff would step silently up and draw the curtains of Miss Amanda Whitwell's room against the night.

The young man had spent the day demolishing the old barn doors from the stable wing, tarred to his elbows with hinge grease. Tomorrow meant hanging the new modern doors he'd paneled and glazed himself in the estate carpenter shop. The stables were being refitted to house the Whitwells' new motorcar and the limousines and electric broughams in which their flow of guests arrived and departed. No favorite in servants' hall and a misfit there, John Thorne was an invaluable craftsman who repaired and maintained Whitwell Hall as if every splinter and stone of it were his.

His territory ceased at the kitchen yard, but it stretched backward to embrace the outbuildings and the pastures of the home farm as far as the distant cottage in the grove. There he'd been born before the Whitwells had come.

Just as the curtains on Amanda Whitwell's window were drawn together and given a final twitch by the invisible hands of one Mrs. Buckle, the Cookes' wagon crunched past the motionless man. He was hardly aware of them, for his head remained lifted toward the high windows. A tremor of dread overcame Mary Cooke just then, perhaps because she was in sight of the kitchen wing. Perhaps something more caused her to turn and glance behind her mother's ramrod back at the shadow of a man between hedge and stable. But the moment passed, leading on to her arrival at the house where she would serve.

The ordered silence of its grounds gave no indication of the fevered activity consuming the lower reaches of Whitwell Hall. The dining-room regime was the only operation functioning close to efficiency. There a pair of gaitered footmen, hired for the house-party occasion, were coaxing flame into spirit lamps on the sideboard, under the scrutiny of a butler with a thunderous face and a twitching nostril. The table was set for twenty-four in a wilderness of French crystal. Autumn roses deepening from pale green-white to darkest black-red burst from a regiment of tall silver cones down the center.

The fanning door to the serving pantry suggested the storm gathering belowstairs. Hilda and Hannah and Betty, in caps like overstarched toadstools, bustled past one another in harried haste that would not subside until long past the dinner hour.

Below, Mrs. Creeth, the cook and empress of the kitchen, was far too overwrought to hear the sound of Josiah's stamping plowhorse on the cobblestones beyond the barred windows. Mrs. Creeth was locking horns—not for the first time—with Mrs. Buckle, the housekeeper, whose sphere of influence ceased at the baize doors separating family from domestic staff. Nevertheless, Mrs. Buckle, whose accents grew hideously refined in her encounters with the lesser servants, had invaded enemy territory during the very time of its most feverish pre-dinner strategy. Mrs. Buckle and Mrs. Creeth stood frozen in combat, each tugging a handle on the same Georgian silver tray.

"Give over, if you *please,* Mrs. Buckle!" Mrs. Creeth shrieked. "I have more than my job to get a dinner out of its pans and onto the table. There'll be no catering to imaginary invalids until Sir Timothy and Lady Eleanor's guests have ate and drunk their fill!"

White with rage, Mrs. Buckle twisted the tray from the cook's grasp. It swung down to rap her own bony knees. Mrs. Buckle's life was a ceaseless struggle against just such indignities as this. She worked her mouth silently for fully a minute in search of a speech to wither the unwitherable Mrs. Creeth.

"If you don't mind," she said at last, "I haven't the least intention of disrupting your culinary endeavors, for I know how exceedingly *difficult* it is for you, Mrs. Creeth, to manage even an *ordinary* dinner —at your age."

The final phrase fell on Mrs. Creeth like an ether-soaked rag. She staggered back against the long refectory table. And Mrs. Buckle swept past her to the stove, where she meant to coddle a nice egg and toast a thin slice for Amanda Whitwell. She shook out a linen cloth to spread on the silver tray. And all the while, Mrs. Creeth stood behind her, yearning to close her reddened hands around Mrs. Buckle's stringy neck.

For her part, the housekeeper seemed to address the toast rack as she arranged the bland meal on the elaborate tray, though her words were distinctly within Mrs. Creeth's hearing. "Poor, delicate darling! Left to the heartless cruelties of some I could name whose only duty is to feed and sustain, Miss Amanda, who has hardly known a well day in all her young life, would lie abed until starvation hastened her end, and—"

"Just how sick *is* Miss Amanda *this* time?" Mrs. Creeth demanded directly into the housekeeper's ear.

But this rude intrusion seemed to pass unheard. "—and who, I should only like to know, would care for her few needs without her dear old Buckle, who was nurse and nanny to her from the day God sent the poor, high-strung creature into this vale of tears?"

The egg appeared to coddle itself with record speed under Mrs. Buckle's efficient direction. The toast received a pale skim of butter, and the invalid's tray lacked only a finishing touch.

Mrs. Buckle turned with maddening calm to Mrs. Creeth, who had evidently forgotten her dinner for twenty-four. "Would you be good enough to locate a silver vase and one small, perfect rosebud for this tray, Mrs. Creeth, before I take it up to Miss Amanda?"

In response to this final outrage, Mrs. Creeth's lips parted dangerously. But there had been a knocking at the kitchen door for some time. It continued. Whirling to grasp the table, Mrs. Creeth howled at Betty, who had just descended from the dining room. "You, girl! See who's at the door, and if it's a dirty, begging tramp, lay the frying pan across his head!"

Betty made a wide and prudent circle around the two women and pulled the door open, revealing Mrs. Cooke and Mary, with her small wicker satchel in her hand.

Mrs. Cooke had only to set foot in the kitchen to assess the electricity in the air. Her years of domestic service had accustomed her to the squabbling snobberies that formed the life force belowstairs.

"Where is Mr. Finley?" she demanded in a ringing voice. "I have brought him the girl he has engaged." For all the kitchen knew, Mrs. Cooke might have been an old friend and trusted colleague of the mighty Mr. Finley, butler above and dictator below. No one knew that Mary's job had been decided in the impersonal precincts of an employment agency in Newport.

"Well, go fetch him, goose!" Mrs. Creeth called sharply to Betty. But the butler entered at that moment, noting that Mrs. Creeth and Mrs. Buckle were standing far too near one another than was good for either of them.

"Ah, Mrs.—Cooke, is it not?" he said, advancing toward the door.

Mary had to discipline herself to keep from stepping back into the twilight. She'd learned the futility of seeking solace from her father. Still, she longed to run back to where he sat on the wagon, as patient as his horse and as work-worn. She had no real reason to doubt that she was born to be a servant, but the effect of the icy Mr. Finley bearing down on her inspired panic.

He never glanced at her, though, saying to her mother, "I see you have brought the girl. Midafternoon would have been preferable, of course."

Mrs. Cooke stuttered. "I—we—she—"

"Quite so," said Mr. Finley. "I have been assured that the young person shows promise of serving in a capacity of some responsibility, given the closest supervision. She is sensible and literate, is she not?"

Mary recovered enough to notice that the left side of Mr. Finley's nose vibrated in little jerks when he spoke. It was as if one of his nostrils detected an especially repulsive odor, while the other nostril refused to become involved.

"She is both sensible and literate," Mrs. Cooke hastened to say, "trained by me, who once personally attended Lady—"

"Yes, yes, I have no doubt. You will have her back if she does not live up to our standards and your—ah—training. You have provided her with sufficient aprons in good repair for rough work and one suitable costume for her afternoon off, if she is granted one?"

"I have," Mrs. Cooke vowed. "The very aprons I myself once wore when I—"

"Yes, used, but in good repair." Mr. Finley spoke like a man whose most pressing duties obviously lay elsewhere. When he finally shifted his stare to Mary, he blinked once, almost in a baffled kind of recognition. "What are you called?" he asked after a troubled moment's pause.

"Mary, sir," she murmured and bobbed from the knee.

"Yes—sensible," he said. "You will find that—"

A deafening cymbal crash and an inhuman howl drowned Mr. Finley's introductory speech. While he had been engaged in this business at the door, the battle of wills between Mrs. Buckle and Mrs. Creeth had moved beyond words. Determined to find a bud vase for Miss Amanda's tray, Mrs. Buckle had begun her own search behind the cupboard doors above her. On the second shelf she had found the very thing, stored among the lesser silver pieces and segregated from the major plate in the strong room. As she reached for the vase, Mrs. Creeth's hand had slipped around her to the countertop, as sudden as a snake striking. A crooked finger hooked the handle on the silver tray and overbalanced it. It teetered for an instant, then crashed to the floor.

Weeks of Mrs. Buckle's accumulated dignity lay in the ruin at her feet. After her last howling cry, she turned on Mrs. Creeth. "WHORE OF BABYLON!" she screamed. "DECREPIT DAUGHTER OF THE DEVIL! BAWD OF BEELZEBUB! B—"

"Enough!" said Mr. Finley, very nearly raising his voice. No stranger to such crises, he advanced on the women and noted automatically that there was still toast on the stovetop and a warm pot of tea. "Prepare another tray for Miss Amanda, Mrs. Buckle. I am astonished at your outburst! You have quite forgotten yourself!" Quivering, Mrs. Buckle reached down her egg-stained skirts to retrieve the tray.

"Accidents will happen," Mrs. Creeth said mildly, folding her hands across her bosom. Estimating the amount of work she had yet to do before dinner could even be thought of, the butler decided against accusations.

"I shall take this tray up to Miss Amanda, and I shall not return to servants' hall this night, though I starve to death in my sleep," Mrs. Buckle announced, kicking aside a broken plate.

"You will prepare the tray," Mr. Finley said evenly, "but you are in no fit state to take it up. You, Mary"—he turned to the door where she still stood, suspended, observing the drama—"you will take Miss Amanda's tray up to her. And we shall thus be in a position to assess the quality of your work at once." Mary's mother nudged her sharply.

"Betty," Mr. Finley continued, "fetch a white apron and cap from the press and show the new girl how they are to be worn."

And as Mary stepped forward to obey, her mother stepped backward into the yard. For Mr. Finley had closed the door firmly in her face, cutting Mary off from all she had known before and from any hope of escape.

Three

Amanda Whitwell of Whitwell Hall lay in the center of a bed carpentered from the best English oak to accommodate Good Queen Bess herself. Like all bedsteads fashioned firmly for the Queen's country house visits during her royal progresses, it was as big as a barge.

Planted in its midst, Amanda felt pleasantly removed from the rest of humanity and its nagging demands. She was nearly overcome by the temptation to jerk the heavy cords and let the side drapings fall. Instead, she drew a hand mirror from under the counterpane and gazed into it, enthralled. Though she was not absolutely fixated on her face, it was a favorite object of her scrutiny.

There was rice powder enough, artfully applied, to turn her naturally pale complexion to pallor. It was a great pity, she thought, that she never used rouge on her lips, for leaving it off would have added still another touch to her invalid's disguise.

Angling the mirror to catch the light, Amanda momentarily forgot the evidences of her artificial wanness. She scanned her white face with violet-blue eyes that returned her look. There was a certain piercing sharpness in the expression of those eyes that betrayed calculation. By a concerted effort, Amanda summoned her powers to soften her gaze. It was a technique she had nearly mastered. She had only to think of the one man in her world who could subdue her and in whose arms she nearly forgot all trickery. Her violet eyes grew dreamy, and she seemed to regain the innocence she had so gladly lost.

Her healthy complexion glowed softly through the white powder. Black hair haloed her head in rather wildly tossed ringlets. Searching for imperfections, she found none. Or almost none. There was the odd little half-moon scar that faintly sliced her right eyebrow. Three and a half years before, when she was just fifteen and rather fat, a docile mare named Sapphire that she was belatedly learning to sit had forgotten its manners and shrugged her off.

Amanda showed no promise as a horsewoman, the despair of her riding master, who never succeeded in breaking her of the habit of hunching forward in the posture of a suicidal jockey. She was not, however, a girl to put a horse at an impossible fence, and so her teacher never feared for her life. They were both surprised on that final afternoon of her equestrian career. She had just breasted a low hill when unaccountably she found herself sprawling awkwardly onto pillow-soft ground. But then she had gone rolling down a gentle incline until a small, sharp stone had neatly divided her eyebrow in two.

When Lady Eleanor was informed of the accident, she shuddered at how near her daughter had come to being blinded. And the stable door was forever closed on Amanda's future as a horsewoman. It had been a great relief to her, for she preferred the comfort of the new motorcars to the perils of a horse.

It was perhaps the idea of motorcars that brought her suddenly back to the present and to the very reason she had invented one of her convenient indispositions. Her small chin jutted with determination. But she was aware that her childhood displays of temper were hardly equal to a situation of growing seriousness. Buckle could still be manipulated and used. But Buckle was beside the point.

On the far side of her bedroom door, Mary Cooke approached, balancing a now slightly bent Georgian silver tray. Betty, quick as a water sprite, had guided her up three flights and past an infinity of doorways before she vanished at the last moment. Mary knocked hesitantly.

Accustomed to Mrs. Buckle's forthright entries, Amanda started in her bed and slipped the mirror out of sight. "John?" she called before she thought.

But it was Mary who entered, trying to remember if it was proper or even possible to drop a curtsy while bearing a tray. Before her stretched a room even grander than Mrs. Creeth's kitchen. The electric lamps cast only small pools of light in the immensity of the chamber. Mary's eyes widened at the sight of a fire burning heartily below a distant marble mantel. The idea of a hearth to warm a bedroom surpassed her imaginings.

The posters of the great bed towered nearly ceiling-high to support a canopy of striped lavender satin. To Mary it seemed a great tufted jewel box, in which lay a girl from a fairy tale, a girl whose eyes were fastened on her.

"Please, Miss, your supper tray."

"Well, bring it along, then." Amanda struggled up against her dozen pillows.

A new servant could not have surprised Amanda Whitwell very much, but her eyes showed momentary astonishment as Mary drew closer to the bed. It was a look of naked surprise not much different from the one Mr. Finley had registered. "Put down the tray and take off your cap. Yes, at once!"

Wondering if the young lady suffered some sickness in her mind, Mary swept off the cap so recently fitted down over her brow. "Yes," Amanda mused, "even the same black hair, though better controlled than mine. You don't dye it, do you?"

"Oh, no, Miss," Mary said, thinking this odd creature, no younger than herself, might require the humoring of an infant.

"Servants have been known to," Amanda said. "Finley dyes his hair, as you may have noticed."

"Oh, no, Miss. I didn't notice."

"Yes, he does. There's no question about it. In his natural state he's as gray as an old rat, I should think. You may move the tray closer to me. What have we here?" Amanda removed a silver cover and wrinkled her nose. "Dry toast? I believe the kitchen is taking the invalid at her word. And no egg? This smacks of punishment!"

"Oh, no, Miss. There was—an accident—in the kitchen."

"A famine, more likely," said Amanda. "Who are you?"

"Mary, Miss."

"Mary what?"

"Mary Cooke, Miss."

"Oh, no, that won't do at all. Quite unsuitable. *Mary* is too ordinary and quite overworked. And the alternative is to call you Cooke, which would be to suggest Mrs. Creeth. What shall I call you?"

"I don't know, I'm sure, Miss."

"Miranda, I think. Yes, Miranda and Amanda—they go nicely together. Would that suit you?"

"I suppose so, Miss."

"And so it should, too. There was a Miranda in *The Tempest.*"

"Yes, Miss?"

"Yes. You know, Shakespeare. I was reading it only this afternoon. Part of it. And Miranda is the heroine. Quite beautiful, too. And let me see, she says at one point:

> *. . . To be your fellow*
> *You may deny me; but I'll be your servant,*
> *Whether you will or no.'*

And I do will it. So there we are, and the matter is decided. Why isn't everything so easy to arrange?"

"I'm sure I don't know, Miss." And then because she presumed she was to show more enthusiasm, Mary continued, "I suppose everything comes right if we put forth our best efforts."

"Oh, dear, how hearty that sounds," Amanda said, running the back of her small hand across her forehead in the manner of Sarah Bernhardt. "I do hope you're not *too* hearty. I have a rather robust friend, and she tires me terribly. I prefer a bit of languor in those about me. But not too much in a servant, of course."

There was nothing in Mary's training to prepare her for this eccentric familiarity, much less the dramatic suddenness of it. She had learned a scrap of Shakespeare herself, but had never heard it declaimed or insinuated into conversation. And she was blank concerning the meaning of the word "hearty." Mary almost longed to be back in the strife-torn kitchens. But Amanda was on the point of shocking her more profoundly.

"You may sit on the edge of the bed while I have my feast, Miranda. I won't be long over it, clearly."

"Oh, no, Miss, I couldn't."

"It's obvious you have been taught to obey. Do so." Mary lowered herself on the extreme edge of the bed and tried to smooth the overstarched apron that hid her own brown dress. She could not decide where to look while the crunching sound of Amanda wolfing her toast seemed to fill the room, crackling like the hearth. "Oh, Lord!" Amanda said at last, tossing down her napkin. "Grouse, I shouldn't wonder. Or ptarmigan. And Dover sole in lemon butter. Or perhaps *saumon d'Ecosse* with a *sauce Médoc.* Roast beef, rich and red. *Petits pois,* of course, in those little pastry baskets that Mrs. Creeth does rather well. And talking of pastry, *croissants,* parchment-pale and light enough to float. Then *gâteau,"* she intoned on a rising note. "There's no point in considering the variety of cheeses."

"Please, Miss?"

"It's what they will shortly be stuffing themselves with down in the dining room. Oh, I would sell my soul for a water biscuit, never mind the wedge of Camembert."

"Oh, I *am* pleased you're feeling better, Miss Amanda. Shall I just slip down to the serving pantry and bring you a plate of—"

"No, no," Amanda said. "I'll play out my hand. You haven't the least notion of what's going on, have you?"

"No, Miss." Without meaning to, Mary leaned near Amanda and stared with open curiosity into eyes precisely the same shade as her own.

"I am having a temper tantrum, and the rather complicated reason is that—"

"YOU, MARY! ON YOUR FEET! The idea!" Mrs. Buckle made a swift and silent entry into the room, cutting off Amanda's confidences. Mary leaped from the bedside. "Where is your cap, you wicked wanton? To the kitchen, and be quick!" Mrs. Buckle commanded.

"No, she will remain with me," Amanda said in a small and steely voice.

"She'll do nothing of the kind! I will not have this sort of familiarity in—"

"Mrs. Buckle, if she lives another ninety years, she will never equal your familiarity. Yes, yes, I know that you nursed and nannied and nagged me from the first. And when I'm feeling quite myself again, I shall remember to be properly grateful. Until then please leave Miranda with me."

"And who might *Miranda* be, if one may presume to inquire?" Mrs. Buckle bristled. She was already aware that this new and entirely too presentable young maid posed a threat to her favored position with Miss Amanda. A dozen underlings had been dismissed for less reason.

"I have decided to rename the new servant, and I trust you have no objections."

Mrs. Buckle smoothed her gray silk front and pursed her lips. "I'm sure my objections would carry very little weight when you are in one of your willful moods, Miss Amanda."

"How right you are, as usual, dear old Buckle. So you may go, for I won't be needing you again—tonight. And do try your very best not to make Miranda's life hell on earth simply on my account."

"Well, really, what language!" said Buckle, withdrawing with such composure as she could muster.

"Such an old trout!" Amanda said in a ringing voice before the door had quite closed.

"Oh, Miss," Mary said, working her hands.

"Yes, yes, a bad beginning, I know. But there is no other sort with Buckle. Come back and sit down. I'll see if I can pick up the train of my thoughts. Well, let's see what you have learned already. Possibly, by mere observation, that I am easily as willful as Buckle claims and that I am also quite amiable until someone crosses me. Then I rather tend to lash out. Oh, do sit down again, or I'll be cross!"

Mary/Miranda settled uneasily on the edge of the bed once more. "Oh, bother Buckle!" Amanda snapped. "She's upset you, and now you won't be able to listen to me properly. If I had my way, as I almost never do, she'd have been pensioned off long ago to one of the Nettlecombe cottages with a purse of gold sovereigns, a pair of my infant boots for a keepsake, and the solitude she so richly deserves.

"But Mother never lets anyone go. They all drop dead in her service. I told her if she kept on a nurse, she ought really to have another baby to justify the expense. She was quite horrified to hear it. Are you?"

"Yes, Miss. I mean no, Miss." Too much was happening for Mary to sort out, though her mind was quicker than anyone had ever troubled to notice. For all Amanda's oddness, Mary found herself cautiously drawn to the girl, whose commanding tone seemed strange in one so young and pale. Then Mary noticed the white powder liberally dusted over the innocent-seeming face. Such observations were out of place for a servant, as Mary well knew. But Amanda left her little time to consider.

"Oh, I fancy I really can smell a roast of beef! I could swear the aroma is seeping up through the floorboards." Amanda eyed her empty tray. "I'll become quite a drawn and desiccated spinster at this rate," she said to Mary, who had eaten nothing since early morning. "I wonder why I bother." Mary wondered, too.

"Have the men returned from Cowes?" Amanda asked. "They were there all afternoon looking at a yacht that someone wants to buy. I hate boats, don't you? Boats and horses and waltz music and small talk and boats again. It's all a beastly conspiracy to drive the women of England mad, don't you think?"

"I couldn't say, I'm sure, Miss Amanda. I've never been on a boat. I should probably be sick."

"I don't mean a yacht or an ocean liner, necessarily," Amanda explained. "But you've crossed on the steamer to Portsmouth or Southampton."

"Oh, never, Miss." Mary's eyes grew round. "I've never been off the Isle. Never. Where would I have gone?"

None of the maids—Hilda or Hannah or Betty—or the women who walked up from the village every afternoon to sew, or the laundress, who was one of the many cousins of Hilda and Hannah, had ever been off the Isle of Wight.

Of the women servants, only the embattled Buckle and Creeth moved back and forth in a seasonal migration with the Whitwell family. London, the Isle of Wight, then London again. And even they were left behind in town or country when the family accepted invitations for a stay in Scotland or a shooting week at Chatsworth when the old Duke of Devonshire was still alive.

Amanda's faintly budding social consciousness had never until that precise moment recognized the lower members of her own sex. The sudden glimpse of their bondage unnerved her. She chose to recoil as if she'd just opened the wrong door and had glimpsed something unpleasant.

"But London," she insisted. "Surely you've been up to London." The very sound of the city's name rumbled like thunder from a distant cloud bank in Mary's mind.

"Oh, not London," she whispered. "It's bigger than Ryde, isn't it, Miss?"

To Amanda, Ryde was the hilly overgrown village where one waited restlessly for the Portsmouth ferry. Ryde, with all its predictable streets leading to the same iron pier where Amanda had often sat, deeply bored, and wrapped in a tartan traveling rug, and cosseted by Buckle.

"Yes," she said, looking away to smile. "Ryde is hardly a patch on London. You have not been here long?"

"I only just came, Miss. Today."

"Then you haven't met—everybody?"

"No, Miss."

Amanda's mind edged forward in a satisfying small move. "I think I shall be wanting you for my own personal maid. It must have been in Finley's mind—and of course my mother's—I'm sure. But they take such a time about everything. I expect they mean to edge Buckle out by degrees, which would be too tiresome. Yes, I'm sure you will be quite useful.

"After all, I am to have a London Season next summer, I suppose —if I am not to marry first. And we shall certainly be going up to London in November for the Little Season. I shall need more than a crotchety nanny to keep track of my clothes and to bring me nice cool tumblers of barley water after dancing until dawn. Buckle has not sat up past ten in all her life."

"It sounds quite exciting, Miss."

"Does it? I suppose it does, if one is diverted by standing in endless receiving lines at the elbow of one's mother. But rather pointless if I am to marry Gregory Forrest, which is the current plot afoot. There's little purpose served in dancing with every spotty youth in London if one is fated to marry an American from New York. One is quite trapped by all these conventions. And marriage is the ultimate snare, though perhaps rather a safe harbor as well. If something can be both a snare and a harbor. You must see me through, Miranda, whatever happens.

"I am feeling quite, quite hopeless just now. But mark me! I am given to sudden bursts of inspiration that can make a perfect muckup of other people's meddling plans. *You* aren't thinking of marrying, are you?"

"Oh, no, Miss." And then Mary remembered the Wisewoman, no matter how unreal her words already seemed. She colored, though, and Amanda noticed.

"Ah, you have someone, haven't you? Tell me."

"Oh, no, Miss. In truth, I haven't. It was never allowed. Only—

I was told—just today it was—oh, please, Miss, it's only nonsense. I see that now."

"Everything is nonsense, but some of it is rather more amusing than the rest of it. Go on, for Heaven's sake!" Amanda showed an unaccustomed interest in affairs not directly her own.

But for the second time the conversation was interrupted. A rattling, uncertain knock announced another intruder. "Oh, I cannot *bear* it!" Amanda twitched with temper. "Yes! Who is it?"

It was either Hilda or Hannah looming there, her large, lumpish figure filling the doorway. Hilda or Hannah, for the two sisters from the village were inseparable and indistinguishable. Neither of them had set her sights above the serving pantry. And so when either was sent or summoned to the upper house, she went in an agony of embarrassment and misery. "Oh, Miss Amanda, if you please, I was sent up to fetch the new one—"

"She's called *Miranda!*" Amanda shouted.

"If you say so, Miss."

"I *do* say so!"

"Yes, Miss." In her anguish, Hilda—for it was Hilda—committed the indiscretion of wiping her nose nervously with the end of her apron, which she had reached down and gathered up for the purpose. "She's to come help at table. They's as busy as bees in bottles down there and flarin' at one another something chronic. The gong's about to go, too, Miss. It was ever such a time ago that the dressing gong went, Miss, and so—"

"Who has sent for her?"

"Mr. Finley, Miss."

"Ah, well, then I suppose you must go," Amanda said to Miranda. "There is little enough one can do against the awesome hierarchy of this house, as I know to my everlasting sorrow. Very well, you may consider your message received. I shall send Miranda along shortly, Hannah."

Hilda sniffled and vanished. Mary adjusted her cap down over her forehead and rose to go. As she lifted the tray from the bed, Amanda's hand snaked out to grasp her wrist. Lightly, but Mary could feel fingernails imprinting her flesh. "As you are to serve in the dining room tonight, Miranda, look sharp and notice the young American gentleman. Then tomorrow you can tell me what you think of him. He will be easy enough to identify, for he is quite divinely handsome and rather better behaved than the rest. Why he should be so besotted by our quaint, archaic ways I cannot imagine. He is the man my mother has decided I should marry. She would mate me to a Zulu to get me off her hands, and well I know it. Can you conceive of anything more *medieval?*"

Mary could only wonder why her young mistress was not downstairs at that moment, dressed in a beautiful gown—white, perhaps, to set off the darkness of her hair. And dining sumptuously beside her fiancé.

"But I am a rebel and will resist the rigors of outrageous fortune. When I am deprived of satisfaction, I can usually manage to withhold it from others. Poor Gregory will have to bear up without me. One of his several virtues is patience, so I imagine he will survive. And I am sustained by the certainty that beneath her unflappable facade, my mother is writhing. No, don't worry. I shan't pine away in my bed, sulking forever and beginning to babble. I fancy I'll devise a plan to foil them all. I can only hope that by some miracle I may become as clever in my scheming as I am difficult in my disposition."

"But, Miss—"

"I know. You're wondering why in Heaven's name I don't meekly obey my family and make a suitable marriage"—Mary had not been wondering anything remotely as intrusive as that—"and I will tell you. I love someone else. Quite hopelessly. And quite madly. And if my mother knew who he was, she would in her serene and gracious manner have me flogged."

$\mathcal{F}our$

⸻❦⸻

When the incisive John Singer Sargent had painted Lady Eleanor Whitwell's portrait, he had scanned her face for days in search of flaws. Finding none, he had pulled at his small pointed beard and stepped up to the blank canvas.

The result hung at the far end of the double drawing room beyond the salon with the painted ceiling. Lady Eleanor in court dress, the paint laid on her cascading skirts in blurred ivory petals. The dress she had worn, the feathers that had crowned her hair on the last day she had appeared at Buckingham Palace in the reign of Queen Victoria. The year before the nation had lost their most durable symbol of monarchy and the year Lady Eleanor had suffered a more tragic, private loss. She had been forty when Sargent completed his work. At fifty-one she could have sat for the portrait again with her beauty undiminished.

Sargent portrayed one hand frozen in a casual gesture as the subject touches the pearl choker inspired by Princess Alexandra's taste. The other hand is invisible in the froth of her skirts. Apparently she is distracted by something in the invisible distance, for her face is turned in slight surprise to depict the line from cheekbone to chin. A haunting, water-lily line. And yet the source of her mild surprise remains an enigma.

The mood of the painting is ethereal, but its strength is faithful to the subject: a woman who distantly knew both Alice Keppel and

Mrs. Pankhurst. A woman with the ripened beauty of King Edward's mistress and the steady determination of the suffragettes' leader.

She stood that long September evening beneath the portrait of herself, entertaining her houseguests and being but mildly entertained by them. The gentlemen had returned from their day's outing at Cowes. The room was thus perfectly balanced between the blackness of their dinner clothes and the languid colors of the ladies' gowns. Though autumn was upon them, the Isle's only social season was late summer, when the London Season gave way to the Regatta at Cowes. And so the ladies clung to the diaphanous pastel gowns that clung to them.

It was all in contrast to the previous summer. Lady Eleanor thought briefly of that season after the passing of King Edward, who had followed his mother, Queen Victoria, in death after a reign of but nine years. The Edwardian years. Of all the elaborate funerary arrangements, none lingered in the mind so much as the awesome Ascot racing meet where everyone, man and woman alike, wore deepest mourning.

The Black Ascot of 1910 had fallen in the midst of a darkened summer. But after a year's mourning, the pall had lifted by degrees. The aristocracy sought out their own kind once again in the outright pursuit of pleasure, as King Edward had taught them to pursue it. While the merely rich rushed to imitate their every gesture. The new King and Queen, George and Mary, seemed to stand aside, stiffly, neither leading fashion nor impeding it.

Death always turned Lady Eleanor's thoughts in the same, the inevitable direction. The captains and the kings might depart, but to her, death was expressed by the austere stone tablet along the wall of the Nettlecombe church. The tablet to commemorate her only son, lost in the African war at Mafeking just before the siege was raised in 1900.

Eleven years had passed since she had received garbled word of her son's heroism. Eleven years in which she had refused to wear mourning for him. Had ceased, almost, anguishing over the one handsome, laughing boy out of so many dead and lost. There had not even been a body to identify, to bury with quiet grief in the casual graveyard beside the church. And so the Whitwells had raised a stone tablet to Lieutenant Gordon Whitwell, 1881–1900, lost to defend the Empire in the chaos of the war against Kruger's Boers.

There were those who muttered against Lady Eleanor's refusal to include on the commemorative plaque a chiseled recital of her son's military glories or a pious tribute to his sacrifice for Queen and Country. She would not even allow his regiment to be named. Only a fragment of a line from Keats's poetry, carved in stark and heavy letters that caught the streams of damp coursing down the church walls:

THOU WAST NOT BORN FOR DEATH

How rarely Gordon was remembered, Lady Eleanor thought in the sea of her chattering guests. Not even Amanda shared her grief, for the girl had been only seven when her brother was lost. And Sir Timothy, already old when Gordon disappeared from their lives, was now old indeed, forgetful, easily moved to tears, but past the time for sharing pain and giving comfort.

Lady Eleanor's mind had wandered down this bitter, solitary path long enough. She returned to the babble welling up in the rooms, the voices that always seemed to rise to lunatic waves of meaningless noise just before the dinner gong sounded.

Voices detached themselves from the general hum, and Lady Eleanor heard the odd snatch of conversation. Apparently she had missed nothing, for the talk was still preoccupied with Maurice Brett, Lord Esher's son, who persisted in his plan to marry the musical comedy actress, Zena Dare. That he should have to resign his commission in the Coldstream Guards was, though inevitable, widely debated.

But Lady Eleanor was nearly obsessed by a problem much closer to her own life. She was reminded of it when her glance fell on Gregory Forrest's tall, immaculate figure as he stood across the room, listening to Sir Timothy. His head was thrust forward from broad shoulders, attentive to her husband's sometimes tedious monologue, the disconnected talk of a man near death without a son to endow with his considerable worldly goods.

Gregory Forrest's hands were clasped patiently behind his back. Unmoving in the room of drifting figures, he seemed as rigidly, conventionally correct as a young Guardsman. But his unlined, open face with the visionary eyes was pure American. Dismissing the memories that clung like cobwebs to the corners of her mind, Lady Eleanor stared at the young man as intently as if he were her lover.

He was not, though she had courted him on Amanda's behalf in a manner that had raised an occasional eyebrow in the otherwise quiet previous Season. During the time when pleasure was dampened by royal mourning, gossip embellished slighter items than this.

But gossip never dealt Lady Eleanor more than a glancing blow. She was elusive, they said, but not furtive, which amounted to eccentricity. She mourned her dead son in secret, they said, which was morbid. She was prudish, they said, for she buried herself in the country while a more adventurous woman would have sought the discreet freedoms of town. She should seize the day in her own behalf, for her beauty wouldn't last, they said, knowing that it would. She had been the third daughter of an impoverished duke, she had married beneath her, a rich man, fifteen years her senior, a tea merchant. A calculated choice, they said, but far from brilliant. And she was faithful to a fault to this monotonous old Sir Timothy, which in itself suggested frigidity. They called her miser, then gaped at her gowns from Worth and Jacqmar.

She had made a religion, they said, of simplicity, running a country place with a skeletal staff, entertaining dribs and drabs of no more than four-and-twenty guests. The numbers that made up her dinners and weekends dwindled in the conversations of those who were never invited. They said a great deal, and it amounted to very little.

It was plain as a pikestaff what she was about with this handsome American, for he was rich into the bargain. American money came, as everyone knew, from sources that had once been unmentionable but were now only unspeakable—trade, Klondike gold, Texas oil pumped from places with such ludicrous names as Sour Lake, sharp land practices. When the rumor drifted across the Atlantic that Gregory Forrest was the only son of a beer baron—German, of course— there were pleasantries passed about the mingling of Forrest beer and Whitwell tea. Even a line or two of doggerel repeated endlessly just out of Lady Eleanor's hearing:

> *And malt does more than background can*
> *To justify Amanda's man.*

Poetic lines that not even the audacious Maude Glaslough had quite been able to repeat to Lady Eleanor.

It was clear enough what she was about with this handsome American. She was as capable of conniving as the shrillest climber, they said. For the man was rich, and if a bit ruddy, not, at least, anemic. His Germanic background would have gone down better in old Queen Victoria's day, but things might have been worse. America was full of more questionable racial strains. Forrest was fair game for any woman, matron or maid. Only the most idle tongues contemplated scandal. And a good many women Lady Eleanor's senior forsook notions of conquest on behalf of their daughters, or themselves, and poisoned their good digestion in the process.

Lady Eleanor was noted for declining the bed of King Edward himself, in his most insistent years. And this was an achievement never forgotten. She'd spared herself this distinction by the combined effect of rigid dignity and agile footwork.

Still, it was remembered that during an entire London summer Lady Eleanor had been unable to set foot outside the door of her Charles Street house in Mayfair lest the royal equipage rumble up and she find herself confronted by her sovereign, whose whims counted as commands.

But she'd made a dead set for Gregory Forrest—everybody said so. And the headstrong Amanda had, for a time, seemed to fit into the plan for her own future. The early stages were measured, of course, though they did not go unremarked. There had been time. Amanda had been only seventeen then and newly emerged from her chrysalis —and the schoolroom, if it could be said she'd ever been schooled. Her formal introduction to society, if she was to be persuaded to endure it, had still stood a season or two off. And one had only to look at Amanda to see that her early promise of beauty was already being fulfilled.

There were purists who preferred to marry off their daughters to squint-eyed third cousins in the interest of family solidarity and allegiance to One's Own Kind. And others who would not look beyond the six hundred families who, by common consent, formed London society.

But the Americans had been flocking in for decades now, since Jennie Jerome had met Randolph Churchill. They had discovered one another at Prince Edward's party on the yacht *Ariadne,* and Jennie had found herself a noble husband. And in time a royal protector. The spectacular Churchill match, as it turned out, was not a notable success. But as the beginning of a trend, it was decisive. After that, male and female alike, the Americans seemed to arrive by the shipload, mingling fresh blood with the blue.

Lady Eleanor rarely considered the world at large in the forming of her own plans, though she felt the tug of time and change threatening her hopes. Amanda, even at seventeen, had been anything but putty in her mother's hands. There were somber moments when Lady Eleanor even stooped to envy Queen Alexandra, who held her spinster daughter, young Victoria, in a velvet grip of steel.

It had seemed to go smoothly enough at first, from the day when Sir Timothy had brought Gregory Forrest home from his London club. An unlikely pairing. Sir Timothy, almost impenetrably deaf, had never quite been able, or even willing, to raise his vaporous thoughts above the tea-importing business. Though Lady Eleanor was far from the most rigidly conventional figure in her set, she did agree with accepted opinion that trade, even on the most successful scale, was better left undwelt upon, particularly once it had served its purpose.

It had served Sir Timothy handsomely, winning him the respectability of riches that could be flung away in acquiring two costly domestic establishments in town and country, a knighthood, and Lady Eleanor. But provokingly enough, Sir Timothy would insist upon talking a good deal of mundane business to the well-bred young American, who listened with the patience of a parish priest while his eye roved to rest upon Amanda.

No one who knew Lady Eleanor seriously considered her a fortune hunter. And no one who knew Amanda could think of her as a commodity for sale. But Lady Eleanor saw strength in the set of the American's shoulders and determination in his apparently dreamy eyes. She was willing to gamble that he might impose a necessary authority over Amanda that her mother could never hope to gain. There was a dark side to Amanda, evident from her earliest years. The wildest heights of childish merriment gave way to the grimmest sulks. It had taken all of Mrs. Buckle's patience to cope with Amanda from her cradle days. And the number of nursery maids who had handed in their notices and fled in the first five years of her life would have populated a children's hospital.

Amanda's rebellion, now playful and merely provocative, might blossom—and soon—into the bright flower of disgrace. Sons committed indiscretions that could be dealt with. Daughters committed indiscretions that had to be lived with. When Amanda felt that no one understood her, she reckoned without her mother's perceptions.

Lady Eleanor gave a last-minute thought to the choreography of the dining room, considering that the guests were as suitably partnered as the occasion merited. For it was another point on which she was faulted by some: that she employed no little secretary-bird of a faded spinster to make her social arrangements. A bit of deliberation with Finley was the only drop of oil in the machinery of her hospitality. A very independent woman, people said of her—so capable.

The dinner gong sounded at last, striking a brassy note across Lady Eleanor's thoughts that wandered across the great divide between dead son and living daughter. At the far end of the room, Sir Timothy clapped his prospective son-in-law on the back in a glancing, rather vague manner and turned to search for the lady he was to take in to dinner, a Mrs. Glaslough, whom he didn't like or understand. And Lady Eleanor waited to be claimed by the dinner partner whom she'd chosen for herself, a Mr. Harry Emerson, whose alliance with Mrs. Glaslough found its way into the more disreputable daily newspapers often enough to require a bit of blunting.

As the double doors to the dining room yawned, Lady Eleanor took her dinner partner's arm and led the way, thinking, as she often did, how different things might have been if Gordon had been spared. If there had been no distant wars to blight the bloom of young British manhood.

It was an evening's work for Gregory Forrest to concentrate on the rippling flow of his dinner partner's conversation. She had a great many teeth and a great many pearls, and he couldn't manage to dredge up her name from memory. But it was enough to smile and incline his dark head in her direction. For she was of the age at which a woman is determined to be charmed. He remembered that she was unmarried. Her hands were covered with antiquated rings, but there was no wedding band among them. She'd long since navigated the choppy seas of an extended mating season—London, Dublin, India —and had reached the far shore untouched and unclaimed. She was in every sense a miss, but Gregory could not remember her name.

He was happy enough not to be paired with the notorious Mrs. Glaslough, though her beauty had stood the test of time. Even when she spoke behind her hand, her voice was clearly audible four chairs away, as it was meant to be. She enjoyed her food, and the lip smacking that attended her eating served as counterpoint to her conversation, making Gregory wonder to what purpose he'd trained himself in decent table manners. And Mrs. Glaslough's laughter for some reason reminded him of the brilliant sparks that sent the new wireless radio messages from ship to distant ship across the empty sea.

Like anyone with one foot tentatively planted in a foreign culture, Gregory Forrest found himself partly attuned to the exotic folkways. The openness with which illicit romance was reported by tongue and pen in England would have knocked crude New York sideways. Apparently this Mrs. Glaslough was the mistress or whatever you call it of the man with the monkey's face on Lady Eleanor's right. They were given adjoining rooms in visits to country houses, passing the days in utter indifference to one another and the nights in one another's arms. But whatever attempts at discretion they practiced must have been to spare the servants' sensibilities, because they were more firmly joined by gossip than by any wedding vows. It wasn't quite the England of Gregory Forrest's schoolbook history or the Harvard course in British literature. He had no ear for gossip, and yet he'd have had to be as deaf as old Sir Timothy to miss hearing it, for what was whispered rang louder even than Mrs. Glaslough's braying laugh.

Forrest's placement midway along the table was no mystery. He'd dined too often with the Whitwells during his extended stay in England to be featured as guest of honor. Moreover, had he been seated on Lady Eleanor's right hand, it would have advertised his role as her daughter's fiancé, a position that still lacked formal announcement. English customs were beginning to seem to him more and more like English cuisine: preoccupied with appearance at the expense of substance. He forked through a decorated pastry shell to find the unyielding flesh of some dead bird beneath—possibly grouse, possibly not.

Cookery aside, Gregory Forrest's basically romantic soul was ignited by the pageantry of England. While still appearing to attend to his dinner partner's words, he scanned the rest of the diners. Glimpsed in a vignette between the tall vases of flowers, each face revealed the assurance of substance and breeding and position secured by centuries.

There was newer money among them, of course. The expansive Edwardian era just past had seen to that. The host himself was not directly descended from Saxon land or Norman conquest. But the pattern was there, and every figure around the sumptuous board seemed to have fitted effortlessly into it. A stately, static minuet without apparent footwork, accompanied by conversational music conducted by Lady Eleanor and punctuated by the cymbal crash of Mrs. Glaslough's presence. The drooping mustaches above the towering winged collars that never seemed to bind the ample necks. The ropes of inherited—or borrowed—diamonds and opals adorning breasts flat or softly rounded or pigeon-ponderous. The heads nodding to conversations that moved cleverly to the brink of scandal and beyond, then retreated gracefully with knowing, toothy smiles.

It was all a good deal for the son of a Brooklyn brewer to absorb. A young man whose shirt-sleeved father had promoted a son into just the sort of fashionable world the father had never wanted for himself.

For some odd reason, Gregory's mind leaped from this select, serene gathering, this murmurous rose garden of wealth, wit, and innuendo, back to the house where he had spent a Brooklyn boyhood. Bushwick, in fact, where the brewery owners' turreted and shingled mansions backed on their own foremen's wooden row houses. The ragtag far reaches of Brooklyn, where German beer gardens sprang up in the grazing land of the older Dutch dairy farmers.

Bushwick, befogged by the heady cloud of malt-flavored air, where even the well water seemed to taste of hops. And where the brewer aristocracy was composed of families named Liebman and Obermeyer and Doershchuck and Lipsius and Forrest.

In the perpetual chill of a great English house, Gregory Forrest was momentarily back on the steaming streets of a Brooklyn summer. The lethal heat that blighted his mother's rows of ferns hanging from the pots along the jigsaw front porch before the stained-glass windows. The summer noons of ice wagons and their retinue of parched urchins. The horses dead of exhaustion in the street, bellies exploding in the relentless heat. The evidence on every hand that the slum had preceded the city in the sudden quest for wealth that eluded all but the few like his father. A father who worked beside his day laborers, a capitalist in steel-toed boots and overalls who growled companionably in German to the employees who needed no other language. A brewer born who could drive the giant cork into the bunghole of a barrel the size of an outhouse with one mighty blow of the mallet.

A canny businessman who read nothing in English, little in German, and every figure in a financial statement.

The most familiar scenes of Gregory Forrest's life glowed suddenly bright and exotic in that moment between the courses. And inevitably his most painful memory struck like lightning in his mind. For to remember the Brooklyn of his boyhood was to remember his best friend, Sammy Bettendorf, the son of the driver of a scavenger wagon.

It was with Sammy that Greg shared his secrets, pinched candy he could have paid for, clung from the swaying backs of horsecars, mingled blood squeezed from slit thumbs to pledge undying brotherhood. Sammy, who lived with his stout parents and four sisters at the top of a frame row house built in the 1840s for Peter Cooper's glue factory.

He and Sammy had plotted an escape when they were both menaced by a certain Miss Swenson, teacher and terrorizer of the third grade. Determined to start a new life as Kansas cowboys, Greg and Sammy had left home and school after one Wednesday recess, trekking as far as the Gowanus Canal and the outskirts of Red Hook before they learned that Kansas lay much farther off. And the pair of them had returned to take their punishment, a total of six whippings between them. One each from each parent and an unforgettable double session with the pitiless, muscular Miss Swenson.

It was a summer's night like any other in the year Greg was nine when his dreams of the following day's adventures were only dimly disturbed by the distant sound of the fire engine's bell. He slept through that muggy night to awaken the next morning with his mother beside him.

She sat on the edge of his bed, her wrapper pulled tight around her, and her hair hanging down to the sheet in an uncoiled braid. The boy sensed trouble, even tragedy, at once. For he had never seen his mother without her corsets, and this was the very hour she had always spent in the kitchen, supervising breakfast.

"There vas trouble last night, Greg," she said softly, running her hand through his tousled dark hair. He wanted to withdraw from her, retreat beneath the sheets, even though the day was already hot at dawn. "Bad trouble in the night, my boy, down Goodwin Street."

"Sammy?" Greg asked. "Trouble at the Bettendorfs'?"

"Yes, my son," she said, and tears welled in her eyes. He saw then she had been weeping long before he was awake. "A fire. It vas very bad, very quick. The engines, they could do nothing. The hoses, they vas too short, and not vater enough."

"But Sammy?"

"Sammy and all his family gone."

"Gone away?"

His mother looked uncertainly at Greg, trying to tell him with her eyes, and still to diminish the full horror of it.

"Dead?" Greg asked at last. "All of them?"

"*Ja.* All."

He fell against his mother's bosom then. They wept together, and she rocked him as gently as she had done when he was a baby, whispering, "My boy, my boy," knowing his boyhood was blighted now.

Fifteen years later and three thousand miles away, Gregory Forrest's memory probed that moment again and found the wound unhealed. But it brought his mother to mind, and other memories of her. He thought of her storytelling, which had fueled his earliest dreams. How her accent always grew thicker as she spun out the familiar tales told to her in a half-timbered pink village above Augsburg forty years before.

They were tales of black forests full of helpless widows and useful elves. Of treasures guarded by faintly comic ogres. And always in the woodland clearing a beautiful maiden—Gretchen, Ursula, Rapunzel —whose blond braids coiled about a ravishing face. A chaste, blond, milk-fed Teutonic beauty who awaited awakening by a hero's liberating kiss.

Gregory Forrest had found quite another Old World maiden at last, though not in a forest clearing. And long after he thought he'd put such boyish romancing behind him. His father had known from the beginning that Brooklyn was no seedbed for an American gentleman. Gregory had thus been sent away to boarding school where a brewer's son might be reshaped along more genteel lines. Then college, where the Arrow-collared sons of older money drank whiskey, not beer, and spoke with easy knowledge about track ponies, not draft horses.

With the shrewdness of a successful peasant, his father had foreseen the family's first gentleman. The father had been content with one small step toward respectability in changing the family name from Wald to Forrest in celebration of his new citizenship. But the old man had reckoned without Gregory's intellect, which led him to law school, where he edited the law review and finished first in the class of 1909.

And he reckoned without his son's creative itch, which drew the young man's questing mind beyond the courtroom and the legal library to a gathering desire for something more. A new goal, still forming, that would express Gregory Forrest's yearning for creativity and the half-sensed need to create a life not merely for himself but for the emigrants still pouring into New York, only to find the dockside streets paved with manure instead of gold.

Gregory Forrest began a dream of houses. Houses to replace the teetering tenements where the spigot at the foot of the stairs was dry from summer drought and from the frozen pipes of winter. A dream of houses to replace the hovels where families slept in the warmth of crowded bodies.

Still flushed with his son's academic triumphs and his immediate placement in a Wall Street firm of absolute dignity, the old brewer could only shake his head in surprise at his equally bewildered wife when Gregory announced his intention to study architecture.

It seemed hardly as desirable as law to the befuddled father. But he was not a man to keep a grown son on a short rein. If it was to be housebuilding instead of the bar, then so be it. The star Gregory began to follow led him to a Grand Tour of Europe to examine the architectural triumphs so lacking in New York, where the hastily constructed houses often fell into the excavations for still more hastily constructed houses beside them.

And so Gregory slipped the bonds of the law firm. And after a brief look at the buxom, strident beauties of Fifth Avenue society and the tennis-playing younger sisters of his Harvard classmates, he had come to England. The *Wanderjahr* was meant only to begin with London. But it had ended there on the day he first saw Sir Timothy's Amanda. He hadn't stumbled into a woodland clearing to confront a Germanic maiden. Amanda had been arranged in a rather hoydenish pose on the sofa of a darkly paneled London drawing room in Charles Street.

Her black hair was still drawn back like a schoolgirl's from a face that foretold a woman's beauty. He'd fallen in love with her beauty before she'd lifted her cool violet gaze, and then he had seen those eyes. He had fallen in love with her, and everything about her. The small hand stretched out toward the tea tray in careless invitation. The voice as commanding as any New York debutante's, but accented with infinitely more appeal. The disturbing sense that she might bolt at any moment, leaving him to stand in the world alone.

Gregory Forrest had worked steadily toward the day when Amanda would cease calling him "Father's American" and accept him for himself, an acceptance she knew how to dangle and draw back. He experienced all the tortures of a young man who is overwhelmed by his own capacity to suffer.

And so, to be loved for himself, he altered himself out of all recognition. He tailored himself from Savile Row, deliberating over the quietude of neckties with all the concentration he had once reserved for the bar exam. He'd spent a princeling's ransom on riding clothes the day before Amanda mentioned that she never went near horses. Forgetting she was only seventeen that year because she never giggled—she laughed outright or sank into remote, somber tones—he dreamed of making her his wife. Of going back to New York with her on his arm. Of rebuilding that sordid sprawl into a shining city. He to plan and carry out; she to inspire and encourage.

When Lady Eleanor reminded him with exquisite tact of Amanda's extreme youth, he contented himself with a more measured courtship. He courted her and her mother and father. He'd willingly have courted all Charles Street and Mayfair and London and the Isle of Wight to speed the passage of time.

He made occasional forays to the Continent to stir himself with its architectural glories and innovations. He puzzled, half-blind, over that sensuous fad called Art Nouveau that was transforming the facades of Brussels with cast-iron bulrushes and serpentine grillwork. Once, he got as far as Barcelona to gaze, momentarily awed, at the Gothic anthill eccentricity of Gaudi's unfinished La Sagrada Familia Cathedral. And everywhere behind the glamorous prospects of famous cities, he found slums more wretched than New York's. Slums centuries old that had accumulated no dignity with age.

In Brussels he'd once followed a woman through what seemed half the city's rain-swept streets. And for no more reason than that the narrowness of her waist reminded him of Amanda. He nearly passed her, lost in his own fantasies, when she stopped, lingered in a blank doorway, and gave him an unmistakably direct look. She was past her girlhood, and drew him with a practiced hand up a flight of stairs to a hall bedroom the shape of a coffin.

He learned, after much travel weariness, that it was easier to be in the same country as Amanda, even when they were separated by the distances of geography or her moods. So he enrolled himself in a London school of architecture in Bedford Square. And there he managed to get through whole days in the pursuit of a subject less elusive than Amanda. The time passed for Gregory Forrest. But it seemed to stand still for Amanda.

She was less receptive to his advances at the end of the year than she'd been at the start. When he grew bold and embraced her almost roughly, she only laughed. When he was driven into a state of frustrated hopelessness, she grew absentmindedly tender.

It was the work of a moment to win him back, and Amanda enjoyed the work, for it was only a game to her. There'd been that day in August just past during the Cowes Regatta. Gregory's face had darkened with an anger that flashed a warning even across Amanda's consciousness.

"But, *dear* Gregory," she had said, running a fingertip across the back of his hand, "you can be quite overwhelmingly *intense.* You must know that I'm truly fond of you. Perhaps the young women of—is it Brooklyn where you come from? Yes, Brooklyn—undoubtedly fall at your feet. But surely you've noticed that we English are rather more cold-blooded."

"I'm in love with you, Amanda. And no matter how cold you are to me, you're a hell of a long way from being cold-blooded."

"I shall have Buckle take my temperature at the earliest opportunity. The point I am struggling to make is that we inhabit quite different worlds. How am I to judge you?"

"I'll tell you what you want to know," Gregory said.

"You are far more likely to tell me what you think I want to hear."

"No, not that. I can't figure out what that might be."

"Ah, you're wiser than I thought. I'm accustomed to people around me whom I can outthink but cannot outmaneuver. You see, it's just as I said. You *are* a creature from another planet—a figment of Mr. H. G. Wells's fevered imagination."

"Damn it, Amanda, stop playing games. If you want to be a child, go back to your nanny, or whatever she's called. You want all the freedoms of being a woman and all the protection of a child."

"I was never a child, not really," Amanda said, and the maddening playful note vanished from her voice. "That's just the point. While you were roaming around the American prairie, having had your independence declared for you, I was a prisoner in the nursery. I was scheming at an age when you were thinking of nothing but—but whatever little boys think about."

"And what was the point of all that scheming?"

"Well, it didn't get me very far, I'm bound to admit. But that's hardly the point at issue. Oh, don't you see? Doesn't anyone?" Amanda suddenly shifted on the long, deep sofa on which they sat. She drew her legs up and thrust her small feet against the cushions at the far end. Then she settled quite companionably with her back resting against Gregory's shoulder. A wisp of her hair swept across his cheek, and he knew that whatever the argument was between them, he was bound to lose it.

"I want the freedom that you men take for granted. You can't understand that, can you? I doubt I'd find that freedom even in the Land of the Free, as you Americans so arrogantly style yourselves. Do your women vote?" she asked in a ringing voice, turning suddenly to challenge him.

"Good God, no," Gregory had replied. "Do you want the vote?"

"Not particularly," Amanda said, settling back against his arm.

"Then what's the point?"

"The point is that I want to make my own decisions. This is the twentieth century. And am I to be bought and sold as chattel—palmed off on some unsuspecting foreigner like a freshly painted yacht?"

"I'm not trying to buy you, Amanda," Gregory said, yearning to reach around and draw her into his arms. "I doubt if I could afford you, anyway."

"Good Lord!" she said. "You aren't crying poor, I hope. If you turn out to be a pauper well-disguised, it will certainly send Mother off the rails. Serve her right, come to think of it."

"No, I'm not poor—at least my family isn't. But where I come from, every generation wants to make its mark."

"How very odd of you, then, to fall under the spell of this particular stratum of England where you've surrounded yourself with precisely the people who are doing their damnedest to pretend that nothing has changed since the Middle Ages. Except, of course, that the chivalric code is stretched a bit at bedtime."

"Meaning?"

"Meaning that women are still meant to be decorative by day and compliant by night, while men seem to have cornered the market on freedom of choice."

"Choose me and you'll have exercised all the rights of the New Woman."

"Don't patronize me, Gregory. You're sounding more like an English country squire every day. What if I *have* chosen someone else already? Has the thought crossed your mind?"

"Has it crossed yours?"

"What pomposity! Perhaps it has."

"Then I doubt that you'd be crying for your emancipation."

"You must have inhabited a very elemental landscape before you came here if you think matters are that cut-and-dried." And then Amanda surprised Gregory by demanding to see his hand. "Yes!" she said, snapping her fingers in command. "Give me your hand." He gave her the hand that was not imprisoned by her back still pressing against his shoulder.

She gripped it with her small, curling fingers, rubbing her thumb across it from wrist to fingertip. "Are you going to read my palm?" he asked, trying to coax her out of a mood grown more intense than any of his.

"I don't need a gypsy's art to see you haven't worked a day in your life."

"Neither have you."

"That's not the point. Behind your facade of American ingenuity and featherheaded idealism, you're as idle as all the men I've ever known. Almost all of them."

"What makes you think I'm an idealist? I'll overlook that business about featherheaded."

"Oh, Lord, you positively *reek* of idealism. You have some master plan about reforming the world that you mean to spring on me when I've finally given way to your charms and am fainting with love in your arms. It's true, isn't it? I'm never wrong."

If Gregory Forrest had not been in love with Amanda Whitwell before, that moment would have turned the tide. This self-centered, icily remote girl, apparently engrossed in her own concerns, had suddenly wheeled to pierce the armor of his courtship. She'd seen through to him.

"Yes, it's true. There's something I want very much to do—apart from marrying you, Amanda."

"Well, go on. I'm yearning to hear what it is. Just because I haven't the slightest intention of telling you everything about myself doesn't mean I won't insist on your revealing all. I want to know about you. You must remember I am but a mere woman and must deal in wiles and artifices."

"You're but a mere girl," Gregory said, elbowing her in the small of her back. "But a clever one—too clever."

"I would spin round and slap your face for that. But at any moment that dry old stick Finley will barge through the door with the tea things, and I won't give him the satisfaction of seeing me misbehave. For the last time, tell me your dream, damn it!"

He told her while Amanda fidgeted only occasionally, seeming to hear him out. He told her of the "elemental landscape" he had inhabited. Of the New York teeming with immigrants, homeless in parks encrusted with villages of tarpaper shacks. He told her of the children rat-bitten in their beds and left to die because their parents didn't know the word for "hospital," much less the location of one.

He told her of narrow, eternally dark streets crisscrossed by lines of flapping gray laundry, of water unfit to drink, of epidemics that raged from room to room crowded with the suffering who longed to die. He came to the brink of telling her how the best friend of his boyhood had died in a tinderbox bedroom. He drew back at the last moment, unwilling or unable to relive the nightmare that had triggered his dream.

But he told her the dream. Modest, perhaps, given the magnitude of the problem. But a dream that was growing in him in this exile from his native ground. The dream to build solid, safe houses that any family could live in, could own. Homes with lawns and plumbing and electricity. Streets of them, neighborhoods of them, free of the filth that bred disease and crime and despair. Free of the shoddy combustible materials that invited fiery death in the night.

She listened, at first against her will. Then with a certain attentiveness. For this was a poverty she had never encountered. It was, perhaps, the blight of East London, where she had never been. But it was a far cry from the picturesque poverty lying beyond the gates of Whitwell Hall. One knew that there were damp and sagging cottages along the back lanes of Nettlecombe, that there were woods full of poachers who ate only what they could kill on moonless nights. The roads were dotted with fatherless brats whose noses ran in all weathers and who would grovel for farthings.

But the impoverishment that Gregory Forrest described awed her for an unguarded moment. She forced her mind away after a time, forbidding herself to hear any more.

She was not precisely shocked by the sufferings of transplanted, faceless Italians and Irishmen who had overreached themselves in crossing the Atlantic. She was more disturbed by Gregory Forrest's idealistic plans to give a few of them a chance for a better life. If he had spoken of them as his personal charges—as a bank of feckless yeomen who tugged their forelocks at his proposed largesse—she could have dismissed his visions at once. But he spoke of these people as his fellow citizens. He saw no distance between them and himself. He seemed to view his future as part of theirs.

She sidestepped this overliteral interpretation of democracy. Everyone knew that America's high-flown posturing about the equality of man had long since sunk under vulgar money-grubbing. One had only to see the unspeakable American women in the Burlington Arcade, buying everything in sight and overdressed in yesteryear's fashions. And behind them their submissive, obsequious, tobacco-stained husbands.

That this upstart plutocracy had bred a Gregory Forrest defied all Amanda's neat notions. When she ceased listening, her last impression of his words was that he was thoroughly sincere. It surpassed idealism; it surpassed anything she had ever heard, and left her behind. In the hour that Gregory was falling more deeply in love with her, touched by the silence in which she heard him out, Amanda added one more reason to resist the suit of Gregory Forrest. She could never rule him, not on her terms. He had a ruling passion already. He wanted her love, perhaps even her help. It would have been a kindness to say to him at that very moment: *You need another kind of woman. Go find her.* But Amanda Whitwell was not kind.

She could send him away at the end of his lengthy speech. It would be withering but effective. But without a suitable suitor, she would be vulnerable. And to send Mother's choice packing would incur every sort of icy recrimination, perhaps a showdown in which

Amanda would reveal a secret that must be kept buried.

And so, against the background of Gregory's words, Amanda thought with immense calculation about John Thorne. Only minutes after she had dropped Gregory's hand she recalled the calloused roughness of John Thorne's hands gripping her naked arms. The workman's hands that kneaded her body as if she were a common little slut he had lured into a dry ditch.

John Thorne, who in the act of possessing her became her possession. And a taunt to the powers of her narrow world that had kept her a pampered prisoner. She thought long and hard about John Thorne, and reminded herself that in a game this perilous, rules were made to be broken.

These were her thoughts when Finley followed his own discreet knock and entered the drawing room with a tray bearing the afternoon tea.

And so Gregory Forrest continued to endure Amanda's whims, hoping she would grow out of them and toward him. But on that evening when he sat through the endless dinner without the partner he would have chosen, he was close to giving up. Just when he'd received from Lady Eleanor the tacit but tangible assurance that she would consent to an engagement. And as the courtship had been lengthy, the engagement need not be.

But it was all going badly, and he could no longer keep it from himself. In this strangely long summer spent among these storybook people who never attended to business, Amanda had spent more and more time unreachable in her room, mildly indisposed. Gregory knew he need not worry about her health. His worries were all centered on their future.

He sat at the elegant dinner table, and beside him, instead of Amanda, sat this nameless woman with her pearls and her teeth and bright chatter about he knew not what. In this setting like a satirical play by Bernard Shaw cast with stock characters, he felt sunk in the helpless trough between idealism and determination. He clenched his square hands beneath the table and longed, just momentarily, for the kind of woman he could bend to his will. But in arrogance Gregory Forrest was no match for Amanda. And well he knew it.

Just at this moment a door, half-hidden by a screen, opened silently opposite Gregory. A maid in one of those absurd English caps bore in a tray of water ices in stemmed silver. She transferred it to the hands of the butler, who in turn passed it to the footmen for serving. What a lot of hired help it took to conduct this not very satisfying meal from kitchen to mouth, Gregory thought.

Then he noticed the maid. Only a glimpse and she was gone beyond the screen again. For a moment he thought it might have been Amanda herself. Nothing was beyond her, not even playacting the role of a servant at a dinner she'd refused to share with him. The same violet eyes in the serene, pale face. And all else disguised by the ridiculous cap and encompassing apron. But this fantasy passed, and he heard his dinner partner's voice rise in some question.

He turned to give her the kind of noncommittal reply he had learned always satisfied the English.

Mary had seen him. Halfway along the table and as handsome as Miss Amanda had said. Faraway eyes in a firmly set face, his thoughts perhaps somewhere else. Mary had never seen an American gentleman before. She'd half expected buckskin waistcoat and coonskin cap. But he was dressed like the rest of the gentlemen. And since she had never seen a baron or an earl, either, she might have thought he was one of those. He was a god among gods, and the vision of the sumptuous dining table and the tinkle of crystal and her own hunger dazzled her so that she very nearly missed her footing on the kitchen stairs.

"You, Mary or Miranda or whatever you're called, be quick with that platter of cheese!" Mrs. Creeth rasped out, shattering Mary's thoughts. The elderly woman watched with an eagle's eye as Mary lifted the vast platter without disarranging the delicate ropes of parsley around its edges. "And hurry along!" Mrs. Creeth added, though the new girl had contrived to be quicker than the cook's commands.

It was well past midnight before Mary found herself alone in the little space under the roof that was to be her cell. As far as she could tell, her room was directly above a portion of Miss Amanda's.

There was an iron bed with a thin, curling pad for a mattress. And instead of a dormer window cut into the slanting wall, only a small window angled against the night. And on the one battered chest, an oil lamp. For the new electrical wiring did not reach as high as the servants' attics.

Mary had worked as hard every day of her life as in the hours finally past. Still, she barely had time to empty the contents of her wicker valise and hang her few clothes on the wall pegs before a terrible weariness overcame her.

She was soon in her nightdress and lying in the bed, staring up through the slanting window above her head. The narrow bed might have been a great feathery eiderdown, for her mind drifted into a half sleep mingling the stars above with the crystal of the Whitwells' dining room. She thought once of Miss Amanda, playing her childish games in her vast lavender room. And of the young American gentleman dining as if alone in the room full of people. Then she must have been dreaming, for she saw him sitting alone, in fact.

He sat at the great glittering table, and she, Mary Cooke of Whitely Bank, advanced toward him bearing a great silver tray, slightly bent. And on it, instead of food, a great mound of flowers. Chrysanthemums, dahlias, Michaelmas daisies, love-lies-bleeding, lobelia, and the wild flowers of the roadside. Her unconscious mind turned from this absurdity, and she slept soundly.

But within the hour she sat bolt upright. She knew she was not at Whitely Bank. The dark shapes of the room were landmarks in unfamiliar territory. Her recent dreaming deepened the sense that she was lost. Thinking she still dreamed, she moved across the patch of cold linoleum toward the door. Her long, white, often-patched nightdress billowed in the drafts. Her feet found their way in the pitch-darkness of the hallway, and she moved on as if summoned by a distant voice.

In her mind it was perhaps morning, and she was eager to do the bidding of her betters. But the house was sunk in absolute quiet, and all the darkened faces of the clocks stood at two.

Still, Mary moved forward, sleepwalking, if that is what it was. Loosed from its tight knot, her black hair hung down to tumble around her shoulders. A curving, treacherous stairwell drew her on, drew her down. Her hand turned on the cold doorknob at its foot, and her feet sank into the deep luxury of a carpeted hall.

She stood, coming to herself now, not a yard from Miss Amanda's door. Frightened, she was turning instinctively back toward the attic stairwell when a hand fell on her shoulder, roughly.

Mary's mouth opened to scream, but the silence of the sleeping house continued unbroken.

Five

———— ✺ ————

I shall be murdered, Mary thought quite clearly as the rough hand tightened on her shoulder. Her own hand, reaching for the stairway door, missed the knob and closed over empty air.

The black hallway seemed rent by the screams within her head. She was spun around and violently embraced. A man's hand caught both of hers in an easy vise behind her back. Her face was half-smothered against his chest. *None of this is happening,* she thought, fumbling in her mind for the right prayers.

His chest was muscled with straining, rigid bands. Then his face sought hers, his chin against her temple, forcing her head back, roughly yet easily. Her mouth was still open in its silent scream when his lips found hers.

His lips and then his tongue. She writhed against him before her bare feet were half lifted from the carpet that would muffle any struggle. The one hard hand closed behind her neck, beneath her flowing hair. The other clamped her wrist. His mouth abandoned hers, searching for her eyes, tight shut in terror.

Mary knew that the hand clenching the nape of her neck could kill her in a simple gesture. Instead, it found its way across her shoulders beneath the flimsy nightdress. A calloused hand moving with an absolutely certain yet lightly lingering touch across her naked shoulder, marble-cold with fear. A hand that moved as confidently as if it had caressed her before.

There was the first sound, as the seam of Mary's nightdress tore from neck to shoulder. The sound of each separate stitch giving way as his heavy hand knotted the worn fabric and wrenched it down, away from her.

He freed her hands then, but they hung useless at her side. She was forced back against the polished door, and her nightdress ripped from her shoulder. The groping hand that drew it down closed over her naked breast.

She felt his lips on her neck—the smoothness of his lips and the sandpaper of his chin that burned across her coldness. His mouth found the swell of her breast. It was wet there, and warm where his mouth tried to encompass it. Then cold in the next second.

When she felt the ridge of his teeth moving across her flesh, tears began to fall from Mary's eyes. She blinked them away, staring madly into the darkness, too stunned for thought or prayer. And too frightened to call for whatever help there might be in the muffled house.

Beneath her chin, his head of pale, thick hair glowed dimly. "Please," she said in a strangled whisper. Her hand, with a sudden life, rose and rested in the thicket of his blond hair. "Please, I beg you —don't."

His fists clenched in a spasm on her arms. "My God," he said aloud, "who are you?"

Mary stood there, free, as his hands drew back from her. Her ruined nightdress left her half naked, but the darkness and his looming shadow covered her.

"I said, who are you?" he whispered hoarsely, and Mary fancied she could see his eyes glowing, though this was only her near-madness.

"M-Miranda, sir—if you please."

"I know no Miranda. Account for yourself and be quick about it before I—"

"I've only just come, sir. To be in service."

The man groaned, seemed to rub an enormous hand over his damp forehead. "Don't call me sir," he said. "I'm lower than you. Be off. What in hell are you roaming the halls for? Did *she* ring for you?"

"No one sent for me. I—I—"

"Creep back where you came from, then," he said, turning aside in an instant when Mary could almost make out his profile. "Forget this."

Behind her, Mary's shaking hand found the doorknob. In the next second she had vanished up the narrow stairs to her attic.

But John Thorne stood staring at the burnished blankness of the attic door before he moved heavily on to the next one down the hall. He stood for a moment, waiting for the animal excitement to subside, waiting until the pounding blood would give way to coolness. Finally he turned the noiseless knob on the door he had oiled himself and strode into Amanda Whitwell's bedroom.

The embers in the hearth still cast a glow as far as the burnished bedposts. Thorne saw Amanda stir and begin to reach out toward the lamp beside her bed. "Leave it dark," he whispered, and in the silence she heard the command and obeyed it.

She threw back the bedclothes, inviting him in. But he stood over her, staring down, whetting his appetite, and hers. Her hair was caught up in a schoolgirl's bow at the nape of her neck and fell down behind her. Impatient, she began to wriggle out of her nightdress, to pull it over her head.

"I'll do that," he said, and she lay back against the pillows. The little minx, he thought, she's only playing at obedience. He threw off his rough coat and began to unbutton his shirt, wondering if she suspected that he thought it unseemly to show his nakedness in the glare of an electric lamp.

It was the way of these upper-crust women, even when they were no more than chits of girls. So pampered and demure and grand. And then ready to show themselves in their beds and to stare at the nakedness of their lovers.

It was a rare enough man of his station in life who stripped off all his clothes to make love, even under cover of darkness. He threw the shirt after his coat and fumbled with the straining buttons on his trousers. Stepping out of them, he stood there, naked, at once both hot and cold.

The silkiness of her sheets was like her body. He reached out for her, and she was suddenly clinging to him like a cat. She grasped his wrists, drawing him nearer, covering his hands with kisses. And then she gnawed almost more than playfully at the fleshy, vulnerable heel of his hand. This maneuver was unseemly to him too, though he tried to mask the effect it had on him by jerking his hands away and grasping at her nightdress. She undulated like a mermaid, helping him slip the smooth stuff of the gown under her body and over her shoulders. Her face, only a white blur in the light of the dying embers, was lost for a moment as he drew the nightdress over her head, catching up her hair, which fell again over her shoulders.

With his hands on her breasts, he remembered the serving girl in the hall and was stunned again by what he had done. But Amanda's responsiveness left him little time for comparisons or chagrin. She had clamped the back of his neck with her insistent little paws and was pulling him down for the first of many kisses. She always demanded a great many kisses, thrusting her tongue down his throat like a Windmill Street tart.

When her body grew slippery with their sweat, she forgot her pretense of obedience. His hunger for her was piqued by her writhing. How little decency she had, never lying quietly with resignation so a man could part her knees and engage in his own assault. He must have her before she had him. Her legs climbed the small of his back, drawing him down. Above him, her ankles crossed and clamped, locking him in. One hand left his neck and guided him into her. But her legs continued to circle him as he moved deeper, his body completely shadowing hers in a decent darkness that released him to throbbing passion.

A moment or an hour later, she whispered, "John, whatever shall we do?"

"What we are doing," he replied, "as long as we can."

"You belong to me. You're mine. That's the way it is, isn't it?"

He could only nod in the darkness, his head locked in her hands, against her breast.

"MY KIDNEYS!" Mrs. Creeth whooped at Mr. Finley in triumph. "I only want you to have a look at my kidneys, Mr. Finley! And treat yourself to a whiff of their aroma while you are about it!"

Mr. Finley obliged Mrs. Creeth by hovering over the copper pan where the breakfast kidneys were browning in best butter. He applied one nostril to the steam rising from the pan and nodded with absentminded, early-morning dignity.

"I have said it on previous occasions, and I now repeat it. There is no one your equal in the matter of really well-prepared kidneys, Mrs. Creeth." Even the wart beside her nose appeared to glow in triumph at the compliment she had wrung from the butler. However, he glanced automatically toward the door lest Mrs. Buckle suddenly appear to hear her enemy praised by one whose position required unvarying impartiality.

The servants' bell had just sounded, at half-past six. But Mrs. Creeth's kitchen was already at midpoint in its preparations for breakfast. A vat of porridge bubbled beside the matchless kidneys, and the bacon hung in strips on a row of hooks above the dripping pan, ready to be thrust nearer the fire.

Hilda and Hannah were giving the meager sum of their concentration to the toast-making. Hannah attacked the loaf with a lethal knife while Hilda balanced the slices against the screened sides of the little device that fitted over the gas ring. She turned the toasting slices constantly, fearing Mrs. Creeth's warnings against charred toast more than she feared charred fingers.

The footman, Abel, was late. But then he almost always was, for he was a local, walking over every morning from Bierley and taking his sweet time about it. As he was employed only when the Whitwells entertained houseguests, he reserved a degree of independence deeply galling to Mr. Finley. One struggles to command an army with even a single part-time soldier in the ranks.

"That Abel," Mrs. Creeth said, pounding the air with a stirring spoon, "will find no breakfast awaiting him in *these* kitchens." But Hilda, who would have thrown herself into the flames for one amorous glance from Abel, silently slipped a slice of toast for him into her apron pocket.

In the small cell between the kitchen and the wine cellar, Betty, her mouth full of pins, was pulling a black uniform down over Mary's head. Betty's small, drawn face glowed greenish in the dim dawn light. But her hands tugged deftly at the voluminous uniform until Mary's face appeared over it.

If the previous night's terrifying encounter showed on Mary's face, Betty was too busy to notice. She grunted softly as she gathered up the folds of the uniform and with a threaded needle took a tuck here and there. Mary's slim figure began gradually to emerge.

"It's best-quality goods," Betty claimed through her pin-studded lips, "but it'll go halfway round you again. Still, you can trim it to size later on. And there's three more like it and some printed ones as well—rosebud-sprigged. *She* left 'em behind in her haste."

Mary looked down at the expanse of black uniform, thinking how suitably sober her mother would find this cast-off uniform. "Whose was it, Betty?" she asked.

"Oh, this was Lottie's, she wot flounced off back to London. Couldn't stick the country, she said. Wouldn't be needin' her uniforms neither, to hear her tell it. For she was set on gettin' married. Didn't even give proper notice. Mr. Finley was that put out.

"Lottie was head house parlormaid, or so they called her. But believe me, she never turned her hand over when her ladyship wasn't about. With her it was always, 'Betty, do them grates!' And 'Betty, turn that carpet in Sir T's dressin' room!' Oh, she was very much above her station, was Lottie, and says she's orf to marry the landlord of a public house in St. James.

"But I happen to know," Betty said, heaving herself up with an effort, "the only chap our Lottie ever walked out wif was the man wot blacks the boots at the Cavendish Hotel. You know, that place up in London Mrs. Rosa Lewis runs, where the nobs give actresses midnight suppers. And then once they've given them poor girls a good meal and a bottleful of bubbly, they sets on 'em and—"

"BETTY! Get the new one into her uniform and report to me this instant, my girl!" Mrs. Creeth's bellow cut across Betty's revelations.

"Anyhow, you're here now, and whether you're Mary or Miranda or wotever you're called, you're a welcome change from that Lottie!" And then Betty gave Mary a smile both shy and sly before bolting to do the cook's bidding.

The citizens of servants' hall sat to their breakfast when gray dawn was only beginning to seep through the twisting bars on the kitchen windows.

Mary hurried in, tying behind her the apron brought from home. Mrs. Creeth was just settling her pendulous weight at one end of the table, while Mr. Finley at the opposite end seemed to be offering up a silent thanks, either to God or Sir Timothy, for the first meal of the day. Hilda and Hannah handed around bowls of steaming porridge. Mary slipped silently into a chair before one of the bowls, hoping it was meant for her.

When Betty, beside her, passed a pot of marmalade, Mary nearly fumbled it in surprise. The servants' breakfast at Whitwell Hall was the most sumptuous banquet she had ever known. Moreover, it was lavishly sauced by her hunger, for she had not eaten a bite in twenty-four hours.

There was the porridge, lumpless and tawny, rising in a mound from an uncracked bowl. Mary stared in wonder at Mr. Finley's hand, which was pouring thick cream over his porridge and then dusting it with sugar. She gazed a moment too long, for he shot her a stern look.

There was toast as well, with both marmalade and butter. The butter in a round wooden bowl was imprinted with a rose design across the smooth yellow top. Mary wondered how the breakfast to be laid in the dining room above for the family and their guests could surpass this feast in grandeur. And then she caught her breath, for a platter of bacon and sausages was being sent around the table and past the empty chair of the tardy Abel.

Amid the clinking of cutlery, Betty leaned toward Mary and whispered, "We don't say nuffin' at breakfast." But mealtime conversation was beyond Mary's experience. Nor would she have ventured a word to these superior beings who seemed to dine like gentlefolk, only faster.

But then all at once Mr. Finley broke the silence, calling out, "I trust you passed a comfortable night, Mrs. Buckle!"

"Fitful," came Mrs. Buckle's complaining voice from a chair drawn up to the hearth. From the tail of her eye, Mary caught a glimpse of old Mrs. Buckle eating a hearty breakfast from a tray in icy solitude. It was clear that she would not place her feet beneath the table at which Mrs. Creeth presided. "And I must say," Mrs. Buckle went on, "this bacon is quite, quite inedible."

"Throw it on the fire, then," Mrs. Creeth barked, and returned to the devouring of a heavily buttered slice of toast.

It required all hands to convey the breakfast to the sideboards of the great dining room. In the morning light the room was a palace of mirrors, dazzling with the reflections from silver covers and urns. Great pierced silver baskets dripped with fruit beneath the Waterford chandelier. But only the pink side lights glowed over a board groaning with covered platters standing on silver legs above the spirit-lamp flames.

Mrs. Creeth's famous kidneys, an entire school of kippers, ranks of crisp sausages, pink beef awash in a cream sea. And hanging invisibly in the room the alluring scent of fresh coffee. Mary wondered as she bustled with the rest of the staff if coffee tasted as wonderful and mysteriously expensive as its scent promised.

By half-past eight no one had yet descended to the dining room. But Mr. Finley stood ready to serve the first who might appear. Beside him stood Abel, arrived at last and already severely reprimanded. The disgusted Mr. Finley had just discovered the hint of grease spots on Abel's lapels when the great double doors opened.

The female servants were sent scurrying to the pantry. But not before Mary saw that the first down to breakfast was the American gentleman.

Even in the serving-pantry gloom, she fancied that her eyes preserved a lingering impression of him. The coat of muted tweeds pulled taut over his shoulders, and the blue-blackness of his hair.

"Ooo, they are such slug-a-beds! Wouldn't it be wicked and lovely to sleep right through the day!" said Betty, who already seemed at Mary's elbow by habit. "And the ladies—they'll be calling for breakfast up in their rooms. All except her ladyship, of course. She's always down for her breakfast, though never this side of nine. Mrs. Glaslough, though, whenever she's stoppin' here, she don't show her face till teatime. She's called a famous beauty, is Mrs. Glaslough, though nobody's seen her in daylight for a donkey's years. And then Miss Amanda—she's in one of her sulks just now. But she'll be ringin' the bell orf the wall, come ten o'clock. They say she's starvin' herself, but not as regards breakfast.

"So we might just as well pull down some of them breakfast trays from the shelf, Mary. Ol' Creeth'll be callin' for 'em soon enough. It's a game, keepin' ahead of *her* commandments, but you can't win it."

There was a curious device mounted on the wall of servants' hall, just outside the door to Mr. Finley's private quarters. It was a board with numbered squares corresponding to the rooms of Whitwell Hall. Whenever the cord was pulled or the button touched in any of the chambers above, a bell rattled and then chimed on the board, and a black card dropped into the square, summoning a servant.

The contraption was Mr. Finley's greatest earthly joy, for he approved of such innovations as promoted the efficiency of his staff. But for her part, Mrs. Creeth, who was summoned by no one but her ladyship, and then by prior arrangement to discuss the menus, regarded the Board with the deepest suspicion. Mrs. Creeth took a dim view of electricity and spoke often of the likelihood that the infernal thing would doubtless one day explode, bringing the wall down on their heads.

"And what will happen when they all ring for us at once—by some evil chance? Answer me that!" she often said. "I shouldn't like to be at my work on *that* dark day!"

Betty referred to the Board as "Old-Buzz-and-Jump."

The Board whirred and chimed, conveying the information that Mrs. Glaslough had rung for her breakfast. Her tray was all but ready. Mrs. Glaslough never took anything but fresh fruit and tea.

"You, Mary—Miranda!" called Mr. Finley. "Take up Mrs. Glaslough's tray. She is three doors beyond Miss Amanda on the opposite side. And, mind you, knock and wait. Do you have that, my girl? Knock and then wait to be summoned. There's to be no bursting in on Mrs. Glaslough."

Mrs. Creeth muttered over her luncheon preparations but was stilled by the butler's glance, which firmly conveyed a very specific warning.

As Mary passed the door to her own attic and then Miss Amanda's room, she remembered too clearly the events of the night before. The odd, undecipherable confidences of the impulsive Miss Amanda. The hint of a man she could be flogged for loving. And then later, the dark encounter in the dead of night. Mary grew cold, remembering the grip of the stranger's hands, the wetness of his mouth. The nakedness of her breast. Her heart pounded, and she tried to take comfort from the daylit hallway. Its ivory paneling already glowed with midmorning light, and the flowers bloomed like great bridal bouquets from the bowls set on small, two-legged tables that jutted from the walls at regular intervals.

Mrs. Glaslough called an answer to Mary's knock almost at once, though the servant entered her room at half speed and with downcast eyes, wondering a little at Mr. Finley's pointed instructions. She thought it was perhaps only her imagination, grown overactive in this strangely foreign place, when she noticed that the door to Mrs. Glaslough's dressing room seemed just to be closing. It might have been a trick of the shadows, but it seemed very much as if someone had lingered until the last moment before exiting.

The scent of patchouli hung like incense in the dim room, though Mary could not identify that aromatic oil. Mrs. Glaslough was just drawing herself up on a haphazard tumble of pillows. The counterpane of quilted satin had fallen over the foot of the bed, and the pillow beside her contained a deep indentation.

"Good morning, madam," Mary said quietly, looking no nearer Mrs. Glaslough's famous face than one creamy shoulder. The lace strap of the lady's nightgown hung by a silken thread far down her arm. "I hope you rested well, madam."

"Don't be impertinent!" Mrs. Glaslough snapped and then caught Mary's horrified eye. Mary stood frozen in the act of seeking out a safe harbor for the breakfast tray upon the disordered bed. The teapot vibrated.

"Oh, madam, I meant no—"

"Of course you didn't." Mrs. Glaslough swept a strand of flame-colored hair from her brow and looked more intently at Mary. "I am sorry to be abrupt. But it *is* rather early in the day. And I'm Irish."

"Yes, madam?" said Mary, utterly mystified.

"Yes. And servants in my country do tend to be rather cheeky and —I suppose *inquisitive*—by nature. Tedious as well. As it happens, I had a somewhat *tempestuous* night, and I am pining for my tea. Pour it out, won't you? No sugar."

When she had performed this duty, Mary stepped back to rescue a dinner gown that lay in a bejeweled heap across a chair arm, a great ruby clip still clinging to the bodice. As she stooped to retrieve a pair of silk slippers, her eye was drawn to a champagne bottle that protruded its uncorked neck from beneath the bed.

"In the names of all the saints, don't open the curtains. I abhor daylight—what I've seen of it," Mrs. Glaslough cried out. She was occupied in dividing a peach with a small silver knife. "I am quite addicted to fruit in the morning," she said in a musing manner. "However, this peach is just the least bit overripe—not unlike myself."

Making no sense of this observation, Mary continued to order the chaos of the room. As she started to withdraw, Mrs. Glaslough said, "What is your name?"

"I'm called—Miranda, madam."

"I suppose you have grown quite thoroughly accustomed to hearing you are very like young Amanda—in appearance, I mean. You have quite the look of her."

"Oh, no, madam. I'm not really accustomed to anything," Mary blurted.

"Really?" Mrs. Glaslough replied with widened eyes. "How extraordinary."

"That is, I only began yesterday, madam. But perhaps Miss Amanda did notice a similarity. She asked me to take off my cap and looked at me."

"Yes, Miss Amanda *would* be engaged by any reflection of herself," Mrs. Glaslough said, intent upon her peach. "With a houseful of guests, I trust you have not met Lady Eleanor yet."

"Oh, no, madam."

"I am one of her oldest friends, though rather earthy for her taste. I have been in the business of shocking her sensibilities since we were girls together. Our families met at the seashore, though nowhere else. You will find her somewhat encased in her own dignity, but human withal. It is Amanda who wants watching. Do keep your guard up, Miranda. And now you may go."

Old-Buzz-and-Jump rattled just before eleven, announcing Miss Amanda's need for breakfast. Betty was directed to carry the tray up by Mrs. Buckle, whose idea of punishing Amanda's impertinence in calling her an old trout was to deny the young lady her presence.

But Betty was back only minutes later. She had succeeded in delivering the tray, but her eyes were wide and beginning to brim with tears. "She sent me packin' wif a flea in my ear, she did," Betty announced to the kitchen. "Sez it's Miranda who's to do her fetchin' and carryin' from henceforth—her very words! Oooo, she's ever so high-handed this morning, is Miss Amanda. Worse than wot she usually is." Then Betty blinked twice and looked around the kitchen to calculate the effect of this report.

Torn between the desire to discipline Amanda and the need to protect her from the loose talk of the lesser servants, Mrs. Buckle observed a rare silence.

Miranda's eyes remained fixed on the snowy linen of the tea towels she was folding. But Mr. Finley, beside her, asserted his command. "I am very much afraid that we must all endure the wrath of Miss Amanda for the time being—at least until the house clears of some of its guests and I have the opportunity to take up the matter with Lady Eleanor. It is our duty—yes, even our sacred trust—to serve all the members of the family to the limits of our capacities and beyond. However, until we have thoroughly settled the matter of the new servant's precise duties, our position is untenable.

"Therefore, until I find the moment to speak with her ladyship at a convenient time, Miranda will find herself occupied in household matters that do not permit her personal attendance on Miss Amanda.

"I charge you, Mrs. Buckle, with the task of attempting to reassert your former authority over the young lady. And while this is no small challenge, I have no doubt that you will find it within your powers to rise to it."

Mrs. Buckle's face expressed guarded satisfaction at this diplomatic decision. Even Mrs. Creeth at her chopping block professed her admiration for Mr. Finley's Solomonlike judgment. "I'm sure I don't know where we'd be, Mr. Finley, without you to command the ship, so to speak."

And so the rest of Miranda's day passed in a flurry of duties that kept her continually occupied below the bedroom floor. The clear soups and roast chicken prepared for luncheon gave way to the watercress sandwiches, rolled ingeniously into pinwheels, for tea. There was just time to join forces with Betty to prune and collect the fallen leaves of the sprays of cut flowers, big as bushes, that adorned the front hall.

The task took them longer than it might have, for at the approaching footsteps of family or guests, the two maids scurried through an all-but-invisible door in the panel wall, there to wait and spare their betters glimpses of themselves.

Miranda found herself listening for the footfalls of the American gentleman. She even wondered briefly if it might be within her powers of observation to locate his flaws. For surely he was flawed in some way or Miss Amanda would not be in love with another man.

But whether they were lurking or working, Betty enlivened the day with a steady, bubbling stream of gossip and speculation. Her only topic was shameful scandal, but she explored it thoroughly. She was too lighthearted and, Miranda decided, good-hearted, to moralize. But she was full of ripe tales of randy tradesmen, servants packed off in disgrace, and an occasional broad hint of irregularity abovestairs. Though she named no names except those of Mrs. Glaslough and Mr. Emerson.

Her favorite theme was the low but exciting life led by the inhabitants of the nearest town, Ventnor, which she portrayed breathlessly as a sort of Sodom-by-the-Sea, ringed by Gomorrah-like suburbs.

"Ooooo, such wickedness as does go on in town," she would repeat, "especially down on the sands at night. You wouldn't credit it, Miranda, indeed you wouldn't. No decent girl would! I'll take you there myself one day, and then you'll see!"

It was only when the shadows grew long across the polished floors, when Abel and Mr. Finley began to lay the fires, that Miranda had an odd momentary sensation of something like foreboding. But she dismissed the haunting feeling like any fancy that might interfere with her duties. She had been equal to the day's tasks, meshing neatly into the machinery of the domestic establishment.

"A new broom sweeps clean," Mrs. Creeth proclaimed, "but we old ones knows the corners." Still, the seasoned veteran could find little to complain of in a servant who kept so busy that she very nearly had to be *invited* to sit to her meals. Miranda was astonished to learn that the entire staff dined as sumptuously at noon and evening as they did at breakfast. She wondered at the bounty of the place. It would be many days before she could persuade herself that she was actually to be paid a wage as well.

The evening duties seemed to be dispatched with greater speed and fewer untoward incidents than on the previous night. The Whitwells' house party had dwindled to half its former number. After tea the curving front drive was continually full of motors conducting guests away. Some to Yarmouth to take the ferry to Lymington. Some to Cowes for the ferry to Southampton. And some to Ryde for the ferry to Portsmouth.

With only twelve at dinner and Miss Amanda firmly planted in her invisible lavender bower above, the house seemed very nearly empty. It was that emptiness and the long, slow settling of darkness that sounded an ominous note in Miranda's heart.

She thought of the enshrouded halls, the echoing stairwells that led to territory she still knew nothing of. Like paths in a forest folded in its own darkness. She remembered the stranger who roamed those halls in the deepest hour of night. And she could feel again his rough, calloused palm cupping her breast, those demanding hands tearing at her nightdress.

She wondered at a household that was run with the efficiency of a newly cleaned pocketwatch by day, given over to such lawless menace by night, a menace she could mention to no one. When she learned that the rooms where Betty, Mrs. Creeth, and Mrs. Buckle slept were all in the attics of other wings, isolation heightened her fears.

It was past nine and just dark before Betty, Hilda, and Hannah returned from the upper reaches of the house, where they had been turning out the rooms of the departed guests. Miranda was setting out the thin china for the next day's early-morning tea trays when the three maids burst in, full of abovestairs speculations. Betty bore aloft the champagne bottle she had fished out from beneath Mrs. Glaslough's bed.

"Lumme!" cried Betty. "That Mrs. Glaslough, she didn't polish orf all that champagne by her lonesome. Oooo, she is a one! No gentleman is safe around *her*—and her bein' forty-five if she's a minute!"

"Mind your tongue, girl!" Mrs. Creeth said drowsily from over her chocolate cup beside the fire. But she fell silent in order to hear more.

"And that American gent, Miss Amanda's Mr. Forrest, he's orf in the morning, by the looks of things. He's doin' himself no good hangin' about with Miss Amanda in one of her states. But I suppose he'll be catchin' up with her again in November when the family's in London."

"He's well out of it," Mrs. Creeth muttered obscurely from the fire.

"Here, stuff this in your pocket," Betty murmured, brushing past Miranda and passing an envelope into her hand. Later, in the apron room, Miranda opened the envelope with her new name scrawled in a careless hand across the flap. A pound note dropped out.

"Blimey!" said Betty, who was again just behind her, peering around her shoulder. "That Mrs. Glaslough, she's as generous with her money as wot she is with her—"

"A pound?" Miranda said in wonder. She had never held anything more than a ten-shilling note in her hand, and that only briefly. "Twenty shillings?"

"Well," said Betty, "it's addressed to you in Mrs. Glaslough's fist, and I found it on her night table, so I guess it's your tip. Perhaps it's to seal your lips. Perhaps you covered up for some of her nastiness!" Betty beamed at the thought.

"I only took up her breakfast," Miranda said, still riveted by the riches in her hand.

"She must've taken a likin' to you," Betty mused. "You never know with the Quality. They're very much give-it-then-snatch-it-away. And money either drips from 'em like rainwater orf the eaves or they're too mean to tip Buttons a tanner."

And so Miranda entered finally into the ranks of the serving class, having received her first largesse from the casual and capricious hand of the mighty.

The hour when she had to make the dreaded climb to her attic bed was forestalled by a suggestion from Betty. Her plan was for the two of them to occupy the deserted laundry long enough to wash their hair and then to dry it by the embers of the kitchen fire. "We don't want to be goin' about wif hair stiff wif muck like them two, Hilda and Hannah," Betty maintained.

And so with a final burst of energy after a long day, the two girls abandoned their caps and drew the pins from their imprisoned hair. They helped each other in the unwieldy process of stooping to scrub their tresses over the low sheet-metal sink. Miranda massaged Betty's scalp with the suds of laundry soap shampoo to the accompaniment of her victim's spluttering amid grunts of satisfaction. Betty produced a half bottle of apple-blossom scent left behind by a houseguest. "We didn't ought to smell like laundered shirts," she said as she sprinkled the scent over both their streaming heads.

Fortunately, Mrs. Creeth had relinquished her fireside post in favor of her bed. And so Miranda and Betty sat on the hearth rug, throwing their hair over their heads to catch the warmth from the banked fire.

Her eyes drooping with sleepiness, Miranda watched Betty by the flickering firelight. Her pertness seemed subdued, though she chirped on in snatches of disconnected conversation. Her hair hung in limp, colorless ringlets about her narrow face. The play of firelight and shadow accentuated the long and narrow nose that she thrust harmlessly into the business of others.

It was a foxy face, Miranda thought, perhaps less wise than quick. There were patches of dark beneath the button eyes as well, as pronounced as smudges of coal dust. Miranda wondered if her new friend was quite well.

"How old are you, Miranda?" Betty asked suddenly.

"Eighteen—nineteen come January," Miranda replied.

"Cor. To be eighteen again and know wot I know now," Betty sighed with worldly conviction.

"How old are you, Betty?"

"Twenty," came the grave-voiced reply.

The candle Miranda carried up the many flights to her attic flickered in sudden drafts. She stepped carefully in the moving pool of yellow light that only underscored the darkness beyond and behind.

But she found the door to the final twist of steps and shot a flimsy bolt behind her. The tiny room above that she had not yet seen by day was flooded with moonlight, falling across the patched blanket on her bed.

The unseasonal scent of her apple-blossom hair filled the room. Miranda lingered for a moment before pulling her hastily mended nightdress on, while the moon bathed her body in white light. Just when exhaustion and a lingering fear of this vast house should have hurried her under the blanket, Miranda was caught up by a strange spell she could neither quite capture nor dismiss. It was compounded of the moonlight and the heady apple-blossom scent of her hair. And something more. A warmth that seemed to envelop her, insisting that she recall memories of moments she had never known. A longing, perhaps, though Miranda had longed for nothing in her life, nothing she could name.

The sea, perhaps. She had longed, even as a child, to stand endless hours beside the sea. To watch the waves breaking over the rocky tip below the headland and fan smooth as oil across the colored sands, thrusting a curl of foam before it to encircle her feet. But there had never been time for the luxury of that idleness, or a more pointed subject for her desires.

But in that moonlit moment Miranda did know desire. And when she crept under her blanket, there seemed no possibility of sleep. Her scalp tingled from Betty's more-than-firm touch. Her feet throbbed from her endless, hurrying steps over flagstone, marble, and parquet. Her heart pounded in a throbbing rhythm of its own, and her eyelids would not stay closed, but fluttered like insistent moths.

As her mind began to drift through only the sketchiest of bedtime prayers, she was aware of someone she could not see. Not a sound in the house below and around her suggested an intruder. The bolt at the foot of her stairs would keep no strong man out, and yet it would sound its own rattling alarm if someone so much as leaned against the door.

Miranda knew with a strange certainty that somewhere about the sleeping house there was someone awake and abroad. She was not given to such presentiments, but never for a moment did she question this one.

She threw back the blanket and rose to her knees, pushing above her at the window set into the sloping roof. There was a latch that her fingers found and flipped open. Then she could push the frame up, with a small hail of grit and dead beetles showering down. As she thrust the window back against the slate roof tiles, Miranda stood up on her bed. She was more than head and shoulders above the level of the windowsill. From above the waist, she stood in the open air, surveying the hundred angles of the roofs of Whitwell Hall. Each surface was either paved or bordered in silver moonlight. And the air was midsummer-still. Even the lingering dampness of her hair gave her no chill.

The twisting chimney pots stood in ranks of three or four, rigid guardsmen with aimless wisps of smoke still lingering above their beaver tops. A soundless mouse skittered in looping arabesques in its attempt to climb the smooth slates to the rooftree. He skidded and climbed, tumbled and recovered, crept stealthily where sharp claws gave him no advantage. And then, in a final burst, charged the peak of the roof and disappeared over the far side.

An arm's length in front of Miranda was a parapet, stretching the length of the roof over one wing of the house and cradling a gutter, filling with the first of the autumn leaves.

Without quite realizing it, Miranda lifted herself up and edged out onto the sill. When she turned again toward the parapet, she could see beyond it down across a side garden. The sudden awareness of the dizzy height of her vantage point made her lunge suddenly for a purchase on the parapet. For a second she balanced between crashing feet-first back through the narrow window onto her bed and sprawling face-down into the gutter.

Edging farther out, she could anchor her elbow along the weathered top of the parapet. There was no sign of either the outbuildings behind the house or the tree-lined drive that approached it from the village. She was gazing out over a side garden she had never seen. It was terraced and scalloped in degrees of darkness. The view was foreshortened by the black shapes from a grove of trees that night had rendered a forest. There was a lawn rolled as flat as a ballroom floor, but its purpose eluded Miranda, who had never seen croquet played. Before the croquet lawn was a long balustrade balanced at intervals by squat, square pilasters supporting empty urns. Beside this stone fence a swept garden walk stretched shadowless, its gravel turned to marble chips by the moon.

One of the urns seemed to alter its shape and move. Miranda's eyes found it instantly in a scene as immobile as a colorless painting. Someone had been standing beside the urn and was moving on.

It was scarely a human figure. Miranda longed for it to be nothing at all—a trick of light. But it was a figure, deeply bent, shrouded. Black skirts fanned out across the path behind it, and a shawl was draped far down and perhaps thrown over one hunched shoulder to conceal a face. Only a hand, small as a white pinpoint in the distance, thrust from the shroud to grasp a cane, or perhaps a walking stick, as the figure moved slowly, painfully along the path. She paused, then hobbled on. The cane was of some highly polished wood, like a crystal wand. There was a diamond spark where the light touched what must have been a metal band near the crook clasped by the twisted hand.

The figure crept on in a silence observed by every nocturnal animal, every hunting owl. Minutes passed before the apparition was lost to view by the angle of the roof.

Miranda slid silently back through the window. Her feet, freezing now, found the thin mattress. She pulled the window over her and twisted the latch tight shut. Then she sought the escape of sleep. As her mind withdrew from the vision in the haunted garden, she sobbed once, giving way to fear at the multitude of horrors that lay about her in the world.

Six

---❦---

"We are in for a bit of a respite, and not before time," Mrs. Creeth said to Miranda in an almost comradely tone. Miranda's cuffs were rolled above her elbows, and her face glowed from the steaming, soapy water in which she was washing the luncheon dishes. There were fewer of them than the day before as the Whitwells' house party continued to disband. "A bit of peace and quiet won't be unwelcome," Mrs. Creeth mused. "You're settling in, then, are you, my girl?"

"Yes, thank you, Mrs. Creeth," Miranda replied. But her thoughts carried her well beyond such a short and respectful answer. How she longed to confide in Mrs. Creeth—or at any rate in an older woman less flighty than Betty who could throw some light on the mysteries of Whitwell Hall. But Mrs. Creeth would bridle at any unsolicited comments. Her faintly friendly air would sour to contemptuous rebuffs if Miranda phrased even a cautious question. Experience with her own mother had earned Miranda insight into the ways of a woman growing gnarled and hard in service.

"It's a pity, really." Mrs. Creeth addressed a bowl of rising dough. "I could have made a first-rate kitchenmaid of you, teach you a thing or two about good English cookery and baking, if I had my way in the matter. You've not tasted any of my Dundee cake, or my spotted dick, but I'm that vain of both recipes. And not without cause.

"Oh, I shouldn't be the worst of teachers, I can tell you! Not like the days gone by. Why, would you believe in my first place—I wasn't the age you are now when I went to work for old Lady Beaumartin at Torfield Court. I was put to work under the head cook there, a Mrs. Tankersley, if I remember rightly. Proper old dragon she was, too. And a first-rate cook in her way, I'm bound to admit. But would you credit it? She did all her sauces in the still room, locked the door behind her and all. And brought the saucepan out covered with a tray cloth. Terrified somebody'd steal her recipes, she was. I call that very selfish. Still and all, I learned despite her. Not that I stooped to *her* recipes, which was all very old-fashioned and commonplace. I learned, though, and never have been mean with my knowledge, though there's little enough kitchen help about these days as could profit by my teaching.

"But they'll have you upstairs, I daresay, once they can get their heads together. Mind you, girl, don't take on the airs and graces of one of them frog maids, once they have you serving Miss Amanda."

"Frog maids, Mrs. Creeth?" Miranda looked up, astonished.

"That's right—you know, French maids. Saucy pieces, the lot of them, flouncing their fannies about with lace on their petticoats like an improper postcard and I don't know what all. Let them stay in Paris and Dieppe and them foreign places. Don't take on no airs, my girl. Miss Amanda has quite enough of them on her own. Quite enough for three or four young women, I should have thought. Keep your wits about you, if you have any. In this house you'll need them!"

Miranda needed her wits about her less than an hour later, but they deserted her at the strategic moment. On her way to polish and tidy the morning room, she took the circuitous path from the kitchens across and under half the main block of the house that Betty had shown her.

A half flight at the end of two subterranean turnings rose to the invisible door set in the paneling of the front hall. From there Miranda had only to cross a few yards of the family's main interior crossroads before reaching the morning room.

She had gone as far as the invisible door and was through it before she realized someone was standing in the hall. It was the American gentleman, as she saw at the first glance, though he was facing away from her and seemed to be staring far up to scan the wall near the ceiling.

Miranda stopped dead, considering retreat. She need only take two steps back to reach the invisible door and be gone. And perhaps she wouldn't have long to wait on the cellar stairs, for Mr. Forrest was surely standing there only until a motorcar could be brought around. There was a pile of gentlemen's luggage, strapped and ready to shift, heaped beside the table.

But Miranda remained, her eyes following the long horizontal line of his shoulders. Then she was staring up, too, trying to follow his gaze, which seemed fixed at a point high on the wall, as if he were searching out a nest of bats. His head of blue-black hair was held well back.

She could see very little in the gloom near the distant ceiling. The chandelier that hung down three floors was unlit, and there were no balconies piercing the high walls. The hall was like a great box, paneled in white below and painted in palest gray above.

But as she searched the twilight heights of the room, she fancied she saw a dim line of decoration faintly visible near the coved molding of the ceiling. The longer she looked, the more the pattern revealed itself. A series of darker scrolls, coiling and uncoiling together and ending at intervals with little festoons that might have been footed bowls of fruit or perhaps very formal little weeping willows. She was quite sure she saw this quaint design by following the slow-moving gaze of the American gentleman.

Then suddenly she felt giddy from stretching her neck and from forgetting for a moment she was skulking there. Her eyes dropped to Gregory Forrest's hands, clasped behind him. They were heavy and square, almost a farmer's hands in shape. But smooth and white, arrestingly pale against the background of his blue suit.

They weren't the work-hardened hands that had groped and torn at her in the darkness of her first night. She had never seen such hands as these, clasped easily, with great strength held lightly in reserve.

All this she thought in a moment, gladly rejecting the American as her assailant. Unless, she thought, growing as lightheaded as Betty, he was like the man in that story by Mr. Stevenson. The man who was Dr. Jekyll by day and Mr. Hyde by night. The tale returned to her with hideous clarity from her days in the spinster's parlor-schoolroom. She even remembered a phrase about the pathetic Dr. Jekyll and "the law of his members warring against the law of his mind."

Miranda shivered and ran a hand over her arm, and the starchy sleeve rustled. Then the scraps of her education in literature vanished, for Gregory Forrest turned suddenly around. She so forgot herself that her eyes met his before she could cast them down to the floor. When she commanded her feet to bolt, they fastened themselves to the floor.

His eyes were very brown. Not spaniel eyes, but as piercing as if they were blue, however without the iciness. "I think it's called grisaille, but I'm not sure," he said to her, very directly.

"Please, sir?"

"The detailing just under the molding at the top of the room. That gray-on-gray pattern that repeats. It's too far off to see very clearly, but that's what it's called, I think. A lot of artistry to not much effect. I'm trying to learn architecture, among other things, and that's one of the more useless tidbits I've picked up." And then he smiled, and his smile was just the least bit crooked.

Miranda smiled back, forgetting everything that had ever happened to her in her life, and all her training.

"I think we've met before," Gregory Forrest was saying. "Or almost. I noticed you in the dining room night before last. You were working and I was eating. That almost amounts to an introduction, doesn't it?"

"Oh—I shouldn't think so, sir," Miranda said, finally remembering to lower her eyes. She stood silently, all retreat cut off, while it dawned on her in stages that the gentleman was waiting for her to tell him her name, as if they were to introduce themselves, in fact.

She was reasonably certain it wasn't proper to introduce herself to a man of her own station. She was positive that it was improper in this instance. It seemed a strange request, and unseemly. But then he was foreign, and perhaps he was as lost in the world in his way as she was in hers. You could notice the foreignness in his voice far more than in his appearance.

"They call me Miranda, sir," she whispered.

"How do you do, Miranda. I'm Gregory Forrest. What is your last name?"

"Cooke, sir—but they don't call me that here." The lunatic idea that Mr. Forrest might call her Miss Cooke at some embarrassing future time, and in the presence of others made Miranda's blood run cold.

It occurred to her that perhaps here was the very flaw that had turned Miss Amanda against this otherwise perfect man. Not that he didn't know his place, but that he didn't know the place of others. Not to know how to speak to servants from a proper remove seemed a grave deficiency, and hardly fair to all concerned. Though, of course, Miss Amanda herself seemed to speak with strange and sudden familiarity to those who were trying their best to serve her. It was too confusing and went against all Miranda's training. And all the while, she was staring great gaping holes into the paving of the hall floor while Mr. Gregory Forrest remained unmoving. She knew she had only to raise her glance to meet his eye.

She did just that when he said, "You gave me a minute or two of surprise the other night. Did you know that, Miranda?"

"Oh, no, sir."

"Well, you did. At the time I thought I might have been influenced by too many glasses of Sir Timothy's wine. But I had the idea that you were Amanda disguised as an honest working girl."

Miranda maintained her silence, already beginning to wonder how often this supposed resemblance between her and Miss Amanda was to be remarked upon. It was shaping up in her mind as a distinct impediment to the discharge of her duties, whatever they turned out to be.

"But now I'm cold sober," Gregory Forrest went on, "and the resemblance is just as striking."

She knew he was studying her. The pleasure in that sensation began to play lightly around the edges of her embarrassment. He seemed to know he was making matters awkward for her. His next words were a change of tack. "It's a very beautiful house, isn't it?"

"Oh, yes, sir." It would have silenced Gregory Forrest to know that her chief experience of it was her attic cell and the rabbit-run of kitchens and tunnels where no guest had ever penetrated.

"Especially Lady Eleanor's own sitting room, which I was honored to visit exactly once. That was when I knew I was being taken seriously by at least one lady in the Whitwell family."

"Oh, sir, I haven't seen Lady Eleanor's sitting room."

"Well, you should," Gregory Forrest said. "I'll ask her to show it to you sometime. In fact, I could ask her now."

There was the sound of silk and a soft footstep on the carpeted grand staircase that descended at the rear of the entry hall. It could only be Lady Eleanor approaching. The foreknowledge that in a matter of seconds she would be discovered by Lady Eleanor Whitwell chatting with her daughter's fiancé at last set Miranda's feet in motion. Gregory Forrest glanced once toward the staircase where his hostess's slippered foot was making its appearance. And when he turned back, expecting to see the beautiful hired girl so like a demure twin of Amanda, he found himself staring at the burnished blankness of the marble floor and the seamless paneled wall beyond it. It was a vanishing act with an oddly supernatural effect that would return to baffle him at odd moments for many days.

Miranda stood on the servants' side of the invisible door, her back pressed against it and her heart pounding. It may have been wrong to dismiss herself, but it would have been dangerous to remain. Lady Eleanor had not yet even summoned her for a first interview. And Miranda's mother had been forcefully stressing to her the importance of first impressions all her life.

She could hardly return to the kitchen—and to Mr. Finley—without having performed her dusting duties in the morning room. Her only hope was that Lady Eleanor would bid Mr. Forrest a brief good-bye and then quit the entrance hall herself. There seemed nothing to do but wait, positioned there between two worlds. And it was impossible not to hear conversation through the thin door.

The voice of Lady Eleanor carried nothing of her daughter's commanding tone. It was low-pitched and as nearly sultry as its cultured rhythms allowed. Miranda first heard Lady Whitwell's voice over the soft, swirling sounds of her gown. She was ever after to remember the mingling of those two delicate, near-musical notes.

"My dear Mr. Forrest—Gregory—I'm afraid we've rather let you down on this visit. The entire situation somehow surpasses mere embarrassment."

Gregory Forrest's reply was too low-pitched for Miranda to hear. It sounded like the husky rumblings of an apologetic man, and he interrupted himself at frequent intervals to clear his throat.

"Something is clearly troubling Amanda," Lady Eleanor continued. "And I'm afraid it is rather too like her to trouble others at such times.

I dislike saying anything at all, and I beg you not to think me interfering. I can hardly apologize for her behavior without making her sound much younger than she is. And yet Amanda is being absurdly childish, but to what purpose I cannot imagine. With another girl it might be put down to mere shyness, but in Amanda's case we both know better than that. I could extol her high spirits to you, but I'm very much afraid my heart would not be in it."

"I'm willing to wait, Lady Eleanor," Forrest said in a voice of gathering strength.

"You are being more than patient. Few men would be. And without sounding disloyal to my own nation, I must just add that most Englishmen would have taken flight long since out of a combination of wounded pride and sheer funk." The lilt in Lady Eleanor's voice, planted there with some care, lightened the tone of a conversation that threatened to sink like a stone.

"My dear man, I think you're quite right to return to London now. You have your studies to think of. And to speak plainly, your presence just now may well be prolonging Amanda's tiresomeness. I should, I assure you, like nothing better than to burst in upon her for the sole purpose and pleasure of dragging her from her bed of manufactured pain. But I have the certain feeling that nothing would appeal more strongly to her sense of the melodramatic. Most girls will cast their mothers in a Gorgon's role—Medusa, preferably—but Amanda is rather quicker to do that than most. And certainly more steadfast. I have been known to indulge a fleeting envy of my daughterless friends.

"But don't think of staying away all the autumn. Now that summer has passed, Amanda will stir herself in a quieter house. She loathes being what she calls *bored,* though I should have thought that most of her monotony is self-inflicted. Still, I have sometimes thought that in the summer a houseful of company bent on enjoying themselves has a dampening effect on her—though I should prefer not to pursue all the implications of that theory. I shudder to think how she—how all of us—would bear up under a London Season for her. But if Amanda is to have her Season, it still lies many months off. Besides, my dear boy, perhaps other arrangements for Amanda's future will be made before she is given the opportunity of snubbing and sulking her way through a long London summer of festivities that everyone else is doggedly determined to enjoy.

"We shall see you when we come up to London in November. I'm not frightfully keen on opening the Charles Street house only for the month. But London is bent on observing a Little Season before everyone goes to ground for the winter. And not to be there invites adverse comment.

"One is either thought too hopelessly bovine to leave the rustic lair, or one is branded a hermit with something to hide. One doesn't mind for oneself, but with a daughter. . . . But never mind. I shall write to you, and perhaps even Amanda will persuade herself to scrawl you a line."

There was a sound at the great double front door then, only a second after Lady Eleanor had finished her gracious speech. Had Miranda ever attended the theater, she would have been struck by the neat timing of it. "Here's Thorne now to collect your things." And then the subdued flurry of good-byes, a silent clasping of hands, perhaps, and a murmured word of added encouragement from the hostess, followed by a response from the guest. And finally the sound of silk subsiding into stillness.

Miranda waited what seemed minutes to her before she eased open the door in the paneling and hurried across to the morning room, through the hall where John Thorne had just carried Gregory Forrest's luggage out under the portico to the circular drive.

If Miranda had dared to linger in the hall to venture a look through one of the long windows that flanked the front doors, she would have seen the two men who were both hopelessly and miserably in love with Amanda Whitwell.

She would have seen Gregory Forrest, a light-gray topcoat over his arm, settling into the rear seat of Sir Timothy's shuddering new Lanchester motorcar. And staring straight ahead with a stoic expression evident even in his profile.

Miranda would certainly have seen John Thorne, stacking the cases along the running board and securing them there with a complicated overlapping of straps. John Thorne, who had whittled shamelessly away at Sir Timothy's arguments against buying a motorcar until he had finally promoted the idea and thus secured a promotion for himself as chauffeur-mechanic. Well aware that Sir Timothy abhorred any kind of fuss, John Thorne was determined to master the motorcar's every eccentricity so that it seemed a sort of flawless perpetual-motion machine, tuned and at the ready around the clock.

He had even rebuilt the greater part of the stables into a mechanic's garage, disposing of the carriage horses at a sale in Freshwater and retaining only a quartette of ponies and Amanda's former friend, the amiable Sapphire, for use with the dogcart and the brougham.

Miranda would surely have noticed Thorne's mildly annoyed expression as he busied himself with the touring car. He would save his expression of wrathful contempt for Gregory Forrest for quieter, more private moments with Amanda. But his disgust was apparent for the motorcar Sir Timothy had chosen. Trust the old man to make an unimaginative choice once he was persuaded to make any decision at all.

Instead of a Rolls, Sir Timothy would buy a six-cylinder Lanchester with side curtains that seemed to admit streams of rainwater if there was so much as a cloud in the sky. And the stubby bonnet that sheltered the thirty-eight-horsepower was no bigger than a breadbox and less fashionably formed.

John Thorne gave the last of Gregory Forrest's suitcases a quick and glancing blow with the side of his boot and swung himself up into the driver's seat. He would have given up the idea of a motorcar entirely if Sir Timothy—not to mention Amanda—had insisted on his wearing livery. And so he settled himself behind the wheel in his corduroy jacket and soft countryman's cap. He engaged the gears, hauled at the great steering wheel, and the Lanchester lurched, then glided around the smooth circle and off down between the rows of Italian pines to the distant gates.

But long before the Lanchester had passed through the gates that divided park from village, Miranda was already at work in the morning room. She was on her knees with her skirts hitched, rubbing down the strange mazelike carved backs of the Chippendale chairs with a polishing rag.

She had worked unceasingly for three-quarters of an hour before she sat back on her heels and ran the back of her wrist across her forehead. Surveying the glassy surface of the parquet floor between the long islands of Oriental rugs, she searched for dust. Instead, she saw reflected there the silver-green of the lawn beyond.

To stretch her legs, she stood up and walked toward the long morning-room windows that gave out onto a terrace paved in a herringbone pattern of bricks bordered in marble. The terrace appeared to descend to a side lawn in a series of steps that ran the length of it, providing an open vista of lawn bordered with flower beds. A gardener was knee-deep in the vegetation to one side. Beside him, a growing mound of late-summer flowers grew in a miniature straw-stack of brown leaves and stems, with here and there the faded vigor of the last August blossoms. He was replacing them with autumn plants from pots wheeled up in a barrow from the greenhouse.

Miranda could not name all the new flowers that ranged through the purples to deepest red and smoldering russets. There were dahlias, of course, and gentians and curly chrysanthemums, and other blooms more exotic. She could imagine them all grouped as tightly as bouquets in the shelter of the boxwood, blooming far into the new year, proof against the winds of winter and the somber grayness of its days.

She looked beyond the nearest lawn to the balustrade that divided the middle distance beyond a swept walkway. The balustrade supported by the squat bases of the towering, empty stone urns. And suddenly it was that soundless night again when she had gazed down upon this very view from the parapet. This was the side garden, like a manicured hidden kingdom, where she had seen the fearful figure. The hunched crone moving soundlessly over the gravel in a shroud darker than the night. The figure of nothing quite human leaning heavily on the wickedly gleaming cane.

Miranda looked again for comfort to the very human figure of the busy gardener, squatting to throw behind him the wrenched-up weeds. And she gazed again at the rich autumn flowers, now nodding in their pots and from the mouths of bulbous bags of earth. But soon to put down roots. Then, beginning to sense herself putting down some tentative roots in this new place, she turned back to her work.

The days that followed confirmed the kitchen in the idea that the new maid showed extraordinary promise, though the staff was wary of newcomers. Ham-fisted Hannah and Hilda only gawped without envy at the amount of work Miranda could accomplish with efficiency. For her part, Miranda found a workday that stretched to sixteen hours less onerous than sudden assaults in dark corridors and grim specters in the garden. She'd grown agile at flying to her attic after her work, and she was never again tempted to push open her window to view the midnight lawn.

The interview with Lady Eleanor she had half dreaded came about with such ease that Miranda hardly had time for fear or awe. Late one morning Mr. Finley slipped into his black coat after Old-Buzz-and-Jump had sent a signal from Lady Eleanor's boudoir. He snapped his fingers once in Miranda's direction, and she followed him up to be viewed and interviewed.

It wasn't Mr. Finley's way to inundate a servant with last-minute advice before such important moments. The ordinary sort of country girl would hardly profit by eleventh-hour advice, and one or two had been known to faint on the stairs after no more than an admonitory word. Miranda merely kept at his heels and was standing in the sitting room above the drawing room with the painted ceiling before she quite knew where she was.

Apart from Sir Timothy, Lady Eleanor was the only member of the household not to comment on Miranda's startling similarity to Miss Amanda. Her eyebrows scarcely rose, perhaps because she had already caught more glimpses of Miranda than anyone realized. Perhaps because it was beyond her to equate the appearance of a rural serving girl with her own daughter. Or more likely, from kindness, she wished to spare a newcomer a personal comment she must already have heard quite often enough. Lady Eleanor welcomed Miranda with warmth and dismissed her almost in the next moment, with the promise that they would speak later, once the house had quite settled down. It was the exercise of a light touch from a subtle mind that was like nothing Miranda had known in her small world, where those with authority exercised it heavy-handedly. Still, Miranda recognized it.

But she was back again on the hall side of the door before she had registered the full effect of Lady Eleanor's chamber, a room so unlike the conventional splendor of the rest of the house that it would challenge a far more practiced eye than Miranda's.

It was more garden than room, suffused throughout with the soft, muted reflection of glass in twisting petal forms in the palest yellows and pinks. Even the ivory lacquered table on which Lady Eleanor rested her arm throughout the brief interview was shaped and turned to resemble three large, overlapping lily pads, supported by twining tendrils. The ceiling had been lowered and replaced by a screen of ebony and parchment, suggesting the austere grandeur of Japan. More than that, Miranda had not noticed, for though she finally remembered to keep her eyes on the floor before her mistress's feet, she had caught a glimpse of Lady Eleanor. Her hair had been more casually dressed than usual, but dressed nonetheless. And her robe suggested far-off heathen places, with the sleeves slit open to the shoulder and the collar high and round like a vicar's, if vicars had ever worn pale-peach silk shot through with threads of lime and silver.

Miranda withdrew, thinking Lady Eleanor twice as beautiful as the portrait she had already dusted from the top of a teetering ladder. For she had found her way through a good deal of the house in that first week. The official list of duties drawn up each morning by Mr. Finley, and augmented in separate interviews with Mrs. Buckle and Mrs. Creeth, grew shorter almost at once. Miranda was able to occupy herself without need for the explicit, dogged direction Hilda and Hannah and Betty required to set them in motion. Miranda had even managed the feat of unhooking the curtains in Sir Timothy's study to exchange them for the heavy winter velvet ones while the old gentleman slumbered undisturbed in his chair at the very foot of the movable library steps.

"Coooo," said Betty when she heard of this, "you might've come crashin' plump down on the old party, killin' him from the shock. I'd've been all thumbs tryin' to work over him!"

"And that, my girl, is why you were not given the responsibility of the task," said Mr. Finley, who was passing at the time.

"Nosy old bugger," Betty said in a whisper. "Everywhere at once, he is. You carn't have a private word anywhere in this house." But she said that some while after Mr. Finley had taken himself elsewhere.

It was a week of triumph for Mrs. Buckle, who let it be known thrice daily in servants' hall that she had reasserted her old claim on Miss Amanda. The food on the tray appeared to be gone after each meal. But it was Mrs. Creeth's loud surmise that Mrs. Buckle ate it herself on the way back from Miss Amanda's room, pausing on landings to gobble down whole lovely cutlets and milk puddings. Those who thought the young lady would dance out of her bed on Mr. Forrest's departure were proved wrong. Apparently Miss Amanda had another cause and meant to sit in invisibility until the powers of the Hall gave in to her demand for a maid of her own.

On the Friday evening in mid-September when Miranda was silently observing the completion of her first week in service, there was a mildly festive air about the table in servants' hall. The subdued gala, however, stopped short of the hearthside settle, where Mrs. Buckle picked at her supper in superior silence.

Mr. Finley showed every sign of bursting into speech—a formal address. Even Hilda and Hannah looked medium-bright, continually digging at each other's ample sides with large, dimpled elbows. When the pudding was cleared away, Mr. Finley extracted his spectacles from his waistcoat pocket. From his breast pocket he withdrew a handful of brown envelopes. He cleared his throat portentously, and Mrs. Creeth rang for silence with her spoon against a tumbler. But the entire kitchen had already fallen quiet at the first sight of the envelopes.

"For the benefit of one among us," Mr. Finley began, rising from his chair, "who is unaccustomed to our—ah—ways and—routines, I shall just take a moment to touch briefly upon the manner of financial —ah—remuneration that is traditional at Whitwell Hall.

"On the second Friday of every month, wages are distributed in the amounts commensurate with each servant's position. As you know, since the—abrupt—departure of Lottie, we are at present endeavoring to proceed without the services of an upper housemaid. Nevertheless, we seem to be holding our own, thanks to the good offices of—er—Miranda—and, of course—Betty—"

Mr. Finley's voice undulated on, catching the rhythm of a zealous missionary preaching to a circle of benighted savages. Betty leaned toward Miranda and whispered daringly into her ear, "He'll go orn and orn like this, even after he's handed round our lolly. He's in love wif his own voice, he is, and it's the only lovin' he knows anyfing about, you may be sure. All this wind and very little wages, the way I see it. And none of us to know wot anybody else gets, but of course we all do. As you've only been here the week, yours'll be ten bob, since you're to be makin' two quid a month, same as me. I heard 'em deliberatin'. Mrs. Creeth, though, she makes—"

"BETTY!" boomed Mr. Finley, nostril flaring. "If you would prefer to take the floor, my girl, feel free to do so, and I shall gladly give way to your superior wisdom!"

"I'm sorry, I'm sure, Mr. Finley. I was only puttin' Miranda here in the picture, like."

"I believe I can manage that task quite competently myself, if you will kindly grant me the opportunity and allow Miranda to listen."

"Quite right, too," nodded Mrs. Creeth, working her neck and pursing her lips.

"*She* makes forty quid a year, the old sow," Betty hissed quickly in Miranda's ear as Mr. Finley cleared his throat to continue. He concluded a quarter of an hour later, sensing that he had lost the rapt attention of even his staunchest ally. Mrs. Creeth's eyes were fixed on the six envelopes he had unwisely chosen to gesture with while outlining the fortnight's accomplishments and rewards.

"And so, in summing up, I can do no better than to quote but a few lines from Mr. Kipling, upon whose poetry we can all depend for a sentiment suitable to every occasion:

> *Creation's cry goes up on high*
> *From age to cheated age:*
> *'Send us the men who do the work*
> *For which they draw the wage!'*

Or as in the present instance and situation, the '*women* who do the work,' " Mr. Finley amended, permitting himself a gratified smile at his own paraphrase.

"Hear, hear, well said, Mr. Finley," Mrs. Creeth declared, though she had given way to an annoying habit of rubbing her hands together in the bald anticipation of her envelope.

The butler made a stately progress around the table, managing with each delivery to imply that the salaries were his personal gift. Miranda folded her envelope into her lap, awed that in her first week she was worth thirty shillings, including the astonishing tip left behind by the peculiar Mrs. Glaslough.

As Mr. Finley left the table to approach Mrs. Buckle with her envelope, Betty chanced another confidence. "Of course, there's no knowin' what *she* draws. Gives herself shockin' airs, but she's not too proud to take her money. Very likely has the first tanner she ever turned hidden away in her mattress!" At that moment Mrs. Buckle was receiving her packet with a curt nod and palming it into an invisible pocket of her skirt.

At that very moment, too, there came a thunderous pounding on the kitchen door. "Who in the world at this hour?" Mrs. Creeth said, starting in her chair. "See who it is, Hannah, but take care!"

Hannah, who looked comically alarmed, edged sideways to the

bolted door, which was still throbbing with a volley of violent knocks.

Mr. Finley froze in the act of placating Mrs. Buckle. His expression wrinkled in vexation at the intrusion of his cherished ceremony. There were several remarks he had held in reserve once the wages were distributed. Admonitions about the wisdom of thrift, the advisability of post office savings accounts. The tucking away of sensible sums against an otherwise bleak old age.

He meant to make a great point to the new girl that a considerable portion of her salary should be set in reserve for the maintenance and acquisition of future gowns, aprons, and caps. For the very reason that Miranda had been amply fitted out by her mother and had fallen heir to the departed Lottie's uniforms, she must not be left with the impression that these necessaries would last indefinitely. How little foresight these young girls had and how much in need they invariably were of firm advice.

But it was not to be, with the kitchen door half pounded down and every eye on it. "What's to do?" howled Hannah through the door, her hand reluctant to draw back the bolt. "Who's out there?" The sound of a hoarse voice barely audible through the oak door seemed to give her courage. She pulled back the door, and a tide of wet leaves blew across the floor, carried on a rain-laden night wind that sent the lamps swinging.

A boy of perhaps fourteen staggered into the kitchen, his eyes starting from his head. He was gasping with cold and something more. Miranda, who had come to fear the darkness that settled on the house by night, stared at the boy. He was an arresting sight as he stood in the room while the swinging lamps threw shadows across his white face. In the moments he fought for breath he was evidently unaware of the sensation he created.

His wrists hung well down out of an old wool shirt, blackened and clinging in wet patches. His hair was plastered in flat curls against his streaming forehead. His exceptionally long lashes were beaded with raindrops, which he tried to rub and bat away. He looked like a gawky angel, with two red and bony kneecaps thrust through the holes in ragged trousers that stopped above his shins.

The boy managed to put down the storm lantern that had guided him to the Hall while Hannah threw her considerable weight against the door.

"It's that cheeky monkey Willie Salter!" Mrs. Creeth proclaimed, on her feet now with hands planted on her hips. "Frightening the wits out of us all!"

"It's the estate agent's son," Betty said to Miranda, not taking her button eyes off the boy, who had never burst in on the Hall staff before.

"Speak up, boy!" said Mr. Finley. "What call have you bursting in on us this way?" The door that divided domestic staff from the estate servants was forever closed and barred in the butler's mind. Those over whom he had no authority were better rendered invisible.

"Come over to the fire, Willie!" Mrs. Buckle said unexpectedly. "Why, he's quite wet through!"

The fire thawed Willie's tongue, for as soon as he had spread his red hands before the grate, he managed to say in a breaking voice, "I've come up to the stables—to the garages—for John Thorne, but he's nowhere about. Likely he's out in the far barns seein' the Guernseys are well sheltered."

"More likely he's over Niton way, swilling in a pub, or worse," Mrs. Creeth remarked.

"It's old Gran," the boy said, his wet face beginning to crumple. "She's been set on and half-strangled with a length of wire. It'll be the old madman's work. I never seen the old madman, but Aunty, she remembers him. Oh, sir, Gran—she needs help bad!"

Mrs. Buckle had rocketed out of her settle, and the butler reached the boy in two strides. "Are you babbling, Willie? Steady yourself and speak the truth!"

"It's God's truth, Mr. Finley. I went down Smuggler's Cottage way to see if John Thorne might let me have a look at his automobile books. And there I found the cottage door off its hinges. And inside Granny Thorne was a-laying on the hearth rug. She was breathing, Mr. Finley, but she—she—"

Willie was seized then by a violent attack of uncontrollable shaking. His teeth chattered as the staff drew closer to him. Nothing was understandable to Miranda except the boy's terrible state and his conviction in telling the fragment of his story. Mrs. Creeth clutched her throat, and Hilda and Hannah gave way to moaning terror.

Mr. Finley was galvanized into sudden action. "Hannah!" he actually shouted. "You know the park and farmland, every bit of it and even by night. Set out with a storm lantern and locate John Thorne!

Send him on the run to the cottage. Get your boots, girl, and be gone!"

"With the ole madman runnin' amok, Mr. Finley?" Hannah gasped, her tiny eyes grown suddenly glassy.

"We know nothing for certain," the butler snapped back. "But take Hilda with you. The pair of you will be proof against anyone. And slip a carving knife into your coat pocket if it will give you courage!"

Mr. Finley pivoted on his heel, surveying the upturned faces of the remaining staff. "Mrs. Buckle, if you would be so kind, please inform her ladyship that Granny Thorne is poorly. Do not elaborate, for after all we are acting on the unconfirmed report of a young boy. But request her ladyship to try to get through to Dr. Post at Ventnor and tell him he's needed. We can only hope the line is not down. The wind is shifting around."

Mrs. Buckle swept noiselessly away up the turning stairs, a study in composure. Mrs. Creeth was left to crouch before the quivering boy. In a quieter tone Mr. Finley said to her, "Get the wet things off the boy when we are gone, Mrs. Creeth. Better not send him back to his father and his aunt. They wouldn't thank us for letting him run free until this matter is thoroughly looked into. And I shall leave it to your judgment as to the advisability of cocoa for him or something stronger. Here is the key to the cellar if you decide on brandy."

"Leave the lad to me, Mr. Finley," she replied, nearly cradling Willie Salter's shaking head against her bosom.

"Betty! You are to make an immediate circuit of the house, securing all the doors and the long windows against—the wind—and any other intrusion. Then return to the kitchen to await any further requests directed to you. We will all be in need of sustenance before this night is finished, I have no doubt. You may assist Mrs. Creeth in the preparation of some hot food to stand ready."

"Yes, Mr. Finley," Betty murmured, her active imagination already running rampant among the horrors of a howling wind, the glint of a flashing wire looped suddenly over old Granny Thorne's head—or her own—and the likelihood that an inhuman face might appear at any of the windows she might be about to secure. She scuttled off, green with fear.

"And, Miranda," Mr. Finley said suddenly, "you'll be accompanying me to Granny Thorne's cottage, where you will be very much needed. Have you the stomach for it, my girl?"

Miranda could only nod.

And after no more than a minute's time, while the kitchen was alive with flapping coats, the acrid smell of hastily located rubber boots, and the smoking wicks of suddenly lit lanterns, it was empty of all except Mrs. Creeth on her knees before the fire with Willie. She crouched there like the image of a prehistoric woman, clasping the trembling shoulders of the silently sobbing boy, calming him with her work-roughened hands.

Seven

———⟨◦⟩———

Since the evening when Miranda had been led up to the kitchen yard door in her mother's grip, she had not set foot outside the doors of Whitwell Hall. But now she was staggering and stumbling over the slick cobblestones in a pair of rubber boots as big as boats and a heavy, borrowed ulster thrown over her head and already streaming. The rain needled her face, so that she could barely follow the bobbing lamp that moved before her in Mr. Finley's hand. The water cascaded down the back of his black rubber coat, and his scarf tails whipped in the wind.

"It will be heavy going along the woodsy path around the mere, but that's much the nearest way," he shouted to her over the howling wind. "Step where I step when you can!"

They crossed the rectangle of the yard, and Mr. Finley led the way through a narrow gate between the outbuildings and down a walled path protected from the wind but turning rapidly into a gutter for the raging rainwater underfoot. Miranda was lost at once.

They crossed smooth, evenly rolled lawn and then rougher ground. Miranda peered from under the flopping hood of the ulster to see the madly thrashing tops of a grove of trees. The lantern described a zigzag route as Mr. Finley wandered a moment, searching for the beginning of the path into the trees. At last he swung the lantern wildly and shouted back to her, "This way! I see it now!"

A branch of prickly holly oak whipped Miranda's face as the two entered an opening that seemed more tunnel than path. At once there was a splintering crack directly ahead of them and the rushing sound of a great limb crashing through the branches of the trees and thundering to earth in an explosion of twigs. Their path was blocked.

The lantern's yellow light revealed a solid wall of drenched vegetation filling up the trail ahead. If they had been there a second sooner, they would have been crushed beneath a fallen limb as thick and heavy as a chimney pot.

Mr. Finley shied like a horse and whirled around. He held the lantern high between them and shouted over the roar of the gale, "That was warning enough! We have no choice but to go back down the front way and along the main road!"

And so the two figures, wet to the skin, retraced their steps, angling across the kitchen yard and along the drive that curved around one wing of the house past the stables. The high boxwood broke much of the wind's force, and the gravel beneath made for more certain running.

It was an eighth of a mile from the portico of Whitwell Hall to the main gates. But Mr. Finley made it in record time, breaking his stride only to avoid entangling his feet in the fallen branches of the Italian pines. Miranda, too mystified to think, swallowed great gulps of air and never fell far behind the man who seemed to shed all his loftiness in a moment of emergency.

Lightning split the night sky as they rounded the towering iron gates at the foot of the drive. The main road was a river, but the high stone wall that separated it from the Hall park guided them on their way the better part of a mile.

Miranda's borrowed boots were leaking badly by the time they reached the end of the stone wall, where an iron fence continued, bordering the road. Farther along, Mr. Finley crashed into the undergrowth half submerged at the roadside. He reached back a hand to help Miranda over the black ditch. Then they were standing before a stile. Struggling to the top of it, Mr. Finley lost his hat in the wind and let rip a rare oath. But he turned at once to lift Miranda up, and the two of them negotiated the fence with near ease, though Miranda's skirts were plastered around her, drenched and heavy.

The path beyond was overgrown with unmown grass, but the woods lay well off to the left, roaring in the wind. There was little danger of being felled by a splintered limb, though the long grass was slicker than the cobblestones.

It was another ten minutes' hard traveling before a yellow light danced in the distant darkness ahead. They were on the stones before a front door when Miranda saw the cottage. It was smothered in a fluttering cover of ivy that curved about the gushing eaves. The sight of the door fallen in with long, raw strips of shattered wood still clinging to the hinges shocked Miranda into remembering why they were there. This was not the work of the wind.

A paraffin lamp in the middle of the room cast a clear light inside, conveying a sense of the ordinary at odds with the door that lay angled against a chair back. One of its panels was completely knocked through. Finley shed his rubber coat and rushed into the center of the room. Miranda kept at his heels, her heart thumping from exertion and sudden fear.

An old woman, no larger than a child, lay on the knotted hearth rug like a broken doll. Her head was wrenched at a curious angle, perilously near the glowing embers in the grate.

Long strands of gray hair had loosened, falling around her face, fanning out on the floor. Her arms were thrown out, and her hands, like tiny paws, lay palms upward, with waxen claws curled. The light in the room was bright enough to reveal the stout baling wire looped around her neck. It had been loosened, undoubtedly by the boy, Willie, but it remained coiled above her wrinkled throat.

Mr. Finley dropped to one knee and took up a thin arm, searching for a pulse. But at once the old woman drew a deep, shuddering breath, and her lips worked silently. "Thank God she's alive!" Mr. Finley said. He drew the gleaming wire away from the fragile neck, saying, "Remember what you have seen here, my girl, in case you are called on to give evidence in a court of law! Let's lift her onto the bench over there." But Miranda had already gathered up the old lady's feet, daintily shod in small, well-polished boots, worn nearly as thin as parchment.

She weighed nothing at all, and as they lifted her onto the bench, Miranda had the impression that she was deeply bent, a hunchback perhaps. Even her high shoes had the strange perfection of a cripple's boots. Miranda had the certain feeling that she had seen this old woman before. But in the next moment she had taken up the storm lantern and ducked behind a curtain separating the main room from the kitchen beyond in search of strong drink to bring the victim to her senses if that was possible.

Alone in the cubbyhole kitchen, Miranda stole a glimpse at a window set in a rotting frame just at her elbow. She forced herself to look through it, fearing what empty, maniacal gaze she might meet outside. But there was nothing except blackness beyond the rivulets of rainwater coursing down the wavering panes.

Though there was hardly room to turn in the kitchen, it was ranked with bottles. Preserved fruit, mostly, but nothing like strong drink in evidence. On a low shelf stood a shepherd's pie, with one wedge neatly removed. Holding the lantern aloft, Miranda saw that along a high cupboard shelf was a row of what appeared to be bottles of homemade wine. She drew down a dusty bottle and hurried into the front room.

"Her own vintage," Mr. Finley said, brushing the label-less bottle with his sleeve. "Perhaps it will serve. There may be damage to her throat, so we must take care." Crouching beside the motionless woman, the two of them managed to get perhaps as much as a spoonful down her. She whimpered and turned her head away, now seeming more asleep than unconscious, though her lips formed unspoken words.

There was little to be done about the remains of the stout oak door. Mr. Finley glanced away from the patient at intervals to cast a worried glance out into the noisy darkness beyond the doorframe.

The two kept watch until the woman grew restless, shifting on her rounded back so suddenly that she would have pitched off the narrow bench if Miranda had not steadied her in time. "It won't do," Mr. Finley said quietly. "We should get the poor soul into her bed. It's very likely upstairs under the eaves."

Miranda took the lantern and headed for the narrow stairs boxed off at one side of the room. She was just starting up to see if she could locate Granny Thorne's bedroom when Mr. Finley said, "Miranda, perhaps I should just have a look around upstairs first." He was touched by the bravery of the girl, whose first thought was of the comfort of the old woman and not of the possibility of what danger might be haunting the attic.

But there was nothing ominous above in the tiny rooms. Mr. Finley searched under all the beds and swung every cupboard door open. The room at the back belonging to John Thorne could not conceal a cat. A desk heaped high with brochures for motorcars and mechanics' manuals, and an iron bed covered by what had once been a steamer rug filled the small cell entirely.

Granny Thorne's bedroom ran along the front of the house, with two dormers, the windows plastered with wet ivy. Her large bed, neatly made, took up half the space in the room. The low room was heavy-laden with the memories of a long lifetime and the aroma of ancient rose-petal potpourri. The only recent touch was the pair of coronation portraits of the new King and Queen, George V and Mary, cut from an illustrated paper and mounted in bird's-eye-maple frames far older than their pictures. They hung in a place of honor from twisted silken cords above the high head of the bed. The butler set down his lantern on the nightstand and struck a match to the wick of the lamp. Then he turned back the bed, wondering at his own lack of dignity in performing this chambermaid's chore for an old peasant woman.

Half an hour later Granny Thorne seemed to rest easy in her own bed. Her small pigeon breast rose and fell regularly. Mr. Finley and Miranda kept watch from a pair of straight chairs on either side of the bed. The butler chanced a bit of conversation in his usual tone now that the situation seemed to be settling down a bit. "She's nearer ninety than eighty," he said at last to Miranda. "And at that age there's no knowing. Still, she's stronger than she seems, or this night would have done for her.

"The Thornes have lived on the land hereabouts since long before Sir Timothy's time, a great deal longer. They were the tenants of old Lord Halsey, who sold to the Whitwells in 1894. I shouldn't wonder if old Granny Thorne hadn't been born in one of the other cottages on the estate. In the old days it ran to a thousand acres and paid its way. The men farmed, and their daughters served in the Hall. I doubt Granny needed to look beyond the gates to find a husband for herself. Of course, it was all well before my time. I came here myself only to serve the Whitwells. It was after the passing of my former gentleman, who served in the cabinet of Mr. Gladstone, with bachelor chambers in the Albany building." Finley grew expansive in the silence of the room, caught up in his memories and heedless of his listener.

"It was bitter medicine for some of the locals when most of the farms were sold off and the Hall became a country place for a gentleman—in trade. Not, mind you, that Sir Timothy is any the less a gentleman for all that. But these country people cling to their old notions and in their primitive way understand nothing beyond farming," he explained to Miranda, who until the past days had known nothing else herself.

"Of course, the tenants only fancied they'd lived here time out of mind on the land. The story is that Granny's husband had been a smuggler before he came ashore. Very likely only folklore, but this place has been called Smuggler's Cottage to honor the tradition. It was hard for some of them, nonetheless, when the new ways came creeping in. There was land they had rented up for sale and no money to buy it with. Of course, there were new opportunities as well, though not many of these people had the wit to grasp them. Why, Sir Timothy employs a staff of fifteen gardeners throughout three seasons, but that is trained work.

"Most of the local help is worth nothing more than to muck out the barns and clean tack. Now these new motorcars are putting paid even to that livelihood. Granny Thorne's grandson, John, of course, is of a new breed. Sees himself as a twentieth-century man, I shouldn't wonder." Mr. Finley permitted himself a spinsterish sniff. "And he's motorcar-mad. No, young Thorne has broken with the old ways, and I will say he's good to his old grandmother. But he doesn't know his place. And there's a wild streak in this family, as wide as the King's Road." He paused then while the new King gazed obscurely down upon him from the heavy frame. Mr. Finley seemed tempted to continue his discourse, but he closed his mouth, pursed it, and appeared to think better of saying more.

After a lengthy silence Miranda was emboldened to ask, "But, Mr. Finley, who would have wanted to harm the old lady?"

"Ah, well, my girl, we don't know that, do we?" he replied very much in his official voice. They might have been back in servants' hall again. The silence descended again, and the storm appeared to have abated. There was only the trickle of water in the leads beyond the windows. Mr. Finley muttered that Dr. Post seemed unlikely to put in an appearance, but that perhaps there was no urgency after all —no medical emergency, at least. Then he dozed, though his chin never dipped.

Miranda slept soundly. The unyielding wooden chair with its slats digging into her back might have been a featherbed. She slept dreamlessly and opened her eyes suddenly at the alien sound of a bird trilling its morning notes. Gray dawn was creeping into the corners of the bedchamber, and someone had turned the lamp down to a minute yellow pearl of light.

Starting slightly, Miranda nearly kicked over the bottle of home-made wine at her feet. She was almost certain that she hadn't even nodded off. But her legs were still asleep, and her neck felt caught in a cold vise. She blinked at the room now transforming itself in the morning light. It was stuffy from the smoking lamp. The blurred faces of a number of regal personages gazed down from their frames all around the room, as if this chamber were a Lilliputian court, preparing for a levee, awaiting patiently the awakening of the minute queen in the overlarge bed.

Miranda hoped that Mr. Finley had not noticed her asleep at her post. They might both have been murdered where they sat if he had not kept watch. And then she noticed the hand resting heavily on the coverlet beside the old lady's slight form. A powerful brown hand, fingernails blackened with grease. It was far from being Mr. Finley's.

Glancing up in terror, Miranda stared into the eyes of the man sitting where Mr. Finley had been settled—how long before? The gray morning and the yellow lamplight played across his face, its strong planes and cragginess revealed, and the tumble of blond hair above his wide forehead. He wore a coarse, colorless shirt with the cuffs rolled above the elbows, revealing forearms firmly muscled and thick with golden hair. It was John Thorne sitting there, impassively waiting for her to wake, gazing at her with eyes the color of dawn.

Here was the man who, except for one midnight moment, had existed just beyond the regimented routine of Miranda's new life. The man who had stepped through doors seconds before she had entered them, except for once before—and now.

She seemed to know in the first moment who he was. And more. She knew that she'd been caught up in those thick arms, mauled by those hands. But she had never seen the gray cool eyes or the set of the chin. Its stubbled firmness was relieved only by the cleft that formed the only boyish feature of this man. She even fancied that the strong, slender nose revealed him as the old woman's grandson.

She knew the urgent need to speak, to flee, and the impossibility of both. And so she sat mesmerized by his eyes. He had the kind of strength Miranda had always feared, though she had suffered at no other man's hands but his. No local lad of Whitely Bank had ever been allowed near her, and she was guileless in the ways of a district where nearly all the girls were wedded and bedded at her age. She could only sit there in wonder, her thought expanding enough to see John Thorne as the old woman's grandson, protective of her. His massive hand never moved from the bed, as if he might send a charge of his animal strength through the tired old body beneath the covers.

But at last Miranda was able to break from his expressionless gaze, though if she had been able to read his thoughts, nothing would have distracted her. She looked around the brightening room. There above a chest of drawers opposite the foot of the bed was a brown-spotted oleograph of old Queen Victoria staring out at a vanished world with sightless eyes above sagging cheeks. A broad band of black crepe knotted in a limp rosette hung across the picture frame, proclaiming a funeral ten years past.

Below, on the top of the chest, a pair of china candleholders, festooned with chipped roses. There was a bowl, too, stained black inside and long abandoned; its use eluded Miranda. It had been more than a decade since Granny Thorne had often carried that bowl full of strong black tea up to her room, there to comb it through her hair to conceal the strands of white. For she had, within her limits, carried a touch of vanity well into her old age.

Miranda glanced down to the far corner of the room, beyond the chest. Leaning against the wall and throwing a pale shadow was the old woman's walking stick, a shiny black Malacca cane banded in silver. It had been almost the only legacy of her long-dead husband, the smuggler.

Like a puzzle piece falling into place, the cane seemed to complete Miranda's knowledge about her companions in this room so distant from the rest of the world. For the cane told her that the apparition she had seen creeping through the moonlit garden had been Granny Thorne—who was not yet a ghost. And her grandson was the man who had assailed her with such confident familiarity on that first night. These two creatures of darkness might well have faded from her memory in time. Instead, they were revealed in bold relief when the sun's first rays fell through the ivy, delivering a new day. Ordinary mortals, after all. Miranda wondered why her fear of them did not ebb at once.

———

When Hilda and Hannah, like two great Valkyries in full flight from a Wagnerian opera, had encountered John Thorne on the home farm path, he had at first made little sense of their repetitious hysteria. The wind screamed louder than they, but the words "madman" and "Granny Thorne" had sent him in full flight back toward the park. Where the path divided at the mere, he hesitated between pounding through the thrashing grove to the cottage or making for the Hall. Knowing enough about Mr. Finley's priorities, Thorne presumed that the butler had already sent help Granny's way. He fought against the idea that she might be beyond help. So he turned down the way leading to the kitchens, overtaking the soaked and squawking Hilda and Hannah, who were brandishing a long carving knife against the unknown forces of the night.

The madman was far from unknown to Thorne. If there was indeed a maniac loose within the grounds, he knew well who it was. He could not have known how near he had drawn to him, however, during that second's lingering where the path forked. For under the great slab of rock beside the mere, the madman was lying, covered in slime, with the rain gusting against his loose mouth and burning eyes. He lay there, feeling nothing of the wet and cold, like some prehistoric creature hidden but unsheltered by the rock outcropping not two yards from John Thorne's booted feet.

The madman's disordered mind had registered the intrusion of footsteps: the headlong stumbling of the two kitchenmaids, the heavy footfalls of John Thorne. His hearing had the keenness of the hunted. Among the bulrushes he lay, as still as death, until these intruders' sounds were lost in the moaning wind. Even then he did not shift his heavy body, only digging his fingers deeper into the mud, trying to bury the hands that had tightened the wicked wire around Granny Thorne's neck. He clung to the earth, inviting it to swallow him where he lay.

In the kitchens where he was never welcome, Thorne encountered Mrs. Creeth at her most imperious. Willie Salter had been stripped and sent to bed with a hot water bottle at his feet and a tot of hot rum in his belly. Tucked up in the boothole, where a page in former days had slept to guard the wine cellar, Willie was far from asleep. Yet Mrs. Creeth disclaimed all knowledge of his whereabouts to John. She planted her hands on her hips in grim finality.

"She'd be better off dead, would Granny Thorne," Mrs. Creeth said to the man she had always viewed with a distrust that was growing by the day to hatred. "If it's a sin to say so, then may I fry for it. But to live with the shame her menfolk have visited on her time out of mind is more than an old woman should have to bear. It's a wonder that business with poor Naomi Barton didn't finish her off long since," she added, reaching far back in time.

'He's back, I have no doubt, for who else would be wild enough to attack an innocent old party at her own hearthside? Answer me that! And, mark me, there's not a lunatic asylum on the island, nor yet on the mainland, I daresay, would hold the old monster! There's a madness in your family, John Thorne, strike me dead if there isn't. And if he's done for Granny, then maybe they'll lock him up in a proper prison from which there's no escaping and swallow the key! Or better yet, hang him! I would. There. Now I've had my say."

"You generally do, Mrs. Creeth. Though if he's to hang, I'd sooner it be for murdering *you.*" Then John banged out into the night. Mrs. Creeth gathered her forces for a stinging reply to this all-too-typical outrage, but Thorne was gone, leaving the door ajar to send the lamps dipping again. She waddled across the room to slam the great door shut. And just as she reached it, in tumbled Hilda and Hannah, still brandishing the meat knife.

She vented her spleen on these witless geese, who set up a howling over the unfairness, the indignity, the sheer horror of it all.

It was in the darkest hour of night when Thorne strode into Smuggler's Cottage, stepping over the demolished door and scanning the room for further evidence of mischief. He had found Finley upstairs in the front room, wide-eyed at his approach. And he found the slumbering Miranda across the room beyond the bed where his grandmother lay.

He and the butler murmured together, the situation drawing them into a kind of guarded camaraderie. After he had told all he knew, Finley added, "The police, Thorne. We had better get through to them. It's their job, after all."

"And what's the point?" John muttered back. "He'd make straight for this place and nowhere else. Not even Nettlecombe. He has no unfinished business elsewhere, and even in his state he knows that much. His mind is ruled by this plot of earth. He'll keep returning to it as long as he's able. And none of the ham-fisted police out from Ventnor could track him across this land, not with a brace of bloodhounds on a dry night. He knows every twig and turning. I'm the only one who could track him down."

This was scant consolation to the butler, whose opinion was that the asylum authorities at Newport had very likely alerted the authorities in any case. "The family," he said, working his hands in anguish. "We must endeavor to do our best not to disturb her ladyship and Sir Timothy with this terrible business."

"Yes, Finley, that should of course be your first concern," John Thorne said with a searing irony as he stared down at the motionless figure of his grandmother.

The butler hurried off then to the Hall to impose a normal routine upon the weary, skittish servants in the new day, while John Thorne sat down to keep watch beside Granny's bed. She would survive this, he hoped, for she'd survived much else in her eighty-seven years. And he spared a thought for the madman as well. For though he doubted that the fugitive could be gunned down like a plunging stag before a hunting party, he longed to see the old maniac under lock and key—and safe from a world he could no longer live in.

These thoughts delayed Thorne's awareness of the girl, who provided a near-humorous scene on the far side of the bed. She sat bolt upright and sound asleep, like a young Life Guard standing his first night watch before St. James's Palace.

But Thorne's eye drifted down across Miranda's unsoldierly form, and he lingered over the soft rise and fall of her breast. He'd cursed himself throughout a week for accosting this girl outside Amanda's door. He'd come near enough taking her where she stood pinned against the wall, thinking she was Amanda, knowing how any variation in lovemaking would divert the easily bored young lady of the manor.

If there was an ugly river of insanity coursing through the Thorne family, John decided it had surfaced in himself on the day Amanda Whitwell had grown up enough to stir his loins and becloud his brain. He was a veteran of too many skirmishes—in battlefield and bedchamber—to have fallen under the spell of this young, highborn girl, scarcely grown, yet as wily as an aging demimondaine. But still she had held him in her grasp from the first moment he had locked her in his arms. If that didn't amount to madness, he was damned if he knew what did. Though it was Amanda, he reasoned, who deserved locking up in the interests of the public good, not himself.

John Thorne had taken Amanda Whitwell's virginity and thus lost his own innocence no longer ago than a night during the previous summer. Yet it seemed she had kept him on a short tether far longer than that. But to what purpose? He hadn't plumbed the depths of her rapacious passion. And he knew in his heart that twenty men could never satisfy her.

Still, she'd shown no signs of tiring of him or of the adventure of him. She seemed continually to gather her languid, devious forces in his further ensnarement. The experience she had gained in his rough embrace was already translating into the kind of power over him that no other woman had ever exercised. When his mind turned toward the imponderable future between them—a future that could not come to any sort of satisfactory pass for any number of sound reasons —his mind grew as weary as his body. Thorne had always taken his strength for granted. His weakness before Amanda's might was more than he could handle. He wasn't a man to nag at himself with fears of his own virility. But he feared in his heart that Amanda was claiming his soul. John Thorne returned with relief to contemplating the girl asleep opposite him, the girl who could be Amanda's double but hardly her match.

He wondered if she would know him. Waiting for her recognition in the slow half hour before first light, he found himself absorbed in keeping watch over her sleeping form. His eye followed again and again the shadowed line of her temple. He memorized the damp ringlets of her hair escaping from their severe restraint.

Something stirred deep inside him and yearned toward her—only her. His eyes began to possess her and then caress her. Then he jerked himself from his trance and knotted his fist against such idiocy. To be inflamed by one woman—so unattainable and so available—and to be drawn to another. That might well be the clinching evidence of madness. It far surpassed straightforward lust.

And so in the last half hour of night, when memories flame up most brightly, John Thorne gave way to a rare spate of recollections. Whatever the way stations of his thoughts, the terminus was always Amanda. But he surprised himself with the clarity of his memories, for he rarely looked back. He'd learned early in life the bitter folly of clinging to outworn creeds. He'd served in a war that had snagged the mighty flag of Empire, and he was one man among the very few who foresaw that the snag might open a rent in the fabric.

He knew, too, how to keep a secret—in war or peace—and that meant closing his mind at most times to memories that might too suddenly surface.

He was shaken to realize that he had very likely been born in the very bed where his hand now rested. Yes, it must have been in this same room in the spring of 1882 where his mother had died giving him life. And that was a decade—no, twelve years—before the estate was fragmented. Before the great house became Whitwell Hall to honor the merchant prince who had bought it as offhandedly as he would have taken a lease on a London house. Thorne had been amply old enough to be aware of the rumblings of the tenants and the retainers when they learned their land was being sold off and that Sir Timothy was to keep on a meager twenty-six acres to play at gentleman-farming. The earth had seemed to shift beneath their feet.

It signified little to John in that twelfth year of his life. Sir Timothy's Amanda was a toddler, a moppet no more than a year old. Young Thorne never ventured close enough to the Hall gardens to see her carried about for an airing by Mrs. Buckle.

But Gordon Whitwell, Amanda's brother, was another matter. A year older than John, he'd made his presence felt from the first day. The young lord of the manor, who was everywhere at once, had in time crossed John's path. Now John turned his mind away from the secret store of memories of the Whitwells' vanished son. And other recollections welled up from Thorne's past.

It was in this very grove of trees that John had staked out his solitary boyhood kingdom long before it was threatened by change and by the cast-iron whims of the two Whitwell children. The uplands and dust roads of the holding had been alive then with neighbors.

Boys his age already switching home the cattle at evening, running the flats of eggs by dog cart into Ventnor to be shipped to London and the North. Embryonic farmers already, trapped in the changeless round of milking stool and hoe and milking stool again. But John Thorne had never sought out these boys. He needed nothing from their companionship and found no time or patience for their dull fellowship.

The only mother he had known was Granny Thorne, bent already in his earliest memories, but with her hair carefully dressed and colored darker than walnut stain. If his raising had been left to her, he might have roamed the landscape at will, playing at poaching, reducing the few mechanical contrivances about the place to their smallest grease-soaked parts. Swinging from rope to rope through the branches of the grove, charting the mild seasons restlessly, and catching the salt scent of the sea when the wind was right.

But his bullnecked father recognized none of the rights of boyhood. Embittered at the loss of his wife, who had died to replace her useful self on earth with this lawless brat, Bart Thorne had turned himself into a beast of burden. And the burden became his obsession. It was the obsession of a man who, working the land, comes to believe it belongs to him. He would hear no more picturesque stories of his own long-dead father, the fabled smuggler who had come ashore to exchange with reluctance the illegal tiller for the respectable plow. He had only contempt for his own mother, Granny Thorne, who took an innocent pleasure in "helping out" at the Hall when the servants of the domestic staff were unequal to their tasks, or summarily discharged. Bart Thorne seemed bent on compensating for the centuries his forefathers had not farmed these sixty acres that formed an insignificant corner of the estate lands. Given permission, he would have wrenched up even the hedges and battered down the stone walls with his bare hands to cultivate one more roadside row of barley or rye for fodder. He would have added hours of sunlight to the already endless days if only he could have controlled the turn of the earth.

When his aging mother shuffled back to the cottage from a day's work at the Hall, full of the kitchen gossip that was her only link with the society of her own kind, he silenced her with a word. When she carried home in her reticule a bit of fine mending from Lady Halsey's lingerie cupboard, he yearned to wrench the silk from his mother's small, skilled hands and throw it on the fire. Possessed by racial memory of a peasant past earlier than the Middle Ages, John Thorne's father yearned for a forgotten time when a man might till his own patch in obscurity, far from the grand posturing of a titled overlord. He might have made his mark at the lonely limits of some remote frontier where a common man's claim might be staked by his own hand, and where there were no near neighbors.

John's first memories were of the sky-blue days when he had scaled the tallest tree in the grove. Its topmost branch became his conning tower. And after he had heard of the great balloons in which the far-off Frenchmen were liberating themselves from the earth, his tall outpost became in his imagination a great gas-filled sack, carrying him wherever the vagrant winds decreed.

From his swaying perch, he could survey more of the world than he'd ever traveled. The roofs of the Hall where the Halseys reigned were astonishingly near. A hollow fist to play the periscope brought every stone of the great house up in bold relief. The smoke from the Smuggler's Cottage chimney curled up a dizzying distance below his naked toes, which held fast around the supple branch. Granny's white Leghorns, lingering in the dooryard for a scattering of grain or probing for earthworms, were only snowdrops. To the south were the rooflines of Ventnor, the houses of the topmost part of a town that descended invisibly to the sea. And, stretching to the hazy horizon beyond, the sea itself, green-gold. His farthest imaginings took him across the Atlantic in a range of craft, from Spanish galleons to the high-speed liners, even balloons that might span the earth in Jules Verne voyages.

It was more than the view the small boy commanded from his perilous perch that set his heart singing. It was the wafting motion of the sap-rich treetop itself, swaying above the lesser trees, waving its graceful finger at the uncharted sky. It was in one of the moments such as these that the widower Thorne's only son fell in love with freedom. A freedom that only movement and an escape from the plodding pace of earthbound man promised. A freedom of wheels and wings and lands beyond the narrow frontiers of an island already shrunken in the mind of a boy who had been nowhere else.

But on one such sky-blue day the wordless dream, the tantalizing exhilaration were snatched from him. The treetop silence was shattered by his father's roar. And there, sixty feet below, his broken boots among the roots of the tree, stood his yeoman father, sixteen stone of red-faced wrath. The sight of his only potential unpaid helper on the farm hanging between life and death far above and beyond him came close to giving the elder Thorne a fit of apoplexy.

His thundering voice brought Granny to the door, where she worked her hands tensely in her apron at the sight of her only grandchild wedged in a branch that could snap at any moment. But there was no talking him down over the roaring of his father.

He was soon down nevertheless, leaving half his skin on the rough bark. The enraged father had flayed him further. The man was inarticulate at the best of times. In anger, a leather strap spoke for him. He dragged the boy down between the sheds and whipped him without mercy. Crediting his son on one point, he knew the boy would not cry out to agitate his fussing grandmother.

From that day on, John's boyhood was transformed into a kind of penal servitude. What book learning he came by, he garnered slumped against Granny's knee, half asleep before the fire in the hour after supper. His education by day amounted largely to what he learned to despise about farming. Harnessed in tandem with the plowhorse, he followed the furrows as the disk turned the unyielding soil. Nor was harvest time a season of thanksgiving or festivity, for the marginal land never quite yielded a sufficiency, let alone an abundance. Market-garden produce sold in Ventnor to the greengrocer for coin was food often enough sorely missed from the Thornes' table. In many a lean season and long winter, the only money the household saw were the coins Granny's sporadic work at the Hall brought in. And each penny of this meager sum became a taunt to Bart Thorne's darkening mind.

Deprived of every moment of freedom, young John found somewhere a grudging understanding of his father's fixation for those pathetic acres. He even saw the twisted logic of a man too proud to accept the helping hands of his neighbors, hands that stretched out less and less often. For John Thorne saw his father as the father never saw himself—a man clinging to the final shreds of an unworkable way of life. A man with too little imagination to alter his course. A man who stood frozen between two generations of a family in flux —between a salty smuggler and a young boy who would chart an unknown course.

John Thorne's hatred for this cruel taskmaster shifted to a hatred of the task itself. He waited with slow-burning patience for the first moment of manhood. And he waited alone, drawn in upon himself. There were tantalizing premature signs of it. At twelve, the year the Whitwells came, his shoulders were as broadly muscled, his upper arms as knotted as a prizefighter's. Because the boy possessed the imagination his father lacked, he dimly foresaw that the brute strength forced upon him by worse than coolie labor would purchase him a showdown with his father one day. He knew as well that in that future moment his animosity toward this father who had never granted him so much as a grunt of approval would give way to bleak triumph.

At fourteen John Thorne was a man in everything but experience. His naked back glistened at midsummer noons when he bent almost effortlessly to weed rows within sight of the nameless brook that fed the mere. The stream was barely deep enough to submerge the boy's massive body. But he had never been allowed to cease his labors long enough to ease himself into this inviting coolness to test its capacity. Though they might be toiling in fields at opposite ends of the farm, his father seemed always to know when John was tempted to slow his pace. Bart Thorne came to him then at a run, brandishing the leather strap, now tattered with hard use and greased with the sweat of both father and son.

It was a scorching July midday in John's fourteenth summer when the rigid routine yielded at a strategic moment. With business in Nettlecombe, Bart Thorne had left his son at work in the field alone. The old man had plodded off to the village on foot, to spare the horse.

In that scant hour of comparative freedom, the boy raced for the cooling stream. Shirtless, he had only to pull off his outgrown breeches to slip naked into the water that had been beckoning to him for all the summers of his life.

In the deepest part, his sunburned back touched, then rested against, the pebbles of the stream bed. Sun-dazzled, he closed his eyes, allowing the cooling waters to seep into his ears, to surround his nose like the floodtide around the headland. His arms were too heavily muscled to float lazily out from his sides. But the water weeds enmeshed his fingers with sensuous tendrils. For a boy in love with movement and distance, this complete immobility was strangely satisfying. Even arousing. His hands drifted with the stream until they brushed his hairy thighs. Hair that had sprung up to envelop his legs in a matter of months. His strong new manliness broke the brook's smooth-flowing surface. John sank into a luxurious stupor, rigid and relaxed.

Half asleep and then blinded at the first suggestion of intrusion, he might have missed noticing that the bulrushes a yard from his shoulder had been parted by a pair of small, grubby hands. But a ripple of mirth followed, midway between a giggle and a low chuckle. John's hands flailed the water to cover himself, which only deepened the giggle to a gale of low-pitched laughter.

"Who in the devil?" The boy struggled to stand, thought better of it, tried to turn on his stomach, and thought better of that. Suddenly standing up among the bulrushes and brush was a girl whose sunburned face showed black between him and the sun.

There was little enough the boy could do, pinioned there but unconcealed in the shallow stream. He would have preferred the sudden appearance of his father, and the inevitable leather strap. But he struggled to a sitting position, muttered the most adult oaths that sprang to mind. He grasped his knees with his forearms and locked his fingers, expecting this saucy girl to go her way.

She stood her ground instead. "I've not seen much of you these past years, John Thorne," she said in imitation of much worldliness. "But I'm seeing plenty and all today!" He recognized her then. She was Farmer Barton's girl, the third one or the fourth—he couldn't be sure and it little mattered. The Bartons of the north farm, all of them saucy and devil-may-care, and somehow better fed than the Thornes.

"It's Naomi, is it?" he said, squinting up at her and struggling for a shred of dignity. It eluded him, for his voice, which had changed two seasons before, suddenly cracked again like gunfire. She allowed that she was Naomi to the life, and shamelessly stared him down, grinning luridly.

"You've—grown, Naomi," he said in confusion, noting how her handed-down cotton dress strained across her breasts.

"You're bigger yourself," she replied wickedly and looked between his legs. "Oh, I've only come down for a bit of a bathe myself, but there's little enough room with a great—gangling—lad to slop out all the water and likely leave the stream bone-dry and mucky with it."

"Then turn your back, Naomi, and I'll get out and be about my business. You can have the ole stream, for all I care."

"I'll save me blushes for a better time," Naomi answered. "There's no sense in hidin' eyes that seen everything there was to see." Without further verbal sparring, Naomi reached down and drew off her light dress in a single gesture.

John's throat tightened as he watched the skirts twitch above Naomi's thin legs, so much whiter than her sunburned face and arms. He swallowed hard and grasped for renewed purchase on his knees when he saw the curve of her white belly and then the breasts like firm apples. She waved the bunched frock wildly above her head as it tangled in her hair. But she soon freed herself completely, casting the dress into the bulrushes. And there she stood at the edge of the stream, naked and grinning like a cat. There was the red V at her throat that the sun had found, and the milky whiteness below. She laughed at his confusion, but fell silent when she met the cool grayness of his eyes.

"Well, give over," she said less saucily than before. "There isn't room for two."

"Isn't there?" said the fourteen-year-old John Thorne, putting his confusion behind him and reaching for Naomi's earth-stained ankle.

It was the autumn a week or so before John turned fifteen that there came a knock on the door of Smuggler's Cottage. Granny started in her chair, for a night visitor to the friendless meant some manner of trouble.

Bart Thorne was asleep at the long oak table where he had eaten his supper, head cradled in his arms. Granny pulled the door wider at sight of Farmer Barton, relieved enough to see a half-familiar face. But Barton's expression promised no neighborly chat. He remained on the doorstep muttering to Granny in a tone blending anger and acute embarrassment. His girl—Naomi. Her grandson. The girl—in the family way. Her mother—raging and beside herself. A poor example for the younger ones and a poor outlook for the girl herself. The disgrace. A family rough but respected, troubling no one. Now this . . .

Granny drew the shawl tighter around her round shoulders, her other hand still unconsciously on the doorframe to bar the way. She glanced back at her son snoring across the table. And she hoped bleakly that this news could be kept from him. But he jerked upright at that moment, whirling to see an outsider at the door.

"State your business to *me,* if you have any, Barton!" he snarled, still befuddled with sleep. And at that, Granny dropped her thin arm to her side, and Naomi's father entered the room.

It was nearly an hour later when young John had finished his chores and crossed the yard from barn to cottage. Barton had left. Thre had been little enough to deliberate, even if Bart Thorne had been a reasonable man. Even if the youngsters were of an age to marry, Barton would not have suffered an alliance with the Thornes. The brutality of the man would likely surface in the son soon enough, if it hadn't already. He went his way, back across the fields to the north farm, embittered but resolved to forgive his wayward daughter. The Bartons could see to their own. And when all was said, had it not been one lad in the district, it would have been another. Barton saw himself clearly as a father who had need of a philosophic outlook.

When John Thorne entered the cottage door, his father felled him with a length of firewood. The boy lay stretched across the doorstep. A black line of blood traveled down from his ear. It was his grandmother's scream that brought him around almost at once. And when he looked up, he found himself lying between his father's wide-spaced feet.

"Get up and tell me Barton's a liar!" his father bellowed. The boy raised himself and balanced momentarily on his hands. The blood gushed more freely, and his head pounded. His blurred eyes fell on the thick piece of firewood, and he remembered Naomi.

He shifted to a fighter's crouch and jerked his father's feet in a gesture too quick to see, much less to anticipate. Bart Thorne fell full-length onto his back, his head bouncing against the oak floor like a vegetable marrow.

"You're dead, boy!" he howled. But John was upon him, a quick knee in the groin. And when the father doubled with this pain, the boy's fists caught him on the chin, the temple, a glancing blow to the ear, and a smashing, final battering of knuckles against teeth. His fists drove like pistons, and Bart Thorne fell back again, gagging on the blood from his crushed lip, spewing slivers of his teeth.

John stood up, straddling the great girth of his father. "Now come for me," he said, almost coaxing. "Come for me again, without the firewood, if you dare." But his father lay still, his eyes burning up at the boy who was no longer a boy.

The recollection of this bitter triumph over his father led John Thorne's mind down other paths of the past. It was a time of life best forgotten, with a thousand small frustrations to overbalance a single victory. But what a victory it had been.

There had been a good many Naomis to follow the first, and only blind, lucky chance had kept more angry fathers from his door. His own father continued on a hopeless downward spiral of brutalizing labor and nights befuddled by liquor when it was available, and nameless horrors when it wasn't. In the two years that followed, John

Thorne never received another command from Bart, never a word. But the farm bound them both. Bart took to sleeping in the barn like an animal. And on the night John turned seventeen, his father set fire to a small outbuilding. The flames danced crazily, throwing mad shadows into the grove. John found Bart standing beyond the ring of firelight, his mouth slavering and his hands drenched with paraffin.

Sir Timothy, the new master, sent for the asylum authorities, and Granny signed the papers for commitment. But John Thorne had already seen a glimmer of a future for himself, a future that would break the cycle of labor that had broken his father. The war against the Boers had already erupted in South Africa, and John had heard of it, and of the glory of soldiering. The possibilities seemed endless, and the chance of returning to these acres remote.

Without ever holding a newspaper in his hand, young Thorne had word of the war in Africa against that ragtaggle of hardheaded Dutch farmers under the insolent command of Paul Kruger. England was seething with the news of this threat to Empire, but John's informant was the new master's son, Gordon Whitwell, of the place now known as Whitwell Hall.

The Whitwells had taken up residence in 1894 when John was twelve and already his father's field hand. News of the new owners filtered slowly to the Thornes. George Salter, the Halseys' estate agent, acted for Lord Halsey in offering the farms for sale to the previous tenants. Two or three of the families on the largest farms were able to scrape together enough credit to buy their acres. The carefree but improvident Bartons turned out their pockets, examined the bare linings, and continued as Sir Timothy's vassals for two or three years more before moving to the mainland. When Salter quoted a reasonable price to Bart Thorne for his sixty acres, Thorne ran him out of the barn with an ax and threw it after the agent's retreating figure. Thorne continued, therefore, as the reluctant tenant of a new landlord who would have preferred to divest himself of all the old feudal estate except the garden acreage nearest the Hall, the grove, and the home farm occupied by George Salter, his spinster sister, Winifred, who kept house for him, and his son, Willie.

Sir Timothy had kept on George Salter, mainly as grounds keeper. The big estates were breaking up into holiday holdings and country homes for rich Londoners. There was little enough opportunity for a proper estate agent's job about, and so Salter was glad not to have to alter his life and livelihood.

Sir Timothy had made the effort to come to friendly personal terms with the remaining tenants. On the first day he had ridden into the Bartons' haphazard barnyard, Barton had come on the run from the fields, waving his sons on behind him. Mrs. Barton had formed a nearly military regiment of the girls outside the kitchen door. Barton had tugged at his forelock in a timeless gesture of obeisance, while the curtsies of the Barton females rippled down the row of them, awkward but cordial. They pressed a glass of beer on Sir Timothy during the ceremonial visit. And hospitality overcoming propriety, Mrs. Barton boasted a bit to him about her seed cake and invited him back on baking day.

He was thus disarmed when he rode on to the barnyard of the Thornes. He could see Bart in the middle of the nearest field, staring back at him under a lowering brow, his hat firmly squashed on his head and his hands on his hips. The man made no effort to walk the rows back to greet his new landlord. And one look at the uncertainty in Granny Thorne's eyes when he saw her in the cottage dooryard was enough to tell the story. She had stepped back into the shadows of the room to drop her curtsy.

A strapping boy, whom Sir Timothy took to be older than his own son, Gordon, stepped from the barn and stared in confusion. Sir Timothy only nodded in a manner meant to be friendly and turned his horse to the road. From that day until the day he sent for the authorities from the madhouse to take Bart Thorne away, Sir Timothy left negotiations with the Thornes to his estate agent, glad enough each quarter day he did not have to wrest the rent from Bart Thorne's massive paw himself.

It was more than a year later when young Gordon Whitwell made his way to Smuggler's Cottage, for he had been warned by his father to let sleeping dogs lie. Gordon was at home for the summer holidays from Charterhouse, where he was an indifferent student. Sunk in the tedious summertime trough between school and the August festivities of the Cowes Regatta, the boy had taken to roaming the estate grounds.

Gordon Whitwell was a year older than John Thorne, though he looked younger. He shared with most boys of fourteen a half-finished look. Red, almost cherubic lips in a colorless face still waiting its first suggestion of a beard. The same curly dark, slightly un-English hair he had in common with his baby sister, Amanda.

He was weedy, and lacking the stature and the promise of a powerful physique, liked to think of himself on horseback. He dreamed obsessively of the cavalry, of being a man among men raising the dust of some Godforsaken plain to put down a native insurrection beyond the Khyber Pass. At seven, he had memorized "The Charge of the Light Brigade," all unknowing that it commemorated a crushing defeat. And he had recited it so often that even doting Lady Eleanor implored him to add another poem to his repertoire.

The Whitwell stables were still ranked with horses in those days, and Gordon set himself a daily regimen of riding. He soon knew half the public roads on the island by heart. But he preferred the notion of riding endlessly back and forth across his father's land—his own land, as he thought of it. The fragmenting of the original estate had made a nonsense of the rides from the Halseys' time. New fences, holiday cottages, and plowed fields barred the former pathways. Low-hanging limbs that no one cut back interrupted the rhythm of a brisk canter.

Nevertheless, Gordon found himself in the midst of the estate only a few hundred yards from the Hall one summer noon. His horse had thrown a shoe on the Ventnor road, and the boy had decided to lead him cross-country to spare the horse's hoof and to vary the routine.

He saw John Thorne at work in a field long before John saw him. Gordon led his limping horse up to drink from the same stream where Naomi had once come down to bathe. In the field bordering the far bank, John was laboring, stripped to the waist and streaming sweat.

He was a magnificent young animal, his muscles bunching and working beneath his deeply reddened skin. His hair plastered his skull, bleached by the sun, then darkened at the ends with sweat.

Gordon Whitwell fell in love with him in that moment, the first of many loves, and the strongest.

He initiated a cautious friendship, playing young lord of the manor, only within limits that John Thorne permitted him. Gordon pledged an undying loyalty he never hazarded to speak aloud. Later, they fought together in South Africa, still hardly more than boys in the battle. And John Thorne returned alone from the war. He returned to Whitwell Hall burdened with a secret.

Eight

Miranda was almost convinced that the blond bronzed man sitting across the room, but quite near enough, seemed unlikely to attack her again. It was broad daylight now, and the setting of an invalid's sickroom seemed hardly the place. His strength was evident enough, but his brutishness appeared to have ebbed away. He seemed lost in distant thought, though his eyes were upon her. They almost beckoned her to speak. She could think of nothing to say. To speak the truth would be to voice her fervent wish to return to the Hall at once, though the grounds might be infested with lunatics. At last she said, "I shouldn't have slept."

"Even the voice is the same," John Thorne mused. "Do you know who I am?"

"Yes, I know you," she said quietly. "They call me—"

"I know what they call you," he cut in. "Finley has told me of you, and so has someone else. They'll be bringing broth down from the Hall kitchens soon enough, and someone to sit with her. I'll see you safely back then."

"I'd sooner go back now," Miranda said, stirring.

"I'd sooner you didn't," he replied with finality. And so they sat minutes more, the birds in full chorus outside and Miranda trapped a second time by the will of this man.

Granny Thorne opened her eyes and turned them to Miranda. The old woman trembled in sudden consciousness of what had happened to her. Consoled by the sunlight streaming in, she blinked sleepily at Miranda and tried to wriggle up against the wooden head of her bed until John laid a restraining hand on her. Still, she didn't look his way, but continued to peer at Miranda with pink-rimmed eyes.

"Why, Miss Amanda," she said in a soft, respectful voice, "you didn't ought to have troubled yourself on my account."

"It's not Miss Amanda, Granny," Thorne said sharply. "It's a maid from the Hall."

"John?" she said, turning toward him. "You know I'm all but blind without my spectacles." Her voice grew tremulous when she realized her grandson was sitting beside her. "Oh, John," she said, trying to control her voice, "he's back. He's back with us again, and whatever shall we do? His brains is twisted still. Battered down the door, he did. Had to, for I knew who 'twas. I looked up from my work and saw his great slavering face at the window."

The old woman was racked with dry sobs, and her small hand closed around John's thick wrist. "And then he come for me, tried to garrote me with a nasty bit of old wire wrapped around his knuckles. Old as I am and near enough to death. But he didn't know me, John. Not properly. He took me for a wicked spirit that had stolen his land. He said that much quite clear, and then he—he fell to his work. I thought I was killed, John, and should never see you more on this earth." She gave way to weeping, drawing her grandson closer to her until she had hidden her small face against his shoulder.

He had been right to let her talk, Miranda thought. There was a gentleness within him that the old woman could draw out, as readily as she had drawn him closer. And while she wept, Thorne returned his gaze to Miranda, who met it with a feeling of sympathy shared.

The room was suddenly full of intruders in the next moment. Three sudden entries, at spaced intervals, joining the three already there. The floor throbbed alarmingly with their footsteps. The low rafters rang with the crossfire of voices.

The first into the room was by far the most exalted, though he cowed Granny Thorne not at all. She jerked away from her grandson and wiped her streaming eyes on the end of the sheet when she first identified Dr. Post. The doctor strode into the room, looking gaunt and brisk and put-upon. He swung his black bag on the bed, glancing nowhere but at Granny Thorne.

"Well, now, old woman, I see the reports of your death are much magnified." Granny sniffed. "I was out all the beastly night," he continued, "in water axle-deep, weather fit for neither man nor beast. Three miles along the Undercliff to the Orchards and not back till dawn, when I had a message regarding you, Granny."

"If you was at Orchards, it must have been to see to Mrs. Parfitt. I knew her time was near," Granny piped conversationally. "What'd she have?"

"A boy," said Dr. Post. "Near enough nine pound and a very difficult birth from start to finish."

"Ah, not so difficult as all that," Granny mildly remarked, "or she'd have cried out in her agony for a proper doctor."

Miranda was startled by this, but saw at once that there was an established bond of chafing wit between the two.

"Well, now," Dr. Post said, "have I been called over only to prescribe idle gossip to an old party who knows plenty on her own? For if I have, I'll be off to my bed instead. What is it, Granny, have you taken one of your turns?"

"Turns! I don't *have* turns, and well you know it, or should! And for my part, you can be off to your bed and sleep the day away, as I have no doubt you generally do!"

"Let's have a look at you, since I'm here," the doctor said, motioning John Thorne away from the bedside. Granny tucked her chin into her small pigeon breast when the doctor drew back the sheet. But he lifted her chin to find among the mass of wrinkles an angry red line encircling her throat. "My God," he said, too loud. And then he turned an inquiring glance toward John, who stood above him.

Any chance of a quiet explanation was doomed by the sound of heavy shoes and wheezing from the stairs. Mrs. Creeth heaved herself up the steps and appeared at the door bearing a cloth-covered basket. She glanced at the occupants of the room with an expression confused between compassion and scorn. "Well, I have come myself, since none of those worthless drabs of girls would set foot out of the Hall. Cheeky baggages! I shall have my own back, see if I don't. There, now, Granny, I've brought you a lovely bit of breakfast and a hot drink if you're feeling up to taking a little something. I don't let the chance of being murdered on my way stand between me and Christian duty!"

"I'm sure Granny will be glad enough for the food you've brought, Mrs. Creeth. But after I've had a look at her, if you don't mind," Dr. Post said firmly.

"Well, I'm sorry to poke in where I'm least wanted, I'm sure!"

"And what's all this about being murdered along the way?" asked the doctor, whose further questions were silenced by a look and a quick gesture from John Thorne.

There was little enough time for further explanations or an examination of Granny Thorne, for at that moment another man ducked his head through the low bedroom door. Miranda had never seen this stranger before, but he looked very much as if he belonged on the estate. A towering, moon-faced man in high boots and a pair of breeches and coat of well-weathered corduroy. He pulled the cap from his head only as he clumped over the threshold.

He would not have crossed Miranda's path in the usual course of events, for he held the now diminished position of estate agent for the Whitwells. It was this George Salter who collected the rents from the summer visitors who took the former farmhouses for the season. And he oversaw the gardeners and turned his own hand at the upkeep of the outbuildings. Salter's dominion ceased on one side of the kitchen door, just as Mr. Finley's began on the other.

Nor was he John Thorne's superior in any official sense. Now that John Thorne had carved out a new niche for himself as chauffeur and mechanic for the new motorcar, he recognized no overseer. It was true that his wages flowed through Salter's hands, but the estate agent could no more dam that flow than he could issue young Thorne an order. When John elected to help out on the home farm where Salter lived, or turned his hand at helping with the cattle or a bit of carpentry, he did so voluntarily. And so a sort of grudging friendship existed between Thorne and Salter, for the agent secretly felt relief that he wasn't responsible for any underling as independent and hotheaded. The damnable twentieth century with its flying machines and motorcars and new-formed gentry was managing to make a perfect balls-up of country living and a decently functioning chain of command. Salter, who had once held absolute sway over the destinies of nearly thirty estate workers, felt his authority sorely curtailed. He eyed with the deepest pessimism whatever future there might be.

It was a minor breach of etiquette for Salter to stride into Smuggler's Cottage, despite the fact that there was no longer a front door to bar his way. For since the day Bart Thorne had been taken to the asylum, no rent had been collected for Granny's home on quarter day. She took great pride in the fiction that the oddment of mending and sewing and turning of hems sent down along the path for her to do was rent enough, though she knew in her wise old heart that she was a charity case. The comparative ease of her old age she attributed to Lady Eleanor, whom she had fixed in her private pantheon, along with Queen Mary—May of Teck as was—the Queen Mother Alexandra, and old Queen Victoria herself.

George Salter knew an uncertain moment, therefore, having made free to stride through the house. An old lady's bedroom was hardly his climate in any case. As a result, his outdoor voice boomed altogether too mightily in the first words he found to say: "I've got the gardeners gathering brush and opening the woodsy path already, even that lazy old coot, Sam. They know no more than that we had a vicious storm last night. Otherwise, the half of them would have flung down their rakes and bolted!"

In a voice nearly Salter's equal, Dr. Post boomed, "In God's sweet name, will somebody tell me what's going on around this place? It looks to me very much as if an old woman's been half-strangled. Mrs. Creeth here chats on confidently about being murdered in the road, and now you, Salter, are carrying around a secret so dark that it would test the phlegm of a brace of hardened old yokels! Just what in the devil—"

"Send out the rest and I'll put you in the picture, Dr. Post," Granny piped suddenly from her bed, gaining an immense advantage over him.

"Not a bad idea, though it does come from you, Granny," the doctor replied with conviction. And the rest of the party was hustled down the stairs. Mrs. Creeth ordered Miranda back to the kitchens, repeating that it was her own Christian duty to give up her half day to the sustenance and defense of Granny. But she looked dubious and thoughtful when she saw that John Thorne meant to see Miranda safely back along the newly cleared path. The watery Creeth eye followed the two young people out of Granny's bedroom, and her expression was not lost on Granny herself.

Miranda and John were deep into the grove on that path she had never walked before when she realized she was beyond shouting distance of help and in the company of her recent assailant.

The path was narrow and full of dips and turns, carpeted with leaves. Miranda's sleeve brushed John's as the two made their way along. The sun was well up. Its rays fell at an angle and reflected in the dripping foliage of the holly pines.

It was a morning to remind Miranda of that day she had walked unthinking across the hills toward the sea. The day she'd met the Wisewoman. A day as warm as this one promised to be, fragrant with the mingling scents of dying summer and autumn at hand, and more subtly of the scent of the soaked earth itself. She nearly forgot to fear her companion in the sudden pleasure of this temporary freedom.

At a sharp turning in the path, there was just sight of a moving figure well ahead. John Thorne threw out an arm and had already pulled Miranda roughly behind him when he said, "It's only old Sam, one of the gardeners. Useless, but harmless." Old Sam was to be seen filling his ancient pipe and luxuriating in the sylvan solitude like a squire. But at the rustle of intruders, he bent for his rake and shambled off.

The milky waters of the mere showed through the trees before John said, "It's my old dad causing all this, if you haven't guessed already."

Miranda looked up at him inquiringly. As if her obtuseness were paining him, he continued, "My father's the madman that set on Granny—his own mother."

"Does everyone know?" Miranda asked.

"Yes. There are a few secrets about the place, but damned few. And by now Post knows as well. This place drove my old dad round the bend. Some would say he'd have run mad regardless. But it was his fixation with this land, trying to make it pay, making it up in his own mind that the holding belonged to him because he'd bought it with his sweat, that finally put him over the edge. They had to lock him away when I was just turned seventeen. Should have done it years before, but Granny could do nothing, and I was only a kid. And the Halseys, who had this place before the Whitwells, never took what you'd call a friendly interest in the tenants. Salter was here then, of course, but he never interfered as long as my dad—and I—broke our backs working the place.

"He was a stern teacher, was my dad, but I learned a lesson from him. As soon as they put him away in the asylum up in Newport,

I was off to the wars. Joined the army just as trouble was breaking in South Africa. I knew even then I'd find no discipline in the whole British Army to rival my dad's."

They walked on in silence until the mere lay like a great saucer beside the path with the mist still rising from it. On the far shore near a great rock where two paths diverged was a kind of Grecian temple. It was a tight circle of fluted columns topped by Corinthian capitals to support a stone dome like an inverted pudding basin.

To Miranda this example of nature refined seemed some water-colorist's rendition of paradise. She lingered unconsciously, forgetting her duties and even the man beside her. The mere and the temple had the sort of perfect, serene beauty that she had perhaps dreamed of but never seen, never envisioned in this blend of water, stone, and sky.

The perfection of the rooms of Whitwell Hall was still beyond her. The Flemish tapestries set in the bleached and silvered panels. The infinity of mirrors set up by the thousand curving silver sides of teapots and urns high on their tripods. The morning room a garden of subtly shaded chintz flowers covering the graceful curves of the chair backs. The great glittering chandeliers. These surpassed in elegance anything she had ever seen. But this rain-washed vista touched her imagination. The mere, perfectly circular and bordered by smoothly mowed lawn, except for the single outcropping of rock and a stand of bulrushes. And the perfect temple rising above it. This was a beauty that made her heart yearn and sing.

"It's called a folly," John Thorne said. "That temple thing. A folly, I suppose, because it serves no purpose." She turned from his side, the moment shattered, and walked at a brisk pace toward the house, whose roofs she could see above terraced gardens.

He caught up with her, sensing that something had gone wrong, and wondering why it seemed to matter to him. It could be no more than her resemblance to Amanda that drew him. And if this girl was showing spirit now, it was a poor shadow of what Amanda could manage at the slightest provocation, she who was continually provoked. He'd thought it would not be necessary to apologize for that first night. And he was damned if he would now. She was a servant, and she knew that much. He had had more than his share of servant girls before he had fallen into Amanda's web. Country maidens who were on their backs before they knew it, and no longer maidens thereafter. Still, he struggled to think of something to say to appease her as he kept up a steady pace.

"You'll be all right now," he said at last, when they started through the passage between the outbuildings. "He'll be caught, my dad. I daresay he'll want to be. And they'll come from Newport for him. It's happened before. When he was first there, he was out half a dozen times before they learned to watch him."

Miranda stopped in the shadow of the overhanging eaves and looked suddenly up at Thorne, wondering at herself as she asked, "Why did you come back?"

"What?"

"After the war. Why did you come back to this place?" There was a challenge in this bold question that neither of them understood.

"I—I suppose it was my fate. I had a hundred plans, but when I was free, I came straight back. I guess it was my fate."

And mine, too, perhaps, Miranda thought, wondering if she, too, was going slightly mad.

When she had closed the door against John Thorne, the kitchen's sudden quiet seemed as ominously strange as the night finally past. Without Mrs. Creeth, there was no bustle. The breakfast trays had gone up, and the hearth was white with cold ashes. Miranda felt close to fainting with fatigue and an emotion harder to recognize. The hour of snatched sleep had been more exhausting than an uninterrupted vigil.

The quiet was broken at once by the sounds of murmuring and footsteps on the stairs from the dining room. Before Mrs. Buckle came into view, Miranda identified her by the rough flurry of her ample, old-fashioned skirts. She was deep in a conversation held over her shoulder with Mr. Finley, who was descending behind her. "Her ladyship is inquiring after Granny Thorne. I left her with the impression that the old woman had taken sick, and I daresay she suspects nothing more. Still, it is hardly my way or my place to practice deceit upon her ladyship, and—"

"And you were quite right, Mrs. Buckle," came the butler's suave reply. "For the present, I wish to spare the family the sad knowledge that old Thorne is back and very likely still within the grounds—"

"Oh, Mr. Finley, never say so! The very thought of it makes my blood run cold!"

"Mrs. Buckle, I look to you, as in all things, to set an example for the others. We will take the proper precautions and on no account give way to disorder. It is just such a steadying hand as your own that is most wanted. It seems far from fair that the family should have visited upon them this—creature—of a past for which they had no responsibility."

"Ah, Mr. Finley," the housekeeper declared with rising composure, "when Sir Timothy and her ladyship acquired this property, I fear they little reckoned on the legacy of—depravity they fell heir to. And my reference is not entirely limited to the old lunatic for—"

"I believe I follow your reference, Mrs. Buckle, and I think the less said the better, even in confidence."

Mr. Finley nearly leaped to see Miranda standing across the kitchen. He had tarried long enough with Mrs. Buckle for their privileged conversation to skate nearer thin ice than a new house-maid need follow. "Miranda, at last! You have done good service in the past hours, my girl, and have shown evidence of your mettle. But I am very much afraid you are only to be rewarded for the moment with further obligations. We have had to press Hilda and Hannah into service abovestairs, and that is always trying—"

"Trying, indeed," Mrs. Buckle echoed.

"They are attempting to cope with the breakfasts, and one only hopes for the best. Good fortune is with us in at least one regard. The only guests at present are some gentlemen from Sir Timothy's Royal Yacht Squadron, expected here for the day. However, it is imperative that we keep up our usual standards so that no hint of the recent—unpleasantness—be allowed to disquiet any but ourselves.

"Unfortunately, we are not up to strength, for Betty appears to be malingering. Your first duty, my girl, is to see to her, and if there is nothing really seriously wrong, which I very much suspect, you are to rout her out at once. It may well be that Betty lacks courage, rather than her usual robust health! Mrs. Buckle, kindly inform Miranda as to the way to Betty's room."

The way to Betty's room lay up half a dozen flights and along a labyrinth of box rooms and empty presses with doors that yawned open to catch the shins of passersby. Miranda had need of all her concentration to negotiate the turnings. But at the same time she was troubled by a number of unfamiliar irritations. For a start, she felt as if she had lived in her wrinkled uniform for a month. The damp night had sent her apron drooping and her hair escaping in strands from under her cap. As she walked, she set about the difficult task of trying to retie the flattened bow in the small of her back.

This flustered feeling about her appearance in these perfectly empty halls was a strange sensation in itself, strange and uncomfortable, for there was little enough time to set about making herself properly presentable.

But then her mind shifted unaccountably to John Thorne, as if his gray eyes were still following her. She sensed that none of the servants approved of John Thorne or even trusted him. Not that they had any reason to. When Granny's room had suddenly filled with people, Dr. Post alone had seemed to acknowledge him as Granny's kin, as one who had a right to be there at her bedside and to have the strongest stake in her welfare. And even between those two men no words had passed.

It was as if the Hall staff had closed ranks against John Thorne. Perhaps they all had evidences of his coarseness, as she herself had. Or perhaps they thought it wiser to watch from a safe distance for the return of the madness that stalked his family. But it was more likely John Thorne's arrogant independence that vexed them all, particularly Mr. Finley.

It was only a show, Miranda decided. Thorne showed every sign of being the kind of man who flaunted a freedom he didn't possess. Had he not told her himself that it was his fate to be drawn back to these acres, he who acted so independent? If he was not the master of his own fate, was he not, after all, a cowering footman, swaggering about in a countryman's clothes? And staying out of the range of the hierarchy of the place as much as possible to spare his pointless pride? Judgments that would have been utterly alien to Miranda a week before flowed through her mind.

Yet nothing summed up the man. The rough edge of his gentle voice. The ring of regret behind his blunt words when he told her of his mad father. The manner in which his hand shot out to shield her at the slightest hint of danger along the path. Nothing fitted about this John Thorne. And perhaps that was the greatest cause of his unpopularity.

There was no time for more of these speculations. They led only to a kind of wary excitement that stirred somewhere beneath

Miranda's breast. As she neared Betty's door, she was guided through it by a sharp and sour smell that cut the mustiness of the attics.

Betty lay across a disorderly bed where she had been very sick indeed, and repeatedly. She scarcely noted the arrival of a visitor. There was a full basin at the side of the bed, which she struggled toward. She was sick again, retching painfully into it. Her hair stood out from her head in a tangled, dust-colored halo.

A pitcher of water squatted on a small, battered, yellow pine chest. Miranda moved quickly to dip a towel into it and set about word-lessly to tidy up the sick girl and to make her as comfortable as she could. She wedged the window open for a breath of fresher air and stripped the sheets out from under Betty, who rolled upon them, moaning pitifully. If she doesn't find strength enough to speak very soon, Miranda thought, I'll be very worried about her.

But almost at once Betty's moans gave way to speech. "Lumme! I thought I'd done with all this bein' sick! It goes on sumpen chronic!" There was enough of Betty's old spirit subdued behind these gasping words to reassure Miranda.

"What is it, Betty?" she asked, applying a wet cloth to the girl's brow.

"What do you fink?" Betty replied, and rolled her eyes a touch dramatically.

"I don't know," Miranda replied to humor her, "but I hope I don't catch it."

"I hope you don't, myself," Betty replied fervently. "If ole Finley wants me at me work, I've a good mind to tumble down the steps to the kitchens and be sick again all down his front! Ever so sick! I fink I could just manage it!"

"Lie still. Mr. Finley won't ask anything of you when you're feel-ing like this."

"There's no end to wot people will arsk of you in this life," Betty muttered.

"The doctor's with Granny Thorne now—that Dr. Post from Vent-nor. Shall I ask Mr. Finley if he can be sent for?"

"Wot? A doctor see me? Not bloody likely! They want payin', doctors do! And he carn't prescribe nuffin for wot I got."

"What have you got, Betty, if you know?" Miranda asked, her mouth twitching to stifle a smile at Betty's reviving manner.

"Wot I've got is a little stranger comin' for company, is wot!" And then Betty gave Miranda a very hard look. Her eyes, glittering like black coals, sought Miranda's to see if the message had been received.

It had. Miranda's smile deserted her. "A baby, Betty? You?"

"That's right," Betty sighed. "A baby and me. Accidents will happen."

Nine

After the night's storm that had kept her wakeful and restless, tossing in her great oak bed, Amanda Whitwell was up at first light. Forked lightning and crescendos of thunder, the splintering of tree limbs far and near, the scream of the relentless wind sweeping the leads along the roofs, finding the chinks at the corners of the windows—all these had combined to make a perfect nonsense of her attempts at sleep. "Altogether rather too theatrical," Amanda said aloud to test the sound of her morning voice, "like the stage effects for *King Lear*." And then she silently pondered the wisdom of talking to herself. For one who might be closeted in her chambers for an indefinite sentence, this could develop into a regrettable habit. "And I have so many already," she remarked, quite audibly.

Amanda flung out of her bed, where the sheets and satin counterpane were twisted into the shapes of cream horns, reminding her, as so much did, of food. She pulled the billowing nightdress tightly around her body, drawing the stuff of it into great bunches at either side of her narrow waist. Unquestionably, she had taken off a few pounds. And this despite an utter lack of proper exercise.

Since the chubbiness of earlier years had melted off her figure, Amanda had kept a careful watch on her weight. The new fashions decreed wasp waists and a gently curving line, rather swanlike, from bosom to hip. The day of the well-nourished, highly colored English beauty had passed, she thought complacently. Out with great lumps of girls like Sybil Ward-Benedict, who trod Bond Street as if she were crossing the yard to a stable. Dear Sybil—that great ten-stone monument to a robustly insatiable appetite, who carried her handbag through all the smartest London shops smacking against her ample thigh as if it were a riding crop. Poor Sybil, Amanda thought, how unfashionable her jutting prow has grown to be. She peered down the front of her nightdress at her own small breasts.

Nor was there any knowing how high hemlines might creep. A pair of trim ankles was already a prerequisite. The day might come, she thought daringly, when a length of calf might well figure prominently among one's charms on continual public display. Another black mark against Sybil Ward-Benedict, she decided with complete objectivity. Sybil, who had thickened and hidden her great milkmaid's ankles for all of sixteen years inside pairs of steadily larger riding boots.

Amanda lifted the skirt of her nightdress to examine her own bare ankles. She scanned them from every feasible angle, rising on the balls of her feet to simulate high-heeled shoes, or better yet, slippers, dancing slippers. Her ankles passed muster. There was very little about herself that Amanda could fault.

The wind had set one of the leaded panels in the window rattling during the night, and so she set off across the long room to fasten it. Pale autumn daylight and the first low rays of the sun drained the lavender hues from the room, bleaching it to shades of funereal gray. The deep amethyst velvet covering of the double seat before the hearth looked quite dismally dingy. The linen-fold paneling, weathered to silver, rose along the walls, only adding to the monochromatic effect. Amanda was beginning to loathe the room she had had done over especially to express her subtle tastes, to provide a proper, somewhat austere setting for her own coloring. She had decided on shades of lavender and time-softened wood tones as a backdrop for her own pale skin and black hair. Now she wondered if the color scheme of the room was not simply another mistake.

The immense room ended in a great bay, glazed in leaded-glass windows set in carved stone. The Hall had been assembled from no fewer than forty more venerable structures at various times. Paneling from a Tudor house rescued from the knock-down crew, whole ceilings on permanent loan from other households fallen on hard times. Amanda's window frames had derived from a seventeenth-century church with a dwindled congregation. But she was no student of past artistry or economics.

The floor of the bay was paved in polished flags, as smooth and as cold to a bare foot as glass. In her plans for decoration, Amanda had kept this irregular area quite free of furniture and those everlasting great pots of depressing ferns. The three-sided bay had always reminded her somehow of the bridge of a great ocean liner, like those one saw sailing from Southampton. No matter that her ship had seemed to go aground in a manicured garden, fussy with stonework and beds of flowers. And no matter that the only water in view was the mere, diminished by distance and quite ludicrously subdued in a perfectly circular border of green lawn and fringed with bulrushes like the lashes of an enormous eye.

The bay had become her sea captain's bridge, and so she had kept it clear of ornamentation, choosing only sets of unbleached muslin curtains for the windows that could be drawn back neatly. The coarse fabric reminded her of sails. She shuddered to think what her mother's advanced and arty tastes would have done with this corner, so pregnant with possibilities. Lady Eleanor would have turned it, no doubt, into a cross between a swamp of water lilies and a shop window cluttered with chinoiserie. Amanda uncharitably imagined her mother choking it with cut flowers in combinations calculated to distract, and scattering about any number of little spindly tables in orange and black and ivory lacquer.

She turned with a shudder to the windows. Instead of latching them against the morning breeze, she pushed them open. The winds of the night had given way to small flurries and minute cyclones that swirled the leaves in spirals from the heaps the gardeners had made. These funnels played across the silver surface of the mere. The mist still rose from this small body of water, revealing and then concealing again the stone temple on the far shore.

It would be, she thought, a perfect day, still balmy yet brisk. A wonderful day for a walk. She half-turned to select a suitable outdoor ensemble from her wardrobe. Light tweeds—and brogues, of course. But she returned to plant her elbows on the window. For she remembered to honor her own resolve not to leave her room until they had detailed the new girl as her own maid.

Life seemed very hard to Amanda Whitwell. The minute one obstacle to one's freedom of movement was removed, another cropped up in its place. Gregory Forrest had gone back to London, no doubt glumly, to pursue his desultory architectural studies. And Amanda was left free to roam the Hall and grounds at will without having to do battle with his earnest attempts at courtship. How free she felt of having to hear his endless plans to make the City of New York over into a safe and decent haven for immigrants. This tiresome, exotic boy-man was gone for a time, leaving her in peace.

But his departure had only cleared the field for another battle. For her mother was being exceedingly tiresome about the new girl—Miranda. If Amanda had been a few seasons younger, she'd have set up an unearthly howl. But she mused bleakly on the subject of her vanished childhood instead. How quickly one passed beyond the tantrum stage. And how quickly one grew helpless just as one should be coming into one's own.

She'd barely been able to endure Lady Eleanor's reasons for withholding Miranda's services. The new girl must find her place among the other servants. The new girl must learn the house thoroughly, top to bottom. The new girl must develop a necessary degree of versatility in her duties. The new girl must . . . It would seem that the new girl must be more carefully groomed than one of Sybil Ward-Benedict's horses, while all the time Amanda must sit in solitude confronting the prune face of Buckle, who clung to her nanny role and practiced her pathetic attempts at discretion. Poor, superannuated nanny, who tried so hard to transform herself into a lady's maid in order to maintain her grip on dear little Amanda. Besides, Buckle knew too much. Behind her pursed lips, the old witch longed to confront Amanda—and anyone else who would listen—with her suspicions about John Thorne.

Amanda had depended upon two factors to keep those pursed lips sealed. The first was moral. It was still all but beyond Buckle's belief that a young lady so carefully reared (by Buckle's own hand) could stoop to share her bed with the rudest underling. It was a crime darker than incest, merging on the murder of all decency.

The second factor was purely practical. To tell was to lose what hold she believed she still had—on Amanda and on her own livelihood.

Amanda felt her own patience drawing to an end. I shall *have* Miranda before the week is out, or know the reason why! This bracing resolve tended to set her up for the day. She beamed with premature triumph out across the lawns, drawing in great drafts of morning air. Perhaps she would have that walk in any case. A very short one, possibly, that no one would remark upon.

Her mind thus occupied, Amanda stared without seeing across the mere. The mist continued to play above the rippling water. And a bit of the great boulder beside the paths seemed to disengage itself and roll free. It was almost surely the stone, dividing itself like an amoeba. But no, it was a living thing, an old turtle, grown impossibly long. Or, more likely, a mud-colored man, crawling from beneath the rock's underside along the edge of the mere, leaving behind him a glistening trail of slime. A man so near the soggy soil he seemed at one with it. Mud-colored all over, even to his head. He seemed to be crawling nowhere in particular, as low to the ground as the cover of mist, and so slowly that his movement made no variation in the landscape.

The small corner of Amanda's mind that was not occupied by more important concerns found the sight of him curious. But she had grown bored with the new-washed morning and turned back to her room, determined to ring for Buckle and then send her back down again for a proper breakfast. Amanda decided in favor of a complete Sybil Ward-Benedict breakfast, from kippers to croissants, with every heavy gastronomic delight laid on.

She turned from the window just as John Thorne and Miranda broke cover and stepped out from below the branches of the grove. Even at that distance she would have identified them at once, and the sight would have been the ruination of her day. She would have compelled herself to watch them as they walked, brushing against one another on the narrow path, pausing to look out across the mere, which was half-concealed again by the swirling mist. She would have seen Miranda hesitate, transfixed by the Grecian temple, only to move on again at a word from John Thorne.

Amanda would have writhed to see them lingering there, the inaudible words passing between them. Had he said those same words to her? For he would certainly talk to a lady just as he talked to a serving wench. He would recognize the difference and then scorn it. She would have forgotten her plans for breakfast if she had seen those two, forgotten even herself and indulged in a tantrum to pale all previous tantrums.

But she saw nothing, for she was standing beside her canopied bed by then, with her thumb pressing insistently against the electric button that would alert the kitchen to one of her lesser desires. Her thumb thrust against the button steadily, as if it were the eyeball of an enemy.

Mrs. Buckle seemed to take her time about coming with the morning tea tray. When she finally arrived, whisking into the room, catching her skirts on the doorframe and then managing a re-entry, Amanda failed to notice that the woman was distracted. She was nearly normal enough in appearance to pass invisibly beneath Amanda's scant notice. The cameo that had lain buried in the black ruffles at her stringy neck longer than Amanda could remember was nestled in its usual place. The bunch of keys hung from a long chain down her skirts. Despite her distraction, Mrs. Buckle was astonished to find Amanda out of bed and examining the contents of her wardrobe. The great mirrored doors were thrown back, and Amanda stood in her dressing gown thoughtfully peering inside.

"Oh, Buckle!" she said. "Tea at last. It will just see me through to a proper breakfast. I am absolutely famished. Do have something quite overwhelming sent up in the matter of solid food. I shall have a bit of everything on the sideboard and—anything else you might suggest."

Mrs. Buckle's eyes bulged at this sudden shift of mood or maneuver. There was a near-affable undertone in Miss Amanda's greeting that had long been absent and had never been usual. It only doubled the surprise of seeing her charge awake at this early hour.

"And, Buckle, if we *are* going up to London in November, it's surely not too early to be making some preparations—simple ones, of course, that you can sort out. I shall need quite a lot of new clothes once I'm there. But I don't see why we can't salvage some of my older things if we put our minds to it, do you?"

"No, indeed, Miss," Mrs. Buckle said with lowered eyes.

"I think I might get another wearing or two out of this gray charmeuse, don't you? It might just do for the odd afternoon at home. But just see here where the lining has pulled away and the corsage is hanging by a single thread. A good job for Granny Thorne. Here, take it and see that she gets it at once. Granny will put it right."

Amanda held out the dress in a casual wad and looked up sharply when Mrs. Buckle failed to take it from her. Instead, the ridiculous woman seemed paralyzed, her mouth gaping and her hands at her sides. It was too sad, Buckle's attempts to keep pace with her now that she was quite grown, with a woman's needs, and even whims. Buckle beyond the nursery was out of her depth.

"Do take it!" Amanda said, waving the dress at her. "And see that Granny gets it. She'll see in a moment what needs doing."

"Oh, Miss Amanda," Buckle said in a sepulchral voice, "I don't think—"

"You don't think what, Buckle?"

"Well, Miss, I don't think Granny Thorne is up to the work."

"Nonsense, Buckle. No one gives up at Whitwell Hall. None of the staff ever grows too old for their duties. Do you?"

"No, Miss, I suppose not." Mrs. Buckle took the dress from Amanda's impatient hand and shook out its wrinkles in her best imitation of a lady's maid.

By midmorning Whitwell Hall was alive with unaccustomed activity. Amanda was busily tucking into a trencherman's breakfast, her mind alive with plans for a day to break the monotony of weeks.

Up in the attics Miranda sat at Betty's bedside, waiting to hear the particulars of the girl's startling news. But Betty had drifted back into a kind of sleep, exhausted from her sickness and relieved at the sharing of news she could not keep much longer in any case.

In the sunless bowels of the Hall, Willie Salter, forgotten by everyone, stirred on his pallet in the coalhole. At that moment he had not presence of mind enough to know where he was. His brains were still addled by the tot of rum prescribed by Mrs. Creeth. He stirred in his slumbers and turned back to nightmares of old Bart Thorne stalking like a great reptile through a dark landscape, delivering sudden death to numberless victims whose last earthly glimpse was of an inhuman face contorted by madness.

Not far from Willie, Mr. Finley and Mrs. Buckle had pushed the breathless Hilda and Hannah to one side. The two senior members of the staff had fallen with a rare spirit upon the duties of the day. With the usual routine at sixes and sevens, and with Mrs. Creeth out of the way, the two old veterans were nearly playing house in the kitchen. Mr. Finley found time only for the occasional directive thrown in the direction of Hilda and Hannah. Mrs. Buckle, who never deigned or dared go near Mrs. Creeth's larders and meat cage, bustled about like a new bride. She extracted the flaky kidney pies that her adversary had baked for Sir Timothy's Saturday luncheon party, and she thought of salads and a nice bit of plaice for an opening course. To display her efficiency, she managed adroit footwork, keeping just clear of Mr. Finley, but never working far from his side. If Betty and Miranda had appeared, ready and able to work, she would have been sorely vexed.

The morning, they agreed, was shaping well under their hands, despite everything, particularly when Hilda and Hannah were banished to the scullery to do the breakfast dishes. Mr. Finley was at work, decanting a bottle of port and another of claret through a muslin cloth, and beginning to expand on a favorite theme: "Ah, Mrs. Buckle, I cannot but think this day's activities are a presage of the future." His more expressive nostril flared importantly.

"Why, whatever can you mean, Mr. Finley?" the housekeeper asked. She loitered over a vinegar cruet, ready to invest his every statement with a meaning designed to draw them closer.

"Simply this, Mrs. Buckle. I foresee a time in a future not far distant when two souls such as you and me will be all that's left to perform the domestic duties of many a household."

"Surely not!" Mrs. Buckle was shocked. "Why ever would that be?"

"The times, Mrs. Buckle, are changing. Consider if you will that this very house, I'm told, in the Halseys' time employed a Hall staff of fourteen. Footmen, pages, grooms, a carpenter, four in the scullery, a man, my good Mrs. Buckle, who was retained to wind the clocks.

"Consider also that this numerous staff was at most times doubled by the servants of houseguests who were stopping. Oh, yes, Mrs. Buckle, we are a sadly shrunken lot now—a race, if you will, confronting extinction. It is a rare houseguest who travels with his man, or a lady with her maid. We do double duty in catering to guests, drawing in such as Abel to perform the charade of a footman or to valet some gentleman who travels quite alone, arriving, perhaps, in a motor with a single valise and departing the following day in perpetual haste. I have heard it said that there are even young ladies about now, driving their own motors and flitting from place to place quite unchaperoned.

"Yes, yes. We are sadly diminished, and our ranks will thin further, you mark my words. Young girls are lured away to a very different sort of life these days. Even decent girls. They are going to the schools now, many of them. And then they are taught the typing machines and various skills and go into the offices."

"I don't call that progress," Mrs. Buckle commented darkly.

"Ah, progress or no, it is the path to the future. We are, though it is hard to believe, better off in the country than a town establishment. For it is the town girl who is led away first—"

"Town girls always were," Mrs. Buckle noted.

"Here, at least, we can find the occasional girl who knows no other option. But soon there will be no place to hide from the great changes, Mrs. Buckle. Even a coarse country girl will seek a different—I don't say a better—way of life."

"Much luck to them." Mrs. Buckle sniffed.

Mr. Finley lowered his voice and continued, now in an ironic vein. "We are graced with Hilda and Hannah, of course, for they are fit for nothing else. And Betty—well, one can hardly picture poor Betty as a female secretary."

"Flighty," Mrs. Buckle said.

"Quite so. On the other hand—"

Mrs. Buckle foresaw that Mr. Finley was about to make an exception of Miranda in this roll call of the maids' shortcomings. She was very much afraid that he would weigh Miranda and not find her wanting. A girl, perhaps, cast in the mold of earlier times. A girl born to serve, who knew it and knew how. Mrs. Buckle saw no good purpose served in hasty favorable judgments of new servants. She had herself served fifteen years, first in the scullery and then as under housemaid, in a damp country house in Shropshire before she had so much as glimpsed daylight, as it were. Besides, she could not suffer gladly praise of a young snip who was even now, in several minds, a possible successor to herself. Her mind moved even quicker than Mr. Finley's pronouncements, and she dared interrupt him. "But I don't see how the gentry will manage without their staffs, Mr. Finley."

"They will not manage well, Mrs. Buckle. You may be assured of that. Not well at all."

In her boudoir two stories above, Lady Eleanor Whitwell's thoughts ran a course roughly parallel to her servants'. She sat at her writing desk, lingering over correspondence that failed to hold her attention. She continually lost the thread of a sentence. For moments at a time, her pen remained poised over a random word, refusing to flow on in the customary way. She sat, unconsciously posed like the subject of a painter more *outré* than Sargent.

In her morning robe of Liberty silk, she might have been a portrait by Klimt. All the rosebud fussiness of her Victorian youth had fallen from her, revealing a purity of line. She thought of the changes being wrought. She thought even of servants, though the same subject tired her as a topic of conversation. Money newer than most of her circle's indeed spoke of little else and thought it smart. How endlessly Maude Glaslough decried her Irish servants, their thieving, prying ways, and how thoroughly dependent upon them she was. How like them, in truth. How silly Maude could be, Lady Eleanor thought, and how silly clever people always seemed to be.

The subject of Lady Eleanor's letter was Amanda, and as it was a difficult letter to put discreetly, her mind drifted among related thoughts. She had every intention of giving way to Amanda's demand for a maid of her own. Heaven knew, Amanda needed one. If she continued her tiresomeness about Gregory Forrest, then she would have her London Season in the summer. She would certainly need a maid then, a skilled one thoroughly indoctrinated. And in the unlikely event that she saw sense and married Gregory, she would certainly need a maid to go out to America with her and to assist in the setting up of a domestic establishment there. Buckle couldn't be expected to make this transition. She was overstrained in her present role. Lady Eleanor lingered over the eventuality of Amanda's marriage, wondering what an American household might be like. The best people in New York, she assumed, lived like the best people in London. And then she smiled at herself, for it was a judgment that might have been made by the most slavish and unoriginal and insular conformist in her set.

It was a mother's role, of course, to give in to a daughter's demands by degrees, pointing out a few home truths along the way. That she herself, for example, managed in the country without a woman to serve her personally. That she had, in fact, grown quite comfortable in the privacy of boudoir and dressing room. That Lucille came from Ventnor to do her hair and went away again. And that Mrs. Buckle, along with Granny Thorne, was quite capable in the matter of keeping up her wardrobe. It would seem—she allowed herself a smile— that apart from the Season, only climbers and the stout required maids. The climbers for the pleasure of ordering some poor wretch about. And the stout, whose elaborate corsetry demanded as many experienced hands as possible, all pulling together.

This was not a line of reasoning to take with Amanda, naturally. That young lady would do her share of ordering a maid about. But Lady Eleanor saw a deeper need. Amanda needed a companion. Life was dull in the country for a girl who did not love the fields and stables, a girl like that rather large and thoroughly hearty Sybil Ward-Benedict.

And even when Amanda was at school—a brief and distressing interlude for all concerned—she had had few friends among the other girls, except for the robust Sybil, who was a friend to all. Amanda was altogether too solitary, though she complained of everything but loneliness. But then it would be like Amanda never to complain about the very problem that troubled her, but to pluck from the air, instead, every imaginary injustice to refashion it into a cause.

And so Amanda would have her Miranda, in time. And if the maid proved no more sensible than Amanda, another would be found somewhere, though help in any form was growing nearly impossible to find and keep. Perhaps a maid in whom to confide would clarify Amanda's thoughts. She remembered that during her own girlhood half the pleasure of a beau was sharing intimations of his ardor with a confidante. Maids, for their part, were quite eager audiences for such girlish gossip. And hardly less trustworthy than one's friends, who were often enough one's smiling rivals.

Lady Eleanor's pen recovered its eloquence. She finished a sentence in her scrollwork calligraphy: *"Your patience, my dear Gregory, will not, I feel sure, be its own reward. And I shall take what steps a mother can to coax Amanda into a more amiable frame of mind."*

A rather guarded letter, Lady Eleanor thought as she glanced over it, but then she was in no position to promise more than she could deliver. The vision of Amanda as a neatly wrapped parcel being shipped to a New York address skated across her mind. She half smiled and then frowned at the lack of maternal feeling it suggested. The picture in the silver frame on her desk smiled back at her in return, ignoring the frown. It was a picture of Gordon, the last one she had of him that was not in uniform. He wore a soft shirt, open at the collar, and his black hair was a mass of ringlets. The sight of him caught at her throat for the thousandth time, but to retire this picture to the bottom of a drawer where it would not cause her continual pain would kill her outright.

With the most difficult letter of the morning finally out of the way, she averted her eyes from Gordon's gaze and turned to less challenging correspondence. She barely noted how quiet the house was that sunny morning and how like a picture the grounds looked from her narrow window.

The heartiest breakfast in weeks fortified Amanda. She had not rung to have the littered tray carried away. Another encounter with the desiccated Buckle would dash her own high spirits. Besides, she meant to slip unnoticed from the house and roam the grounds at will. She harbored no hopes that she would run into John Thorne by chance. A country place is not a London street where every coincidence can logically occur. They had been very cautious. Except for the first meeting, their trysts had been made under cover of night and a quiet house.

Amanda jerked a tweed coat and skirt from her wardrobe. It would not be long, she thought, before she had a proper maid to lay out her clothes and to help her dress. She considered going hatless, but thought better of it. She rummaged through half a dozen round boxes and settled on a small three-cornered hat, like a French shepherdess's in a painting by Fragonard, but rendered in twill. She started from the room, but turned back to find a long scarf of loosely woven Irish wool and wound it around her neck. Then she turned the silent knob of the door, scanned the empty hall, and slipped out.

Past her mother's door she crept with exaggerated stealth, while a part of her half longed to be discovered. Resigned to meeting some busybody servant with an overloud voice on the stairs, she encountered no one. Amanda stood undecided beneath the great chandelier of the hall. From the back of the house the sound of braying merriment drifted. Sir Timothy and his Yacht Squadron cronies were sampling a glass or two before lunch. Amanda was accustomed to think of Sir Timothy, if at all, as "poor Father." Communication with him was all but impossible. And appeals to him on any matter were met with a glazed lack of comprehension. Nevertheless, poor Father seemed to be passing a very pleasant morning with the gentlemen from the Squadron, who were talking around him at a great rate and drinking up the excellent claret that was his chief social asset.

Amanda made for the front doors, but decided against that direction. She turned and wandered through the morning room instead, for the pleasure of easing out of the house by the same way John Thorne used when he came to her by night.

She ran across the terrace and down the steps to a lawn that was like the Sargasso Sea. Water filled in the prints Amanda's small brogues made as she strode past the autumn plantings. The dampness would find its way through the stoutest shoes. But Amanda was determined to steer clear of the walks. To follow one straight line of crushed rock after another was no improvement on sitting in her room while her thoughts ran along their usual rails. She made her way in the general direction of the mere, as she knew she would. And all the while her brogues made amusing little squishing sounds as she planted them in the soaked earth.

The mere was almost above its banks, and the lawn was nearly under water. Still, Amanda pressed on, almost splashing. Halfway around, a small bit of sharp gravel worked its way into her shoe. She sat down on the great slab of stone that jutted above the water and pulled the brogue off impatiently.

The little diamond of gravel fell out, and Amanda took her time about wedging her shoe back on her foot and tying the wet laces. She seemed to have thought about this very rock on which she was sitting. When was it? Sometime earlier in the day as she'd gazed down from her window. But the thought escaped her now.

She was within a few yards of the temple. It very naturally claimed her thoughts for several minutes because it was there last June, during Coronation Week, that John Thorne had first made love to her.

She smiled to think how little appeals to his reason mattered in those moments leading up to the temple. She had led him on shamelessly. The very techniques that had driven poor Gregory to the brink of distraction had worked in a very different way on John Thorne. Nor was one ever drawn into earnest conversations with this man of the soil who smelled of sweat and earth and axle grease. It had been a triumph to be seduced by him and in this place. This too-perfect temple that some early and rigid romantic had planted there a century before. These columns that had surrounded them like a cage of their own choosing within sight of the brilliantly lit house. The house where Gregory Forrest had been a guest that very night.

She had given herself to John Thorne on the very night of a Coronation party with the music from the Hall wavering across the mere. She had broken every rule she knew on that breathlessly warm night when John Thorne had first fallen on her. He had taken her superbly, she thought, remembering the crumpled dancing frock beneath her, the moment of searing pain given way to a pleasure combined of passion and satisfaction. The spattering of blood she had rinsed away herself from her underclothes.

If she lived to be a very old woman, which she meant to do, she would know no greater triumph than to be set upon by that rough, experienced underling. As he had torn at her beribboned gown that evening, she had thought of the thousand inaccurate versions of the wedding night she had heard whispered of. She had despised her innocence nearly as much as she despised the conventions that bound her.

Young girls, of course, were meant to know nothing—to have no opportunity of judging for themselves the sort of man who could give them pleasure. Young girls were not even to know that after a suitable interval following marriage it was now quite the thing to take a subtle afternoon lover, as long as he was of their own class. A married woman, people hinted, was free to pursue a life of—diversion after she had married well and produced an heir or two. But there were rules even for infidelity. First the marriage nonsense. Then the agony and bother of bearing a child—and by a child, people meant a son, naturally. And only then when one was quite thirty could one turn a veiled eye toward some conventional cardboard lover as dully discreet as oneself and no more interesting in the long run than one's husband.

To play the game by all these rules was to forfeit in advance the satisfaction of winning, Amanda had thought, lying there in the straining arms of John Thorne.

The temple of this bright autumn morning seemed to keep her secret with stuffy discretion. It was a veritable Mrs. Buckle of a temple. The tiled floor where they had lain was a mirror of rainwater, with here and there a tiny galleon of a leaf scudding across the surface.

She walked on, running her hand along one fluted column and still remembering. Then she stepped beyond onto the higher ground toward a more secluded part of the garden.

At one side the grove of larch and holly pine had been allowed to grow in a dense tangle almost as close as the mere. But beside it a long greensward of mowed grass stretched in another direction into the distance, between rows of rhododendron, grown as top-heavy and softly rounded above as thatched cottages. The broad green walk between them was as level as a carpeted hallway. But within the rhododendrons were entire invisible networks of twisting passage-ways—highroads for voles and shrews for whom the arching branches opened at points as great cathedrals. Roots writhed from the ground, and here and there at the heart of the leafy greenness were irregular open spaces as big as rooms with ceilings of glossy leafwork higher than a crouching man's head.

Amanda strolled down the middle of the rhododendron-lined lawn, for at the end it gave onto a large circle of garden land she had played in as a child. It had always seemed to her then that this part of the garden was the end of the world, since it was well out of sight of the Hall.

The secluded garden was a choice example of Victorian pomposity. Between the grass circle and the belt of trees beyond stood a regiment of stone animals on their lichened pedestals. This ring of monuments to the Middle Ages had been carved in the Halseys' day, and none too artfully, by some local stonemason. They represented the symbolic beasts of medieval legendry, crouching on their hindquarters with claws raised stiffly to hold heraldic shields.

The shields of Angle and Saxon and Norman names were in the paws and claws of griffins, leopards, tigers, one chipped unicorn, and a brace of lions in several unlikely, attentive attitudes. Some of the stone monsters mangled stone serpents at their feet. Others were capped with crumbling crowns. And several turned blind, pious eyes to heaven.

These grotesques had been Amanda's childhood favorites. Often enough she had nagged Buckle to walk her this way so that she might play in the broad ring of stone beasts that were toys to her. And Buckle had always grumbled, for no one walked that way very much after the Halseys' time. And thus no one had provided a convenient garden seat. Half of small Amanda's pleasure in gamboling there had been to watch from the corner of her eye Buckle's discomfort as she stood with a great show of patience in the middle of the round lawn, just a touch more stony than the statues.

Positioned in the circle's precise center as Buckle had once been, Amanda felt as if she were standing at the middle of a clock's face. Each weathered stone beast appeared to mark the hour of the day, and though the hazy sun stood almost at the top of the sky, it seemed perpetual afternoon in the garden. Amanda indulged in a bit of nostalgia for her childhood, which had been lonelier than it needed to be because of her fractious ways.

She seemed to remember once when she was so little that the walk this far had tired her and she had been carried the rest of the way to greet these beasts. It had been afternoon, for the statues along the western curve had thrown long shadows across the grass. And her mother—for yes, it was her mother with her that time, not Buckle—had held her in her arms, thinking that the bizarre sculptures would frighten her. But she must have shown bravery, for she remembered squirming from her mother's arms and slipping down her voluminous skirts to the grass carpet.

It was curious how all Amanda's thoughts seemed to return to her mother if she did not halt them in time.

If she ever married and had children of her own, Amanda thought bleakly, she would interfere with their lives as little as possible. Her mother's great mistake had always been meddling. And it was all due to the fact that her mother didn't truly have a life of her own, but lived in that perfection that no one could approach or imitate. Amanda would not burden her children, if she had any, with this unpleasant combination of meddling and perfection. She would lead her own life and deposit her offspring in the care of some nanny more enlightened than Buckle.

But then she wondered if there were to be nannies in her children's futures. For if she eloped some night with John Thorne, they might have to forgo the luxury of servants. Amanda's mind approached a paradox then. She was longing for a lady's maid to call her own, to see to her every need. And she was longing for John Thorne as well, who was, when one thought of it, less than a servant himself. Still, the passion she felt for him was more than a knife to cut her free from polite society. They would live, perhaps, in a world where love replaced comforts. Amanda considered life with John in quite a small cottage somewhere, out of the way of the fashionable world.

No, that sounded like her mother, this affecting to snub correct society even as she entertained a few selected members of it. Amanda's thoughts were growing muddled, perhaps from all this fresh air. She nearly began to argue with herself aloud, as if she were in the midst of one of those verbal sparring matches with Gregory Forrest.

Behind her the shadowless stone leopard moved. The motion was so silent and swift that Amanda sensed nothing. The leopard remained on its plinth, of course, smiling a fanged smile into the grove and rolling its pitted eyes upward. But from behind it Bart Thorne had stepped. He had lain all night beneath the rock at the mere's edge and had crept all morning among the rhododendron roots. Because of him, there was not a bird or a small furry animal in all the bushes. The creatures of nature had seen or scented or sensed him, had warned their own kind, and fled. Only Amanda would have missed noticing the eerie silence enveloping the gardens in the absence of birdsong.

Bart Thorne had shambled along the turning paths within the rhododendron leaves, falling once to gulp brown water from a cradle of mud in among the roots. For hours at a time, he scarcely moved, his mind turning slowly upon events that stirred the past into the present.

He had known a moment of clarity toward dawn when he realized he had tried to garrote his own mother beside her hearth. But the eye of madness blinked against the thought and blurred once more. If there was a sane corner of his brain, it was fixed upon the asylum he had escaped. The asylum where he had spent many a timeless day and night stripped naked, hanging by bound hands from a hook on the back of his cell door.

But the memory of punishments for earlier escapes fell from him, though the wrists from which he'd hung were ringed with bracelets of scarred flesh calloused as smooth and hard as ivory. He was back on his own land again, though it had meant dashing a slop jar against the head of a new keeper who had defied all the rules by turning his back on the old maniac. Bart Thorne had run like a deer through the yard of the asylum and scaled the walls, for years of imprisonment had not shortened his breath or his stride.

He had made for his land, traveling across country and lying in brakes when footsteps sounded so near he might have reached from the undergrowth and broken the ankle of an innocent hiker. And now, returned, he was befuddled, for the past seemed to have dissolved about him. The grove, the mere, Smuggler's Cottage, this double row of rhododendrons leading up to the old bits of stonework were as they had always been. The roofs of the Hall and the chimneys spiraling smoke looked right enough. But he could not find his acres. The patchwork of his farmed land had vanished in just the season when they should have been yielding their harvest. Fields his feet had found from old habit were overgrown with wild flowers and worthless weeds. Cattle grazed where his much-mended fences had kept them out. The barnyards of his neighbors were to be found by patient, quiet searching. But they were farmer's houses no longer, and there were strangers behind the windows sitting in the glare of electric light. Where the feckless Barton family had once gathered around a dim yellow paraffin lamp, some unknown couple sat, dressed as Londoners chose to dress in their country cottages. And before the barn squatted a motorcar streaming with rainwater where once a horse would have stood to be shod.

His land had been bewitched, Bart Thorne knew. Even the woman who sat in his mother's place beside the cottage fire was a witch grown impossibly old, humped, white-headed. A crone who had used unspeakable powers to rob him of—everything.

Bart Thorne prowled in the rhododendrons. He feared no pursuit, no challenge. He had forgotten the son who had once bested him in a decisive battle. Though the past gnawed at him like hunger, great portions of it were lost.

He was barely aware when his solitude was first invaded. Standing almost upright within the bushes, he caught only a glimpse of Amanda when she strolled up the open green carpet, hardly six feet from where he stood. Thorne froze, and even his animal panting subsided as she passed. Then when she seemed to continue to the end where the stone creatures stood in their ring, he began to move forward, to stalk this easy prey.

In the shadowless noon Bart Thorne was standing directly behind Amanda before she felt his presence. To him she was some young hussy in a skirt too short, giving herself airs on his hard-won acres. His knobby hands closed over the ends of her woolen scarf.

Amanda's head jerked suddenly back. She was blinded by the sudden flash of the sun at which she stared, screaming soundlessly as the hat fell from her head and the scarf cut off her breath. She felt nothing but surprise until the noon turned dark.

Ten

———◦◦∞◦◦———

One of the more sensational London morning newspapers broke the story of the attack on Amanda Whitwell through a tip from an enterprising young reporter on the staff of the Isle of Wight *Observer*. And so most of England was treated to the account with their break-fasts on an otherwise unremarkable Monday morning in September 1911.

At the Surrey estate of the Ward-Benedicts, Sybil strode to her breakfast in mucky boots after an early-morning session when she had taken a favorite Arabian stallion through his paces. She had only to unfold the morning paper to see her school chum's name embla-zoned across the top of page one. "Good God!" Sybil thundered, and her elbow swept a coffee cup to the floor.

Twenty miles to the northeast in the heart of Mayfair, Mrs. Maude Glaslough was half-awake in the veiled light of her bedroom at Brown's Hotel. She was recuperating there between house parties. With difficulty she scanned the front page of the newspaper, and then she saw Amanda's name and the murky photograph of the sculpture garden at Whitwell Hall. Suddenly she was awake.

KNIGHT'S BEAUTIFUL DAUGHTER
ESCAPES DEATH AT LUNATIC'S HAND

Amanda Whitwell, only daughter of Sir Timothy and Lady Eleanor Whitwell of Charles Street, London, and Whitwell Hall, Isle of Wight, was set upon last Saturday by an escaped inmate of a lunatic asylum. Miss Whitwell, who has been in uncertain health, was taking a solitary stroll in the grounds of her wealthy family's island estate at the time of the outrage.

Her walk had led her to a secluded quarter of the gardens embellished with a ring of allegorical stone figures. In this remote and ominous location, the young lady was surprised by the escaped lunatic, identified as Bart Thorne, an inmate for many years of St. Luke's Asylum in Newport. Thorne had all but succeeded in strangling Miss Whitwell with her own woolen scarf when her rescuer interrupted an assault that would otherwise certainly have resulted in her murder.

The hero was the son of the attacker, John Thorne, a retainer of the Whitwell family, who was searching the grounds for his father at the time. The two men struggled over the unconscious Miss Whitwell, the lunatic turning his attack with superhuman fury on his own son. At length the crazed assailant broke from John Thorne, who pursued him through the grounds. The battle was resumed on the shores of a small body of water. The elder Thorne then suffered an apparent heart attack, staggered into the shallow lake, and fell dead. A forthcoming inquest is expected to return a verdict unprejudicial to John Thorne, who was forced to defend the daughter of his master against the unreasoned violence of his own father.

While no members of the Whitwell family have made themselves available for comment, it has been learned that Miss Whitwell is suffering severely from shock and has not fully regained consciousness following her ordeal. Local constabulary authorities in the Ventnor vicinity have been besieged by concerned residents whose own safety is called into question when the daughter of the district's most prominent family is not safe within the grounds of her own . . .

On that Monday morning when Gregory Forrest strode down the steps of the Kensington house where he had taken rooms, he heard Amanda's name being shouted in the rich Cockney of the urchin who hawked newspapers along Gloucester Road. Gregory broke into a run to overtake the newsboy and dazzled him with a half crown as he tore the newspaper from the small, grimy hand.

Amanda drifted between nightmare and nothingness. At moments she seemed to be lying in the wet grass of the garden, struggling for breath. All the stone creatures appeared to have come alive, lunging at one another in an epic battle that shadowed the sun. She dreamed then that the sculpture garden had been transformed into a great chessboard with a surface as smooth as the floor of the Greek folly. And herself a fallen pawn on a field of tumbling chessmen. At other times she was wrapped warmly in her own bed, drowsing with the comforting crackle of a fire in the bedroom hearth somewhere beyond her feet.

Voices came and went, hushed whispers that demanded nothing of her. Once, in the middle of the night, she found herself quite awake, but so tired she could not bring herself to open her eyes. She thought of John Thorne then, and almost believed that she had been lifted in his arms and carried through the garden—an immeasurable distance—through the bright sunlight. She smiled at the thought of this absurd boldness, of being cradled in his arms in broad daylight where any prying eye might discover them.

There were times, days later, when she grew restless and fevered, drawing back with cries of panic at something too monstrous to remember. She clutched at her throat and writhed until hands comforted her and cool cloths were pressed against her forehead.

She awoke fully at last and thought she must be dead. It was evening, for the lamps were lit, and she was lying in the middle of her own bed, gazing up at the rosette of lavender silk at the center of the canopy. She had only to turn her head slightly to one side to see her mother sitting there, her face serenely beautiful and yet not remote. And on the opposite side sat Miranda, very upright and proper in her chair. Miranda in an abbreviated white wisp of a cap unlike the caps of the kitchen staff. And no apron over her dress, as if she were already Amanda's own lady's maid. Miranda seemed subtly altered, as people often are in dreams, less a timorous mouse and more confident in her role. But what could her role be?

At the foot of the bed stood a figure that convinced Amanda that she had left one world for another one, far better. John Thorne seemed to be standing there, in full view of the others, with his cap in his hands and the blondness of his unruly hair burnished by lamplight.

Though her eyelids seemed only to flutter, it was daylight again, and Amanda felt cramped from hours more of motionless sleep. Pale sunlight fell across the floor, and while the chairs that flanked her bed were empty, there was activity in the room: Opposite, the mirrored doors of the armoire were ajar, and a maid—it was almost certainly Miranda—was busying herself among the shelves. Her practiced hands moved over an utterly transformed interior.

Where once there had been haphazard piles of underthings and unmatched gloves and puddles of stockings—with the slightly soiled slipping continually into the newly laundered by some perverse magic—all was in astonishing order. The shelves were ranked with fat silk pouches of neatly sorted items, each envelope tied in a length of lavender ribbon. Above, the hats had disappeared into towers of round boxes. Amanda just noticed the efficient label on each box and the scent of sachets drifting from the shelves before she was overcome once more with an unaccountable weariness.

She stirred again, certain that it was the evening of the same day. The fire was laid again and popping merrily. She had dreamed in ominous abstractions, to surface to the mingled scent of tobacco and claret. Through half-opened eyes, she was amazed to find Sir Timothy there beside her. He was nearly asleep, but his grizzled fist lay against the satin counterpane as if he had been holding her hand. Dear, dim Father, Amanda thought idly, whatever has brought him to my bedside? He had not done such a thing since she was in the nursery. With a moment's wonderful clarity she was back again in that nursery on a night when both her parents had entered, younger then and very glamorous in evening clothes, to kiss her goodnight before going down to receive their guests.

She was indulging a warm affection for her father when the scene shifted again. Someone was urging a curved straw between her lips, and she drank a glass of warm milk, though she was nauseated by it. She struggled to see who was holding the glass, but it was only Buckle. The old fool's face was contorted with silent encouragement, willing Amanda to speak. And so she closed her eyes and fell back on the pillow until the milk was taken away.

In the middle of another afternoon Amanda awoke, her mind utterly clear and already beginning the task of sorting through the blank pages of the previous days. She felt unrested, but alert and rather as if she'd had a bout with tonsillitis. A charge of newfound energy surged through her. She sat bolt upright and very nearly threw her legs over the side of the bed before she saw Gregory Forrest sitting there. Perhaps it had been those intense brown eyes that had willed her to wake. He reached for her, and to forestall his embrace, Amanda drew her hand from beneath the coverlet and took his.

"My darling."

"Oh, Gregory, I must have overslept."

At that he grinned, disarming Amanda, who would have been proof against a look of grave bedside concern. "Whatever has happened that Mother has allowed you unchaperoned in my room? Or is she lurking under the bed?"

"It's my own Amanda restored to her old spirit," Gregory replied.

"Account for all this, Gregory! What are you doing back on the island again so soon? Or is it so soon? I'm in an awful muddle, and I've had the most extraordinary dreams. If I've had an attack of brain fever, it will be one up on all those who think me brainless. Don't sit there so patiently, Gregory. Interrupt me and tell me everything!"

"That would be a good deal. More than you're ready to take in all at once."

"Never mind that cosseting-the-invalid talk, Gregory. How long have I been drifting in this bed?"

"More than a week. Closer to ten days."

"Good Lord. Then I have been ill. I remember . . ."

"Yes? What do you remember, darling?"

"I remember it was a lovely day. The morning after the storm. I decided to go out. Yes, that was it. You had gone back to London, and so I felt quite free. I know that sounds rude, but I must say everything as I remember it. I dressed and slipped out of the house. I went out through the morning-room window where—where I knew I would slip away unnoticed. And I went walking. It was frightfully damp, but I was dressed for it. Surely I didn't catch a chill. I never do. I walked. Yes, I remember that quite clearly. Down to the sculpture garden, though I was only wandering, really. A stone worked into my shoe, and I stopped to shake it out. I was by the mere then and—and—"

"Go on, darling, if you can."

"Don't humor me. I'm thinking. I walked on until I came to the sculpture garden. It was lovely there, with the sun on the wet leaves and my dear old dragons and grotesques standing in their circle just as they were when I was quite a child. And then—something extraordinary happened, and it all changes into a dream. And such an exhausting one, too. Something—something happened to me, Gregory." Amanda suddenly tightened her grasp on his hand. "Gregory, do you know what happened to me? Do you?"

"Yes, Amanda."

"Then tell me."

"Maybe—maybe it would be better if you remembered on your own, Amanda. You've been in shock, and you've been sedated. It might be better if you let it come back to you in your own time."

"That's nonsense. Perhaps I fainted and can't remember. Gregory, if you don't tell me, someone else will. If you love me, surely you'd prefer I heard whatever it is from you."

Gregory sat staring away at the hearth, feeling bested again by Amanda's demanding spirit. "All right," he said finally, "you win. Just promise to hear me out and don't upset yourself. Remember, it's all over now." And then Gregory told Amanda the story, as it had been pieced together by John Thorne, by Finley, by the asylum authorities and the Ventnor police. He told her of Bart Thorne, whom she had known nothing of—Granny Thorne's son growing old in the lunatic asylum during the years Amanda had grown up at Whitwell Hall. John Thorne's father, who she had assumed was dead because John had never mentioned him and she had never thought to ask. Gregory came at last to the end of the story, encouraged by the first sustained attentiveness Amanda had ever given any of his conversation.

She lay very quiet against her pillows for a long while, her hand limp in his, and he thought she had withdrawn a great distance from him, though she had attended his every word.

"Then John killed his own father to save me," she said.

"The man was old and sick, Amanda. As a result of the fight, he had some kind of seizure and died. You mustn't think you had any responsibility. He was a menace to his own mother. He was never going to have his sanity back. It was—"

"John saved my life," Amanda said, as if she were alone in the room. She turned then to Gregory, and he was relieved that she had taken the story so well, for she smiled at him. "Gregory, it takes something like this to bring me to my senses. I've been very stupid and childish about—about a great many things. I have been quite willful, and to absolutely no purpose, and I've made you perfectly miserable."

"Amanda, don't. It's enough for now to see you your old self."

"You sat with me when I was—unconscious?"

"Yes, there was always someone with you. You looked beautiful lying there, like Sleeping Beauty waiting for her kiss."

"You may give it to me now, Gregory," Amanda said very quietly. But Gregory Forrest was already out of his chair and enfolding her in his arms. She returned his kisses with a degree more abandon than ever before. Her eyes shut, she thought of John Thorne and tightened her grasp on Gregory's shoulders. Even then she began to wonder how long the news of her recovery would take to reach Smuggler's Cottage. "I owe a great debt to John—to Thorne."

"We all do," Gregory whispered.

"I want to thank him."

"When you're up and around again—"

"Nonsense. Showing gratitude to someone for saving one's life isn't the sort of thing to be put off until it's quite convenient."

"Your mother allowed Thorne in to pay his respects when you were still unconscious."

"Did she indeed! And I thought I had dreamed it. How unlike her. She must have thought I was dying."

"She loves you very much, Amanda."

"Does she? I'm glad, for I need a great deal of love, Gregory. More than you can quite realize. But we were talking of Thorne. Perhaps a note. Surely that would be very suitable. Go over to my writing table and bring me paper and an envelope and—oh, a pencil will do. I shouldn't think an automobile mechanic would stand on much ceremony."

While Gregory rummaged in the writing desk, Amanda smoothed the counterpane he had rumpled. She ran a hand through her hair then and found it disorderly in the extreme. She must look a fright. If Gregory found her desirable at that moment, then love was blind indeed. In Gregory's case, she mused, it might have to be a great deal more blind in future, and deaf. For there was no doubt now in Amanda's mind that Thorne's sacrifice of his own father in saving her had bound them together in some final way. A way that at last took precedence over all convention and simplified the future. In the past months Gregory had been an annoyance. That was over, too. Henceforth he would be a convenience, one way and another. The last doubts and girlish skittishness fell away from Amanda. She marked their leaving. From now on, she would use every device—and everyone—to have John Thorne.

When she had the paper in her hand, she ordered Gregory to stroll around the room while she composed a proper note of gratitude.

But he was too heartened by her recovery to allow her to scrawl even a few words in peace. He stood impatiently on the hearth, going on and on. Something about alerting the rest of the house to her restored health and spirit. Something about Sybil Ward-Benedict.

"Horrors!" Amanda said as she sealed the envelope with a small red tongue. "You don't mean Sybil is *here!*"

"Yes, she came as soon as she heard and has stayed on."

"Oh, Gregory, how beastly for you. To be saddled with her all this time. I underscore the word *saddle.*"

"She's a very nice girl—"

"A bit bluff for your tastes, surely, Gregory."

"—and a very faithful friend. You'd have done the same for her."

"How little you know me, Gregory. If the roles had been reversed, I'd have sent her flowers and perhaps a book of horse stories in the event she ever grew lucid enough to read. Here, do see this note finds Thorne. I'm told he haunts the garages most of the time. Be an angel and deliver it yourself. Servants are so unreliable." Amanda handed over the sealed envelope. The note inside was terse and to the point:

> *John,*
> *Come to me tonight.*
> *A.*

Miranda Speaks

$\mathcal{E}leven$

———⋅⋅⊰∞⊱⋅⋅———

My mother taught me subservience but not survival. And so I was less prepared to be a servant than she foresaw. But I was a willing worker who held my tongue. Perhaps my longest suit was my need to succeed, for I knew I had no home to go back to if I failed.

I came to serve at Whitwell Hall expecting to remain there all my life. I remained seven months. Later I had ample reason to remember the first day, if only because of my strange encounter with the Wisewoman. Her prophecy was veiled, like all prophecy, in language that obscured what it revealed. But what I heard of it on that September day was too fantastic to stay with me in any case.

Even in my ignorance, I thought the woman was prattling about husbands and marriages only because that is the subject most likely to stir a young girl's imaginings. She spoke, too, of death and rebirth, and I thought that was only to startle and thrill me. And so it did for the moment. But she charged me nothing. Indeed, she even gave me a gift.

If it had not been for the coin the Wisewoman gave me—an American Indianhead one-cent piece, it was—I might have forgotten her words in the busy and bewildering days that followed. But I carried the small copper, not as large as a halfpenny, about with me as a talisman, as something of my own. Even after I exchanged the voluminous kitchen apron with its capacious pockets for the quiet gray frock with the frilled cuffs that I wore as Miss Amanda Whitwell's lady's maid, the coin was forever somewhere on my person.

The first days at Whitwell Hall passed in a whirl of new impressions and the endless duties for which I was well prepared. I wonder now what my future might have been had I stayed on in the kitchens or had risen to head house parlormaid. But after the first, I was never to blacklead a stove or rouge the silver again. I was being drawn along a different and far more dangerous course.

As I think back, my life at Whitwell Hall truly began on that Saturday morning after I had spent the night at Granny Thorne's bedside. It was just past noon, and I was at work in the kitchens, performing Betty's duties along with my own. When I answered a thumping at the yard door, John Thorne stood there, cradling Miss Amanda in his arms like a baby. Her head was thrown back, and her hair was unpinned and swung free. She seemed to be dead, and I stifled a scream. John Thorne did not push past me to bear his burden into the house. Instead, he thrust Miss Amanda into my arms, and I staggered, for she was as heavy as I, and a dead weight. In the next moment he was gone.

It was Mrs. Buckle coming onto this scene who screamed. But when she saw that Miss Amanda was breathing, she regained a portion of her composure, and between us we managed to carry her up all the flights to her room. As we lay her across the bed and began to undress her, I saw the marks on her neck already turning from an angry red to dull purple. It was clear enough that the madman had struck again. I said nothing to Mrs. Buckle, however, who was near the breaking point. If she had been herself, I have no doubt she would have sent me from the room. But her fingers fumbled so over the buttons and fastenings of Miss Amanda's clothes that she could not do without me.

From then on for many days, the household was caught up in chaos. I was given to think then for the first time how difficult life is made for a family served by protective servants. All in a rush Lady Eleanor was forced to learn that her daughter had been half-strangled by a lunatic whose very existence had been forgotten by the family, even through the dark night when he had roamed free over their grounds. Moreover her ladyship had to learn that this same madman was lying dead and spread-eagled in the mere. It was John Thorne who waded out and carried his father's body to shore while Sir Timothy and the gentlemen of the Royal Yacht Squadron looked on in horror from the terrace, their claret cups in their hands.

After that, the drive was full of policemen and the coroner's van and an ambulance with barred windows that had been belatedly sent from the asylum. Later the newspapermen swarmed about the place and were too many for Abel, who had been assigned the thankless task of keeping them back beyond the gates. As it happened, one photographer got through and made a picture of the sculpture garden, and another was thrown bodily through the gates by Mr. Finley himself when the man tried to bribe Hilda to steal a picture of Miss Amanda from the photograph album.

I saw little of John Thorne in the days that followed. It confused me to think of him. I wondered if his father's death and the manner of his dying had left him remorseful or relieved. And I thought more than was good for me about the uses to which John Thorne put his brute strength.

There was a funeral of sorts for Bart Thorne. Sir Timothy had given his permission for the burial in a long-abandoned graveyard on the grounds. There had once been a chapel built for the Hall that had later been a church for the tenants and the staff. But it had fallen into disuse and had been dismantled. The graveyard remained, however. It was thought best to put Bart Thorne there, for if he had been buried in the Nettlecombe churchyard, it would have been a Roman holiday for the newspaper people, who lingered on for days after.

All the Hall staff attended except me. I was directed to sit with Granny Thorne that afternoon. She had not left her bed since the stormy night that Mr. Finley and I had put her in it. I was happy enough not to attend the burying, but I feared the old woman would be grief-stricken. I was very young and inexperienced and did not know how I would find a way to comfort her.

But she was resigned to the death of her son, saying only that his mind had died long before and she had already spent her lifetime's store of tears. In her kindness, she said that much to me at once, to put me at my ease. I made her tea and warmed the scones that Mrs. Creeth had sent with me from the kitchens. I was lavish with the butter.

It was nearly a festive time, for Granny was determined to banish the silence with a conversation that would take both our minds off the events of that long afternoon. Even then I found myself listening for any mention she might make of her grandson. But John Thorne never arose in her one-sided conversation. She was as sane as her son was mad, but her ruling passion was the royal family, whose pictures surrounded her in that tiny room. I suspected that when she was by herself, she carried on spirited conversations with their portraits, for she spoke more familiarly of them than she did of the Whitwells.

Lowering her voice and gesturing with one hand at the portrait of Queen Alexandra, she said, "The Queen Mother is quite as deaf as Sir Timothy, you know. She is quite clever at covering it up, but everyone knows, and it is very hard for her. I well remember the day she came over from Denmark to be the Prince of Wales's bride—in 1863, that was. And as lovely today as she was on the day of her wedding. The Prince—King Edward, as I should say—was naughty, though. In the way men always are naughty. I ought not to speak of it now he's gone, but it was true, and Queen Alexandra had a burden to bear, and bears it still in her heart, I shouldn't wonder. Deaf though she is, she isn't blind, nor ever was."

The conversation moved on to Queen Victoria, as all Granny Thorne's thoughts always turned in the direction of her idol. Her quavery, piping voice grew quite strong, and she gestured grandly in the direction of the old Queen, who seemed to meet her gaze. "She never put a foot wrong, did Queen Victoria! She was first and last a ruler. I saw her once myself when she was here on the Isle at Osborne with all her dear children about her. She was happy here, happier than anywhere else. Oh, she was beyond anything! The most loving wife, the dearest mother, the greatest monarch! And never a moment's ease. That I lived in her age to be her subject is my greatest joy! It has seen me through many a sad day. It sees me through today."

I was to return at odd moments to pay visits to Granny Thorne. She grew very far in my mind from that first frightening glimpse, creeping along the garden walk by moonlight. She never failed to greet me warmly, and as soon as she was up and about again, she was eager for work to occupy her hands and thoughts. As Miss Amanda's maid, I had many an excuse to bring her a basket of mending or a bit of embroidery to repair or a hem to turn. She seemed to know that I could do this work as well as she and welcomed me the more for it.

When Dr. Post declared Miss Amanda out of danger, her ladyship summoned me to say that I was to be Miss Amanda's maid. My duties began when she still lay quiet in her bed. There was much whispered talk that her experience might have driven her into a permanent catatonic state, that she might lie for years unmoving in her bed. But from what I had already observed of my young lady's temperament, I thought this unlikely.

I had my work cut out for me, putting her wardrobe to rights. It was in just such a disorderly muddle as any young girl's, though I was in awe of the quality of her silk underthings and the great quantity of her stockings and the variety of her shoes. I had always thought that my mother exaggerated the size of a lady's wardrobe, but Miss Amanda's would have clothed an entire village of young women, though much of it was at first in disrepair.

There was usually someone at her bedside in those first days. When I was alone with her, though, I busied myself in putting her shelves in order. There were times when I thought she might be awake, watching me from her bed. But each time I turned around or caught a glimpse of her in the mirrored doors of the armoire, she was breathing regularly, and her lashes were fringed on her cheeks. There are times even now when I feel her gaze on me when I am in a room alone, so far from Whitwell Hall.

A friend of Miss Amanda's, Miss Ward-Benedict, journeyed to the island as soon as she read of the trouble. I looked after her, too, while she was there, though she brought only a change or two of very practical clothes and required little attention. Indeed, she tolerated very little. She brought only one dinner gown, and that was a well-worn corded silk in gun-metal gray with curious fur tippets as the only decoration. The visitor who interested me more was Mr. Gregory Forrest, for he was at Miss Amanda's bedside within hours of reading the newspaper. He was vexed, too, that her ladyship had not sent him a telegram at once, but she was so near panic that he made allowances. It was hard work to persuade him to leave the bedside for his meals and of course at night, for her ladyship thought it improper for him to spend so much time in the room alone, particularly in the evening hours.

It is easy enough to say that I was already in love with Gregory Forrest and had been from the day I encountered him in the front hall. It was a love that did not trouble me for the very distance that existed between our stations in life. I had never been to the pictures then—the cinematograph, it was called—and so I knew nothing about how a silly young girl might fall in love with the image of an actor on a screen. But that was very much the kind of idolizing love I felt for Gregory Forrest. An innocent, make-believe love that did not interfere with my duties or tempt me to confide in anyone, though I was not given to confidences in any case. Nor was I, even after I had befriended Betty and found myself in possession of a willing listener.

Gregory Forrest always spoke to me with great kindness and always remembered my name. I attributed this to my resemblance to Miss Amanda, which clearly interested him, though it unnerved me severely.

For all his civility to me, he remained in my mind a figure from a storybook. Many an endless, weary day was lightened for me by thoughts of him. It was to be a long time before I understood that Miss Amanda did not love him, though she told me as much on the first day that ever I set eyes on her. Not to love him seemed an impossibility. I even took the opportunity to examine Miss Ward-Benedict's responses to him, though it was not my place. I thought surely she, too, would fall in love with him. But she talked only of geldings and Arabian stallions and racing meets to him or to whoever was in sound of her voice.

I had barely time to sleep during that first week in my new and exalted position as Miss Amanda's maid. I ate my meals in her room, which sorely tried Mrs. Creeth's patience and sent Mrs. Buckle into a decline. I was glad enough not to have to take my meals in servants' hall. I feared the older women would cut me dead, and even Mr. Finley would not have been a moderating influence, however much he might have tried.

It came as a great surprise to me at the end of that week to be taken aside by Mr. Finley and told I was to have a half day off. If I had not feared him, I might well have protested, for I did not know what to do with myself.

That was to be solved, for Betty was to have a half day as well. Such a plan ran counter to the staff routine. Mr. Finley never tired of remarking on the inadequacy of our numbers to run a house of that size. Still, I suppose he sent Betty and me off on our half day together so that we would keep an eye on each other. Which of us he trusted less I did not know.

Since my duties no longer ranged over the whole house, I'd seen little of Betty, and no words had passed between us. I guarded the secret of the baby she was to have, and as far as I knew, no one else had discovered it. It could not long remain a secret, and her days of employment were clearly numbered. With this in mind, I dreaded an afternoon with her. In my innocence, I thought Betty would be desperate about her future and the future of her child.

When we met to go out, though, she was wreathed in smiles and wearing her day-out clothes as if she were going to a gala. She had a decent coat and an extraordinary hat. She'd turned its brim up in front and skewered it with a peacock feather that had once figured in a flower arrangement in the upper hallway. Betty inspected my own outfit, which consisted mostly of the clothes left behind by the former maid, Lottie. Betty pronounced me respectable but not smart. There was only a little spark of envy in her of me in my new position, which she soon extinguished with her usual flood of good humor. We set off together down the drive and were at the gates before I broke in on her bubbling and inconsequential talk to ask where we were going.

My own speech was plain and unsophisticated enough—when I spoke at all. But it is beyond me to reproduce Betty's ripe and incurable speech. It grated on the ear, but she left her listener in no doubt as to her meaning. "Why, to Ventnor, where else?" she replied to my question. "We'll have a look round the shops and take our tea at the hotel. Did you bring money? The tea's one and six, but it's slap-up."

I'd brought a pound of my thirty shillings and was loath to part with any of it. But Betty's enthusiasm was infectious. And though we had a long and dusty walk before us, I caught much of her excitement. After many days of duty and the untoward events that had taken place, I was suddenly in seventh heaven at the prospect of a few hours away. And I thought us both rich women on the strength of the twenty shillings in my bag.

Though the holiday season was almost past, the road to Ventnor seemed crowded with traffic. Motorcars blared their klaxon horns at farm wagons and dog carts. We were forced into the ditch a dozen times before the roofs of Ventnor loomed up before us.

The people of that town compare it favorably with Italy. I cannot speak to the truth of that, but it struck me as a vast and wonderful place. All the buildings seemed to cling to a zigzag of streets that descended the cliffs to the sandy beach. The houses were brightly colored, and here and there in a little garden carved out of the incline a ragged palm tree blew in the Channel winds. The sea beyond was lost in mist, but there were the ghosts of ships far out and pleasure craft nearer in, clinging like limpets to the quays. There was even a covered pleasure pier stretching far out, and music drifted up from it. Music during the day! I stood in wonder at the sound.

Betty hurried me along, though I yearned to rest my feet and drink in the view from the top of the town. She was in such haste that I began to wonder if there was a purpose in our visit beyond pleasure.

We threaded our way down steeply pitched streets past fine villas in shades of orange and umber and puce. I was limping, for the heels of my shoes were run over and made walking down a hill more trying than climbing up. But Betty all but dragged me along, and her conversation ceased to bubble.

We came at last to the first street of shops and were engulfed in a tide of people. I had never seen so many people in one place, and I wedged my handbag under my arm. Without Betty, I would surely have fled back to the Hall.

The street was choked with motorcars, and I was wondering how one crossed from curb to curb when Betty grasped my elbow and we were suddenly in the middle of the street, dodging between all manner of vans and wagons. I did not have breath enough to shriek, though I knew both our lives were in her hands. We fetched up on the far side and strolled on without a word. Betty loosed her grip on me to straighten her hat and to tuck up her flyaway hair. She began to catch glimpses of herself in the shop windows. But she never stopped, though I would gladly have lingered at the rich displays in every window.

Just past a silversmith's there was a shop with a sign proclaiming that it was Sampson & Son, Drapers. Betty slowed her pace and altered her gait, stepping along with exaggerated daintiness. I was quite diverted by her sudden change, and it seemed we were to take our time over this particular shop window. Within, lengths of fine woolens hung in festoons and fanned out in a muted rainbow. There was hardly a bolt of cloth I didn't admire, though I was appalled at the prices.

We tarried so long that Betty finally turned reluctantly away to continue along the street, dragging her feet. But then the bell sounded, and the shop door was thrown back. A tall, exceedingly pale man stepped out into our path. A dark salt-and-pepper suit hung on his gangling frame. His arms seemed imperfectly attached to his shoulders, and he appeared to be lathering his hands with imaginary soap.

It was clear that the two were acquainted, though when he addressed her with some nervous excitement as "Miss Prowse," I realized I had never before heard Betty's last name. I wondered as well how a Ventnor draper had come into the possession of it.

Sampson & Son, Drapers, was clearly the planned destination of our outing. We were both ushered into the shop, where Betty introduced me as Miss Cooke to Mr. Sampson. It appeared that he was the son proclaimed on the signboard and that Mr. Sampson the elder was long deceased.

An agony of shyness overwhelmed me, and I missed much of the conversation pursued with vigor on both sides. I had been trained to serve the upper class, and I had come from the lower. But I was on uncertain ground between. I had rarely been inside a shop of any kind, and certainly not the sort of draper's establishment that retained the services of two shop assistants.

Mr. Sampson's enthusiasm at the sight of Betty nearly masked the fact that he was well past his first youth. Presently he escorted both of us through a doorway at the rear and up a flight of stairs to a small parlor above. The room was cluttered with more objects than I had ever seen before in one place. It was more like a shop than the room below it. The rugs overlapped one another on the floors, and the light was dimmed by a series of flouncing curtains. Even the mantel and the top of an upright piano were covered and skirted. Before the fire sat an enormous woman who viewed our entrance with annoyance.

"Mother!" Mr. Sampson boomed. "Just see who I noticed passing the shop!" There was a terrible moment of absolute silence before Mr. Sampson plunged on. "It's Miss Prowse—and a friend of hers, Miss—Cooke."

"I see," said his mother, glancing at us and then away. She was dressed in a vast gown of old-fashioned design, and she sat throughout the painful interview so immobile that a taffy-colored cat who lay coiled asleep on her knees never stirred.

Mr. Sampson tried gamely to cover his mother's coldness with his own geniality. Betty, for her part, struggled as hard, phrasing her speech with agonizing care.

"Me and Miss Cooke," she said when we were seated, "was—were just on our way along to the—hotel for our tea, it being such a lovely day for a stroll, and us—having a—half day."

"But surely you'd rather have tea here," Mr. Sampson broke in, edging out to the very tip of his chair.

At that, Mrs. Sampson said, "It's too early by far for tea, and I won't have Mavis hurried. She never serves before five o'clock. You know how she is, Hubert, and good servants are hard to come by."

She gave Betty a piercing look then, to remind her, I supposed, that she was herself a servant and thus had no rights whatever. Hubert Sampson seemed to wither under his mother's rudeness, but there was defiance in his eyes. It gave me to think that the old woman who meant to cling to her bachelor son might be going about it all the wrong way. Her spitefulness was clearly drawing him closer to Betty, for they would have need of combined strength.

All this must have been as plain as a pikestaff, or I should not have noted it. I was utterly unschooled in the sort of scheming Betty was engaged in. I never once thought that Mr. Sampson was the father of her unborn baby. He was no one's idea of a seducer, and I strongly suspected he knew nothing of the child. He was also very much taken with Betty. And indeed, though she was a somewhat sorrowful sight, her eagerness to make herself presentable was touching. She was by nature agreeable, and I hoped at once that Mr. Sampson would marry her despite everything—and quickly.

At last we rose to leave, some while after we should have. Mrs. Sampson's parting shot caught me off guard, for she looked directly at me and said, "I am pleased to have met you, Miss Cooke." Then she turned her face to the hearth, ignoring Betty completely.

I hurried on ahead, down the steps and through the shop. Betty dawdled as long as she dared, and murmured to our host, who seemed to murmur apologies in reply. I had little desire for a "slap-up" tea after this interlude. But Betty surprised me once again by her high spirits. She all but skipped along the paving stones and dragged me up the steps of a fine hotel with terraces and a sign above the door in gilt letters.

Inside, we were bowed to a table in the winter garden by a waiter as icy as Mr. Finley himself. And before the bread and butter could be brought, Betty began again to bubble. "Of course, Miranda, I know he's miles above me and the—circumstances is difficult. And isn't his old ma septic? But still, I think he rather fancies me, don't you? It's orful I'm not better spoken. I wouldn't mind in the usual way, but he's such a well-spoken gentleman—almost a real gentleman. And I don't know wot he sees in me, indeed I don't. But—but I do need him, Miranda."

Betty struggled with herself a bit, and her eyes glistened as she drew a handkerchief out of her belt and blew her nose heartily. But she was beaming in the next moment when the tea trolley was drawn up. "I talk this way," she said, "because I was raised in the orphanage. The Girls' Home, they called it, and it was all the home I ever knew. Still, it was an orphanage and no mistake. Right here on the island, it was, though some fink I talk like a Londoner. 'A real little Cockney,' is wot Mrs. Creeth called me when first I come to work, and she didn't mean it as no compliment, either. But I got my talk from the other orphans. It rubbed orf on us, like lice." And then Betty issued a sigh and dove into her tea.

When a three-piece orchestra began to play, she was quite carried away by the music, and so was I. They played selections from *The Merry Widow,* but of course at that time I had never heard this music and would have been thunderstruck to know that one day soon I was to see the operetta myself. Betty summed up the effect the music had upon us by saying rather too loudly, "Lumme! If we aren't a couple of proper ladies!" The approaching waiter blanched.

The sea outside the hotel windows had turned from green to rose before Betty brought up the last crumb of cake with a moistened finger. But we both longed to extend our half day. I was dazzled by what seemed playacting to me. And perhaps Betty knew that in future as Lady Amanda's maid I should see more of worldly life and would never after be awed by an outing with another servant.

We made our way back up to the top of the town as slowly as we dared. Our half day did not excuse us from our evening duties, and so the end of the afternoon took on the bittersweet quality of stolen moments.

The last shop in the town was no wider than the sort of kiosk where tobacco is sold. But a sign outside it somewhat grandly proclaimed it a photography "studio." We lingered at the display window as all young girls will do before the pictures of brides. They were rather stiff portrayals of plain young women. Yet Betty ate the pictures with her eyes, following every fold of the veils and not noticing, perhaps, that each bride carried the same armload of waxen photographer's flowers.

Then, as I was turning away, she plucked my sleeve, and somehow we were inside the place, with the bell above the door sounding. Before I knew it, Betty had driven a sudden bargain with the photographer, or his assistant, for it was a boy of no more than sixteen. We had our picture made that day, for sixpence each. And I remember thinking that at the rate our money was dropping from us, Betty might prove to be a luxury I could not afford.

My concern shows in the photograph. It is a pitiless likeness of both of us, though less studied than the brides'. Our hats rather dominate everything. Betty's feather unfurls above both our heads like a banner, and our brims overlap. There was no hand-coloring in the bargain, and so Betty's hair, standing out beneath her brim, looks gray. My own, drawn up under an untrimmed hat, is inky black, and I stare out upon the world with Miss Amanda's eyes. Neither of us thought to smile in that frozen moment. When I found the picture again after many years, I was again unable to smile. I wept over it instead.

We were well along on the road to Nettlecombe before Betty said anything again relating to her own situation. The silences had been lengthening, though Betty never quite ran short of her chirping conversation. At last she said, "It isn't Mr. Sampson—Hubert. He's not the father-to-be. It was a chap from the Wild West Show."

This information nearly got past me, for at that very moment I was considering the possibility that Betty had been seduced by John Thorne. In a way it seemed unlikely, but then I knew little about him except that he had made free to roam the Hall in the middle of the night. I had only enough imagination to think that he waylaid any unsuspecting servant girl. But Betty broke through my thoughts by explaining that she had been swept off her feet by a man who had courted her avidly in the summer. "He was a cowboy for that Buffalo Bill Show that set up in tents this side of Ventnor. I went on my half day, though it wasn't a proper Wild West Show and no Buffalo Bill in sight, as far as I could see. Still, that's where I met one of the cowboys, though he wasn't a real one. Only a Cornishman who could ride. I slipped out night after night and met him at the Hall gates. I slipped out once too often, if the truth be told."

By the time we reached the gates of Whitwell Hall, the shadows of the Italian pines had cast the drive into utter darkness. Betty and I made our cautious way along to the lane to the kitchen wing. The murmurous night cast a pall over our talk, and we ended our half day with Betty's future hanging in the balance. I may well have been more concerned by it than she was herself.

Twelve

Later, I was to wonder how early in our time together Miss Amanda had conceived the scheme she laid for my future and for her own. I had thought her merely willful, and I reckoned without her guile. She seemed simply a spoiled young miss, given to tantrums and notions. And my greatest fear was that her recent ordeal should continue to haunt her and that I would have to deal with her outbursts of emotion. But she rarely referred to the incident of Bart Thorne. After all, it had won her a maid of her own without further difficulties from her ladyship. It seemed quite clear that once she had her way, Miss Amanda was inclined to adopt an amiable manner for a time.

She had clearly determined to rise to the occasion by treating me as she thought a lady dealt with her maid. She was very much on her dignity, so much so that I believe Lady Eleanor was nearly amused. Miss Amanda ordered me about imperiously. But for much of the time, I was ahead of her. I had a better idea of servitude than she did. When I brought up her breakfast each morning, her eyes glittered thoughtfully at me. At the time I attributed this to the plans she had for filling my days with duties—and for occupying my half days as well.

It would have made a great difference in both our lives if I had known how clever she was at covering her tracks. I did not suspect that John Thorne crept night after night to her room and lay with her there until the moments before dawn. There were no clues. When I entered with her morning tea, she lay in the middle of her bed with the counterpane drawn smoothly up and her pillows neatly plumped. It would have been beyond me to realize that she had taken a lover. Nor did Betty's nattering gossip ever touch on the single item that would have held significance for me. Though she took much consolation in her own trials by speculating on the circumstances of others, Betty was as ignorant of Miss Amanda's secret as I was myself. If the other servants harbored deep suspicions, they never gave voice to them when Betty was near, for they knew her to be indiscreet.

My early days were thus preoccupied with duty rather than suspicion. Miss Amanda changed her clothes thrice daily and often enough four times, even when she had little to do. She tested me by examining her newly ordered and laundered wardrobe and by wearing every garment in it as quickly as possible. When she changed after lunch into an afternoon frock or a three-piece ensemble suitable for the outdoors, she left her former attire in heaps around the room. I needed all the skills of a clairvoyant and a contortionist to find and retrieve items of apparel that worked their ways beneath the bed or behind the dressing table.

During her stay, Miss Ward-Benedict made free to enter Miss Amanda's room at every odd moment. And so my duties were complicated by the presence of the two young ladies, who sat gossiping while I endeavored to make ready my mistress's next outfit.

I well remember one late afternoon when Miss Amanda had resumed changing for the evening and dining with her family and guests downstairs. I had had a difficult time pressing the folds in a mauve dinner gown, which had occupied more time than I had to give it. At last it was hanging on a padded hanger from the door of the armoire, and I was in search of the high-heeled slippers that completed the effect. I had found one slipper in its place at the bottom of the armoire, but the other one was missing.

The two young ladies were sitting in a pair of facing chairs, giving the sum of their attention to an experiment in smoking cigarettes. There was a fearful fog of blue smoke throughout the room, and Miss Ward-Benedict was seized with such a fit of coughing that I was very nearly distracted. I must have shown my disapproval, for the two young ladies were rather subdued and gave more attention to the angle at which they held their cigarettes than to any sustained conversation. Shooting an occasional glance Miss Amanda's way, I noticed that she shifted uncomfortably in the small armchair. In a brainstorm, it occurred to me that she had taken the very slipper I was turning out the room to find. And unless I was very much mistaken, she had thrust it into the back of her chair and was sitting on it.

Continuing my pointless search, I wondered how I might retrieve the slipper and retain my dignity. That she was testing me and provoking me at once I had no doubt whatever. At last I spun around in mock alarm and was in front of Miss Amanda before she knew it. "Oh, Miss!" I cried. "A spark from your cigarette has fallen into your skirt and is burning a hole!" I swept down, pretending to beat smoldering flames from the hem of her frock. Of course she rocketed out of the chair in fright. The slipper lay wedged beneath the back cushion. I merely took it up, held it high, and said, "Thank you, Miss."

Miss Ward-Benedict choked mightily over her cigarette, but Miss Amanda held her tongue, though her eyes followed me as I went about my duties until I was half afraid they would burn real holes in my back.

There was very little real sympathy between Miss Amanda and her friend. The conversation of the one seemed of small interest to the other. But this did not strike me as out of the ordinary. For much the same was true between me and Betty. However, on the evening before she was to depart, Miss Ward-Benedict came in for a chat one last time, and their conversation, directed by Miss Amanda, took a more personal turn. I must have lingered over my duties, for I eavesdropped at length. By then their secret cigarette-smoking had become ritual, and I could smell the nasty fumes in the curtains and the bedclothes.

"Sybil," Miss Amanda said in a tone that seemed to mock her own friend's voice, "I have looked into my crystal ball to survey your future."

"What in the world!" Miss Ward-Benedict replied.

"Yes, I have, and I must say your future is a great deal clearer than my own. As I see it, there are only two sorts of men you can marry."

"Marry! What rubbish. I probably shan't marry at all. I'm quite happy as I am."

"Yes, but you'd be quite happy married, too. Marriage wouldn't be such a—prison for you."

"Prison? What rubbish! Don't be a stoat!"

"Because you'll marry some hearty country squire—madly tweedy and probably old enough to be your father—"

"What drivel!"

"Or . . ."

"Yes, well, go on, since you've begun."

"Or you'll run off with a jockey or a horse trainer," Miss Amanda finished in triumph.

"Don't talk such rot!"

"It isn't rot, and you know it. Those are the only sorts of men you know—or notice."

"Or the only sorts that notice me, you might add."

"Well, it all comes to the same thing, doesn't it?"

"It needn't come to anything as far as I know," said Miss Ward-Benedict. "Father will probably leave me the country place. None of the boys looks like being the least bit keen on it. And I shall run it as a breeding farm, make it pay."

"Oh, I should think you'll be breeding babies long before your father pegs off."

"Don't be coarse," Miss Ward-Benedict said, throwing one leg over the other in an unladylike manner.

"It isn't what your father does or doesn't do. Your mother will shortly find you heavy on her hands, and then you'll either marry or be made to suffer."

"What absolute twaddle. My mother can't be bothered. She isn't the least interested in that sort of thing."

"That's where you're quite wrong, my dear Sybil. Mothers are always interested in 'that sort of thing.' "

"Are we discussing my future or yours?"

"You may well ask. My mother—"

"Your mother can't do a thing with you and never could. Why go on about her?"

"Ah, but you only see her as everyone else does. You have absolutely no idea how insidious she can be. If I go downstairs to confront Gregory Forrest, I am playing directly into her hands. And if I sit sulking in my room, she courts him on my behalf. Oh, how I long for those blissful hours of unconsciousness after John's—after that old maniac, Bart Thorne, tried to murder me. I drowsed along as in a lovely dream world where all mothers are barred. How I wish my brother Gordon had not been killed in the war! By now he would have produced grandchildren for Mother, and then her mind would be thoroughly occupied."

"You do talk such a lot of nonsense, Amanda. You needn't marry anyone if you don't want to. You have money of your own and more to come. The trouble with you is you're obsessed with men. You're an absolute mare in heat—"

"Talk of coarseness!"

"Yes, you are. An absolute mare in heat! You positively stink of it. Any mother would be alarmed at the prospect of you. What you need is another interest to give your mind a balance. You can scarcely imagine that. You cannot conceive of my being interested in horses without conjuring up a lurid picture of me making passionate love to a stableboy—or a jockey, forsooth! And I'm half again the size of the largest jockey in England!"

"Now who's talking rot!"

"Not I. But I have no patience whatever with this conversation about your tortured life, Amanda. You wouldn't suffer ten minutes over anything or anybody, so what are we talking about?"

"Nothing at all," Miss Amanda said, suddenly very mild, and the conversation shuddered to a sudden halt.

From that evening on, Miss Amanda stood less on her dignity with me. Miss Ward-Benedict was off the following day, and Mr. Forrest was persuaded to return to his studies in London. Left to herself again, she seemed inclined to talk to me on somewhat friendlier terms. Perhaps she felt that Miss Ward-Benedict had let her down by not being very sympathetic.

I tried to maintain my distance, but this seemed only to fuel her efforts to draw me in. She took to hovering about when I was at my work. It occurred to me that it might be quite pleasant to be in the employ of Miss Ward-Benedict instead, who seemed to spend much of her time out from underfoot in the stables, and whose simplified wardrobe would simplify my duties.

Miss Amanda spoke more and more about London as the day for going there drew nearer. I took this as a sign that she was warming to Mr. Gregory Forrest, for I assumed that he would be much in the house when the family was in town. But she never mentioned his name. Instead, she recited the wonders of London, though all this was lost on me, for I could not imagine such a place.

"The shops, Miranda! Such lovely shops full of the most beautiful gloves and jewels and hats! We shall have long mornings in Bond Street!"

"Then, Miss," I said innocently, "does that mean that you are an earlier riser when you are in London?"

"Oh, Miranda," she replied, sighing, "are you getting as snappish as ordinary servants? Indeed I hope not, for I need you as a friend. You little know how much."

By mid-October the fiction that I was employed solely as Miss Amanda's maid had given way to the fact that I must also assume a share of household duties. I was therefore expected to dress my young lady for dinner, hurry to servants' hall for my own meal, and then to serve in the dining room under Mr. Finley. His notion of lightening our burdens by conversation once occasioned him to say that in the days of the late King Edward female servants were never allowed to serve a dinner where the King was guest. This was scant consolation to me in our hurried routine, for the Whitwells did not entertain royalty.

My return to the staff dinner table was met with mingled respect and resentment. Before I grew accustomed to this, I began to understand why Mrs. Buckle continued to take her meals a few feet away from the others, being neither quite of them nor quite anything else. She treated me as civilly as she treated anyone else. Lady Eleanor had devised the title of housekeeper to mollify her at the loss of Miss Amanda. And Betty, who was eager enough to whisper confidences during our brief dinner hour, was firmly silenced by Mr. Finley. Despite the additional work, I enjoyed being in touch with the house again. And I indulged the servants' age-old vice of listening to scraps of conversation overheard in the dining room.

The talk there and in servants' hall was preoccupied with the beginning of the fox-hunting season. I knew no more of foxes and hounds than I had seen depicted in the prints that hung in Sir Timothy's library. And I was much surprised at the enthusiasm with which Miss Amanda entered into the conversation over dinner. I thought it possible that she had taken Miss Ward-Benedict's advice quite literally and had embraced a new interest that would take her out of herself. It dawned on me later that she had quite a different motive.

In dribs and drabs, I learned something of the hunt from the excited conversation above- and below-stairs. It was to be held right across the island on the land of a Mr. Forbes-Ledsmar, who was Master of the Hunt. He was evidently the owner of a large holding where the rides and footpaths had been kept open to accommodate the hunters.

The prey of the season's first hunt, it appeared, were fox cubs. And the purpose was to train young hounds in their life's work. All the gentry would be there, along with anyone else who had a horse. Those who did not ride would follow on foot. There was unending speculation upon the likelihood of decent weather. There was no matter so minor that it did not fall as a novelty upon my ear. The notion of weather as either decent or indecent had never entered my life. Weather simply was. It might ruin the crops, and farmers such as my own father would have had less to say about it than this group of people endlessly worrying the subject. I don't think I disapproved of the frivolity—the luxury of speculating about a few hours of sunshine days in advance. I was simply learning the language of a race of alien beings. At the time, I thought that nothing they might do or say could really surprise me.

On the night before the hunt Miss Amanda set me the task of searching out her walking boots, an array of wool jumpers, her heaviest tweed skirt and coat, and a leather-lined mac. She dressed herself in these and her stoutest undergarments and examined the effect in the mirror.

When I had thought my long evening's work at an end, she summoned me back from the door. "But, Miranda, we haven't given a thought to what you will wear! You can hardly follow on foot in flimsy shoes and your gray frock and—and whatever coat you have."

"I, Miss Amanda?" It had never crossed my mind that I would be attending my young lady at a fox hunt. I had never even considered what I would wear in pursuing my duties out-of-doors. Another hour was consumed as Miss Amanda joined me in digging at the back of all the cupboards and into the recesses of her dressing room for more outdoor clothes. I was in an agony at the thought of dressing in her things, however rough and outdoorsy they might be. It was common enough for ladies to pass along their worn castoffs to be used or sold at the maids' discretion. Still, this was rather another matter, and I thought it improper to wear anything that would be returned to Miss Amanda's wardrobe. Moreover, I dreaded the judgment the Hall staff would deliver if they saw me parading about as if I thought myself Miss Amanda's equal.

"Never mind," she said, reading my thoughts with one quick look in my eyes. "None of the other servants will be going. None of the Hall servants, at any rate." She insisted that I model the outfit once we had assembled it. And such was her eagerness that she very nearly jerked my gray frock from my shoulders as I pulled it off over my head.

The mustard-yellow sweater and the lavender-and-green heather-mixture tweed coat and skirt were hardly worn and were of the quality to promise a lifetime's use. I had already grown quickly accustomed to assessing the effect of a lady's clothes on her. But I had never indulged in the fantasy of myself in similar attire.

Miss Amanda grasped my arm and drew me over to a looking glass. I pulled back after the first look. I was not so much Miss Amanda's equal as her double. The effect, I believe, startled us both, but Miss Amanda recovered first. "We shall have to find you some suitable walking boots. I know there is another pair—somewhere," she said in a voice that trailed off. "Have you a hat of your own?" she said thoughtfully. I saw what she meant at once. Though her press was ranked with every sort of hat, any one of them would have completed my disguise as a lady.

"Yes, Miss, I have the gray one that Lottie left behind," I said, referring to the respectable but not smart hat I had worn on my half day in Ventnor with Betty. "I believe it will be suitable." And thus we came to an understanding without the need for further discussion.

That night I hung the tweed skirt and coat on pegs at the end of my bed. And I arranged the walking boots on the floor beneath them, for the pleasure of looking at the effect they made in the flickering lamplight. Miss Amanda's boots were a size too large for me, but I had not mentioned it for fear she might think me vain. As I slipped off to sleep, my last thought was to avoid servants' hall while I was dressed in this finery.

The day of the hunt dawned gray, threatening rain. The sky was the color of lead above my attic window, with liver-colored streaks across. Breakfast for the family had been set well ahead. I wore my usual frock down to the kitchens to make up Miss Amanda's tray, and took a bit of toast directly from Hilda's hand for my own breakfast. I piled the morning tea and Miss Amanda's breakfast all on one tray, for I expected her to need hurrying along.

But when I took it up to her room, she was up and darting about, half-dressed, as if she were already scenting the fox. I was vexed to see her in this state, making a nonsense of the clothes I had laid neatly out for her. When I had settled her to her breakfast, I must have gone about my duties with a pursed mouth, for she vowed that it had taken me scarcely a fortnight to turn myself into as dry an old stick as Mrs. Buckle, though she only called her "Buckle," in rather a rude way. At that, we both set to laughing, and instead of keeping me busy up to the last minute, she sent me off to my attic to dress myself.

When we gathered on the front steps of the Hall, Sir Timothy was already there, swinging a gnarled walking stick with every knot left in, but highly polished. He wore breeches and gaiters, and on his head a tweed hat with a brim turned down all around that fitted his round old head like a bonnet.

There was merriment in Lady Eleanor's eyes each time she looked at him, and at length she said, "Timothy, you look like nothing on earth!" But he affected not to hear his wife and only cleared his throat a number of times and complained that the motors had not been brought around in time.

Though I did not know the routine of a hunt day, I was rather sure that Lady Eleanor had no intention of "following on foot," though I was uncertain about precisely what that activity would be. While I always thought of her, and still do, as an indoor woman, she had selected an outfit that suited herself and the season perfectly. But it was hardly practical enough for anything more demanding than standing on a dry porch. On her head was the most magnificent hat I had ever seen. The brim was deep and stiff and folded in front behind a great sweep of pheasant feathers that were held at one side by a cairngorm brooch and fell on the other to brush her shoulder. Her coat was loosely fitted, though her waist was shown off as well as if she had worn a ball gown. The great lapels were buttoned back against her shoulders, and the entire ensemble was of a russet-colored wool banded at the hem just about her boot tops in several rows of black braid.

Miss Amanda was somewhat more practical in her attire and had snatched up at the last moment the small three-cornered hat she had worn on the day Bart Thorne had set on her. The mother and daughter made a lovely picture, and I was given to think that perhaps in future they might be easier in their dealings with each other.

Shortly a motor appeared at the end of the drive, and then Sir Timothy's automobile swung out of the narrow lane that led from the stables. I started when I saw John Thorne at the wheel of the Lanchester, though I don't know why I had not thought before that as chauffeur he would figure in the day. Behind him a smaller, open machine drew up, driven by Mr. George Salter, the estate agent.

It had been agreed that Sir Timothy would ride with Mr. Salter, while the ladies and I were to be driven in the Lanchester. John Thorne stepped down from the driver's seat to hand Lady Eleanor and Miss Amanda up into the back seat. And I stood in the drive, pulling at my woolen gloves and wondering what I was expected to do. I had never stood so near a motor before and could scarcely credit that I was to be riding in one.

Though it was an immense automobile, or at any rate seemed so to me, it throbbed all over to the rhythm of the engine. The brightwork on it was polished to a mirror finish and gleamed wickedly. It occurred to me that the mechanism might blow up at any moment and scatter our bodies all over the park.

Miss Amanda leaned across her mother and called out, "Come along, Miranda! You're to go up front with—Thorne." He did not conduct me around to the far side of the machine, and so I made my way on my own, hitching my skirts to step up on the running board. They would all have had my gratitude if they had left me behind.

John Thorne gave me no more than a sidelong glance and perhaps a bit of a smile at my nervousness. I should have felt an uneasiness around him in any case, but that sensation mingled with my fears at being perched so high from the drive in a contrivance that might, with a will of its own, leap off down the road. Somewhere I had heard the term "horsepower," and so I darkly feared that beneath the bonnet of the Lanchester there might well be a dozen speed-crazed steeds ready to gallop off in all directions.

Lady Eleanor inquired if the picnic hamper had been put in the boot behind, and John Thorne replied in a rather grumbling voice, "Yes, my lady, though they don't generally bother with lunch on hunt day."

"Perhaps those who pound through the woods on horseback,

mud-covered to the eyes, do not. But I shall certainly bother!"

The hunt ground lay in the west of the Isle of Wight on Mr. Forbes-Ledsmar's land between Newbridge and Freshwater. It was quite ten miles from Whitwell Hall, and I had never been so far away before. As automobiles go, the Lanchester was quite comfortable. While not absolutely weatherproof, it protected us from the wind, and the ladies did not need to have their motoring veils.

John Thorne had pulled his cap well down over his eyes, so that the blond hair at the back of his head stood out in curls. He drove with hands and elbows on the great steering wheel, as if he were quite alone and savoring his solitude. His driving was expert and steady, and I was relieved he was no "scorcher," as fast and reckless motorists were called then.

Carried away at last by the adventure and the sensation of speed, I quite forgot that I was along to attend to Miss Amanda, and to Lady Eleanor, too, if she required me. They both might have toppled out of the rear seat, and I would not have marked their going. After the first mile or two, I imagined that I was in a winged chariot, so smooth was the road and so far from the ground we seemed to be. The rolling fields were full of men harvesting grain. And in the crossroads hamlets small children crouched in the weeds like half-closed pocketknives. They had assembled to watch us pass, for they could hear the sound of the approaching motor from far off. We swept through the village of Godshill, where the thatch roofs on the cottages seemed enormous loaves of bread. Before we reached our destination, I wondered at the immensity of the world. We had driven for miles and were still not in sight of the sea.

At last we drew near another scattering of houses, and even in the distance it was clear that here the hunt was assembling. The road was filled with capering horses, and on them were the riders in the bright red coats that are always called pink. Other motorcars lined both sides of the road. But John Thorne drove slowly into the midst of the riders and drew up in front of a public house.

Sir Timothy and Mr. Salter had just arrived. Already they mingled in the crowd, enjoying the drink provided by the hunt secretary. Not even in Ventnor had I seen such a crush of people. The mounted gentlemen in their pink coats and black velvet caps surveyed the scene, nodding to one another across the heads of those on foot. There were horsewomen among them, dressed in much the same sort of habit, except for their long black divided skirts. They all raised their pewter mugs and talked loudly over the baying and yelping of the hounds and pups who were being held somewhere farther off.

Among the quality were the lesser gentry in their tweeds. Even a few ordinary folk, mounted on draft horses, milled with the rest. Lady Eleanor's plan was to remain in the motor, where Lady Orton would join her, the two to be served their picnic lunch by Lady Orton's maid.

Miss Amanda slipped down from the automobile before John Thorne could come around to assist her. She was to join a group of young people who planned to follow on foot until the going got rough. And then they meant to finish the day drinking claret cup at one of the great houses in the neighborhood. "Now, Miranda," she said to me, as precise as a schoolmistress, "I shall not be needing you at all. You're to go with Thorne, who will show you the hunt and explain—whatever there is to explain about it. Won't you, Thorne?" she said as he stepped up beside her. "And then you can call round for me at Cygnet House in the motor when the hunt's over and Mother is ready."

"Yes, Miss," John Thorne said, giving her a very direct look until she cast her eyes down in confusion. He waited until she strode off into the crowd without a backward look. Then he took my elbow in a rather familiar way and propelled me in a different direction.

"You needn't bother about me," I said, but the din about us may have drowned my words, for he made no reply.

"The great thing at a hunt," he said in a firm voice, "is to have the drink they offer around first." The hunt secretary had sent around all the barmaids from the public house with trays of ale in mugs, and I could only suppose that even servants were allowed their portion.

We edged our way through the mob. "Now, over there," John Thorne said, "is the hunt secretary himself collecting the cap." The "cap," as it turned out, was the sum of money each of the hunters paid, collected in a leather pouch.

Thorne had by then slipped his arm under mine to lead me along, but he spoke as if we had never met before, as if I were a foreigner who had engaged him as a guide. Nearby all the hounds were gathered and straining on their leads, a great choppy mass of wildly wagging tails and howling mouths and steaming breath. In the midst stood the huntsman, chatting up the animals in a kind of gibberish never heard on land or sea. The huntsman was dressed in the black cap and pink coat of the gentry. For something to say, I asked, "What is the difference between the Master of the Hunt and the huntsman?"

Thorne explained that the Master of the Hunt was Mr. Forbes-Ledsmar himself, a largely ceremonial figure, while the huntsman was his servant in charge of the kennels. "Master and man, as you might say."

At that, the crisp air was split by two shrill notes sounded by the huntsman on his horn. It was a rare sight to see the hounds leave off their milling about and to surge all in one direction, suddenly free. The pups paired off with the old and experienced hounds, and away they all flew down the road, leaping a ditch and then a stone wall.

I should have been trampled by the following horses if John Thorne had not drawn me aside. The Master of the Hunt had somehow indicated the direction. All moved according to plan, though all seemed dreadful confusion to me. We held back until the horses had cleared the fence. Then the first of the foot-followers managed to negotiate the first damp ditch and then the stone wall. I caught a glimpse of Miss Amanda in a knot of young people shrieking with laughter at the difficulty one of their number had in clearing the ditch.

Thorne and I came along just ahead of the stragglers. He more than half lifted me over the fence, leaving our empty ale mugs on the topmost stones. Then we made off across the field. The "draw," it seemed, was the place where the foxes were known to lurk. It was a wood some two fields away. I had thought that horses and hounds would leave us behind straightaway. Nor did I much care for the notion of being left out in a secluded field with John Thorne. But that was not the way of it at all, for the hounds grouped and regrouped, darted in various directions, only to return and lift their muzzles to "speak." The horsemen reined up behind them, endeavoring not to get between the hounds and the foxes and thus destroy the scent. Though it was not at all a scent the hounds were trying to find, as Thorne explained to me, but a "line."

Instead of a mad dash, then, it was rather leisurely, with more wait than hurry-up. The fine horses cavorted and quivered and stamped in the distance while the horsewomen arranged and rearranged their skirts and fitted their velvet hats more carefully down over their heads with their riding crops fixed firmly under their arms. Those on foot stood in groups around the stubble field, chatting. Some, seizing the advantage of a dry patch of ground, sprawled about. It was a scene of such luxurious grandeur in the wonderfully clear open air that my heart nearly sang with the beauty of it.

Being very young and perhaps foolish behind my stiff facade, I was struck by a coincidence. The last time I had strolled out in the morning air, this same John Thorne had been beside me. It had been the morning after I had sat up with Granny Thorne, and a troublesome time for all. But it had been a morning with moments of great beauty. There was a need growing within me, I felt sure, a need to grasp at such moments in the hope there might be more. I had been raised to expect nothing for myself. Yet the expectation was rising in me, and I was powerless against it.

Then, suddenly, we were running, and all those about us who had been dawdling were in full flight. The hounds had set off through a thicket and were calling with a strangely purposeful cry. I shall always remember it as the nearest sound to the human voice. The horses were slower at finding their way through the thicket than we on foot. I could feel my cheeks burn bright with excitement as John and I pounded across the field. When we came to the lashing limbs of the cover beyond it, his hand slipped down my arm to grasp my hand. Even through the heavy woolen glove I could feel his warmth. But I saw no impropriety in it. Nor would I have pulled away if I did.

On the far side of the undergrowth was a sloping pastureland. John pointed out a herd of Frisian cattle all grouped together at one spot near a distant fence—a great black-and-white mass. "They know, cattle do," he said. "They've a line on the old foxes themselves. See how all their snouts turn in the same direction."

The horsemen were making a detour around this field. But some of the foot-followers made a headlong dash across it. "Damn fools," he said, "rushing a herd of Frisians. They'll soon have the cattle after them, and a cow can run as fast as a bull!" I only hoped that my Miss Amanda was not one to be singled out by an enraged Frisian. But the cattle seemed more drawn by the hint of invisible foxes than the two-legged intruders. Still, we slowed our pace and made a prudent circle to bypass the livestock. But my heart was thumping. If John had dropped my hand just then, I should have seized his.

In the next cover I had thought we were sure to find a nest of foxes, with brushes bristling, all grouped together, offering their necks to the hounds. Belatedly, I wondered if I had the stomach to be in at the kill. But of course foxes are cannier than that. If they had been near, they were farther off now. And as John unexpectedly said, laughing up their sleeves.

The day sped along in bursts of pursuit and long waits in the freshness of the brisk outdoor air. The sun never broke through, but the exercise had kept us warm. It grew harder to follow the progress of the hunt, as we described a great circle around the village where we had begun, occasionally crossing and recrossing the same main road.

At last the hunters and the followers were dispersed over a wide area, and the speaking of the hounds came from farther off. We sat to rest, John and I, just inside the lych-gate of a small stone church shadowed in elm trees. We found a dry resting place on one of the tombs that stood up out of the ground like a great marble table. In the first moments I was so winded by the outdoor exercise that I remarked neither on the solitude of this place I shared with John Thorne nor the impiety of dropping down to rest upon a tomb, however ancient. I came to myself when I saw my hand was resting on a carved death's head against crossed bones cut into the top of the tomb. I drew my hand away, noticing that another design was carved in the far corner, an hourglass fitted with angel wings, deep green with moss against the stained white marble top. Because I could think of nothing to say, I rose and walked round the tomb to see if I could make out the lengthy message on a brass plate set into the stone top. It seemed to run to many lines, most of it legible. I stood there, silently mouthing the lines, until John Thorne said suddenly, "Read it aloud."

It seemed an unlikely pastime, if not unseemly, but I supposed that whoever had left such a long eulogy had meant it to be read. It was the grave of a young girl, a Susanne Barford. I read:

"DEPARTED THIS LIFE THE 20th OF AUGUST 1652
AGED TEN YEARES THIRTEEN WEEKES,
THE NON-SUCH OF THE WORLD FOR PIETY AND
VERTUE IN SOE TENDER YEARS."

There was a rude cutting of a young girl's face below these words to separate them from more lines below. John Thorne turned around to follow my reading, though he could only see the words upside down.

"AND DEATH AND ENVYE BOTH MUST SAY 'TWAS FITT
HER MEMORY SHOULD THUS IN BRASSE BEE WRITT
HERE LYES INTERR'D WITHIN THIS BED OF DUST
A VIRGIN PURE NOT STAIN'D BY CARNALL LUST,
SUCH GRACE THE KING OF KINGS BESTOW'D UPON HER
THAT NOW SHEE LIVES WITH HIM A MAID OF HONOUR
HER STAGE WAS SHORT, HER THREAD WAS QUICK SPUNN,
DRAWN OUTE, AND CUT, GOTT HEAVEN, HER WORK WAS DONE
THIS WORLD TO HER WAS BUT A TRAGEDY PLAY
SHE CAME AND SAW'T, DISLIK'T, AND PASSED AWAY."

After a pause while the wind rattled the last dry leaves on the elms above us, John said, "Looked at the world, disliked it, and passed away. Simple enough in the old days, to hear them tell it." He fell silent again then. I stole a glance at him, emboldened perhaps by the past hours. His profile was very fine, I thought. Not in the way an aristocratic gentleman's is said to be. But very strong, with the jutting chin of a quiet man. The tip of his nose was touched with red from the cold day, but his skin was still bronzed from summer sun.

I was so much at my ease with him that my guard was down when he broke his silence again in his usual abrupt way. "You're settling in, then, up at the Hall?" It was the sort of question put time and again to a new servant, often some time after she was no longer quite a newcomer.

"I am that," I said, like any callow young person ready to show capability.

"They've made you the young miss's own lady's maid, have they?"

"They have." I wondered who of the Hall staff would be on gossiping terms with him. But then I supposed he gathered as much since I had accompanied Miss Amanda to the hunt.

"And how do you like her, then?"

"It's not for me to say, I'm sure." How I writhe now at memory of such rectitude!

John Thorne turned to me and fixed me with his eyes, which were the color of the overcast sky. "Come now, Miranda, you must bend a bit or you'll be broken by the gale." The autumn leaves swirled across the graves as if to illustrate his warning. "Both spirited children, those Whitwells had. Something way back in the blood, maybe," he continued, looking away.

"Both?"

"Yes, a son. Young Gordon. I say young, though he was born before me. We were in the South African war. Same regiment, though he was a lieutenant and I slept in the mud."

I had heard of this Gordon Whitwell. I struggled to remember where. Perhaps Miss Amanda had just mentioned him in her conversation with Miss Ward-Benedict. "Was he—"

"Yes. He didn't come back. And I did. It's funny how some are spared. And others come, see the world, dislike it, and pass away."

I gazed at John Thorne, trying to see into him. Was he relating the epitaph where his hand still rested on cold marble to the death of young Gordon Whitwell? Was there poetry and sentiment in John's heart, or was he merely being cynical? Why was he not exactly what he was, like the rest of the servants?

"Did Mr. Gordon die a hero's death?" I asked, mainly to erase my own thoughts.

"Are there hero's deaths?" he asked, cocking an eyebrow at me, and I knew enough to keep silent. There was a broad strain of bitterness in John, whatever else was there. He was hard, and I thought it might have been the war that had done that.

"What was Mr. Gordon like?" I asked to shift the subject back.

"Like? It's hard to say. We were lads together, in a manner of speaking. He was something of the young toff, but a bit short when it came to character and backbone. Like his sister, come to that."

I wasn't having any talk against Miss Amanda, so I cut in pretty sharply, "That's a wicked thing to be saying about a young gentleman who gave up his life for his country."

"Yes," John Thorne said. "I suppose it is. Why is it," he went on, "when such as we can get away from our work for a rare bit of peace and quiet, we can think of nothing to talk of but our betters?"

"What else have we?" I asked, truly wanting to know.

"Only what we can take."

In the distance the huntsman's horn sounded a long blast and then another. "Gone to ground," John said. "The foxes. They've got clean away. They've won. I'm glad when they do. It sets the day in a proper perspective."

And with that he stood and offered me both his hands as I stood up from the cold tomb top. And then he kissed me lightly on the cheek. I would have been proof against anything but that. It took me by surprise, the suddenness and the gentleness. We strolled off then, through the lych-gate and back toward the road. Arm and arm, as if something had been decided between us.

Thirteen

Miss Amanda seemed to know before I did myself that John Thorne and I were courting in a quiet way. When before it had seemed sensible that I should spend my life in service, keeping myself to myself, now it seemed just as sensible that I should enjoy the company of a man who attracted me strongly.

From the very beginning I never flattered myself that I would ever capture more than a part of John Thorne. He was as remote from me in his way as Mr. Gregory Forrest was in his. But John Thorne was a man of my own station in life, near enough. And I was awakening to my own desires far more suddenly than those girls who start early to indulge the luxury of dreaming.

I was still drawn to John half against my will. But that only added some mysterious element that I was hard pressed to identify. "A bit of spice," Betty might have said, though I did not confide in her. The condition she found herself in was a cautionary tale in itself. I was determined that I should never find myself in the same straits. And so I went about, a trifle weak in the knees, though cautious, and asked nothing more from life. I scarcely dared survey the future.

It is said that young girls are transformed by love. And so it was to be with me, though not in the way usually meant. Without quite noticing it myself, I began to copy Miss Amanda's ways. Those that I admired, at any rate. The rough edges from my country speech fell away from my words. I had never been to a school with other girls of my own age and had never known the hopeless yearning for gentility that infects the manners and speech of the suburban girl of the middle classes who hopes to rise a single notch in life. I simply watched Miss Amanda and began to be a part of her. After all, she had Mr. Gregory Forrest eating from her hand. And while I could not entirely admire her for that, I would not have been quite human if it had not given me an idea or two of my own. Still half afraid of John Thorne, I kept a distance that bought me time to refine my methods.

I see now that Miss Amanda was too obliging by half. She had dressed me in her clothes for the day of the hunt as if it were the inspiration of the moment. And after the hunt day was past, I scarcely realized that my presence there had not been needed. Indeed, Miss Amanda stayed out of the way the entire time and seemed to enjoy a rare friendliness with a group of the neighboring young people, about whom she didn't care a snap and never so much as mentioned again.

From that day forth, she seemed more and more determined to turn me into a sort of mirror of herself. None of her clothes were really worn out, but she began to pass along to me quite new things, saying only that she would never wear them, that she had had them made in a weak moment. I could think of nowhere I would ever wear most of them, but it was impossible to refuse them. She was in good spirits, and I dared not cross her. She seemed to know this all too well and to trade on it.

We spent an inordinate amount of time preparing for the London month, which was nearly on us. A dressmaker from Ventnor was summoned and came to the Hall in the afternoons to see to the fittings for both Lady Eleanor and Miss Amanda. Miss Semple was her name, and she bristled with pins.

Miss Semple bore watching. She was inclined to get above herself in the unholy pride she took in her position in life. Seeing herself as an independent businesswoman, she was short with servants. And there was a look about her that suggested she would like to give Miss Amanda a piece of her mind on general principles if she dared. She invariably wore the same dress when she came for the consultations and fittings. A black crepe with a lace-trimmed fichu and a skirt that was fashionably hobbled, though she didn't have the figure for fashionable clothes. "She looks rather as if she were hanging on a peg," Miss Amanda once remarked.

Miss Semple was pleased enough to be engaged by the ladies of so grand a place as Whitwell Hall. Pressing her luck a bit, she often dawdled in the hope of getting her tea. Whether this was an example of her frugality or her snobbishness, I am not sure. Very likely a combination of the two. On one rather dismal afternoon she had outstayed her welcome. Miss Amanda had stood for quite an hour as a rather unexceptional afternoon frock was being fitted on her. Miss Semple was making a mountain of a molehill, and Miss Amanda knew it. Whenever she complained, Miss Semple always seemed to have a mouthful of pins and only shook her head impatiently. There was an element of "artist-at-work" about her that was getting Miss Amanda down. At last she said, "Semple, stop, I say! I cannot go on with this charade another moment. I am fainting on my feet!"

"Well, Miss Amanda, I'm sorry, I'm sure," said Miss Semple bitterly. "But you won't get this kind of work done in London for any money. And if it's to be done right, I must—"

"In London," Miss Amanda thundered, "there would be four assistants at work who would have everything done in a quarter of the time!"

"Yes," flared Miss Semple, "and charge ten times the price!" But her shoulders sagged the moment she spoke, for she had taken quite the wrong tack altogether. She was in the presence of a young lady who could pay twenty times Miss Semple's fee, and no one to say her nay. Miss Semple had forgotten herself. She was revealed as the local seamstress that she was, whose regular custom was the ladies of Ventnor, like Hubert Sampson's dreadful mother, who would haggle with her over thruppence. She fingered the pincushion at her belt and seemed to realize for the first time that she was on her knees with Miss Amanda towering above her.

"I think I have had quite enough for today," Miss Amanda said in a grandly dignified voice. "Moreover, I do not fancy putting this interminable task off to another afternoon. Take this frock off me and have it fitted on my maid."

"Really, Miss Whitwell!" Semple said, clawing at her heart.

"She is precisely my size in every particular. To fit her is to fit me. And have it done today. I am going down now to have tea with my mother." (She never took tea with her mother; I don't know where she went.)

When Miss Amanda was gone and Semple was left with the unfinished frock across her arm, I feared for her sanity. She gobbled for a time and wrenched at her pincushion, which was shaped like a tomato, until it came away in her hand. I stood by with maddening calm until she screamed, "Well, am I to fit this frock over your uniform? Take it off! I haven't all day!"

"Excuse me, Miss," I said. "I thought you had."

From that afternoon on, for many more, as Miss Amanda's stand-in I was to see altogether too much of Miss Semple. Miss Amanda never again deigned to receive the dressmaker, transmitting all her instructions through me. It would have been kinder to send her away than to demean her, but that was not Miss Amanda's way.

To give her credit, Miss Semple put a good enough face on the new situation once she saw the inevitability of it. From gobbling, she turned to grumbling, and finally to civil conversation. She was, beneath her thin, genteel facade, quite like Mrs. Creeth in her kitchen. As we were closeted together and I was a more patient subject than Miss Amanda, she even grew chatty. She called me "my mannequin" and praised me for the unmoving stance I took while she worked around me. She even went so far as to say that I had "a better figure for frocks" than my employer, though this was only a pleasantry, for indeed we had identical figures. She pumped me as such people will about the family, hoping for gossip to carry back to Ventnor. And when she got nothing from me, she praised me for my discretion. There was really no displeasing her after a time. And as she was not as cautious with her pins on me as she had been with Miss Amanda, she worked somewhat faster.

Miss Semple's crowning achievement was an evening gown that Miss Amanda had seen in a French magazine and wanted copied in a somewhat simplified form. We were, Miss Semple and I, three afternoons on the setting of the sleeves alone. Though she was vain of her own skill on "anything out of the ordinary way," the gown very nearly defeated her. I grew bone-weary at the sound of the sleeves being ripped from my shoulders and tried yet another way.

Finally the gown that Miss Amanda had wanted for dancing began to take shape. It was in powder-blue Utrecht velvet with panels of ivory lace that Miss Amanda had ordered from Brussels in advance lest Miss Semple foist inferior stuff from Ventnor on her. The neckline was deep and square, and the sleeves were three-quarter, endeavoring to look demure and sophisticated at once. I could hardly bear to see myself in the looking glass before me, for the gown was so beautiful that it wrung my heart.

Standing like a statue with my eyes cast down, I wondered at a world where one might wear such a gown. Only a month or so before, I would not have had the wit to wonder. And all the while Miss Semple praised me lavishly for my patient immobility, little knowing or understanding that I was transfixed.

When she had passed the crisis and had nearly solved all the problems that the gown posed, Miss Semple grew voluble on the topic of "ball gowns for galas." Most of her gossip about Ventnor life fell lightly on my ears. But she returned so frequently to the topic of an evening dance and supper party to be held there that at last I took notice. It was an annual event, held each October by an organization of Ventnor tradesmen. A sort of celebration for the local business people after the end of the busy holiday season. "Absolutely no outsiders," Miss Semple declared. "Very exclusive." It was good, she said, for seven or eight commissions. She had all the work she could handle, and this despite the annoying habit that many Ventnor ladies had of wearing the same gown, but lightly retrimmed, year in and year out.

Already the germ of an idea must have been lurking in my mind, for I asked her, "Are you making a ball gown for Mrs. Sampson?"

Miss Semple sat back on her heels with a start and looked up at me as if a statue had spoken, wondering how I would be on terms with such an august personage. "Mrs. Sampson of the drapers, you mean? Hubert Sampson's mother?"

I nodded.

"Well, as you ask, no. Mrs. Sampson's dancing days are over." And then she observed quite five minutes of silence, refraining from wondering aloud why I had asked. In that quiet interval it began to dawn upon me why I had.

I had not seen Betty alone since our half day together. Miss Amanda did not recognize the servant's rights to regular time off. I occasionally managed a part of an afternoon and an hour or two in the evenings. But I was so absorbed in my duties that I hardly noticed the passing of the days.

When I caught a quick glimpse down the staff table during the meals I took there, Betty was more woebegone than ever. She sat drooping at her place and picked at her food. Mrs. Creeth shot her suspicious looks and often enough told her to buck up. It seemed that Mrs. Creeth was not far from discovering Betty's secret. That would mean a very unpleasant scene into which Mr. Finley would be drawn as our commander. The end of it would be that they would pack Betty off. I was overcome with guilt that I had left her too much alone in her misery.

Late one night when the house was quiet, I threaded my way up and down the staircases I was coming to know by heart. Only half-way along the corridor in Betty's attic, I could hear her sobs. Fearing I would startle her, I lingered at her door, which she had not bothered to shut and latch. The lamp in her room was still glowing, and Betty lay half in its light across her bed. She wept with real despair and hardly stirred when I sat down beside her. "Oh, Miranda," she said when she realized I was there, "if you'd been a thief in the night come to kill me, or old dead Bart Thorne to strangle me, I shouldn't have cared tuppence. I'm that bowed down with grief."

The words I tried to comfort her with sounded hollow enough, but she was beyond that kind of consolation. "It's no good with Hubert —Mr. Sampson. He don't take any notice of me whatever." She sat up then and scrubbed the end of the sheet across her face. In the dim yellow light she looked too ill ever to rise again. "It's the nights are the worst," she said. "I can get through the days, keeping busy, but oh, these nights."

In bits and pieces she told her somber story. On each of her half days she had made her way to Ventnor, there to linger outside Sampson & Son, Drapers, in the hope that Mr. Sampson would step outside for a bit of a chat. But not since the day we had gone there together had he acknowledged her presence. She had seen him through the glass on two occasions. On the third she had drawn herself up and actually entered the shop, but he had beaten a hasty retreat, and a shop assistant had tried to serve her. She was inclined to think that his mother had talked him out of her. I was inclined to agree.

Throughout, she repeated that he was her last and only chance. She didn't need to point out that time was drawing short, for she looked down every other moment, smoothing her nightdress over her front.

Despite her usual plumpness, she was beginning to show, ever so slightly. To keep her from another storm of weeping, I found myself assuring her that between us we would find a solution to her problem. It was even in my mind to put the situation before Miss Amanda, though this seemed an unwise and very likely pointless course to take.

Perhaps at first I thought of going to Ventnor alone to try to reason with Mr. Sampson. But that vague impulse gave way to the need for a more elaborate scheme. I was preoccupied for days with the urge to make plans for which I had no experience. At length Miss Amanda drew me up short and demanded to know what was on my mind. It was clear that my duties to her did not claim my undivided attention.

"Oh, Miss," I blurted out, "it's Betty!" And then I caught my breath, for I had no right to spread another's story abroad.

"Our Betty?" Miss Amanda said. "That shapeless little mouse with hair like a cactus in a conservatory?"

"Yes, Miss. But it isn't anything, really," I said, too late.

"I'm very glad to hear that," Miss Amanda said, "for servants' problems are so dreary, and they always end with their leaving or remaining to stalk about with faces as long as a wet week, and they tend to break things."

"Yes, Miss."

But then she reversed herself as she often did and began to show the liveliest interest in Betty's case. The damage had been done, and so I was guilty of telling her all, or mostly all, of the story as I knew it. Even to the man from the Wild West Show and to Hubert Sampson's wretched old mother. I found myself sitting on Miss Amanda's bed while she ate her breakfast, never taking her eyes off me.

She looked quite startled when I found a way of telling her that Betty was expecting a baby. For a moment I wondered if Miss Amanda did not know where babies came from. But then I had heard enough of the gossip that passed between her and Miss Ward-Benedict to determine that she thought herself quite worldly.

"I would stay clear of the whole business if I were you," she said, though there was a look about her that indicated otherwise. "I can have a word with my mother, who will surely know how such things are handled. She'll be quite alarmed that Betty's morals might corrupt the rest of you. Just imagine Hilda and Hannah both pregnant at once! They wouldn't be able to get through the doors, and the floor would be in danger of collapse. And best of all, it will give Mother something to think about."

I knew it was useless to dissuade her. She was only saying the conventional thing. Once she realized it was conventional, she would reverse herself. Waiting for the right moment, I finally suggested that we might between us devise a more clever plan. She was all ears at once. As the plan matured, it was evident that Miss Amanda thought she had conceived it herself.

On the following day I quizzed Miss Semple shamelessly, but rather indirectly, as to subscriptions to the Ventnor Tradesmen's Ball. It seemed that as a gesture of goodwill a number of worthy people bought sets of tickets that they did not use. Indeed, the financial success of the occasion depended on the gentry's subscriptions, though no one expected them to put in appearances.

Miss Amanda had only to inquire of her father to learn that he had bought a pair of tickets every year and always passed them along to the estate agent, Mr. Salter, who generally attended with his sister. It took no effort for Miss Amanda to ask Sir Timothy if he would order another pair. He could deny her nothing and never bothered to inquire into her reasons.

As a result I was armed with two tickets to the ball before the week was out. And on a half day that Miss Amanda granted me for the purpose, I was dressed in her best and setting forth for Ventnor to beard Mr. Sampson—and his mother, if need be—in their den. I left Betty behind, assuring her that great plans were in the works. Where I found the assurance I cannot think.

As I made my way along the road to Ventnor, it was in my mind to captivate Mr. Hubert Sampson if I could. I might have taken another tack, confiding in him that I was speaking on Betty's—Miss Prowse's—behalf. My plan was to lure him to the Ventnor ball, where Betty would be waiting, got up as alluringly as Miss Amanda and I could make her. At that point I meant to vanish in the crowd, leaving the pair of them to their own devices. I only hoped Betty could discover a device or two up her sleeve. She would have to take it from there, to improve on the situation in any way she could. It was just the sort of scheme silly young girls dote on. I suppose the hoped-for outcome was less large in my mind than the challenge and the adventure. And I was rather sure that Mrs. Sampson would pose a formidable enough challenge.

Once I had reached the paving stones of Ventnor, I nearly lost heart, finding myself quite alone in this vast city of two or three thousand souls. The palm trees in the walled gardens were tattered by the heavy winds of October, and the town was considerably quieter and more dismal than it had been on my first visit there. I lingered along a street of private houses, brushing the roadside dust from the smart dark-blue serge skirt that Miss Amanda had given me. I had worn my own shoes because of the long walk, but they were still in a respectable state of repair. Once I wiped them clean, they gleamed with new polish. My coat matched my skirt, and I even had a fur tippet that one of Miss Amanda's elderly aunts had given her. The hat she lent me was rather severe, being untrimmed. As my tastes in these matters were still forming, I had little idea how fashionable it actually was. I only thought the effect was one of rigid respectability, and this gave me the added confidence I was shortly to draw upon.

When I entered Sampson & Son, Drapers, Hubert thrust aside an assistant in a rush to serve me. He took me, I could see, for a well-fixed patron. Expecting to be remembered for who I was, I hardly found words to speak. But he soon recognized me, and even came up with my name. In the next moment he had asked me to step upstairs and renew my acquaintance with his mother. Hubert danced attendance on me in a way I had never known from any man before. There was nothing of the stern and silent countryman about him, and I had to take care not to become flustered. Though if I had simpered and fluttered, it would not have been out of keeping.

Our invasion of Mrs. Sampson was nearly a repetition of the earlier time. The taffy cat lay coiled on her befrilled lap, and she stirred only slightly from her hearthside post. She was quicker than her son to recognize me. But she waited silently until he had reintroduced "Miss Cooke." Her appraising eye went at once to my hat, and throughout the visit her old and watery eye was fixed on me. Friendliness was beyond her, for any young woman must have posed a threat to her comfortable life with a doting son. However, she was better disposed to me than to Betty, whom she had cut. Hubert Sampson rang for tea, and his mother said nothing.

There was suspicion in Mrs. Sampson's eye, nevertheless. Being a woman, she saw there was a motive lurking behind my manner. Her son might have thought that I had entered the shop to finger the lengths of wool, but his mother knew better. Fortunately, I was armed with a plausible reason.

She surprised me only a little by already knowing that I was Miss Amanda's own maid. Clearly, Miss Semple was a bearer of tales. Though Mrs. Sampson cherished the snobbery of her class regarding servants, she saw my position as somewhat exalted. I was nearer the gentry than she was herself, in a manner of speaking. And my appearance proclaimed it. Before a lull in the conversation might occur, I murmured that Miss Amanda Whitwell had presented me with two tickets to the Ventnor Tradesmen's Ball. Mrs. Sampson's eyes narrowed. I pressed on, saying that I would much appreciate her advice as a lady of the town regarding the propriety of the event. Then I cast my eyes into my lap and fingered my gloves, which were laid primly across my knee. Mrs. Sampson was caught off-guard, but she was forced into a reply to show her superior knowledge.

"It's quite a proper do—affair, Miss Cooke. You may take my word for it. I quite see how being buried in the country, as you might say, you wouldn't have known this is quite the event of the Ventnor season. And quite a gala it is, too. My late husband, Mr. Sampson, was among them—those who set it in motion some years ago. And now it's a tradition for all the best people hereabouts. Your Miss Whitwell done—did quite right in giving you the tickets. Thoughtful of her. There's some in her employ I could name who wouldn't merit such a favor, I'm sure."

Before she had finished this speech, Mrs. Sampson was patting the great bun of hair that rode high on her head and preening herself generally. She was also delivering her son into my hands, and she even appeared half-reconciled to that. Hubert was on the edge of his chair, scarcely able to anchor the cup of tea on his knee.

"You'll have a suitable escort, I take it," Mrs. Sampson said in a very different voice.

I colored, more from nerves than modesty, saying, "I thought to have a suitable escort, but now I learn that it is a very fashionable occasion, I'm not certain. It's difficult for a girl in my position to know." My voice grew very small, and I had the decency to chide myself at this deceitful performance.

Hubert Sampson at last broke in. "Perhaps you'd allow—"

"Perhaps you'd allow my son to take you in," Mrs. Sampson finished, causing her son to swallow and look pop-eyed.

"Oh, I hardly think I could presume," I said, almost in a whisper.

"Well, you'll have to find your own way there. Hubert can't be traipsing right out into the country to collect you. But I daresay he would give you his arm for the first set and into the supper room."

Hubert Sampson beamed in the manner of a boy twenty years his junior who sees the world suddenly opening up for the first time. The suspicion was banished from his mother's eyes by a gleam of triumph. She had managed to dispel Betty by means of me. And her look clearly said that she would deal with me later, if need be. Each of us was suffused with a different triumph, and I was urged to take another cup of tea and the remaining watercress sandwich.

"Of course Betty will have to have a suitable frock," Miss Amanda said, advancing the plan by her own scheming. "And I do hope she has not lost too much of her figure. It could be awkward if we had to fix a great bouquet just at her waist. Still, it happens in the best society. And you, Miranda. What will you wear?"

I told Miss Amanda that I would surely find something suitable among the things she had passed along to me. But this did not satisfy her. She insisted that we come to a conclusion about this weighty matter even before poor Betty was to be outfitted.

After long deliberation, it was decided that I was to have an absolutely new frock, made in great haste by Miss Semple. It was to be white with bands of purple velvet to outline a deep, square neckline. "This will be your opportunity to display your bosom," Miss Amanda said, hard at work with a bit of crayon and a sketching pad. "And a corsage of purple velvet violets at the shoulder. Otherwise quite simple, though the skirt must be ample for dancing."

"But, Miss Amanda, I don't know how to dance." I had every intention of slipping away before the musical portion of the evening.

"You will manage perfectly well among the village clodhoppers. Now be still while I finish this sketch. It must be absolutely foolproof, or Semple will never manage to fathom it. In short, it must be simple for Semple." I had even then the distinct feeling that the project was out of my hands and running amok.

Miss Semple was temporarily speechless with rage at this last-minute job of work, directed to her in Miss Amanda's tone of command. When the dressmaker learned that the frock was for me, a maid, and not for Miss Amanda, she nearly gibbered. The brief flurry of friendliness she had earlier shown me vanished, never to return. Miss Amanda closeted herself with Semple after my fitting, but at the time I did not, for some reason, think that odd. I had enough on my mind as it was.

Scarcely two days before the ball, Miss Amanda ordered me to bring Betty to her. When I had first told Betty that she was to have an entire evening to work her wiles on Hubert Sampson, she had been less delighted than I had hoped. The idea of the ball awed her, and I rather think she feared Mrs. Sampson would find us all out. I even had to choose my words carefully lest she think I wanted Hubert Sampson for myself. If I had ever been tempted to confide to anyone my growing feeling for John Thorne, it would have been then. But the moment passed. We observed a second crisis when Betty learned that she would have to confront Miss Amanda, whom she feared from afar, over the matter of a party dress.

I nearly dragged her by the upper arm to Miss Amanda's room.

Betty entered it as my shadow, cowering, and could hardly be persuaded to drop her hands, which were clutched beneath her apron. With all her witlessness, Betty was more prudent than I in her fear of Miss Amanda.

"Oh, Miss," she moaned, "if Mr. Finley finds me here instead of at me work, there'll be the devil to pay, pardon the language, Miss."

"Never mind, Betty," Miss Amanda said, striding about the room and examining her from every angle. "You have little choice but to deliver yourself into our hands. Mind you, you must snare this Sampson man on your own. We can do no more than put a winning card or two into your hand." Betty goggled.

Miss Semple was to be kept out of the proceedings. If she heard that Betty was being groomed for a public appearance, the word would unerringly find its way into Mrs. Sampson's ear. Then we would all be undone. This left us with the problem of finding a gown among Miss Amanda's castoffs that could be tailored to Betty's quite different figure. "And it will require more than a nip and a tuck," Miss Amanda mused.

At last a frock several years old that had somehow lingered, folded away, was produced. It dated from a time when Miss Amanda had been shorter and more plump. Thus it came close to fitting Betty. It was of pink silk with rosettes set about the skirt, a bit of a little-girl's-first-evening-party frock and a touch too summery. But it could be made to serve. We sent it and Betty along the path to Granny Thorne's for a fitting. And suddenly the evening of the Ventnor Tradesmen's Ball was upon us.

I dressed for it under Miss Amanda's supervision. Immediately following dinner, she had retired to her room. When I arrived there, she wore an old dressing gown. I supposed that this was to indicate that she was on the point of going to bed, if we were discovered by Lady Eleanor.

Miss Amanda had at the ready a pair of silver kid shoes, and stockings to match them in color. My dress was already hanging on the door of the wardrobe. Once we had both drawn it over my head, I avoided looking at myself in the mirror. It was hardly necessary, for Miss Amanda inspected me as severely as a sergeant major. Belatedly, she fussed about my hair, which was drawn back in its usual bun at the nape of my neck. But as she always had Mme. Lucille up from Ventnor to dress her own hair, neither of us had the knowledge or the time to experiment. Yet nothing would do but that I unpin my hair, allow Miss Amanda to brush it and recoil it. In those days it was not the fashion for young girls to paint their faces or to transform their eyebrows into arching strokes of charcoal with a surround of plucked gooseflesh. Still, Miss Amanda dusted my naked neck with pink powder and handed me a handkerchief of her own, damp with French scent.

At last she stood back and examined the full effect of her achievement. For a moment I had forgotten myself, reveling in being fussed over by the young lady I should have been serving instead. "Aren't you going to have a look at yourself in the glass?" she asked.

"Oh, no, Miss. If you say I will do, I am quite satisfied. It isn't as if I was going to enjoy myself." But that sentiment rang so false in the air that we both gave way to muffled laughter. She threw a wrap over her dressing gown and saw me all the way down to the drive, where the Salters were to collect me. And as luck was with us, we met no one in the passageways or on the stairs.

There was a harvest moon that evening, and the weather was winter-crisp. Miss Amanda had arranged for me to go to the ball with Mr. Salter and his sister, Winifred. Perhaps a girl of different background would have been shamed to be sent off to a party without a proper escort of her own. But such a thought never entered my head. I had worked at double my usual pace during the day, discharging my regular duties and serving at dinner with particular efficiency before I slipped up to Miss Amanda's door.

She had told me that John Thorne would see Betty to the ball a half hour after it was well under way. I had spared a scrap of time to help Betty dress, but she had shooed me out of the attic, suddenly beside herself with excitement. "You'll see me in me glory when I march into that hotel ballroom, Miranda, and not before!" Grand ladies to be presented at court could not have matched our mood.

On the way to Ventnor I sat huddled on the back seat of George Salter's rattling motorcar. Swathed in a coach rug and a motoring veil, I was intent on not crushing my lovely bouquet of velvet violets.

The howl of the wind and the clanking of the machine made conversation impossible. I was thankful for this, as I was shy with the Salters. Though George Salter could not have been more than five-and-forty, I thought him immensely old. He had the weather-worn look of a man who has lived entirely in the out-of-doors and always in the country. His eyelids drooped in a great moon face that was nevertheless not dull. He seemed a man of towering strength. As his domain lay outside the Hall, I had hardly ever spoken to him or heard him spoken of. He had been at Granny Thorne's bedside on the morning after she had been attacked. But he had lingered uncomfortably on the fringes of the crowd in her small bedroom and had said little. He was a fixture of the estate and lived quite outside its crossfire of personalities and the thousand little tensions that were already enlivening my days.

Though I had never seen his sister before, I had heard mutterings about her in the kitchens. It was Mrs. Creeth's opinion that Winifred Salter gave herself airs, since she was nothing but an old maid who had been left on the shelf and taken in by her brother. I supposed they were envious of her in the kitchens, for she was not a servant at all. Moreover, she presided over a large cottage on the grounds of the home farm and looked after Mr. Salter and his son, Willie, whose mother had long since died.

All I knew was that Miss Salter never came up to the Hall to do odd jobs of work as the other women of the neighborhood often did. She had given me only the briefest nod when I entered the motorcar, and the darkness masked her face. I thought she must be a cold and withdrawn woman.

The ball was held in the same fine hotel where Betty and I had taken our half-day tea. The approach to the place was dazzling with arching arbors of twinkling lights and floating flags. Townspeople crowded up the curving drive, their finery muted by sensible winter coats, for the wind whipped directly off the sea.

Drawing up in a motorcar made us the object of some attention. Two doormen leaped from the steps and opened the auto's doors for Miss Salter and me. As I was being handed down, I heard an unknown voice from the crowd say quite clearly, "Just look, it's Miss Amanda Whitwell!" I stumbled on the running board and nearly fell into the doorman's arms.

Once we were inside, I had expected the Salters to leave me to find Mr. Sampson the best way I could. But Winifred Salter ushered me off to a ladies' retiring room where we were to leave our wraps. I would never have known of the place without her guidance. It was a lovely jewel box of a room with electrical torches set along the walls, and mirrors at every angle where one might examine and repair oneself.

When Miss Salter handed her coat to an attendant, I saw that she wore a very plain wool dress. Her only concession to the formality of the occasion was a necklace of small garnets in a black setting that lay within the collar of her frock. She was one of those persons one sees very rarely; her figure was awkward and angular, yet her every gesture was naturally graceful. She had a countrywoman's look about the eyes, as if she were gazing into the distance against a strong wind.

When she turned that gaze on me, I wanted to draw my dark coat around me instead of taking it off. To be dressed as I was, even at the whim of my employer, was an impertinence. And what this plain woman with her severe look might say I did not know.

She said nothing at all, and while she gave me and my dress a penetrating look, it was not Mrs. Sampson's sort of appraisal. If she knew the game that Betty and I were playing at, she gave no sign. She said only, "My brother and I don't stay on late, for we always keep farmers' hours. Will it suit you to leave early?"

I told her it would suit me very well. I expected the evening to be over for me before it had quite begun. But in that I was quite wrong.

———

My heart leaped when I saw the size of the ballroom and the confusion of people. The place was ablaze with light, for in those days people saw no advantage in dancing in utter darkness. The great thing was to see and to be seen. High along the walls were festoons of evergreen and magnolia leaves, and great paper chains hung in garlands from one chandelier to another. I had never seen anything remotely like it, though I thought of the engravings in my books at school that depicted the great Christmastide parties of Charles Dickens's time.

Miss Salter had gone directly to a gilt chair set among the potted palms. She clearly meant to sit there, observing the scene, until the supper was announced. But I feared that if I joined her, as I very much wanted to do, Hubert Sampson would never find me.

Suddenly he was at my elbow, breathless. In his long, mournful face a damp ruddiness warred with a natural sallowness. He was by way of being the best-dressed man in the room, in black evening clothes with a boiled shirtfront below a tight collar that reached nearly to his ears. "Oh, I say, Miss Cooke!" he gasped and bowed deeply.

His freezing hand cupped my elbow, and I was deluged by a storm of compliments. I had no difficulty persuading him that I did not care to dance. Even as he asked me if I "wished to essay a waltz," he glanced uncertainly down at his own feet. I knew it would be a kindness to us both to stand to one side as observers. Nor was I eager to leave our post near the doors to the room where Betty was soon to enter.

Mr. Sampson never flagged in his compliments on my appearance, and I never ceased blushing. At the end of five minutes' time I was certain that an hour had passed and that Sir Timothy's Lanchester had fetched up in a ditch along the way.

But suddenly, just as the orchestra had finished a set of waltzes, an arresting couple stepped into the ballroom. Betty had arrived, and she was clinging to John Thorne's arm. It had not occurred to me that he would see her into the ballroom, nor that he would be dressed for the occasion in a dark suit and high collar. I could scarcely tear my eyes away from his blond and unsubdued hair and the set of his chin to observe Betty, who was, after all, meant to be the chief ornament of the evening.

She stood hardly higher than the elbow to which she clung. But her hair added inches to her stature. It was elaborately dressed and clearly by her own hand. To give it color, a pink bandeau was wrapped around her brow in the manner of a tiara. On her, Miss Amanda's pink silk gown was an almost alarming fit. Somehow or other, Granny Thorne had been persuaded to lower the neckline nearly to the point of no return. Betty looked a delicious version of herself.

Mr. Sampson had been gripping my elbow to give emphasis to his steady flow of conversation. At once his grasp weakened, and his hand fell away completely. As the two newcomers paused in the doorway, I was perhaps the only person in the room who spared a look at John Thorne. The rest were riveted by Betty. There was a ripple of awe and disapproval from the women. A somewhat deeper collective sigh issued from the men.

Mr. Sampson breathed, "Could that be—Miss Prowse?" The world seemed turned on its ear that night, and the room was filling fast with real-life Cinderellas. Mr. Sampson was overcome.

Of the four of us, only he was confused. In a sort of elaborate dance step, we were all in a knot and then paired off differently. Betty was beside Mr. Sampson, leading him onto the ballroom floor before he quite knew where he was. And I was standing beside John Thorne in the shadow of a potted palm. There I waited until Betty and Hubert were swallowed by the crowd, for until Betty was quite out of sight, I sensed that John's eye was one of many firmly fixed on her extraordinary bosom.

The underside of his chin was nicked here and there by a razor, and I never thought to see his strong neck so thoroughly imprisoned in a collar. I grew weak in the knees again and even thankful that his small store of conversation would not break in upon my mood. He nearly moaned with relief when I declined to dance, but we seemed buoyed by the music out onto the terrace. There a good number of couples were all standing in the shadows. Dim forms pressed together in silhouette.

We lingered there, looking out on the quicksilver sea, watching the path the moon made. When I laid my hand on the stone balustrade, I felt the cold through my glove and remembered the clammy stone of the tomb where John and I had rested on hunt day. Again, we were thrust together by unlikely circumstances. I took it all as a sign from heaven.

I forgot that meeting John at the ball was not part of our plan for Betty. Nor did I give a thought to Winifred Salter's determination to return home early. I stood there sheltered from the sea wind by the figure of John Thorne, while his arm slipped around to lock my waist. And then I was in his arms, being kissed with all the roughness of that first dark night. But this time I returned his kisses, forgetting even the corsage of velvet violets at my shoulder crushed against his chest. Everything that had ever happened to me seemed to have been pointing to this moment. If I remembered anything at all, it was the Wisewoman's words when she said that I would die and live again. I only thought this must be the moment she had foreseen.

I cannot—will not—recall the first few words that passed between us. The musicians ceased their dance music, and the other couples straggled from the terrace in to the supper tables, but John and I stayed on. Later, he fetched us cups of cider, while I stood transfixed by the sea and the mingling of salt and verbena that hung in the crystal air.

We left the empty cider cups on the balustrade and walked down into the garden of the hotel, where the wind had trained the shrubs all in one direction. "Not yet," I whispered to him as his rough hands grew eager.

"When?" he whispered, touching the curve of my ear with his lips.

When? I wondered to myself, for I was awash with the sort of passion that must have overcome Betty. I thought in that moment that I understood everything. All the secrets of life seemed to have revealed themselves.

I could recount all the moments in the past days when I had lingered at the kitchen door for a glimpse of John's tall figure striding to the garages. The few words that had passed between us in the errands I had manufactured to take me out of the house for a stolen minute. I had felt alone all my life, and I had thought it natural that I must be in love alone. But John Thorne was pressing me closer and asking when we would be together. That I might be drawing close to being in the same desperate situation as Betty never entered my mind. It must only be marriage, I thought, as millions of girls had thought before me. I was willing to mingle my fate with this stranger more readily than I might have dreamed possible. After all, are not two people always strangers until they are one?

"We'll be married, then," John said abruptly. The gruff sound of his voice became the pounding of the surf below and then the throbbing of my heart. "Married then," as in all the storybook romances. I had read too few of them to be skeptical. We had been freed by love, both of us. Free to be and to do. Not a rough mechanic that no one approved of. Not a servant girl. Not bound by anything or anybody.

But that was a thought I could not indulge in for long. "But will they allow it?" I whispered. "Miss Amanda might not—"

"Miss Amanda will allow it," John said, when I might have expected him merely to sneer at the notion of anyone controlling our fate. That she *willed* it was beyond any thought I might have had.

"You don't know Miss Amanda," I said wisely. And then, though the garden was dark and the nearest Japanese lantern bobbed in the wind far off, I met John's gaze. Or rather he was looking through me with his gray eyes, and I saw in them a message I could not read.

One or the other of us determined that I should return home with the Salters for the sake of appearances. Much as I wanted that evening to last, there was something as insubstantial as a dream about it. I was ready to flee from John's side and from the party lavish beyond my experience. I longed to rush home to my own attic and to pursue my dream in the way I knew best—alone. And so we parted at the doors to the terrace with nothing more said between us.

I made my way through the room that was filling again with music and dancers. A vivid flash of pink silk proclaimed Betty's untiring presence in the middle of the dance floor. She was engaging Hubert for still another set. I wondered in passing where she had learned to dance at all. Perhaps she was learning then, and teaching him.

When I found Winifred Salter, she was just rising from her small gilt chair. She gave me a look that comprehended where I had been, and with whom. But if she disapproved, it did not show in her distant eyes. She nodded once to Mr. Salter when she saw him emerging from the smoking room, and then she and I disappeared into the retiring room. We were a long time finding our cloaks. The spirit of a ladies' retiring room must have overcome both of us, for we were another long time adjusting our motoring veils over our hair. It was a room that invited vanity.

When we came out, Mr. Salter had fallen into conversation with someone just at the mirrored doors to the ballroom. Winifred made straight for his side to remind him of the hour. I noticed that she glimpsed into the ballroom and froze for a moment. She seemed so shaken that I stepped up behind her to follow the direction of her piercing gaze. Perhaps Betty had disgraced herself somehow. The ballroom whirled with colors from a kaleidoscope, brilliant and changing. I felt dizzy from the cider and the scene and my own emotions. But I caught a glimpse of two phantoms. They were there only a moment before they were hidden from view again.

It seemed I had never left the ballroom. And that somehow I had learned to dance and was dancing that very moment with John Thorne. My heart began to hammer almost aloud. It was as if I had stepped outside myself and were looking on. For there I was, in spirit and in flesh, on the dance floor in my new white gown, banded in purple, with the velvet violets blooming on my shoulder.

And I was in John Thorne's arms, and he towered over me, and we were turning in the music of the dance, swirling like autumn leaves. I thought I must be mad. Winifred Salter turned to find me behind her. And there was something so startled in her expression that I thought she must have seen my madness. But no, it wasn't that. She took me by the arm and marched me to the door, as if I were a sheltered child who had just opened the wrong door to see something unspeakably obscene.

I longed to shrug her off and run back to the ballroom. I was certain when the crisp night air hit my face that I was sober and in my senses. I knew I must go back, for it had been John Thorne on the dance floor with—

Winifred Salter felt me slipping from her grasp. We were on the steps of the hotel, and she was nearly in full flight. "Don't let them make a fool of you," she rasped at me. And then we were hurrying down the drive behind George Salter, and the shrieking wind caught at our veils and whipped our coats around our ankles.

Betty did not return from the ball until dawn, by her own admission. She had to be dissuaded from proclaiming this latest shameless act to Mr. Finley himself. She went about her duties all that following day tireless and triumphant, bursting into song at odd moments.

And I went about my duties in the preoccupied state of a young girl who knows already what she is unwilling to admit. My mind hummed with unthinkable thoughts, and I was already exhausted by them before ten o'clock when I took up Miss Amanda's tray.

In her room I found the dress hanging from a corner of her wardrobe door. A white dress banded in purple, with a skirt ample enough for dancing, and a bouquet of velvet violets at the shoulder. It sagged there, its skirts smeared green with grass stains. A dress precisely like my own.

Fourteen

In a week's time, the upper reaches of Whitwell Hall were to stand empty and echoing. But what a week it was, with the trunks yawning open throughout the rooms of Lady Eleanor and Miss Amanda. And such chaos reigning that the annual exodus might have been a sudden and original whim—a "midnight flit," as Betty might have put it. Orderly routine was the first victim. Mr. Finley himself was pressed into fetching and carrying and sitting on trunk lids to close them. The dinner gong was stilled in favor of the tray meals that often went uneaten, served wherever a family member might be perched at the moment. By burrowing into his library, only Sir Timothy escaped the worst of our preparations for London and dined off his tray in comparative tranquillity.

London! From distant thunder, the name of that magical place rumbled increasingly louder in my ears. I was more than vexed with Miss Amanda throughout the week. I thought she had lowered herself to play a silly trick on me. Deigning to appear on the ballroom floor, got up in a dress like mine, on the arm of her own chauffeur might have been amusing enough to her. Or to anyone of her own class observing from a distance. But my newly released feelings for John Thorne had bubbled to the surface, and I felt mocked. It did me no good to reason that Miss Amanda could not know what I felt. I was as cold as I could well be in her presence. But most of my starchiness went unnoticed. She chirped so happily at the prospect of leaving that I thought she had begun to miss Mr. Gregory Forrest and longed to renew their acquaintance. She was even quite companionable with her mother, and they were in and out of each other's chambers like a pair of young girls together.

I was, as I say, a less amiable companion. But Miss Amanda chattered on about the impending journey and cast me the occasional look that seemed to promise me some future reward if only my disposition improved. Though we spent the week in packing, she was wise enough not to bring up the subject of clothing suitable for myself. That might have been a difficult reminder of a pair of duplicate party gowns.

On the morning of our leaving, the family and I were driven by John Thorne and George Salter in the two motorcars to the railway station at Shanklin. The trunks had been sent on ahead, but still, both automobiles were heavy laden with valises. The rest of the staff assembled on the front steps of the Hall, a sign of the ceremonial occasion. Mrs. Buckle and Mrs. Creeth found themselves standing elbow to elbow. Hilda and Hannah formed a great mass together on the bottom step, and Abel followed Mr. Finley's snapping fingers in the securing of the last case to the running board of the Lanchester. Betty stood a distance apart from the others, though she started the general waving of us away with a dusting cloth held aloft. On her face was preserved the satisfied smile that had wreathed it since the night of the ball.

Miss Amanda was not so anxious to mollify me that she allowed me to ride in the Lanchester beside John Thorne. Once she and her mother were settled on its rear seat, she waved me away to the small auto driven by George Salter. Sir Timothy shared the rear seat of this machine with a number of reticules in a welter of lap robes, and he complained of drafts throughout the hour's journey.

At Shanklin, John Thorne transferred the luggage into the goods carriage of the train and rode with it there. The train that took us to Ryde, where we would cross to the mainland by steamer, was a wonderment to me. But when it paused briefly at the Ryde town station and then rumbled right out across the choppy water on an iron bridge as wispy as a cobweb, I was horrified. When it made its last stop, the sea was all around and beneath us, and the Channel ferry loomed high over our heads. I had never seen a ship at such close range before. The gangplank leading up to its only deck looked perilous in the extreme.

But we were soon aboard, and I bustled about, settling Lady Eleanor and Miss Amanda in the enclosed saloon section. Long upholstered seats ran the width of the ship with an aisle at either side, rather like a seaworthy church. I prayed that I would be as seaworthy myself. Though I felt queasy and miserable when John Thorne was ready to leave us.

He had settled the baggage in a heap that we should be able to find when we got to Portsmouth Pier. Then he just touched his cap to Lady Eleanor and mentioned that a small dressing case of Miss Amanda's was missing. With a nod to me, he walked back toward the gangplank against the tide of passengers still coming aboard, and I followed him. The dressing case was just where he had left it behind, to offer us an excuse to say our good-byes. When we were out of sight of the family, he caught me in his arms and kissed me full on the mouth. In the next moment, he had placed Miss Amanda's case in my hand and was striding down the gangplank without a backward look. I wondered how I would endure a month away from him. And I wondered what, precisely, I had to look forward to when we would be reunited. A bolder girl would have asked him. A brazen one would have told him. How much I wondered then, and to so little purpose! For plans I could not have guessed at were moving well above my head like clockwork.

When I returned to Miss Amanda across the lurching deck, she showed no particular relief at sight of her straying dressing case.

Ryde, the town that had once seemed to me the largest city in creation, fell away at once. We were never out of sight of land, for Portsmouth, truly a city, lay already on the eastern horizon. I would have liked to watch our approach with the deck passengers who stood in the open and ate their fish-and-chip lunches from papers with frozen blue fingers. But my time was consumed in handing around the contents of a picnic hamper to the three Whitwells and fetching them steaming mugs of tea from a little counter in the saloon. Before I knew it, the ferryboat was nudging Portsmouth pier, and I was folding the traveling rugs once again. We were on the mainland—that other, larger England I had never thought to see.

I smile to think of it now. But when the train from Portsmouth drew into Waterloo Station, I thought the great iron-and-glass roof of the terminus covered all London. Though a light rain had fallen on the train through most of the journey, we stepped out on perfectly dry pavements. It seemed ingenious that the city fathers had completely enclosed the Heart of Empire. Motorized taxicabs drew into the station on a roadway of their own. There were curbs and walks, shops, restaurants, even a hotel, and their signs gleamed in the day-long twilight of the vast, smoky station.

But once the four of us were in a taxi, we rolled out of Waterloo. Then awesome London stretched along endless streets, at the mercy of the elements. Miss Amanda and I sat together in a seat facing Lady Eleanor and Sir Timothy. I scarcely dared glance from the window at all the traffic: The brewers' horses rolling their wild eyes just at the level of my own. The snorting motors and the cursing draymen. The policemen braving death at every crossing, and the flower women darting out to sell nosegays to the occupants of limousines that crawled as slowly as the oldest horse.

Lady Eleanor's glance fell on me again and again. I was aware of it without meeting her gaze. It was the first time I had been gathered into such a tight grouping with all the family. I knew she was remarking to herself how much I resembled Miss Amanda. And so I suffered both from self-consciousness and the terror that we might all be crushed to death in a sudden converging of the traffic on either side. Frozen as I was, Miss Amanda must have thought me still rigid with disapproval of her. I had managed to maintain most of my show of injured dignity through all the novelty of our journey.

"Oh, do look, Miranda," she said, pointing past me to an omnibus with passengers riding inside it and on top. "Just see! There's one of Father's signs!"

And indeed there were advertisements all along the front and sides of the omnibus: TAKE A CUP OF WHITWELL'S TEA: MORNING NOON AND NIGHT. Before that moment I had not clearly realized that the source of the Whitwells' great wealth was measured out by the quarter pounds and spoonfuls of tea drunk in the million drawing rooms and kitchens of London. I saw that Miss Amanda's reference to vulgar trade was a minor thrust at her mother, who straightaway drew down the shade on the window beside her. But mention of the Whitwell tea empire seemed to animate Sir Timothy, who broke into an aimless conversation, chiefly with himself, upon the traffic and London weather.

After an hour's crawling, our cab rounded a great intersection that I found out later to be Piccadilly Circus. Then we were edging down a broad boulevard, and I was finally drawn to the passing panorama.

We approached the Burlington Arcade, which Miss Amanda had often mentioned for the shops within it. Like Waterloo Station, it was covered over with a glass roof, and fine ladies issued out of it, followed by servants burdened with parcels.

We turned into a quieter street, and Miss Amanda, who persisted in instructing me, pointed out that this was the Mayfair section, where the Whitwells' town house stood. By this time Sir Timothy was so lively that he burst into poetry:

> "Dear to my soul art thou, May Fair!
> There greatness breathes her native air:
> Of dinners fix'd at half past eight;
> Of morning lounge, of midnight rout,
> Of debt and dun, of love and gout,
> Of drowsy days, of brilliant nights,
> Of dangerous eyes, of downright frights!"

It was as if an aged and squat teapot had suddenly begun to spout verse. The effect sent both the ladies into a sudden gale of laughter that I could hardly keep from joining.

But the taxicab was drawing to the curb just past a cornerhouse pub with a curious name: "I Am the Only Running Footman." A few doors beyond, the cab stopped, and we had arrived at the Charles Street house where the Whitwells were at home in London. I thought it strange to call it a house at all, for it seemed only windows and a door cut into a long wall with many other windows and doors running to a distant corner. Flights of identical steps interrupted a long iron fence not three feet from the basement windows. This much was as I had always heard: that Londoners lived on top of one another. I wondered how they managed to draw breath.

If I had ever stopped at a hotel, I would have been struck by how much the Charles Street house resembled one. It was furnished fashionably, of course, in a style called Queen Anne. This muddled me considerably, for I knew that Queen Anne had been dead almost two hundred years, and all the furniture was quite new. But there was little that was homelike about the house. All the bedrooms were identical, even to the reading lamps. Even Lady Eleanor's own bedroom reflected none of her taste. And the house being very deep, there were whole rooms at the center of it without windows. There the electric lamps blazed even at midday.

But once I had sampled the brisk routine of life in town, I hardly wondered at the impersonality of Charles Street. Here, when there were not guests, everyone was always out. Even Sir Timothy had transferred himself to his club before the end of the first day.

Not that we were short of gentlemen. They called every afternoon between four and six. There was an anonymous old man who sometimes answered the door. But he was often enough in the depths of the house wrapped in an overall apron and polishing the silver, or drinking strong tea with the deaf cook. And so I was allowed the privilege of letting in the visitors or turning them away. There was an etiquette governing "calls." I was not to relieve a gentleman of his hat or his stick. He was to carry these with him into the drawing room. There he had to leave them on the floor at his feet while he took his tea. This signified that he did not take the liberty of presuming himself a closer family friend than he was. It was also meant to protect the reputation of the hostess somehow. But this nicety remained a mystery to me. It was a custom I never grew used to. I always feared I would tread on a hat or stumble over a stick when I approached with a heavy-laden tea tray.

But the most notable thing about "calls" was that the gentlemen came to see Lady Eleanor, not Miss Amanda. Of course, they were of all ages, and some might have hoped for a glimpse of the daughter while they lingered with the mother. But their compliments to Lady Eleanor seemed to show that they were all half in love with her. Five or six seemed more than half. But perhaps this was only the way men in London talked. Some of them even blushed, a thing I thought men could not do.

Even when we arrived, the house was fragrant with flowers sent by Mr. Gregory Forrest. And he was soon calling as often, I think, as Miss Amanda allowed. And I never approached the front hall to admit a caller without hoping it would be Mr. Forrest. Whether I was betrothed to John Thorne or not, the thought of Mr. Forrest lightened my step. I was absurdly pleased that he remembered my name. But he was always looking past me up the stairway, for Lady Eleanor granted him the privilege of seeing Miss Amanda in her upstairs sitting room. The mother was willing to permit anything to encourage her daughter's courtship.

If the house seemed a hotel, the servants were even stranger. At Whitwell Hall the staff had been more like a quarrelsome family led by a stern father than anything else. In town, without a Mr. Finley for figurehead, they appeared to go their separate ways, and most of them were let go when the family was in the country. As often as not, servants' hall and the kitchens were silent when I chanced to be in them. Only a very elderly cook held forth down there, and she was stone deaf, or pretended to be. Her only regular help was a whey-faced scullery maid who slept most nights in a hole behind the stillroom, a place where the walls streamed with damp. I did not know this pathetic creature's name, and she thrust me furtive glances before scuttling away.

The man who valeted Sir Timothy went home at night. The parlor-maids spoke a dialect so shrill and Londonish that I gave up trying to understand them. Betty might have managed better. In the evenings a shift of waiters headed by a caterer or someone of the sort came in to serve. It was still considered smart to have waiters to serve at dinner parties because the late King had insisted upon manservants when he dined at his friends' houses.

In this bewildering establishment so like a railway station, I found my duties less burdensome than in the country. Rarely was I expected to be in two places at once, and this was luxury indeed. Still, I had been warned by Miss Amanda that I would have my hands full in coping with her more complicated London wardrobe, with its unfamiliar, newfangled sophistications. We were two days getting all her clothes out of the trunks and in a proper state. Miss Amanda used this as an excuse not to see Mr. Forrest on the first evening. But when her mother noticed, Lady Eleanor herself invited him to dinner on the second. And she told her daughter in my hearing that arranging a wardrobe was no excuse for slacking hospitality. And that Amanda would receive Mr. Forrest even if she had to be wrapped in a horse blanket. I nearly choked when I heard that, but there was no hint of humor in Lady Eleanor's voice.

The housekeeper at Charles Street was the only retainer who lived in when the family was not in residence. She was so unlike any idea I had of an upper servant that I could hardly credit her as a servant at all. She was very efficient, or she would not have kept her situation. She oversaw the ebb and flow of maids with great skill and maintained a quiet authority over the menservants as well. She even managed to communicate with the deaf cook by means of a slate and a bit of chalk. It was her manner that confused me, for she lacked the fussy propriety of a Mrs. Buckle. And I could not really imagine a household staff with a woman in what amounted to Mr. Finley's role at the head of it.

If she reminded me of anyone, it was the manageress of the only pub in the little village of Whitely Bank, where I was born. The housekeeper had the independent air of a woman running her own business. She always inclined her head to her betters, but she never bowed.

Her name was Mrs. McCall, and though she may have been married to a Scotsman at one time, she was a Londoner through and through, with the Londoner's look that seems to know all. She had a fine figure, always encased in good corsetry beneath a black dress, again like a woman who presides over a saloon bar. And her hair was flame-red, unlikely for a woman of fifty. Its unnatural color reminded me again of Mr. Finley and of my first night in service when Miss Amanda had told me that the butler dyed his hair.

In the first days, Mrs. McCall had few words for me, and on all but one occasion they were civil. She showed me to my room herself, which was at the back and the top of the house, but twice the size of my attic at Whitwell Hall. It was approached not from the corridor but through a sewing room admirably fitted up, where I was to spend a good part of my days. There was no hearth, but a curious electrical contrivance heated the flatirons. I had a sink with a water tap and waste pipe, though the hot water for any hand washing I did there had to be brought up from the kitchen, four floors below. Withal, a sewing room to myself with every convenience was as good as a sitting room to me, for good working conditions halve the work.

Though I saw little of Mrs. McCall in the usual way, something took place in that first late afternoon that hung oddly in the air. When we had been all over the flatiron-heating contrivance and the warming cupboards and all the other features of the sewing room, I glanced out the single window and far down to an unexpected sight.

There was no garden or lawn behind the house, only a foreshortened yard of cement, swept clean and enclosed by brick walls studded at the tops with broken glass. But beyond lay what seemed an entire country village lining one side of a narrow street. All the cottages had run together in a mass. They were the coach houses for the town houses in front of them, of course. But from that angle the two-story buildings, each with an iron flight of stairs leading up over the barn doors to the former grooms' and coachmen's quarters above, looked like a village of cuckoo clocks. I thought at once how odd London was. Everything was either larger than life or, like this tiny hidden street, smaller. One was dwarfed and cramped by turns.

"What is this street just below?" I asked Mrs. McCall.

"Not a street at all, *reelly,*" she replied, stepping up behind me. "It's a mews—Hay Mews, it's called. It gives onto Chesterfield Street on the west and angles round to Charles Street just at the pub to the east."

As Mrs. McCall spoke, a figure appeared out of the door of the coach house directly below. He stood for a moment at the top of the steep flight of stairs that led down to the cobblestones of the mews. But after a wet day it was a fine evening, and he lingered there almost as if one could enjoy a sunset in the canyons of London. I was looking almost directly down on him. At that angle he seemed extraordinarily tall and thin, with a headful of black ringlets that looked nearly like a cap in the gloom. As if my eyes had drawn him, he threw his head back and looked up at the sewing-room window. His face was only an ashy blur, as mine must have seemed to him. But when he perceived that he was watched, he whirled around and lifted a small satchel off the threshold. Then he banged the door shut, turned a key in the lock, and started off down the iron steps. He wore a dark cloak, though not cut like the cape a gentleman wears over evening clothes. I thought melodramatically of a disguise.

He wore no hat, and so he could not have been a gentleman, even presuming that a gentleman would live in rooms over a stable. Still, I watched him, intrigued because he moved in a manner that would not appear hurried. His satchel betrayed him, though. It caught in the stairway railing, and he jerked it loose in awkward haste. His pace quickened as he walked off through the mews until by the corner he was almost in flight. Then he was lost from view as he followed the angle around in the direction of the pub so oddly named "I Am the Only Running Footman."

"And who was that?" I asked.

"*That* was no one at all and nothing to do with you," Mrs. McCall said firmly, and jerked the curtains across the window. Oddly, I thought of Winifred Salter drawing me down the steps of the hotel in Ventnor after my evening had been shattered by an idle glance in the wrong direction.

In those first London days I was very much "Yes, Miss" and "No, Miss" and "I couldn't say, Miss" and little else when I attended Miss Amanda. I dared not be sharp with her, but I was curt. I could not rid myself of the vision of her dancing with John Thorne, nor could I keep from thinking it had been meant to make a fool of me. This hardly got at the problem, for when she had replaced me at the Ventnor Tradesmen's Ball—and in John Thorne's arms—no one could have noticed the quick exchange. Even that gave me a nagging chill, as if a goose had walked over my grave. To possess a double —an alter ego, as the saying goes—sharing the world with you and thus narrowing it is a worrisome thought. But when the double is a mischievous spirit, there is promise of more trouble ahead.

Of course, none of the gentry was at the Ventnor ball, and so none of the party-goers noticed the difference between us. Except for Winifred Salter. Miss Salter was not likely to gossip. She had been incensed at the scene and was quick to assess it in her own way. And a quick mind rarely runs a wagging tongue. But her noticing gave me added pain.

How strange it is to me now that I did not blame John Thorne at once. Servant though he was—and to Miss Amanda—was he not a man? Could not men decide what they would do and what they would not? I had always thought men enjoyed limitless freedom. But John Thorne had not come into my slow-burning anger. I laid all the blame at Miss Amanda's feet, though it only gave me extra trouble.

She would never put up with sulkiness in anyone but herself. Very soon she had devised a subtle, innocent-appearing scheme to rattle me thoroughly and to display her power over me.

I had been promised many an inviting excursion about London with her—to the shops and fitting rooms and milliners. There was even heady talk of stopping for strawberry ices at Gunter's and cups of tea in the small cafés that Miss Amanda said were to be found in South Audley Street. But none of this had yet come to pass. And in truth, I would not have been very amiable company for outings.

It took no genius in her to see that I was terrified of London. The very thought of setting a foot out on Charles Street by myself filled me with fear, and I even dreamed about it.

In the evening of our third day, when the darkness that falls early on London had already descended and the street lamps were long lit, Miss Amanda summoned me to her room. She sat with her back to the door and her face thrust into the triple mirrors of her dressing table. Her eyes never left her own as I stood behind her with my hands clasped before me, an attitude that I had recently taken up.

She let me stand as long as she could and then said, "Miranda, I have decided to keep a sort of journal. Not a diary of engagements. A proper journal in which to record my thoughts. Do you not think this an excellent way to occupy my mind?"

"I couldn't say, Miss."

"I could and do," she replied, arching her eyebrows. "Perhaps I have unexpected literary gifts. Writing will clarify my thoughts, and I shall be able to examine my life. 'The life which is unexamined is not worth living.' Socrates said that, I think."

"Yes, Miss."

"So I have ordered a book of blank pages from Asprey's. It should be quite gorgeous, with silver corners and my name on it in leaf. I expect it to be a work of art in itself as it cost twenty pounds." She occasionally mentioned the prices of things, for that was something her mother would never do. "Run round and collect it for me now. I have had word that it is ready."

I stood there, frozen. I was being ordered out into the night. If she had discharged me outright, I could have felt no more pain. "But, Miss—"

"Yes?"

"But, Miss, surely the shops are closed at this hour." I was grasping at straws.

"This is London, Miranda, not Ventnor. I would not send you out to a shop that had shut for the night. There is little sense in that."

"Yes, Miss."

"Well, be off, or the shops *will* be shut. And be quite firm with them if they try to put you off. I want to begin my journal tonight —tomorrow at the very latest. We are entertaining Mr. Forrest again, it seems, and perhaps I shall want to record some of his better turns of phrase if he makes violent love to me."

"Oh, Miss," I said, annoyed at the desperate tone entering my own voice, "where is this—this place?"

How she must have enjoyed that! "Asprey's? Why, at One Hundred and Sixty-six Bond Street, of course, where it has always been. That will be all, Miranda."

If she had expected to break my spirit, I thought as I went for my coat and hat, she had succeeded. And then I lost ten minutes' time searching the house over for Mrs. McCall, who might tell me where Asprey's and Bond Street were. But she was nowhere about, and I would not burst in on Lady Eleanor. Her voice drifted from behind the drawing-room door, where she was entertaining a last, lingering gentleman left over from tea. I stood before the front door, wishing it would fall from its hinges and crush me to death. And when I finally pulled it open, a sulfurous London fog billowed in. It encircled the street lamp opposite the house in a yellow halo, seeming to drink up the light from the street instead of casting more on it.

I turned left along Charles Street, only because the "I Am the Only Running Footman" pub showed its lights from that direction. But once past it, I was like a sleepwalker. Only pride carried me as far as Berkeley Square and a policeman who was walking ahead of me, running his stick along iron palings as he went. I was emboldened to ask him if I was going right for Bond Street. Though he gave me a very familiar look, he gestured to Bruton Street, which ran out of the square at the opposite side. Then he touched his helmet in salute as I departed. I was well along the path that cuts across the grassy center of the square when I heard the sound of feet pounding heavily behind me. If I had thought for a moment I could outrun them, I would have been across the square like a fox before hounds.

A hand fell on my shoulders, nearly crumpling me. It was the policeman, and he was sorely vexed. I should know that it was not safe for a lady to walk straight across the square, but keep to the crowded pavements around it. Why was I acting like an ignorant country girl?

"Because I *am* an ignorant country girl," I replied with some spirit.

"Then London will gobble you up," the bobby said, looking down at me from eyes hidden by his ridiculous helmet. And the end of it was that he walked me—marched me, in fact—right along Bruton Street and into Bond and never left my side until I stood opposite the windows of Asprey's.

They towered two floors over me, blinding with electric light. And what a profusion of wonders those windows held. Gold cigar boxes, silver urns for champagne bottles, crocodile-skin dressing cases yawning open to reveal the brushes and bottles within, all sunk in nests of suede. And leather-tooled and embossed and braided and sewed by ingenious hands. A king's ransom in the windows, and what could be left inside?

I dreaded entering to find out, and held back to read the gold letters above the door:

C. Asprey & Sons

Dressing Case, Traveling Bag & Writing Case Manufacturers
by special appointment
To H.M. King George V and H.R.H. Queen Mary
Prize Medal for General Excellence, 1862

At last the door was drawn open by a sort of footman, who may have taken me for a lady who was not accustomed to opening doors for herself. I was bowed from one figure to another through the shop, and each employee appeared more august and important than the one before him. Finally I was before a man who I thought must be at least a cabinet member. When I could manage to inform him of my business, he took down a book for my inspection. It was Miss Amanda's journal, buttery leather colored sky-blue, with silver corners and the narrowest line of silver leaf for a border. "Amanda Whitwell" was embossed across the lower portion. And while I gaped at a perfectly blank book that cost twenty pounds, he fluttered its snowy pages and drew my attention to the quality of the vellum. I was quite speechless, but then I suppose that even the most experienced client could not have found fault with such perfection.

"You are in the service of Miss Whitwell?" he asked quite pleasantly. "We are very pleased to make the acquaintance of those who attend our patrons." And then he paused, waiting to hear my name.

"I am Miranda Cooke," I said, summoning up a London tone from somewhere.

"It is a pleasure to know you, Miss Cooke," he said. "We hope to have the honor of continuing to serve the Whitwell household and to welcome you to Asprey's. Although another time we will gladly deliver any item to Charles Street if you will but ring us up or perhaps send round a note." (Ah, if I had known that in advance, I would have saved myself an hour's anguish.) The personage delivered his cordial speech without a hint of condescension. Still, he must have seen through to my countrified heart to know full well how little experienced I was.

When he saw me to the door of the shop and bowed me out, I began to think that a servant in London might well play an exalted role among the lofty tradespeople there. Reflected glory is, after all, better than no glory at all. Perhaps this was why Mrs. McCall was such a commanding figure. What a lot there is to learn about the world, I mused. And then, tucking up the wrapped book under my arm, I set off back along the way I had come. I shan't be afraid of London another time, I thought with bravery. I also imagined that I had removed another weapon from Miss Amanda's arsenal.

Charles Street is nearly the only Mayfair thoroughfare of any length without shops, so it was as dark as a pocket when I found it again. By the time the lights from the pub's colored windows penetrated the fog, I was almost beside its corner entrance. A half-familiar voice raised in anger made me stop suddenly. It was a woman who was standing just out of sight in the entry hall of the pub. She was railing at someone. "How could you *be* such a fool?" she said, almost in a shriek. "I *reelly* don't know how you could take such a risk and be in your right mind. You were told time and again to be out of the mews and well away before the family came up to town. Must I never know a moment's peace and waste my time following you about to keep you decently hidden? I don't know if it's worth going on this way. *Reelly,* I don't."

A man's voice, high and whining, replied, "It's no good carrying on like a fishwife with me, Margaret. There's no harm done, and the odd moment of danger keeps the head clear."

"If you only *had* a clear head!" the woman scolded. "You're thoroughly muddled now, as any fool can see. You're half drunk."

"I am always half drunk, Margaret," the man said, "though I should prefer to put it the other way round. I am always half sober."

"And I am *completely* sober!" the woman barked.

"Which is to mean, I take it, that you have the upper hand. But then, Margaret, you always do. And sobriety does not particularly become you."

"If you must drink in a pub," the woman said, "can't you find another in the thousands in London? You've been drunk in them all."

"I am often lonely," the man said. "I go to a pub—and always the saloon bar, mind you, nothing common—for the companionship of the place. The drink is secondary."

"You've an odd notion of companionship, drink or not."

"Ah, well, my dear Margaret, it takes all kinds. And I am feeling particularly lonely tonight, forced out of my little home in the mews and nowhere to go unless I can light on a kindly stranger."

"You disgust me," the woman said in a lowered voice.

"Then I shall leave you in peace. Ten shillings should see me through until closing time. And then who knows what wondrous adventure awaits?"

I stood there, still listening, now to the crinkling sound of a bank note being passed from one hand to another. "That's a dear," the man said. "I know I can count on you, Margaret, my darling, when others fail. And others so often do."

"Mind you stay clear of here for the rest of the month," the woman said.

"We must live a day at a time, Margaret, mustn't we? I make no longer plans."

And without waiting for a reply, the man stepped from the doorway almost in my path. But he did not see me, for he was looking back into the vestibule of the pub, flashing a ghastly smile to the woman who was standing there. It was the young man with the cap of black curls and the long, strange cloak I had seen on the coach-house stairs. In the next moment he was lost in the fog.

I stepped off briskly myself, not knowing if the woman was still standing in the pub doorway. I hoped she was not and would not see me, for I knew from her voice that it was Mrs. McCall.

Miss Amanda's sending me out to Asprey's began an evening of mysteries and marvels. So pleased with myself was I at having survived the experience that I bore the new journal into her room triumphantly. She looked a bit startled to find me back and delivering the goods in such a short time. But then she gave way to enthusiasm over her new gift to herself. And I permitted myself to join in a bit. "Only think, Miranda, what awful secrets will soon fill these quite virginal pages once I have unleashed my pen. You must never dream of peeking at the contents yourself. Perhaps I should have had it fitted with a lock! Servants do pry." With that she gave me a sly sidelong look meant to be amusing.

"I shall be glad to take it back to Asprey's, Miss Amanda, if you want a lock put on. For, of course, now I know the way perfectly well." I glittered at her, and she had the good humor, at that moment, to glitter back at me with very little malice.

Once I had dressed her for dinner in a lovely gown and her grandmother's pearls, she dismissed me for the night. I had expected to sit up as late as need be to undress her and to see her into bed. But she made a great point of saying she would not need me again and that if I had nothing better to do, I was to finish up some mending. Hours later, I was nodding over my needlework up in the sewing room when a knock came at the door. It was Mrs. McCall in another of her handsome black dresses and her flame hair as neatly dressed as always. It seemed hardly possible that she had been the same woman at the pub whose snarling, quarreling voice I had heard earlier.

"I always like a cup of tea at the end of a long day, don't you?" she asked, as if we had already established a friendship. With that, she carried in a small tray with cups and a brown pot and settled herself in the other chair, pouring out off an ironing board that she made do as a tea table.

Then she sat back, nursing her cup like a lady in a drawing room. She even crossed her legs at the knee, which is not done among servants, nor among real ladies, I might add. It occurred to me that she wouldn't have minded a cigarette, either, but was making some concessions to my primness.

I cannot recall where her conversation began. Perhaps she talked of her husband, a Mr. McCall, who was dead, or perhaps had never lived. I do remember that her talk was sprinkled with references to Lady Eleanor, whom she greatly admired. There was no errand too small to run for her ladyship, she said, though as a rule she held herself above that sort of thing.

Mrs. McCall was by way of being a sort of sham lady herself, and perhaps she held Lady Eleanor up as an example of what she would dearly have loved to be. For all that, she spoke more emphatically of her own independence than of anything else. It only crossed my mind how easily the wicked young man in the black cloak had relieved her of ten shillings.

I was glad enough that she did not see me as her underling. It was well established that I was Miss Amanda's maid, and the housekeeper was as cautious in her comments about Miss Amanda as she was fulsome about her mother. Before we had drained the pot, I thought I had taken the measure of this exotic Mrs. McCall. Fluent though her conversation was, she gave very little away. I found myself telling her of my own background, for it would have been useless to pretend to be more experienced than I was. Naturally I did not tell her how terrified I had been to walk halfway across Mayfair to Asprey's. She would have thought that half-witted. But somehow we got onto the topic of Betty, and Mrs. McCall showed a real interest in both Betty's sad situation and the efforts that had been made to help her snare a sudden husband. "However it ends, she will fare better in the country than in town," was Mrs. McCall's only comment.

Then an awkward pause fell upon our conversation, and words hung unspoken above our heads. Our cups were empty, and I nearly slept where I sat. Still, Mrs. McCall sat on. There was a matter waiting to be aired, and that had been the purpose of her visit. At last she said, "You were out this evening, early?"

I nodded, but she talked on. "I needn't have asked. I knew. You passed the door of the public house just after—"

"Yes," I said, making a clean breast of it, "I heard voices and stopped to listen. I thought one of them was your own."

"And so it was. You saw—the person I was with?"

"I did. It was the same young man of the coach house below. But as you said before, it's nothing to do with me." This did not appear to comfort Mrs. McCall. After all, I was little more than a stranger to her, and she did not know how well I could keep a secret, or if I could keep one at all. And Mrs. McCall seemed to bristle with secrets.

"It would be worth my job if word got out. And much worse than that, *reelly.*"

"Then tell me nothing," I replied.

She considered that for a moment. Indeed she must have considered it before she had come in. "No, that solves nothing. You have no more than arrived, and already you have seen—him twice."

"But you have sent him away, and surely that's an end to it." I thought perhaps the young man was an unofficial tenant of Mrs.

McCall. Someone she let out rooms to in the Whitwells' coach house and then pocketed the rent for herself. That reason did not, somehow, fit all the circumstances, but I did not think beyond it.

"I have sent him away, as you say. But he won't stay away once he finds out who is coming. . . . There! I've said enough." Mrs. McCall was suddenly on her feet and mistress of herself once again. She swept up the tea tray and looked down at me. "I can say no more. But I only ask you this. For the sake of the family, please mention nothing of this—young man to anyone. Believe me, I am not asking for myself. I am thinking of Lady Eleanor."

If this was a performance, it was a convincing one. I was quite sure that the woman towering over me was not trying to save her own skin, nor that the situation was petty. I told her I would not say anything about it, and she was abruptly gone.

And there I sat, bolt awake from the tea and the curious conversation. Restless, rumbling London thundered distantly above the quiet alleys and streets that lay beyond the sewing-room window. Tired as I was, I knew I would not sleep, not even if I recited all the duties I would have to be equal to on the following day.

At that, a sound detached itself from the background of London's night music. Only a whisper at first, though I heard it in the first moment. Then louder: a wheezing rattle. The sound of an engine— a motorcar bumping down the cobblestones of Hay Mews. And not just any motorcar. I knew to a certainty the sound of Sir Timothy's Lanchester, the throbbing clatter of its engine, hardly muted by the breadbox bonnet. But it wasn't possible. The Lanchester and John Thorne were back on the Isle of Wight. We had left the auto at Shanklin, and John at the Ryde pier. They were miles away in a different world.

I was at the window, nevertheless, staring down. And there the Lanchester was, just pulling up and making a sharp turn toward the coach-house doors. An invisible hand set the brake, and a dark figure stepped down from the chauffeur's side. Then the feeble light of the headlamps caught John Thorne as he threw back the garage doors. And I waited for nothing more. I darted from the room and flew down the flights of stairs, my feet not quite keeping pace with my leaping heart.

John was just closing the great doors against the rear of the Lanchester when I crossed the mews and stood silently behind him.

There was no moon that night, only the glow of the city high above the jagged roofs. I stood there until he would discover me. In the next moment he did, turning suddenly. "Amanda," he said quietly.

No, I thought, he could not have said that. I rushed into his arms, to stop his lips with my own. But before I could do that, he whispered, "Miranda," and his arms closed around me.

Fifteen

John led me up the iron stairway to the loft rooms above the garages. And taking me by the hand, he slipped through the door for which he had the key. We stood on the verge of a jet-black room. He knew his way well enough, never stumbling, though my foot grazed the sides of softly rounded furniture as we moved deeper into the darkness. At the far end of the room he reached for the chain of a lamp, and the room sprang to life.

I nearly cried out in amazement when I saw the place where we were. It might well have been nothing but rough boards and the sour smell of the last of the bales of moldering hay left from the days of the horses. Or it might have been a plain barracks room to house a chauffeur. But John and I were standing in some incredible picture-page torn from *The Arabian Nights*.

In its eccentric way the room was furnished far more grandly than the house. Low mounds of furniture, like great piles of pillows, covered in diamond-shaped patterns in orange and brown velvets. A great India brass tray on lacquered legs littered with curios. A dozen lamps, some that hung swaying from the beams and others like Chinese vases. And around the walls, drapings of satin fabric shot through with gold threads that shimmered and rippled like water. And all this evil-looking luxury cast in a pink glow through the gossamer veils thrown over the shaded lights. Something even more unearthly was there: the scent of incense faintly clouding the stuffy air of the place. The only things that seemed of this earth to find their way into this astonishing room were a litter of empty ale bottles lying beneath a hideous table that was carved to look like a dragon, complete to green scales.

"Too much of an opium den about the place to suit my taste," John said, as if this were meant to explain everything.

Perhaps—very likely—it was the taste of the strange young man I had seen twice. I nearly said so, for surely John knew who he was. As I opened my mouth to speak, I remembered my promise to say nothing. The promise I had made not an hour before to Mrs. McCall.

But I longed far more for other answers. Why had John suddenly materialized in London? What did it mean, and, more precisely, what did it mean for the two of us? "John, do explain!" I said suddenly, in just the tone of voice I must have unconsciously adopted from someone else.

He was bending to examine the ale bottles with a preoccupied expression on his face. But when I spoke, he jerked around as if a stranger had spoken. How oddly large and rawboned he looked in that cramped, unearthly place. His head was in danger of being knocked about by the hanging lamps. His well-worn tweeds were going threadbare at the elbows and were bound in cracking leather to save the cuffs. His blond hair was windblown from the drive, and his forehead ruddy and healthy in this decidedly unhealthy place. "What's there to explain?" he said after a moment. "I'm up here for the same reason as you. To serve the family. At the last minute Lady Eleanor and the Duchess took it into their heads that they'd sooner be driven about London than to hire a car here. So they sent off a wire, and here I am. I'm back and forth between London and the Isle at their whims, though I'd sooner never set foot in London the rest of my days. And a proper old muckup's been made of these rooms I'm to stay in." His lip curled at the disorderly gaudiness of the absurd chamber that closed in on both of us. "Great, silly, idle town," John grumbled with a heavier-than-usual country burr in his voice.

The *Duchess,* I thought. Did he say the *Duchess?* Who might that be? He was in no mood to be questioned, I knew. Yet I pressed on and asked him.

"It's only a name I call her—Miss Amanda. The 'Duchess' for all her high-and-mighty ways."

There it was again, the defiant tone in the voice of a man who had the look of a trapped animal in his gray eyes. "You'll never let Miss Amanda hear you calling her that!" I said, truly shocked.

"Oh, not I," John replied, looking away. "I watch my *p*'s and *q*'s around that young lady."

"Ah, but you've not always been so careful," I said boldly, ready at last to unleash accusation.

"And what's that supposed to mean, then?" We stood opposite each other across a Turkish ottoman. It seemed a greater barrier between us than it need be.

"Only that you were quick enough to dance with her at the ball in Ventnor, and very unseemly it was, too."

"You know about that, then, do you?" He ran a heavy hand through his hair. There was the look of a sulky boy blurring his manly face. "I wonder what busybody carried that tale. Not Betty, I'll be bound, for she was taken in herself. It was as good as a play, hearing the comments she flung to Miss Amanda, thinking it was you."

My face burned, and tears started in my eyes to think that Betty had been deceived as well. It was too unfair. When John chanced a look at me, he kicked the ottoman aside and took me in his arms again. "Forget it," he said. "It makes no difference. The Duchess—Miss Amanda was in it with you, anyway. She knew all there was to know about Betty. And she took care that Betty never knew it wasn't you. Betty had other fish to fry that night, in any case, and only flipped a glance or two in our direction."

The talk was running too much to Betty and too far from ourselves to suit me. "I saw you and Miss Amanda on the dance floor with my own eyes, so you needn't worry about busybodies that carry tales. How could you forget your place and dance with a lady? Have you no pride?"

"Not much," John said, showing a rock-hard chin. "Besides, when you went out and she came in, I thought you had come back. She was in my arms before I knew the difference."

"You're a liar, John Thorne. I couldn't have coaxed you onto that dance floor in a million years. It was the young mistress who called that tune, and you danced to it."

"Have it your own way," John said. "When you know more about men than you do now, maybe you'll find out they don't take much to being accused of dancing to a woman's tune—any woman, high or low."

Especially when that's precisely what they're doing, I thought. But fear or prudence kept me from speaking my mind. And I turned away from my own wondering about what other tunes Miss Amanda might call, and what other dances might be dictated. We could not go on quarreling at our reunion while her ghost intruded on our privacy, as it always seemed to do.

Moreover, it was beyond me to hurl hard words at a man whose hands were cradling my elbows, a man with strength in reserve either to crush me in anger or in desire. I felt suspended between the two.

John was right enough when he challenged my small store of knowledge about the way men's minds work. I knew too little to dissemble. Nor had I ever known envy of another woman before. And so I had not even tried to mask my feelings. But I did know that if a green-eyed display of jealousy might intimidate or flatter another kind of man, it would be worse than useless with John. I took another tack, stretching my meager knowledge of the masculine mind in another direction. "If I know so little of men, how am I to learn more if not from you?" I asked. To follow this pale scrap of coquetry with a saucy, bold look was beyond my capabilities. But I had no need for more artfulness. My hastily chosen words had an immediate effect. John Thorne's arms gathered me nearer, and we had seemed to skirt a small lovers' quarrel. I had no premonition of a greater crisis ahead.

It was not long before we were lying amid the scattered pillows of his peculiar quarters. His hands moved over my body in their assured way, and the blood sang in my ears.

"My dearest . . ." he whispered hoarsely. But though I waited for more words of endearment, and perhaps more promises for a future I could not envision without his help, he said nothing more. He was never a man easy with words, whether they be arguments or compliments or whispers of devotion. His hands spoke for him, and my whole body heard and answered in its way.

As I felt the length of him, like a fallen tree, pressing me down and down, I banished the vision I had of us there. A view of a chauffeur and a maid writhing in the early moments of passion on the floor of a servants' loft, stealing moments together and robbing each other of any dignity in them. I drifted on until the notion of dignity had nearly vanished as I felt his mouth at my neck, sending electric charges through me. And then his lips moved down beneath the collar of my dress, and his tongue explored the hollow at my throat.

I drifted nearly a moment too long, my mind withdrawn to his once-murmured mention of marriage, not quite a proposal or a promise. For marriage was the safe haven in all the stormy seas of life.

But I could pretend no longer that this alien floor was our marriage bed. I summoned what was left of my resistance and braced my trembling hands against the vast, muscular shoulders that hovered over me, shadowing my face from the dim, pinkish lamplight and casting me into a darkness of desire and confusion and the need growing more terrible and intense to be loved.

If I was to be married, I meant to stand before the altar of a church an honest woman, neither shamed nor desperate. Perhaps a sudden sharp thought of Betty gave me the strength to control my own body. I went rigid just as I began to move completely in the rhythms of the man whose knee pressed insistently between my legs.

"No, John, wait," I said, not choosing my words. "We mustn't. What if—what if *he* comes back suddenly and finds us like this?"

There! I'd blurted it out, for all my promise made so easily to Mrs. McCall.

"What if who comes back?" he said, groaning a little as if the passion he felt were giving him pain. Then, in the next moment, his body grew as taut as mine, as if time had suddenly stood still, freezing us only half together and quenching our passion. We both seemed to catch our breath, and the room waited.

I lay silently in the curve of his arm, my forehead prickling with damp. The muscles in John's arm encircling me changed from solid to rigid. One of his hands closed around my wrist, and the other cupped my chin. I was forced to look into his shadowed eyes. "What if who comes back?" he asked again, evenly, and his closed hand wrung my wrist just enough to send a message of pain along my arm.

"I don't know," I said. But I knew enough not to try to move, for I was lying in a vise.

"I think you do. Somehow you know," John said, darting a glance at the outside door as if it might suddenly open. Without looking at me, he said a third time, "What if who comes back?"

"The young man," I whispered, frightened now. "I don't know who he is."

Again my wrist twitched, and hot pain branched up my arm.

"I—I only saw him coming out of here, carrying a valise, that's all."

"All?" John echoed. "I wonder if you aren't learning well your young mistress's devious ways. You saw a young man coming out of this place and never again?"

I must have hesitated a second too long. John's hand slipped down from my chin to lie easily, heavily, on my throat. My mind went blank for a second, and a portrait of Bart Throne replaced the face of his real-life son so near to my own.

"Once more," I whispered, "just this evening as I was coming back from Bond Street. I was passing the pub at the corner, and the young man was there, outside. He was arguing with someone." My throat was bone-dry, but I dared not swallow.

"Someone?" John asked, pretending patience.

"It was Mrs. McCall. She's the—"

"I know who Margaret McCall is."

I lay quiet then, hoping I had told enough, and knowing that I'd told too much. But John was not finished with me. "And what were they arguing about?"

"Money," I said. "He wanted ten shillings from her."

"And got it, of course," John said.

"Yes."

"He would. And did she call him by name?"

"No." Suddenly, I was released. John drew away and stood towering over me. But I might not have been there at all. He balled a fist close to his own chin and whispered hoarsely, "The bastard. The sniveling, bloody little bastard." Then he paced the floor, kicking at the ottomans, which sent up clouds of dark London dust in the unwholesome place.

And I lay where he'd left me, forgotten, wondering how many lives John Thorne was a part of and what mysterious roles he played in them. I shall never marry him, I thought. I am nothing to him. I cannot see into his world, and he sees nothing of value in mine. When I struggled to my feet at last and my wrinkled skirts fell into place, he was standing with his back to the room, staring into the cold hearth. His heavy country boot nudged at the fire irons, and his fist gripped the flimsy mantel. I wondered how this remote, pitiless man, so quick to hurt me casually, could have inspired passion in me. I walked to the door, free from the hold he had so quickly had upon me.

But I did not reach it before I heard his voice. "Say nothing about this."

"There is nothing to say," I replied. He might break me in all the ways a man can break a woman. He might cross-examine me like his prisoner and silence me like a child. But there was a small spark of spirit within me that I was learning to nurture. Only a spark that had always been there, glowing brighter now for all the shadows that shrouded it in this unfamiliar place, among all these shadowy figures.

John Thorne must have perceived the spark that struck a little dim fire in my short answer. He said in a voice almost too low to carry across the room, "It is better to say nothing because of the family."

It was so nearly an echo of what Mrs. McCall had said that I wondered at this new connection—between her and John. But I was weary of mysteries. I had known few enough moments of tentative ecstasy, and they lay buried now beneath the weight of dark figures —and probably dark deeds—that I was expected to be blind to.

The night air struck my face, and the mist-laden breeze swirled my skirts as I made my way down the stairs to the cobblestones. I fled across the mews and up to my rooms near the top of the house and fell onto my bed. The early-morning sounds of the knife-grinder and the rag-and-bone man, and the first of the barrow boys clattered distantly out of Queen Street to signal a new day.

I looked for escape in sleep. Instead, I could hear Margaret McCall's voice merging with John's and then parting from it again. The sharp knife edge of her London speech blending in an odd duet with John's husky growl. I heard her again as I had overhead her outside the pub. "You disgust me," she'd said to the unknown young man. And, "You were told time and again to be out of the mews and well away before the family came up to town."

The family. The entire dim universe turned on them. How many dark plots must be concealed in their name?

If I hadn't been warned to forget the young man, I might well have done just that. The comings and goings and dealings of millions of Londoners were meaningless to me in any case. But I found myself conjuring up the man from the mews. And the more I concentrated, the greater the hold over my thoughts he had. The furl of his cloak as he swung a satchel down the stairs of the coach house—a house he so clearly thought was his home. The moment—strangely sad— when he stood looking up at the blank windows of the family's house. His blurred, whining voice outside the pub, blending insolence with a simper. The tight black curls on his skull and the weakness of his red mouth. Before I drifted to sleep in the dawn, I was convinced that I had known the young man all along. Long enough, at least, to fear him, and to pity him.

In the days after that, I was to lose myself in the work and the novelty of the Little Season. London would never be an easy place for me. But the distractions of that November touched even my life, for all my hurried days and preoccupied mind. Whether I was or was not betrothed to John Thorne—whether or not the thin cord that might have bound us had snapped at our last parting—all this quandary became for whole hours at a time less important than my duties in the routine of a house that teemed with activity.

How Mrs. McCall managed to keep any sort of order in the rackety Charles Street establishment was a minor miracle. The doorbell sounded every quarter-hour or oftener from mid-afternoon on. The anonymous man, who was neither butler nor footman, and I alternated in the announcing of callers, who sometimes filled Lady Eleanor's drawing room beyond its capacity. The floors were a minefield of cast-down gentlemen's hats and walking sticks. On the mews side, the scullery and cellar doors fanned all day long before a rushing stream of tradesmen. Whole young gardens of off-season flowers continued to come from the florist, bearing Mr. Gregory Forrest's name.

As these arrived, I arranged them myself in vases and planted the cards among the stem tops where Miss Amanda could not miss seeing them. Then I placed these tributes nearest the mirror on her dressing table, where she was most likely to take notice of them. It seemed noteworthy to me that she flung neither flowers nor cards out. Mr. Forrest, I fancied, was gaining ground with her. His afternoon visits lengthened, and within days Miss Amanda was making less of a show of being otherwise engaged for evening parties.

She might have wished for a sunnier servant than I, but she could not have hoped for a more efficient one. I found myself on duty nearly around the clock, for in London the engagements overlapped. And there seemed a quite different costume for nearly every hour of the day and night.

I would not have believed how thoroughly Miss Amanda allowed herself to be caught up in the whirl of town. She had put aside her country sulks. And she was often enough so exhausted by dinners, balls, receptions, theater parties, and late suppers that she fell into bed at half-past one in the morning. I found it easier to sit up for her than to go searching all over the upper house the next day for her clothing and jewelry when she was left unattended. Indeed, many a night I undressed her while she sat like a collapsing doll on the edge of her bed and was fast asleep before her head hit the pillow. As we were in London and not on the Isle, she did not depend on me for company. And so she seemed indifferent to my frame of mind.

But she was not wholly changed. I still felt her appraising eye on me at odd moments. There were late evenings when I knew she was less tired than she seemed. For I had come to believe I could nearly hear her thinking. Though I was still a long way from following the trend of her thoughts to their goals.

One morning she startled me by being bolt-awake and in her morning robe when I brought her early-morning tea. As a rule the cup went cold before she could be coaxed to bestir herself short of ten-thirty. She turned her full attention on me before I could collect myself.

"Mr. Forrest is taking me to the ballet tonight, Miranda," she said, busy with her own reflection in the vanity mirror, "and I shall want you to dress me with particular care on this occasion. What do you think would do?"

"I don't know, I'm sure, Miss Amanda. Is the ballet like the opera?"

"Near enough," she said, and the image of her violet eyes shifted in the looking glass to me. "You have never been to the ballet, of course?"

"No, Miss. Nor inside a theater. Would the wine satin do, with a string of pearls? Mr. Forrest has not seen that gown."

"Yes, I should think that would do—with Mother's sable-trimmed cloak, the brocaded one that grasps at one's ankles. But I am not dressing to meet Mr. Forrest's approval. I am more interested in suiting you, Miranda."

"Me, Miss Amanda?"

A little girl's smile played across her lips, and I saw I was to be cajoled and flattered. "Yes, I want to make it quite clear in advance precisely what I am wearing to the ballet tonight, for you will be going as well. And you're not to think I have any devious plan afoot to impersonate you. I refer to the Ventnor Tradesmen's Ball, a prank that I seem never to end paying for." She dropped a hairbrush on the glazed tabletop and gestured in the air as if to wave away imaginary cobwebs threatening to entangle her.

"I'm to go to the ballet as well, Miss Amanda?"

"Yes. You will be sitting in the gallery, and so what you wear need concern neither of us. This is only a little treat. You have been too much in the house and have seen nothing of London." She contrived to make this circumstance sound as if it were my own fault, but quickly passed on. I listened with care, for once she mentioned that she had no devious plan afoot, I was reasonably sure she did.

"Mr. Forrest and I will be sitting in the stalls. But I am told that you will have a better vantage point up in the gallery. Apparently, this is where the students of the dance sit, and other serious types. Do you know what ballet is?"

"A sort of dance, Miss?"

"Yes. I hardly know more myself. It's quite new to London this year—from Russia. Very soulful, and possibly overdramatic. They are doing, among other numbers, *The Dying Swan* tonight, and Anna Pavlova is dancing it. I have persuaded Gregory to take me, for the talk at all the parties is of dance and Pavlova, and I am tired to death of not being able to offer an original opinion."

She was on the point of dismissing me to go for her breakfast, a moment I always tried to anticipate. As I began to withdraw without being told to do so, Miss Amanda said in a very airy tone, "And you need not worry about attending the ballet unaccompanied. John Thorne will take you. I have a ticket for him as well and have engaged him on your behalf."

I descended to the kitchens of the deaf cook with my mind anywhere but on my work. The ballet meant little or nothing to me. But I was in deep thought about Miss Amanda's timely plan for John to take me there. It would have required a far more sympathetic mind than hers to perceive unaided that a coolness had fallen between John and me. I had not gone about my duties with "a face like a wet week," to quote Miss Amanda herself. And even if I had been obviously languishing, she would not have noticed. I was all but certain she knew that John and I had not gone near one another since the night he arrived. But how could she have known this with such certainty?

No mention had ever been made of our courting. And I had not dreamed of confiding in her or in anyone else that John had mentioned marriage to me at the Ventnor ball. She seemed never to consider that I should have a life of my own. And I had nearly forgotten the day of the fox hunt, when it seemed likely that she had thrown John and me together. How slow I was to see her plan unfolding!

But in London, that labyrinth of intrigue and crooked passageways, I began to suspect—perhaps I began to know—that Miss Amanda heard things that only John could have told her. Had I not seen her in his arms once in the ballroom at Ventnor? Did this not narrow the distance between them? But I resisted knowing why it would suit her purposes to smooth things between us. To be laughed at by her for loving anyone seemed a far easier thing to imagine.

But there was no more talk on any subject that morning. When I returned with her breakfast, she lay in a chaise with a pink swansdown throw across her knees. And she was deep into *Three Weeks,* a novel by Elinor Glyn that her mother had expressly asked her not to read.

That evening when I had dressed Miss Amanda in her wine satin, I had little enough time to ready myself for my first evening at the theater. At that, I lingered over her longer than I needed, for she had never looked so lovely before. London that season was undergoing a great change in matters of fashion. The strange and foreign-looking details of frocks and gowns and fitted coats and hats had some connection I could not quite fathom with the arrival of Diaghilev's Russian ballet. These madmen and madwomen had descended upon London from their remote, icebound homeland in a sort of Russian invasion. And with them they brought all manner of outlandish and Oriental trappings that began to be copied by all the dressmakers and milliners in the kingdom. Skirts were cut and gathered like vast pantaloons, fixed at the waist by wide sashes in barbaric colors. And brimless hats called turbans rose straight up from the forehead, boldly and unveiled. And the egret feathers that rose straight up in previous seasons gave way to peacock plumes dyed a spidery black that swept both up and down.

Evening gowns were festooned with silken cords that ended in tassels, as if the curtains of some Eastern palace had been jerked quickly down and swagged around the female body, revealing and concealing in unexpected ways. Even the toes of slippers peeping more boldly from beneath hemlines that year were curled just enough to suggest the footgear of *The Arabian Nights.*

Lady Eleanor, whose wardrobe did not bow to every passing breeze of fashion, made a concession nonetheless. The impersonal drawing room and morning room in Charles Street suddenly bloomed with new silk lampshades that recalled the onion-bulb domes of Russian churches.

Miss Amanda's wine satin evening gown reflected the season without drawing attention away from its wearer. It had been made and then remade with Russians in mind. The skirt was gathered at the hem, and the train first planned had been taken up. Broad bands of gold outlined the low neck. And Miss Amanda's black hair was drawn back and up into a luxuriant twist that looked nearly lacquered. Looping strands were allowed to escape as if by chance and stray down to curl at her cheekbones. She and I had even dared to experiment with a touch of mascara, which drew her downy eyebrows into darker, more definite arching lines with more than a hint of boldness about them. This bit of black art erased even the small scar across her eyebrow left from her long-ago tumble from a horse.

We'd rummaged together through her jewel case, a product, like her new journal, from Asprey's in Bond Street. It stood with pale pigskin lid yawning open while we selected first one and then another of the pieces that might be set to advantage in her hair. At last we settled on a diamond cluster in a Regency setting fixed to a long silver hairpin. It rested on the crown of her head like a gleaming miniature tiara.

She carried a Chinese fan of gilt rice paper. And when I set her mother's evening cloak about her shoulders, she was encased in cloth-of-gold as thin as tissue, with the sable trim glistening as darkly and richly as her hair.

Both of us basked in the vision in her mirror. Standing behind this almost Oriental princess, I looked like nothing but what I was, a maidservant and English to the core. If our voices had not rung in the same pitch, no one would have confused us. But we were silenced in the presence of the magnificence of one of us. Then we burst into laughter together at the pleasure of this isolated moment.

A half hour later, after I had seen Miss Amanda make her descent down the stairs to where Mr. Forrest waited for her, I met John

Thorne in the mews. He lingered on the black cobblestones, smoking a cigarette. The smoke from it bit through the heavy London night air, and I knew it must have come from a little carved box set with opals in the strange coach-house room. I could not imagine John Thorne buying a packet of black-paper cigarettes. Following its orange glow, I never looked up at the rooms over the garages where we had last met. If I had decided how I should act, I cannot recall now. I was growing ever more easy in playing a part that had been written for me by other hands.

He flipped the cigarette away when he saw me, and it fell in a bright arc among the stones. My wrist quivered where he'd wrung it at our last meeting. But this time his hands found mine and held them lightly for a moment, inviting me to draw back if I would. I felt his warmth through my thin gloves. Then I was in his arms, and his calloused, enormous hands spanned my waist and then pulled me to him. He kissed me with a gentle insistence until I turned away to catch my breath. But only for a moment.

Our arms entwined, and after a time we walked away. The slick stones made our feet in town shoes uncertain. I hoped we were moving silently and that the darkness of the deserted mews hid us from prying eyes, though in London I could never be sure of that.

As we turned into Charles Street, the lamps revealed John in a greatcoat that threatened to split at the seams pulling over his shoulders. His chin was square and resolute above the high white collar I had seen him wear only once before, at the Ventnor ball.

In the public street I tried to pull away, but he only gathered me nearer, gently still, for he was certain of me once again. Midway along the little length of Queen Street, he drew me into a shop door and kissed me again. His tongue played round my lips until they opened, and we were wrapped in each other until I grew faint and forgetful. A sharp wind promising winter sent pages from a castaway newspaper scudding up the street past our doorway. But I was far away from great, dismal, dirty London. I pressed my hot face deeply into John Thorne's lapels and savored his stern silence and the strength of his body. I was not, after all, likely to be proof against the force of his animal passion much longer. He had awakened the woman in me. And whether or not he felt the obligation in this was not important to me in that moment.

Our path to the omnibus that ran along Piccadilly Street lay beyond the maze of small lanes and walks of Shepherd's Market. In all the daylight hours, the market was alive with the barrows of vegetable vendors, crying out the beauty of their cauliflowers and marrows and plump Brussels sprouts. The hundred small shops buried behind this noisy cornucopia fed all the households of Mayfair with the choicest cuts of British beef and lamb and delicacies from every corner of the Empire. By midmorning the scent of fresh-baked bread from a dozen bakeries drifted up as far as Charles Street.

But at night Shepherd's Market was a much different place, though far from deserted. Beneath the pools of lamplight women stood in tense idleness. Cigarettes hung from their black mouths, clenched into nutcracker jaws. And the teetering heels of their broken boots jittered on the paving stones from the cold. I felt their hard eyes on us. Others stood in the gloom of thresholds, and I barely dared glance at them from under the brim of my unfashionable hat. Those who would not stray into lamplight were older and more haggard than the others, like the encrusted, half-shattered birds that picked in the dooryards behind the houses of this ashen city.

My mother had told me of women who sold their bodies. But her stories meant to frighten me into a life of submissive virtue had been too remote. Wickedness and hopelessness had never taken their proper form in her stories. She had known desperation and cruelty without looking beyond herself. But she had never looked as far as this shadowed quarter of London. The forms that never figured in her stories loomed up around us on every side in a dark market of human flesh.

I gripped John's arm tighter, and we were well along the twisting passages before I realized that these women took me for one of their own. They thought me one luckier than they, who'd snared a man this early on a cold night. And by all the arts I did not possess might keep him until dawn. At the darker turnings, some ravaged crone alerted by John's heavy footfalls would step out directly into his path. Then, catching sight of me, she would withdraw again, muttering words I tried not to hear.

Only when we reached the narrow bottle-shaped canyon of Whitehorse Street could I see far ahead the brightly lit bustle of Piccadilly Street and the sway of omnibuses above the quick-paced crowds. I longed to break into a run and to leave this degradation behind us. But I knew John would only laugh. When we stood at last in the little shelter along the broad boulevard, I trembled with more than cold. Though what threat those painted, toothless hags posed to me, I could not think.

On the top of the tall omnibus that staggered along through the traffic, I felt more than a pang of homesickness for Whitwell Hall, where one planted feet on solid floors and in the reassuring earth itself. All London reached for the sky with grasping hands, and I remembered a snatch of schoolroom poetry about "the topless towers of Ilium." We lumbered past the upper floors of buildings that thrust forever up into the dull night glow of the sleepless city. And the omnibus appeared ready at any moment to overbalance in an explosion of twisted metal and flying glass. It swooped down on every corner to gather up queues of more passengers, willing victims of this infernal machine. Looking from above on their hats as the impatient queue swarmed aboard made my stomach turn over. But I was reminded of that first day in a motorcar and managed a smile to banish giddiness in a burst of bravery.

"And what's brought the ghost of a grin out of all your solemness, then?" John asked, quick to notice my smile.

"I was only remembering my first ride in Sir Timothy's automobile on the day of the hunt. And how far I thought I was from the ground that morning."

"Ah, you were bright green with fear, and no mistake," John said, nodding wisely.

"I never showed it!"

"Oh, no," John said, "but you quivered from head to toe. I worried for the Lanchester's upholstery."

"You never did!" I cast my coolest glance down from the omnibus window on the taxicabs and limousine roofs swerving well below us.

"One day I'll have you out in Sir T.'s auto when we're by ourselves. Then I'll show you what life's like at thirty miles an hour."

"Never!" I said.

"Or better yet," John went on, as his arm found its way around my shoulders, "we shall have our own motor one day. Not a Lanchester, perhaps, but a better one than George Salter's heap of tin."

"An automobile of our own?" I said in astonishment. "When I am Miss Amanda, and you're the King of the Belgians!"

"Ah, not so long off as that," he said, after a quick look at me. "One day the motorcars will be thicker on the roads than sheep through a broken fence, and even such as you and I will raise the dust."

While I pondered all the possible meanings of this fanciful talk from such a plain-spoken man, the bus labored around the nighttime magnificence of Piccadilly Circus. There, the million lights of a hundred signs burst like Catherine wheels, imploring the public to buy this soap and that ale. All these urgings burned like the sun, and I goggled again, forever the country girl. As the bus wheezed and lumbered on in a sickening curve, the lights glared without pity on the herds of people crowding every curb. Their city faces showed sallow in this unnatural daytime.

Every third one of the women below us reminded me of Betty. And I was brought up sharply, for she had been too far from my thoughts in the past busy days. There were a thousand Bettys there on the Piccadilly pavement. Girls with their tattered coats pinned tight at the neck and gaping open below, who thrust out frost-burned bouquets of twopenny flowers from the baskets on their arms. Shop girls and serving girls on the threadbare arms of their beaux, with faces set grimly in the pursuit of nighttime pleasures. Girls in twos and threes with linked arms and hats trimmed in cast-off finery. Girls whose lips turned back in doleful laughter, revealing their darkened teeth. Girls with Betty's own sallow look of hopeful desperation. Mrs. Creeth had once called Betty a proper little Cockney. Now I saw the meaning behind this. For she had been misplaced among chawbacons in the countryside by some fate that had yet to prove whether it was cruel outright or belatedly kind.

"A penny for them," John said, as I scanned the crowd, almost anxiously.

"I was thinking of Betty again." For all I knew she had played her last card, and it had won her nothing. It seemed more than likely that Hubert Sampson had slipped through the hasty net that she and Miss Amanda and I had tried to cast over him. And surely by now his mother had risen up, all alert to the danger of losing her only son, and losing him to the likes of Betty. I had written no letter to her. I would not have dared commit in writing anything that might be read by eyes other than hers. And I had received no word from her, and abruptly wondered if she could write at all.

"She won't be the only girl left standing," John said, more deeply into my thoughts than I'd supposed.

"It's more than that," I murmured, unwilling to say how much more.

"Because she's got herself in a fix," John said. Of course he knew Betty was pregnant. He knew everything. "Well, she's had her bit of fun. Now comes the day of reckoning."

I struggled to find words to defend Betty against this heartless judgment, so typically masculine and so unfair. But I had little enough experience of answering a man on his own terms. Perhaps my only answer was not to be formed in words at all. I strengthened my small store of resolve never to find myself in Betty's "fix," to be sneered at by the very sex that had put me there.

John listened at the the door of my thoughts for a moment and then said, "I expect Betty led some poor toad or other up the garden path and then a step or two past that."

"Ah, yes," I replied, folding my hands in my lap and giving over as much of the bus seat as I could to John Thorne, "Betty's a wicked girl indeed to let some unsuspecting man ruin her. It's a lesson to us all."

But John was ill-prepared to hear words of such seasoned irony from a servant girl. He cast me another of his sidelong glances to remind me, no doubt, of how quickly he could make me melt in his arms. But I kept myself from returning his gaze and only hoped I was not making myself ridiculous.

The bus swerved again to a stop in a street lined with theaters. John had me by the hand, pulling me down the curving steps at the back of the bus and out on the pavement. We stood nearly under the marquee of the Palace Theatre. The crowd milled around us, blending every sort in a free-for-all, surging toward the various entrances. Limousines and the new, chugging taxicabs drew up to deliver ladies encrusted with jewels, handed down by gentlemen in tall silk hats and white silk mufflers with fringes that the night breeze whipped over their shoulders.

Darting among them were those Miss Amanda had called serious students of the ballet. Young, pinch-faced persons far more thread-bare than John and I nipped around in a pack to the darkened side of the building to scramble up the many flights of thundering stairs to the gallery heights.

I would gladly have loitered under the glowing marquee until the last person entered the lobby. This street scene was more theater than

I had ever experienced, and I caught the first hint of the exciting electricity of London. Always before, even when I had conquered the highly polished interior territory of Asprey's shop, London had been no more than a grimy hazard. But this democratic display of the rich and the poor flocking toward an evening given over entirely to pleasure was a window on a different world. I was at one with the earnest students and the richly garbed ladies. And I was in danger of forgetting myself and the impatient countryman beside me, whose idea of entertainment was clearly not an evening at a theater. But John and I both dawdled there, goggling guardedly at the crowd through rustic eyes.

We lingered long enough for me to sense that he and I were both scanning the throng in search of the same person, the small, shimmering figure of Miss Amanda. I had sent her off much earlier and knew she must be inside the theater by now. But I had become enough of a lady's maid to review the other ladies and compare them to her favor. And I yearned to see her in the crowd for the pleasure of preening myself at dressing her to outshine all others.

But John broke his mood of watchful waiting and soon pulled me away. We jostled along the dim passage at the side of the theater to the gallery entrance. Even in this gangway there was entertainment to beguile the crowd surging past. "Pearlies" stood in straggling groups bellowing out such bawdy songs as "Blow Away the Country Dew." While one of their urchin children, his costume bristling with white buttons sewed in fantastic patterns, held out a limp cap for coppers. There were acrobats in their motley, too, doing sudden backflips along the narrow passage wall, and jugglers, and beggars outright, crouched in their crippled state and wheezing at mouth organs that rasped a countermelody to the Pearlies' roaring songs.

Then we were making the dizzy climb up the stairs to the gallery, where the sixpenny seats were long, rough benches. The hungry-faced Londoners tumbled into this lofty arena and fell over the benches to find a vantage point among their friends.

I staggered when I saw where we were, tucked up under the dome of a room that fell in wedding-cake tiers far below. We were on the level of a great crystal chandelier that exaggerated the distance to the stalls beneath. And the entire cavernous place glowed with golden light while the musicians below the lip of the faraway stage tuned their instruments that put an edge upon anticipation.

I clung again to John's hand when we had fought our way too near the front row of the gallery for comfort. And when we had made a place for ourselves in the squirming mob, it was as if we dangled at the very edge of a cliff.

Only the hope of spotting Miss Amanda and Mr. Forrest at the bottom of the vast well gave me the stomach to stare down upon the distant diamond tiaras and the pelts of fur thrown casually over the backs of red plush seats.

But I soon grew as confident as a bird on a branch in pursuing a glimpse of Miss Amanda's lacquered hair. At last in the second row on the aisle, I caught sight of the burnished gold of her evening wrap. It was certainly Miss Amanda, with her head slightly inclined toward Mr. Forrest. His black shoulder bulked large and protective beside her. And the liquid light from the tiny diamonds in her hair glowed and winked. To me she did outshine all the others, though she sat planted in a galaxy of bobbing heads crowned with tiaras that radiated like the Milky Way.

I was lost in the vision of those two remote figures as the orchestra moved from a disorganized cacophony and was suddenly gathered up by the conductor's baton into a swell of music unlike any I had ever heard before. It touched my heart before my mind could respond. A wave of sudden sound crashed upon a distant beach. It was as if I had spent all my eighteen years in deafness and could only now hear. This was the music of the sea, with the tides ebbing and flowing through the rows of the violins and the sob of the deeper instruments hidden in the murkiness below the stage. My heart seemed to soar out beyond the perilous balcony and glide on its own wings above the waiting crowd. I seemed to leave Miranda Cooke behind in all the smallness of her days and ways. And all this before the great brocaded curtain rose upon a world of more beauty and fantasy than I had known existed.

Years later, in the great museum of a foreign city, I was to come upon a glass case filled with objects that reminded me of that night. They were the intricate, bejeweled porcelain and malachite Easter eggs that the master jeweler Fabergé had created for the Russian royal family. Works of art too intricate to explain away as the products of human hands. Fantastic eggs that opened like curving books upon scenes inside: Russian winters rendered in small branching crystal, grottos of lapis lazuli to shelter small, chaste altars of namelessly precious metals, minuscule coral palaces housing regal figures clad in fragments of stiffened silk. Minute worlds within worlds both too small and too vast to look upon without a sense of hopeless, exhilarating confusion.

These private, perfect universes so superior to earthly life took me back to the first moment I had ever witnessed a curtain rise upon a stage. My mind grows misty at the recollection of the porcelain woman alone on that stage—Anna Pavlova. She was part woman, part swan, and the helmet of her headdress was a swan's own wing. Even her hands feathered against the black velvet backdrop. And she flew, as I had felt myself in flight moments before, above the waves of music, buoyed up by some great gift.

Her feet served only to free her from the stage, which was not a stage at all, but the smooth surface of some northern mere, inky and bottomless. The light that threw a shaft from above us bathed her in whiteness. Light like water played over her sharp profile. She looked more bird than woman, more goddess than human.

I sat swaying in the rhythm of her art. I had not known that it is art's function to transform not a stage but an audience. It was as if one small woman had made order from the disorderly world. As if she had drawn all the strains of life—its joy, its haunting memories of regret, and its hope for an eternity of love—and had woven this skein of yearning into a sort of poem told by her body.

At the end, when the swan she had become and had made us become lost all the life she had given it and fell dead on the stage, I wept. The tears streamed down my face at the dead rag of lost life Pavolva had become. She sank, it almost seemed, into the depths of the polished stage.

The great dancer was to become this mystical swan a thousand nights before uncounted admirers. But she could have given none of them more than she gave one obscure girl.

I must have left the theater in a spell composed of Pavlova's art and the sort of music I had never heard except deep within myself. Certainly now I cannot remember what might have passed between John and me, if anything did. All too temporarily I was withdrawn into a precious privacy where my thoughts did not turn on him or on Miss Amanda. I could manage just so much independence without deluding myself. But I must have known a scrap of time that I now forget that was mine alone.

Certainly John and I must have made a quick return to Charles Street so that I would be ready to attend Miss Amanda when she came home. I must have struggled out of my dowdy hat and my handed-down coat. I must have touched up my hair in passing a hall mirror. And I must have descended to the damp kitchens to warm Miss Amanda's midnight milk with no one to break across my thoughts. In every earthbound step I took across the cold floor, I must have felt the lift and freedom of Pavlova's weightlessness, her suspension in the magic air. And all this quiet turmoil turned in my heart while the old deaf cook sat deeply asleep beside the embers, dreaming older dreams than mine.

I remember nothing about that midnight hour except the way it ended. Miss Amanda must surely have been seen to, for I was in my nightdress, closing a window in my sewing room against the cold. I looked down without thinking to the carriage house below in the mews. There I saw a shape of yellow-pink light that fell across the iron stairs and the wet cobbles. The door of John Thorne's rooms stood open. I saw his silhouette, as if he were blocking the entry.

Movement rippled the light. And I saw there were two forms there. John stood confronting another man. And though I could see nothing of him except his frail shape, I knew who it must be. The mysterious stranger meant to be invisible to me was half-visible again. I pulled back the curtain, since I was protected by the darkness in the sewing room. And I stared down at the wedge of lamplight that made my eyes dance. The two men stood in the door above the garages. They were locked, it seemed, in muttering combat. Or perhaps they were engaged in some silent struggle that dealt in neither curses nor fists.

The man who remained largely in John's shadow was smaller than he was. Yet he seemed ready to do battle. John appeared to shake him off again and again and was on the point of flinging him down the steep iron stairs. Surely he could have done just that if he had chosen to. It would have been all too easy for a man far more gentle than John.

But the smaller man seemed to grip John around the chest and to cling there. Not so much as a wrestler as like a beseeching child. I thought that if I had been within earshot I might have heard him sob.

At last, as I watched without more conscious thought, John stepped back suddenly into the room. The dim interior light flashed across his hair and played briefly over him except for the dark recesses of his craggy face. The young man pitched forward, inside, nearly dropping to his knees. And then he scrambled upright. And I saw the shapeless black cape hanging askew over his narrow shoulders. Then the door closed behind them both. For John Thorne had allowed him in, had given this mysterious stranger some sort of mysterious welcome.

Sixteen

First and last, Miss Amanda loved a sly game. She perfected the art of indirection in communicating with me. Any important matter or any situation that made her feel uncertain of herself could never have a straightforward airing. Instead, she caused me to learn what she wanted me to know by that time-honored servants' means: overhearing a conversation that seemed not meant for my ears. Thus I was the one made to appear underhand and devious.

Her spirits had mounted with each passing day. On the morning after the ballet when I took in her tea, she inquired in good humor if I had enjoyed my evening out. I was unequal to expressing how much it had meant to me and grew painfully tongue-tied, and she seemed to understand even that.

"I daresay Pavlova's art was a more memorable experience for you than for that great clodhopper Thorne!" she said lightheartedly. Then she added, "I must ask him if he has been converted to the world of the dance next time I have occasion to see him."

I might have foreseen the news she was about to reveal because she had summoned up to town her friend, Miss Sybil Ward-Benedict, who was due to arrive that morning. Miss Amanda would not have interrupted her busy round for Miss Ward-Benedict, who was no lover of London, unless she had wanted an audience for a specific announcement.

In accepting the invitation, Miss Ward-Benedict had grudgingly agreed to come up for a day and night of gossiping and a dinner party. But she would not commit herself to a longer stay. Her horses claimed most of her time and all her attention. This much she made quite as clear as the sprawling handwriting in her note permitted.

She arrived at midmorning, blustering like the weather, and she filled up most of the front door. Handing over her small traveling case, she greeted me as an old friend and equal. Her hearty conversation echoed up the stairwell as I led her to her room. "And how is Lady E. keeping?" she boomed. "And Sir T.?" I had to tuck my chin well down to keep from laughing aloud, for she sounded far more like an overbearing elderly aunt than a young girl a year and more short of twenty.

She held forth at some length about what nonsense it would have been to bestir her own maid to come up to town for such a brief visit. The thought of her traveling with a maid, or even having one, though I suppose she did, nearly put me over the edge. I could hardly imagine her traveling with any servant except perhaps a groom. But unpacking for her was the lightest duty of my day.

I found only a change or two of the same clothes she wore on visits to the country. And while these, I was coming to realize, were quite as expensive as anything in my young mistress's wardrobe, they were luxury of quite a different order. I wondered again at the unlikelihood of two such different young women maintaining any sort of friendship. Miss Ward-Benedict stalked about the bedroom with her hands clasped behind her back as if such a cramped, indoor place were closing in on her. "I'm like that gelding of mine in a loose-box," she declared. And when she left off pacing, she stared with distaste down into busy Charles Street, rubbing her forehead where the band of her sensible hat had left a rather raw-looking groove.

"And you, Miranda? Bearing up, are you? I shouldn't think the so-called Little Season is much to write home about for a maid. Particularly young Amanda's!" But this seemed to require no response. She was by then poking into an enormous handbag, and she slapped a ten-shilling note down on the dressing table, causing the small glass bottles there to chatter. "I shall tip you now while I think of it, for I never can remember to do the right thing at the right time! I deplore thoughtlessness, even in myself!"

She waved away my thanks with a large hand and thundered, "You had better show me straight in to Amanda. I daresay she has some bee in her bonnet, or I shouldn't have been commanded to her royal court! What a self-important little baggage she can be—and with what a talent for getting other people to take her seriously! Though I suppose I shouldn't be saying such a thing to one in her employ. Mum's the word. Lead on, then! I trust she's still in bed."

She was, indeed, with the early-morning tea tray adrift on the silk coverlet and threatening to crash onto the floor. She greeted her friend with boisterous cries, and I left them to their reunion. Only at eleven did I return with morning coffee and charcoal biscuits. Miss Amanda had embarked upon a dieting regimen in the hope, she said, of setting a good example for the ponderous Miss Ward-Benedict.

When I bore in this lightly burdened tray, they were still talking nonsense in their chaffing way. Though short on content, it was conversation I eavesdropped on without compunction. Such verbal swordplay was nearly a foreign language to me. It seemed to toy with the truth through the medium of outrageous insult.

"No, truly, Sybil," Miss Amanda was saying, "you must really take care not to live day and night in the paddock. A bit of unhealthy London air will do you no end of good. You know it's said that frightfully keen horsewomen come to resemble the animals of their choice in time. And time may well be running out for you. Indeed, I feel sure it is."

"What rot!" boomed Miss Ward-Benedict amiably, throwing one large leg over the other. "You never give up on this topic! I was *born* with the look of a horse, and damned proud of it, too!"

"Sybil! What language! Must I remind you there is a servant hovering nearby?"

I was pouring out the coffee then, and sober of expression in fear of being drawn as a pawn into their brittle nonsense. The conversation seemed in search of a scapegoat less invulnerable than Miss Sybil.

"What Miranda must have heard from you," she roared, "would leave me and all the stablehands standing at the gate! Do leave her alone!"

And mercifully Miss Amanda did. Her talk veered, as it often did, onto new ground at once. I sensed her eyes on me only when she said, "I am quite done in with London and cannot face the thought that this month is only a sort of dress rehearsal for the real Season next summer."

"Then I shouldn't go through with next summer if I were you," Miss Ward-Benedict said gruffly. "I shan't."

"No, I suppose you won't, Sybil. Though I should find it all worthwhile if I thought there was the least chance of seeing you at court, caparisoned with your mother's dusty old opals and garbed capaciously in virginal white, making your bow to Queen Mary! What a picture you two would make at close range. She an ironclad battleship and you the Rock of Gibraltar! I see it all as a sort of *tableau vivant* to commemorate Victorious Britannia Ruling the Waves! What a celebration of Empire!"

"You may spare us both your fertile imaginings. I shan't be having a London Season, and that's flat. I said as much to my mother, and she went quite giddy with relief."

"Lucky Sybil!"

"Lucky fiddlesticks! If you really thought that, Amanda, you might well follow suit. The fact is, London's your turf. You like nothing better than changing your clothes six times a day and being universally admired the minute you reach the bottom of the stairs. London is heaven on earth to you. I wonder you can face up to the prospect of a quiet winter down on the Isle. It surely gives you less scope than London. Talking of that, it does seem to me I saw your glamorous face in one of the picture papers only this past week, looking both languid and predatory. You were done up to the nines, and they'd decorated the borders of your photograph with steel-engraved orchids and laurel leaves."

"Yes, that was me, as you perfectly well know. Memory serves you uncommonly well, Sybil, when you are attempting to be acid and clever."

"If you can but extend yourself a bit," Miss Ward-Benedict went on, "they'll be selling your photo on cards at tobacconists as they used to do with Mrs. Keppel and Lillie Langtry and that actress— what's her name? The one with the limpid eyes—Mabel Love!"

"Rather passé, but an intriguing thought," Miss Amanda said, wriggling pleasantly against her pillows. "But, Sybil, you have sold me short in your usual brusque manner. I am not railing in my old way against the narrow confines of convention. When I say to you that I cannot face a Season next year, I mean that I *will* not face it, and I have taken steps."

I had lingered to carry away the coffee cups and was just removing the tray from Miss Amanda's bed when her small hand shot out and grasped my wrist. She knew I was on the point of withdrawing. And she meant for me to stay. Her hand pinned my wrist with surprising strength while she continued. "You see, Sybil, I am through with waffling and have decided to get engaged to Mr. Gregory Forrest."

Miss Ward-Benedict choked on a crumb of her charcoal biscuit. Her hand, bearing a napkin, flew to her face. She made rather a business of elaborate coughing, perhaps to cover her surprise. Only then did Miss Amanda release my hand. But I knew I was meant to stay and hear more.

She lounged against her pillows, smoothing the sheet with one hand and thoroughly enjoying the effect of her bombshell on her friend. However much we were said to look alike, I saw on Miss Amanda's face an expression thoroughly foreign to any I had ever had. A mixture of youthful glee, mature self-satisfaction, and a hint of something quite elderly and unfathomable about the eyes. I thought fancifully of the play of winter sunshine across an uneven landscape. And I was too struck by this strange, even worrying expression to absorb Miss Amanda's news at once, or to calculate how serious she might be.

Miss Ward-Benedict was red in the face but in possession of herself again when she withdrew the napkin. She shot Miss Amanda a stern, schoolmistressy look. "Just how seriously is one to take this, Amanda? Where is this particular charade meant to end?"

Miss Amanda met this question with an arch look. "As I understand such things, an engagement ends with marriage. And marriage is terminated only by death, except in unusual circumstances of the sort two such blushing young Girl Guide types as ourselves are not expected to know about."

Miss Ward-Benedict must have been alerted by the gravity in Miss Amanda's eyes, despite the smoke screen of her words. "So it's to be Forrest, is it?" she said in an exploring way. Many another young woman would have raised the question of love, particularly in the society of those who bandied the word as freely as songwriters. But to ask Miss Amanda if she loved Mr. Forrest was beyond her friend. The question seemed to hang in the air in a moment of silence. But Miss Amanda left it there. She said instead, "Yes, it's to be Gregory. What do you think of him?"

Miss Ward-Benedict looked startled and caught short all over again. "Me? What has it to do with me? I hardly know the chap. Good, solid sort, I should think. Not English, of course, but no nonsense about him. Has he spoken to your father?"

Miss Amanda hooted with exaggerated, almost manufactured glee. "Oh, Sybil, you are too quaint to live! Nobody has spoken to Father in years, on any subject! But you may be sure that Gregory has 'spoken' to my mother and she has 'spoken' at length in reply. It seems more than likely that when I have been in some of my less forthcoming moods, Mother has fired off daily bulletins to poor Gregory, all phrased with immense discretion. She should really have been a figure at some minor Central European court, scheming endlessly behind screens. I shall be more than glad to put paid to all this subterranean maneuvering."

"Ruddy odd reason for marrying," Miss Ward-Benedict remarked in a thoughtful mutter.

"Ah, but there are odder reasons—I daresay," Miss Amanda replied. "And never think I am so reformed a character that I might pass muster as a dutiful daughter in a three-volume Victorian novel."

"Never entered my mind," Miss Ward-Benedict said pointedly. Then she stirred herself and sat up with something of a start. "See here! If you *are* to be married—and mind you, I am taking you at your word—I suppose I shall have to act as your bridesmaid."

"How gracefully you offer yourself, dear Sybil."

"Well, it's hardly my line of country, but I suppose it must be done."

"I shouldn't dream of going through the sacred ceremony without your—reassuring presence. And I mean to see you decked out in all possible finery. No tweeds or divided skirts or riding boots, mind you." Miss Amanda was as near grinning as she ever allowed herself.

"Riding boots," Miss Ward-Benedict echoed. "No, I suppose not. I shall have to see if they can make satin slippers in my size. What a bore. Still, I shall manage somehow. Is it to be a summer wedding? I shan't be at my best in floating chiffons, you know. Nor anything in the way of a deep-brimmed hat."

I was not able to tell if Miss Ward-Benedict was spinning out a joke at her own expense or if she was truly alarmed at the prospect of herself as a bridesmaid the size of an heroic statue. If she had had a scrap of subtlety about her, I might have thought she was angling to learn if Miss Amanda had set the wedding date.

But no, for she turned abruptly back to Miss Amanda and said, "Well, then, when *is* it to be, Amanda? You won't convince me that you're serious unless you can name a date at once!"

Miss Amanda shifted uncomfortably in her bed and lingered before answering. "Then you will have to hang in an agony of suspense, Sybil, at least for a time. For I haven't set the date, and you know perfectly well I cannot be hurried. There is so much to pull together so that everything will come right, you see."

"Frankly, I don't see," Miss Ward-Benedict said, puffing a bit. "Your mother could pull together quite a slap-up wedding in no more time than it took to tell it. She's a great marvel at such things!"

"*Slap-up?*" inquired Miss Amanda. "My dear Sybil, you do pick up the oddest turns of phrase from those stableboys of yours! But of course you're quite right. To see me off her hands, my mother could have a special license as early as this very afternoon and me all in old lace and marching to Mendelssohn by teatime!"

"Not the worst idea I've ever heard put," muttered her visitor.

"But I was not thinking of all those tedious plans for the wedding itself. Indeed, since I am to marry an American, I might well slip away to New York and be wed there, depriving my mother of the hour of her triumph! And, of course, sparing you the need of satin slippers." Miss Amanda's eyes glittered and then darkened abruptly. Her brow was positively knitted now, and her expression pensive, not mocking. "No," she murmured to neither of her listeners, "I still have much to work through—and even miracles to pray for."

Miss Amanda moved the conversation away from herself so sharply that I nearly swept all the ornaments off the chimneypiece in shock. For by then I was going through the motions of tidying the room while eavesdropping outright, as I was expected to do.

"There is another wedding that must be executed before mine— it's far more pressing. One wedding, and who knows? Perhaps two." Then she listened herself to the silence that followed this languid remark. And the breath caught in my throat.

"Whose, for Heaven's sake?" Miss Ward-Benedict demanded.

"It will have escaped your notice, Sybil," said Miss Amanda, coy and maddeningly playful once more, "for it's been a bit of a household secret. And it still looks like being scandal if matters do not fall right."

"And therefore none of my concern," Miss Ward-Benedict broke in.

But Miss Amanda's talk flowed on, for she knew she could quite easily engage her friend's curiosity with another word or two. I listened with growing apprehension.

"It seems that one of the servants down at the Isle, quite an insignificant little belowstairs type and quite pathetic with it, has got herself into an interesting condition. Betty is her name, as I recall it. She is, not to put too fine a point on it, far advanced in pregnancy. An indiscretion of the summer likely to burst forth as a sort of amusing tragedy in the winter. Assuming, of course, that it hasn't already and the servants down there are keeping us in the dark. Miranda's a great friend of the poor little wretch—aren't you, Miranda? And it is lucky for our little Betty that Miranda and I have come to her rescue. At least we have done our best to ensnare a likely man to marry her. However, whether our best is good enough remains to be seen. Truly, the situation is so absurd one doesn't know whether to laugh or cry." Miss Amanda laughed merrily.

And I watched my own face go nearly black in the mirror above the mantel. It seemed cruel beyond measure to blurt out anything about Betty to one outside the family. Cruel and unnecessary. John Thorne had been this heartless, but I persisted in thinking that any woman—even Miss Amanda—would have some pity for another woman's plight. And Miss Amanda's half-spiteful tone brought me as near to rage as I ever dared to be.

"Fancy your bothering yourself over such a thing!" Miss Ward-Benedict said in all astonishment.

"You mean it doesn't sound a bit like me?" asked Miss Amanda.

"Well, of course, the meddling part does," Miss Ward-Benedict said heavily. "But I'm amazed you remember any of it long enough to gossip to me about it. Why bring it up at all? I wonder this servant of yours hasn't been packed quietly off in disgrace!"

"How cold-blooded you are, Sybil. Perhaps *you* would have had poor Betty shot, like a mare gone lame. Luckily for the little fool, I am of a more compassionate nature."

Miss Ward-Benedict snorted, and my hand trembled, endangering the china clock on the mantel.

"Servants are often on my mind," Miss Amanda continued. "I did mention there might be more than one wedding before we can give my own the complete attention it deserves. Didn't I mention another, Sybil?" she asked her friend while her eyes trained on me.

"I doubt I was listening. Did you?" Miss Ward-Benedict was giving her no quarter.

"Yes. I shouldn't be in the least surprised if Miranda didn't marry soon."

Miss Ward-Benedict heaved herself around in her chair to look in my direction. I had been trained never to look a guest in the eyes, never to glance higher than the lips. But Miss Ward-Benedict and I exchanged glances then. And I saw in hers what I never saw in Miss Amanda's. A pained kindliness that seemed to wish me protection that was not in her power to give.

"If Miranda is thinking of anything along the line of marriage," she said, as heavily as before, "then it is surely her own business."

"Ah, but that is where you go so wrong, Sybil," Miss Amanda said. "What a servant does and does not do is, alas, all too much our business. We are drawn in quite against our wills."

"Poppycock!" Miss Ward-Benedict said.

"I rather think," Miss Amanda went on, "there really is something between Miranda and our man-of-all-work down on the Isle. Thorne is his name. And of course one must either *encourage* a servant's marriage or *discourage* it. Letting matters drag on simply leads to difficulties. Difficulties of Betty's sort, more often than not."

"Stop bullying the girl!" Miss Sybil said. She was embarrassed enough on my behalf to turn her head away from me.

"Please, Miss," I heard myself saying. My face was blank of all emotion when I turned to Miss Amanda, and I was looking as grim as I knew how. "May I withdraw?"

"There!" Miss Amanda slapped down one careless hand. "All our frank talk has brought Miranda's disapproval down on us. And all in the interests of helping her friend and in contemplating quite innocently a happy future for herself. I do wonder if servants are capable of friendship and gratitude as we understand such matters, Sybil."

"For their sakes, I hope not," Miss Sybil grunted in reply.

Miss Amanda leveled a look at me. "Yes, by all means do withdraw. I cannot bear a glowering servant!" And so withdraw I did, bearing away the shreds of my dignity.

For the rest of the day I shook with useless rage. Though why Miss

Amanda's small, calculated cruelties continued to have the power to hurt me I cannot think. Perhaps because I still did not know that her petty cruelties only masked far greater ones. My eyes stung for hours, and I rattled the trays and the china in the underground kitchen loudly enough to startle the old cook out of half her deafness. I might even have taken time to wonder if some of my young mistress's fits of uncontrolled temper were beginning to rub off on me. But by evening I had quite another matter to occupy my mind. A matter that plucked me from the lofty, artificial world Miss Amanda inhabited and drew me into far lower depths.

I dressed my young lady in a cloth-of-gold gown in the last moments before the dinner hour. And I went about that duty with a face as frozen as an Egyptian slave's, while she sighed audibly at my dourness. But I was not to be allowed to get away with it. Just as I was completing my task by handing her a lightly scented handkerchief, she fixed me with a look meant to seem free of all guile.

"Miranda, you must not take to heart everything I say when I am attempting to be amusing. It is not meant to be taken so seriously. There is something in Sybil so pompous that I often say things meant to shock her out of her immense complacency."

I meant only to nod curtly, but found myself murmuring, "Yes, Miss," instead.

"I confess to you," she went on, "that I don't take poor Betty's situation as seriously as I might if—if I were nearer her station in life. I daresay this is a very human failing in me. But you are quite a different matter indeed, Miranda." Her voice had fallen as it could do into a quiet register that commanded attention far better than a shouted order. "To say that I would be quite lost without you does not even begin to express it. I am quite serious when I say that I shall want you with me always. And I can see no reason why, in the long run, you and I should not have everything that—will make us both happy."

And then she dismissed me with nearly as much quiet, self-possessed charm as her mother.

I went my way with my head ringing with ill-assorted thoughts. Her words, which held out the promise of benevolence to one servant while denying it to another, failed to have their intended effect on me. I had never been so much on my guard, for her kindly moods were always more threatening than her usual manner. When she voiced the wish that I would remain in her service always, I nearly shuddered. In a few short weeks I had grown away from a need for the security of servitude. With such an employer as I had, a lifetime of service seemed a prison sentence to me.

The future was, of course, shrouded in darkness. But one thing was as clear as daylight. The idea that I might marry John Thorne was firmly fixed in Miss Amanda's mind. I did not wonder what had put it there. She could always seem to see through my defenses to the hidden thoughts behind.

But she seemed, in her heedless way, to have overlooked something. If she was to marry Mr. Forrest and go off to New York with him, I could surely not both marry John Thorne and remain with her. One could not be in two places at once, no matter how often Miss Amanda expected exactly that from me.

There were many imponderables in this. It might be that she had no intention of marrying Mr. Forrest at all. She was foolish enough to let the perfect man slip through her fingers while her attention was all on meaningless scheming. Then we might well go on as we were. In that case, I meant to marry John Thorne if I was able. To be married, even to this underling of her household, would leave me a degree less at her mercy.

And if she did marry and go off to a foreign land, I would choose to stay behind and live on the Isle of Wight as Mrs. John Thorne. The thought of three thousand miles of choppy gray water between me and Miss Amanda Whitwell was immensely reassuring at that moment.

And I was not to know that life rarely offers anyone such an easily made choice.

I was so lost in these thoughts that I found myself standing stock-still outside Miss Ward-Benedict's door. But I pulled myself together and went in to see if I might put the finishing touches to this young lady's toilette.

She was half into her heavy faille gown of gun-metal gray with fur tippets hanging down curiously from the bodice and the sleeves. There was nothing much to do for her except to button her up the back. As her gown concealed more of her figure than it clung to, this task was easily done, no matter how distracted I was by lingering thoughts.

I stood like a statue at the head of the stairs, watching both young women descend to their dinner party. Faintly, I noticed Mr. Gregory Forrest standing below, for a secret part of me always longed for a glimpse of him. But when he stepped up to the foot of the stairs to lead Miss Amanda away, I was hardly stirred. There was also a young man got up from somewhere to see Miss Ward-Benedict in to dinner. But I paid no more attention to him than Miss Sybil did herself.

Later I sat over a bit of mending in my sewing room. I remember even that unremarkable part of the evening. For as I sat squinting over the needle, music welled up through the house. It was the age when dancing after a dinner was coming into fashion. And of course this was well before well-bred young people went out to dance in cabarets and other public places where they might jostle among strangers in rooms where anyone might go. It was American music, played on the gramophone. It must have been American, now I think back on it. For it rang strangely on my ear. Music that repeated its jingling themes over and over, with an undertone of mournfulness like a quiet cry in the night beneath all the surface noise. Music that invited you to rejoice, and all the while sobbed. I had listened to it for so long that I ceased to hear it. Abruptly, Mrs. McCall, the housekeeper, was standing at my open door.

"May I come in?" said she, who was free to go anywhere in the house that she ran. And as I nodded, I noticed she was not carrying a tray and a teapot as she had done before. There was purpose in her visit, and I sensed some sort of trouble in her first words. The electric bulb overhead flashed hard on her flame-red hair. She crossed the room in two strides and hesitated a moment before settling uneasily on the other chair. I felt the full force of her personality and put down my sewing as I was surely expected to do.

"I shall come to the point," she said directly, though she looked away from me as she spoke. "I want to ask you a question. And I wouldn't blame you if you told me it was none of my business. Still, I must ask it."

Her face was haggard in the hard light. I had thought of her before then as heavy-burdened with secrets. And I had never thought they were of the trifling sort that many servants nurture to make themselves seem more important. But now there was a look about her of desperation. She was like a volcano at the point of erupting. Though my heart wasn't in it, I told her she could ask me anything she needed to.

"Do you and John Thorne plan to marry?"

"He has spoken of it," I said. Indeed I could say no more, though my answer sounded stiff.

"I am not prying to satisfy my own curiosity," Margaret McCall said.

"No," I replied, for she seemed a woman who would be too little surprised at anything she might learn to bother prying into the business of others. "John Thorne knows I will marry him if he wants it."

She lingered over my answer and worked her hands in thought. "Then I suppose it will be," she said at last. "I could not be sure without asking you outright. If you had—other plans, I wouldn't have troubled you further. As it is . . ." Her hands were clenched together then. A well-worn wedding band, which she might easily have bought herself, winked in the light. "As it is, I wonder if you would come out with me for half an hour tonight."

It was not a question. "Out? But I must see to Miss Amanda—"

"Only for half an hour. You'll be back in plenty of time to see to her—to Miss Amanda. I wonder if you will come round to the pub with me. I know it's irregular, but—"

"Is John to be there?"

She looked startled. "No, indeed, he's off to the Red Lion. It's where the chauffeurs go. I made sure he was out of the way. We— you and I will go down to—where you saw me once before."

She meant the pub with the curious name, the place where I had overheard her arguing with the mysterious young man from the mews. Arguing with him, and in the end giving him money. "Will he be there?" I asked, and she knew whom I meant. She nodded quickly and rose from her chair.

I was so struck by her manner that I did not stir in the first moment. She turned, impatient to move me, and said, "If you are to—marry into the family, in a manner of speaking, you will have to be told some things. It's pointless to keep them from you. You're no fool. In time you'd find out for yourself. But before you did, you might say or do something in all innocence that would endanger—other people."

"Including yourself?"

"You shall be the judge of that," she replied. I stood up then and went for my coat. The intrigue surrounding this matter-of-fact woman would have sent me out into the night with her. But I knew the matter was of deadly seriousness. I knew, too, that I was at last to learn who the strange young man in the coach house was. Perhaps I would even learn the hold he had over John Thorne.

The pub called "I Am the Only Running Footman" was fogged with blue smoke. I walked in Mrs. McCall's wake, shrinking at the atmosphere of the place. Along every wall, people sat packed together around small marble-topped tables, swilling drinks and talking in the overloud tones of London.

It was impossible to know who was at one's elbow, a thing I could never be comfortable with. Servants were there, nursing a pint of bitter through a long evening. And well-dressed men and a few overdressed women. And even the sort of rough workmen who mend the streets. All their differing societies were flung together in a low-ceilinged set of rooms. It was the other extreme from a village pub that is everyman's club, where darts are played and where every drinker's name and family history are known to all. In this noisy, anonymous place the smoke bit at my eyes, and the smell of malt seemed almost wet against my face.

Mrs. McCall made for a pair of glazed doors, and we found ourselves in the saloon bar. There was a degree of privacy in that room, for which the drinker paid twopence more for his drink. A carpet was laid on the floor, and the lamps were shaded, all to give it someone's odd notion of home.

The housekeeper found a corner table, half screened from the rest of the room. She sat down heavily in a sort of upholstered settle. And even before she threw back her coat, her eyes were already drifting toward the doors we had just come through.

We sat like graven images until the two tankards of ale she had ordered were brought. I lifted my drink, determined to take a few sips of the acrid stuff and to leave the rest if I could. Over the rim of the tankard I saw Mrs. McCall shift her searching gaze to me. Our eyes met, and I knew she could not keep her thoughts quiet much longer. There was something uncertain in her gaze, though I judged her to be a woman who despised uncertainty of any sort. There was an invitation in her look as well, and it was scarcely veiled. It told that she would be glad to spare us both what was about to happen and that it was not too late for me to draw back.

If I had taken fright and bolted out of the place, I was certain she would have let me go. She might even have fallen back in relief. But all my training had given me an outward composure and the talent for waiting. My silence drove her to speech.

"There's many who say servants are irresponsible these days," she began in a distracted way. "I daresay many are. Still, if it weren't for servants who go well beyond their assigned duties in looking after the families who employ them, many a noble house would fall." Her eyes slewed again to the doors that she could see, though I could not.

"What is it you're saying, Mrs. McCall?"

She sighed and shifted uncomfortably. "I would go to the stake for Lady Eleanor!" she exclaimed with startling emphasis. "And I bow to no one if it doesn't suit me! She's a lady, through and through, and if her daughter lives to be a hundred, she won't be able to touch her! And Lady Eleanor has not had an easy life. I've known hunger and hard work, but she's had heavier burdens than mine." Her mouth snapped shut then. She ran a long finger in the rings of wet on the table, making little, nervous patterns.

"Yes," I said, "Miss Amanda's older brother was lost in the South African war."

Her head jerked up. "You know about that, then, do you?"

I nodded. "Some of the servants down on the Isle remember him as a boy. And there's a memorial to him on the wall of the village church."

When I said no more, she went on almost easily, as if words were safer than silence, though they never are. "That's right, young Gordon Whitwell, the apple of his mother's eye, went off to soldier when he was no more than eighteen. Out to Africa, burning to prove himself. Lord Kitchener of Khartoum was the hero of the day then, and so was Lord Roberts of Kandahar. Many a young lad who could barely sit a horse flocked out to die in a war thousands of miles away at the end of the world. I remember those times well. We all sang 'Marching to Pretoria,' and many who marched that way never came back. And many who did come back would have been better off buried in foreign soil. Gordon Whitwell and John Thorne went out to fight together. Did you know that?"

I did. The day of the fox hunt John had told me that much. I nodded at Mrs. McCall. "I asked John once if Mr. Gordon had died a hero's death."

Her eyes narrowed, perhaps against the smoke in the room. "And what did he answer you?"

"He only asked me in return if there was such a thing as a hero's death, and would say no more about it."

Mrs. McCall nodded, as if John's answer passed some unknown test. "Hero or not," she said, tapping the table, "he's dead to his family, and so he must stay!"

A shadow fell across the table. *"Who must stay where?"* The question was asked in a high-pitched, demanding voice. It jarred me almost into shrieking aloud. In part because in its womanly tone there was something familiar—a version of a voice I had often heard. Mrs. McCall's head twisted around and up in something like fear. I saw standing over us the young man from the mews. He wore the same cloak. Though I was nearly as caught up in the strong emotions coming from the housekeeper as she was herself, I noticed details.

At close range, the black cloak appeared to be the sort of lined cape that gentlemen wear to the opera. It had the look of a hand-me-down, hanging too loosely from narrow, sloping shoulders around the young man's wasted frame. Since he wore no hat, his black hair lay in flat ringlets glistening with the evening mist.

I hazarded looks at these particulars, for I couldn't in the first moment look him full in the face. His hands rested on the table as he loomed over us. Hands white and soft with blackened nails at the ends of long, yellowed fingers. "I ask you once again, Margaret, *who* must stay *where?"*

"Servants' gossip," she muttered in a voice robbed of half its strength. "Nothing to do with you." And then she edged over to make room for him to sit. I could not fathom her. She spoke rudely, and yet there was a degree of deference in her manner. He slid in beside her and snapped a finger at the waiter who was already beside us, having followed him to the table. "Another round and the same for me. Mrs. McCall is paying. I trust her credit is still as good as ever here."

Only after the waiter left us did the young man allow himself to notice me. In mock surprise he said, "And whom have we here, Margaret? Surely a young woman of some importance. We don't admit every stray into our magic circle, do we?"

I was staring at him by then in spite of myself. He was the sort of person you would rather watch than turn your back on. For there was something more menacing about him than his easy insolence. I could see the skull beneath the skin of his deathly white forehead. He was clearly not as young as I had thought. And there was something so familiar about him that I wondered if I had not known him all along, long before we had come up to London, where there were so many dark corners where he might lurk. Perhaps I had known him in some earlier lifetime. He seemed just the sort of malicious spirit that might pursue those he chose to plague throughout life and even beyond.

He and I both waited in vain for Mrs. McCall to make a civil introduction. Instead she said, reluctantly, "This is the young woman John Thorne will marry."

The stranger's eyebrows flew high on his forehead. Again he drew himself up in manufactured surprise: In other circumstances I would have been writhing in embarrassment. But we had come past that now. And we were all uncertain of our footing and ready to conceal the fact. I was riveted by the man's eyes. They were hooded and lifeless in the smoky light. But there was something in their shallow depths that suggested color—violet. And this glimmer struck me as another familiar feature.

I was inclined to concentrate on those eyes, for the rest of the face was weaker than a child's, and mottled gray on white. His mouth, curiously black and moist about the lips, was still pursed with lingering surprise, and I dreaded what he might find to say. "John Thorne will take unto himself a wife? Well, I suppose stranger things have happened in this badly arranged universe. And when will you collect your brawny, sun-struck prize, my girl?"

"Hush!" Mrs. McCall murmured, covering her mouth with a hand that almost shook.

"What a grand manner we are all expected to affect in your august presence, Margaret! You are poorly placed in life. You have all the priggish impulses of a Scottish missionary's wife. Very well, then, I rephrase my innocent question. When are you to be married to our much-admired Thorne, Miss Whatever-your-name-might-be?"

I looked away from his sneering face, noticing at the edge of my mind only that he was in as much pain—perhaps more—as he was able to inflict. My gaze settled on Mrs. McCall. She had the look of one who has led others beyond her own depth. Apology and disgust played over her face, but she was forced to say, "Her name is Miranda Cooke. And like most women, though you would know nothing of them, she will marry when she decides to."

Her words struck the man a glancing blow. He smiled too quickly and seized upon my name. "Miranda Cooke," he said, stroking his beardless cheek. "A conjunction of names curious enough to remember. But somehow I don't. There is something distantly familiar about her all the same."

At that I nearly did writhe, feeling pinned by his gaze like a stifled moth. But silence, which was my only defense, seemed not to serve Mrs. McCall. In a rush, she said, "You don't know her and never did, or anyone like her. Put that from your mind!"

After a pause he answered, "How very certain you are about everything, Margaret. I wonder how you can be so cocksure about a world that includes the likes of me. But never mind, I have been summoned to meet this fortunate young person who will shortly share John Thorne's bed, if she has not done so already. And so I assume you are going—how would you phrase it, dear Margaret— to 'put her in the picture'?"

Mrs. McCall brought up a shuddering sigh. "I have little choice if I'm to do my duty to those who deserve a little peace of mind." She gave him a deeply troubled sidelong glance, though she had avoided looking at him since he had sat down. Then she began. "Miranda—"

But it was not to be. He was only flushing her out so he could cut her off. "No, no, dear, plodding Margaret, you will only depict me to the poor girl in the worst light possible to you. But my depravity is far more profound than your most fanciful turns of phrase. You always turn ladylike in a pinch. And after all, my life is *my* story, and only yours insofar as you have chosen to involve yourself in it. You are almost certain to turn from *my* biography to your own. Then we shall have to sit through another interminable sermon about how self-righteous you are. I shall tell Miranda all, and I am sure we will all be edified by the story."

I would have run then, all curiosity quenched. But I was sure that this time a hand would shoot out from a black cloak and draw me back. Did I fear this? Perhaps. But something else froze me where I sat—and sealed my fate. I knew in the long run that I was about to hear confirmation of something that a small, buried part of me already understood. He had already begun talking in an insinuating whine before I was collected enough to hear. ". . . hard indeed," he was saying, "to be born and bred a gentleman to my fingertips and to be robbed by fate and youthful indiscretions of my rightful place."

He laid claim to far better breeding than he displayed. And all the while, Margaret McCall sat shrunken at his side, one hand over her mouth and her eyes staring sightless at the tabletop.

". . . my share of weaknesses, of course. Who does not? A love of beauty has, along with alcohol and certain narcotic charms, been my undoing. Did you know, my dear Miss Miranda Cooke, that there are some men—I am speaking of myself, of course, as I often do—some men who are so inflamed by beauty that their desires transcend all womanhood and settle upon the masculine ideal?

"No, of course you knew no such thing. Being a woman, you are cursed with the self-centered blindness of your sex. For all your comely exterior, you are, beneath the surface, like all the Margaret McCalls of this world, convinced that the fate of all rests in the palm of your hand."

A third tankard of ale was before the stranger now, and he nudged the empty ones aside with a hand growing vague. His speech was slurring, too, though I was still hearing more clearly than I wanted to.

"When I was young and innocent of all vice, my eye fell upon John Thorne. What a pity for you, Miss Miranda Cooke, that you will never see him through my eyes! You will, if you can manage it, only have the roughened man. But my eyes consumed the untouched boy as simple as his own animal beauty. Did he return that love with more than matching glances? Did we lie together in the ecstasy of flesh upon flesh? Ah, that, Miss Cooke, you will never be able to know for sure, even if you have the wit, the poor taste, and the courage to ask the question. And I daresay the past is safe with John Thorne, who would beat you half to death for inquiring into his manhood. He comes of quite a savage tribe, as I suppose you know."

Margaret McCall plucked suddenly at his sleeve. He jerked, and I thought he might round on her and strike her in the face. But his elbow caught an empty tankard that clanged to the floor. "Enough," she whispered hoarsely to him. "How hateful can you be?"

"More hateful than you would know, Mar-gar-et," he said, carefully phrasing his words against his drunkenness. "But not nearly as hateful as the world has been to me.

"They put me out of the army," he said, turning his glazed eyes back on me. "Did you know that? It is not gen-er-al-ly known, but still the world is full of secrets, and servants take pride in knowing most of them. They put me out of the army. They said—oh, how they bristled with medals and braid—they said I was a coward and bolted in my cowardice when we were cooped up and surrounded at Lady-smith. They said I had endangered my command! Ten thousand of us under siege in that stinking caldron called Ladysmith, and they settled on me as a scapegoat. And why? Because to the military mind I was a dubious character. My eyes roamed in the wrong directions. They despise beauty and fear its seekers. And so they gave me back my pistol and an empty room and told me to blow my brains out in the national interest. Is that not the greatest, the most—Olympian jest you have ever heard, Miranda Cooke?"

His eyes burned with a low violet flame, flaring out one last time before they grew milky and as vague as his gestures. I had thought he might be done, but he had more to say. Margaret McCall and I both stiffened to hear him to the end. "Luck was with me," he said, with some of the insolence drained from his voice. "John Thorne, who had seen me into and out of scrapes before, spirited me away. Did I tell you he and I went off to the wars together, and he had served as my batman? Oh, yes. Very faithful in his way, John Thorne, and he knows his duty and his place. Born to serve, as I was born to *be* served." He gave me as direct a look as he was able and then said something that I was to remember time and again. "It is the weakness of the wellborn, and not their strength, that commands obedience. That is the great secret, Miranda Cooke."

His eyes filled with tears then. He was telling the only story that could move him—his own. "I eluded my fate as an honorable suicide. I vanished instead. But it comes to much the same thing. I vanished too thoroughly—across the veld, out of the tedious land of the Boers, on and off a dozen repulsive tramp steamers and Port Said-bound gulf-going slums. They—that glittering British Army that took such pride in finally besting a bunch of old Dutchmen brandishing wooden hay-forks—made me a martyr in my absence. I had fallen, they informed the world, on the field of battle. But they are great lovers of the lie. I had, instead, fallen through a crack in their defenses.

"I made my way back to my dear old native land, where I remain as you see me—more dead than alive. Returned on a freighter, as it happens, and leaped out of its stinking hold when it was passing under Tower Bridge. We docked on the day old Queen Victoria died. The streets were thick with mourners. And I have been passing in crowds ever since."

His eyes were quartered by then, and I was able to hear him out by concentrating on the livid patch of his forehead below the flattened black ringlets. I could confront him only by concentrating on portions, as if he were a puzzle I was loath to complete. But I suspected that there was too much missing to complete any real human pattern. And I had gone beyond suspecting who he was, though I was ready to admit nothing to myself.

"Spare us more," Margaret McCall said, pleading with him. "She knows who you are."

"She knows nothing!" he shrieked, drawing back from her as if she had fastened herself to him. "She is as ignorant as the day she was born or she would not be here! You've brought her here to be educated because you haven't the courage to tell her yourself. Because you must draw her into your little conspiracy to protect us all!"

His shrieks drew the eyes of others to our corner hideaway. Margaret McCall spoke in a voice so low I hardly heard her, but it was stronger in its way than shrieking. "I shall give you up one day," she told him, "and wash my hands of you."

"Never," he replied. "I give your life a shape, a purpose. What would you be without your petty intrigues—an aging, vulgar drone with no earthly purpose to get you through your pointless days."

He gave her his shoulder then, and his head thrust like a snake's halfway across the table toward me. In a hissing whisper he said, spitting his words, "I must speak sharply to Margaret at times. She's a great bully, is Margaret. I have never been able to stomach bullies. Useful though she is, I would not be able to stomach Margaret, except, you see, she fears me."

"Fool!" Mrs. McCall said suddenly, breaking the hold of the man's eyes on me. "What have I to fear from you? You could never give me away without giving yourself away into the bargain, and that you would never do."

"Would I not, dear Margaret? Would I never choose my rightful place again—in what is ludicrously known as Society, and that pious outpost of it called Whitwell Hall? Can you be so sure?"

Margaret McCall's hand slapped down on the tabletop. "No. Never. How could you feed your low tastes at Whitwell Hall? You, a respectable country gentleman? It wouldn't last long. You have more satisfaction from the odd shilling got off me and who knows what others than you could have as the respectable son of a decent house. *There* you would be called to account." She turned from him, her lips curling in an expression as ugly as his own.

"How eloquent you grow, Margaret. But such bravado is surely born of fear."

"I *am* afraid," she said to him, controlling her voice to a quiet that almost cajoled. "I fear *her,* not you."

She pointed across the table at me, and I pulled back. He considered her words, and after a moment a blurred light glowed in his eyes. "Ah, yes, Margaret, I begin to see your reasoning. You know me too well. But you cannot be so sure of this young woman, so you must enlist her in our little regiment of lost souls. How may I advance your case? Let me think." He ran tobacco-stained fingers over his chin, pretending to be lost in thought though his eyes returned to me and lingered.

At last he said to me in a wheedling tone that excluded Mrs. McCall, "You see, my dear, how we are situated. Margaret is selflessness itself, caring neither for her own skin nor mine. It is the Family she means to protect, not from me but from you who in your innocence might betray us with an unwitting word.

"*You* will surely not give me away and break my mother's heart. Surely you will let me live in this poor nest of mine in the mews, which Margaret has so conveniently provided. Surely I can throw myself on your mercy with perfect confidence." The irony grew as he spoke until his mouth seemed both turned down in mock dismay and up in a sneer of contempt. And then in a different tone he said, "You know me now, don't you, my dear?"

The skull beneath his drawn flesh grew suddenly evident again. He leered at me like a death's-head. But I had replaced his face with words carved on a stone tablet.

"Thou wast not born to die" was engraved on the memorial to him in the village church beside Whitwell Hall. How strangely true those words were, what an "Olympian jest." For he had not died any real death at all, neither a coward's nor a hero's.

"That's right, my dear," he slurred, reading my face. "I am Gordon Whitwell."

Seventeen

———⟨∞⟩———

I had encountered Gordon Whitwell, that creature who haunted the dark underside of London. I saw him in his ghastly flesh when before I had been only half aware of his existence as a memory lingering in the heart of his mother, Lady Eleanor.

But now I saw the easy power the living man had over Margaret McCall and John Thorne. And I could half comprehend the dread he might well inspire in them. That such a woman as Margaret McCall might fear me was harder to comprehend. That anyone should fear me or have reason to was an idea both novel and strange.

I knew, though, that Gordon Whitwell feared no one. If I had given him away to his own mother, he might have found some satisfaction in the revelation. Perhaps he hated both his parents because he had fallen so far short of all their expectations. Perhaps the unnatural monster would have seized the opportunity to make them pay. But he would have no such opportunity through me. His secret was safe with me, and whether that pleased him or not I shall never know. There was no following his thoughts, for he had the mind of an insane child.

I would have forgotten him if I could, but it nagged at me that he was Miss Amanda's own brother. I recoiled from the truth that brother and sister, one blood, might have more in common than their parentage. Yet in the first moment I saw her in him.

I coped with my unwelcome, unasked-for new knowledge by

searching in it for something of advantage to myself. Whether rightly or wrongly, this is a servant's way. And perhaps a merely human way. Almost at once I found—or manufactured—that advantage.

The shared secret, in all its ugly darkness, was another bond between John Thorne and me. If he wavered in his intent to marry me, my knowledge that Gordon Whitwell lived—at least in part through John's deceit and servitude—rendered me less easily cast aside. My knowledge was by way of being a marriage license. For, in Margaret McCall's words, I must know it as I was to become a member of the family.

She was easier with me once I had been admitted into the mystery. I was never to confront Gordon Whitwell again. Ironically, I never even caught a glimpse of him, not even the furl of his cloak. But the reason is very likely that I never allowed myself to stand at my sewing-room window again, peering down into the dark mews in the attempt to unravel the intrigue that lurked there.

Gordon Whitwell had hinted at an unnatural love that festered in his heart for John Thorne. But in even considering to imply such a thing, he greatly misjudged the effect on me. I was far too ignorant of the world, and so the insinuation gave me less trouble than it was meant to. Besides, I knew that Gordon Whitwell's every impulse was twisted and that he would sow suspicion in any direction that occurred to him. There are people who measure their satisfaction by the misery they create in others. I had already begun dimly to know this because I was beginning to know his sister.

It was not in me, of course, to think of John Thorne as less than a man. To me, men were still great towering unassailable fortresses, armored against doubt and too solid to waver. I had never yet truly seen beyond the roughhewn facade. Mrs. McCall possessed more seasoned wisdom. When she cautioned me in the strongest terms never to confront John Thorne with a display of my knowledge, I agreed in large part to please her. I see now how John might have turned on me for flaunting my awareness of the weakling who had such a hold on him. It would have shown his servitude as even more abject than mine, and it would have thus attacked his manhood at its roots. Still, he needed to be told discreetly, and perhaps with some care, of the interlude I had gone through in the pub. Margaret McCall took this duty on herself. "The less you say, the less can be held against you," she advised. And I was glad enough to leave matters in hands more practiced than my own.

When I suggested to her that despite all our closed mouths the secret was certain to come to light one day, she was ready with an answer for that as well.

"No, God willing, the family need never know. Gordon Whitwell will play out his hand, but he won't make old bones. You don't know just how he lives and the company he keeps. When John Thorne is not about for him to slobber over, he mixes with the lowest scum he can find. One day he'll end up in a gutter. If drink and drugs don't do for him, he'll have his throat cut. He's died once, and he longs for it again. And those who hanker after death down the night streets of London will find it."

She scarcely mentioned the subject again. Since she trusted me, she would not run the risk of a conversation that might be picked up and worried at over and over. She was not the sort of companionable woman who warms her face at the hearth of endless, useless talk. And she thought it both dangerous and unseemly to raise the subject of the son beneath the roof of his family.

With no one to talk to about it, I marveled in silence at the horror of a son supposed long dead who walked beneath the night-shrouded windows of his still-grieving mother. But in time, the nightmare receded into unreality, and I had other, more immediate concerns. Once John Thorne had been told that I shared what I thought in my innocence to be the central secret of his life, a change came over me. And what did not sweep over me of itself I cultivated with a rather wicked pride. I felt less insignificant than before. This was only a young girl's pathetic delusion, but it buoyed me up through the last remaining days of our London stay and even for a time beyond.

Like many a young person on whom a scrap of new awareness dawns, I thought myself utterly transformed by worldliness. Though I blush red to think of it now, I became remarkably and quite suddenly grown-up in my manner. Whenever John Thorne caught my arm and drew me into a darkened pantry for a stolen, wordless moment of embraces, my lips sought his a degree less readily than before. If I melted, I melted a bit more slowly, and my reserve increased. I composed my face in the tranquillity that I supposed befitted my sudden maturity. And I kept from my eyes the questions that they sought to ask John, even supposing the darkness that protected us would allow him to see. Still, he must have sensed my proud attempts at self-control and my studied aloofness, for I heard his muffled chuckle at my new dignity.

With Miss Amanda, this new manner was a greater challenge, for I could never lower my guard. But it quickly became an even greater source of satisfaction. I fancied it was evident enough for her to notice and too subtle for her to question or correct. When before I had wavered between girlish companionship when she indulged me and injured coldness when she hurt me, now I sailed forth to serve her on a more even keel.

I was more the well-regulated, clockwork servant than before. My step was always measured, never hurried. When she sulked, I cosseted her just a bit absentmindedly. When she raged, I clucked audibly in my throat in patient disapproval. And when she was being particularly childish, I played the role of nanny instead of lady's maid. This effrontery conjured up the memory of the real nanny whom I had replaced—the Mrs. Buckle whom she had loathed and longed to outgrow. She caught unmistakable sight of Mrs. Buckle's ghost in certain of my attitudes, and they seemed to cure her of her worst outbursts so quickly that we were both surprised. The real Mrs. Buckle would have been astonished.

Nor did I permit myself to be caught up in her enthusiasms. Now, instead of endless bantering about the proper wardrobe for any of several occasions, I took to laying out the right frock, the underthings, the stockings, the slippers, the jewelry with military precision. She was often enough confronted by my suggested outfit without having to consult me. At times my young mistress looked rather lonely. But she could find no way to criticize a servant who was only growing more silently efficient. Nor was I quite so withdrawn that she might bring me up short. Though when I bowed wordlessly when she retired instead of wishing her goodnight in a more cheerful way, she stared from her bed as one who has just been slighted by an equal. I am sure that from the first indications of my newfound propriety, she was plotting how to bring me down and show her power over me. But I gave her a few weeks of indecision.

So caught up was I in the new protective mask that I hoped would grow naturally into my face that our last London days slipped quickly away. I moved through them with my ears stopped against much that went forth about me. I believed that I had learned quite enough as it was. Still, it did not escape me that Miss Amanda was quite as serious as she had been when she had ordered Miss Ward-Benedict up to town—serious about becoming engaged to Mr. Gregory Forrest. And the great day came, rather like the breaking of a long fever—an unheralded relief to all concerned.

On one of the last days of our London stay, a parcel was sent around from Asprey's. I bore it into Miss Amanda's room as proudly as if I had fetched it from the shop myself. It could hardly be an engagement ring, for the package was nearly two feet long and half that in width. I could barely manage it and the knob on the bedroom door, and made rather an abrupt entrance with it.

But while her room was in its usual morning shambles, it was empty of Miss Amanda. I found her at last in the dining room below, breakfasting with Lady Eleanor, an indication in itself that unusual events were going forth.

"Yes, well, do come in and unburden yourself," Miss Amanda cried out, all her attention seemingly given over to a large breakfast from which she could not be distracted. She waved me in the direction of her mother as if the parcel were certain to be for her. She was often casual in this studied way when her mother was near. There was an air of controlled excitement in the dim room nonetheless. Lady Eleanor suppressed a smile when I placed the Asprey's box beside Miss Amanda's place. Miss Amanda's calm ebbed as she tore through the wrappings with mounting anticipation. I stood behind her, my hands folded, pretending to linger only to receive further instructions.

Nestled in tissue paper was Mr. Forrest's card, with a message written on it. Miss Amanda palmed the bit of pasteboard and turned a final sheaf of tissue to uncover a large traveling jewel case in the same buttery leather as her book of blank pages. I thought the box bound in brass, only because I had never seen such a lavish use of gold before. She opened it at once to reveal an interior lined in suede the pale blushing color of a tea rose, with a dozen drawers and trays that sprang up.

"How very suitable," her mother murmured behind a smile, "for an ocean crossing."

Miss Amanda closed the lid again, running a luxury-loving hand over its soft surface. A gold handle was fitted ingeniously into the top of the lid. Beneath it were stamped the initials that Miss Amanda wanted me to see. She gave the box a quarter turn, for she sensed me staring over her shoulder from one side. A small *A* and a *W* flanked in swirls of gold, the center initial more boldly emblazoned: *F* for Forrest.

This was Miss Amanda's only announcement to me of her engagement. She said nothing, either to honor my recent self-possessed manner or to punish me for it. Being told nothing, I did not know how to tell her that I wished her well. Thus I felt boorish, as I was meant to do. She let the moment linger and then dismissed me. The monogram was meant to speak more loudly than words in its golden silence. I went my way as reassured about her future, if not my own, as this elegant gift could make me.

Another noteworthy thing took place in the evening of that day. A party at home had been planned, and I had noticed more than the usual bustle down in the kitchen. Though there were evidently to be no detailed notices of the engagement in the newspapers just yet, the dinner party was to advertise to the family's closest friends the young people's intentions.

An early arrival that afternoon had been Lady Eleanor's friend, Mrs. Glaslough, who greeted me as an old family retainer and swept directly up the stairs in a flurry of dyed cock feathers. She disappeared at once into Lady Eleanor's sitting room for an hour's gossip before the arrival of the rest.

Early that day I had laid out a new dinner gown for Miss Amanda. I barely knocked before entering her room in the evening to see to her hair and to put the finishing touch to her costume. I was well into the room before I saw Mr. Forrest was there. Miss Amanda had dressed herself in the elaborately beaded yellow gown. She stood with her back to Mr. Forrest, one hand raised to the sweep of her black hair coiled above the neck. Behind her in immaculate black, Mr. Forrest loomed over her, fastening the clasp of a single strand of pearls around her neck. It was the second of his engagement gifts in a single day.

Miss Amanda's gaze was on the floor, and she affected not to notice my entrance. But Mr. Forrest met my eye as soon as I could bring myself to look at him. He had made progress indeed to have gained entry to her bedchamber. I had no doubt that he was there with the blessing of Lady Eleanor. My confusion was very great, though, when he favored me with a somewhat crooked smile and then, of all things, gave me an unmistakable wink. It would have melted a far stiffer servant. I managed a smile in return before composing myself.

"Gregory!" Miss Amanda was saying. "I cannot think what my maid will do if she finds you anywhere near my bed. You simply have no idea how high-minded she can be about other people's moral standards!"

"How can she be less than an angel when she looks so much like you?" he asked, but Miss Amanda was not to be shaken from her pose. She still refused to notice me. Mr. Forrest gave the back of her neck a perplexed look, for he knew perfectly well that she was aware of my presence. He took her shoulders in his square hands and turned her a bit abruptly, which made her gaze sweep over me.

"Great heavens!" she cried. "We have been discovered." She spoke in just the tone of mock surprise I had heard from the brother she thought dead. Once she acknowledged me, her eyes rested on me, seeming to appraise. But I saw in her look only a kind of sullen triumph that looked in on itself.

Like any man truly in love, Mr. Forrest cherished his blindness and sought to make perfect a less-than-perfect moment. "I hope you wish us well, Miranda," he said to me.

I was dazzled by him, as I had been in all our previous brief meetings. I even marveled at how different an American gentleman made the English language sound. And I contrived to find something new to admire about his appearance. The little line beside his mouth that held promise of an unmocking smile even when he was being serious. And with all this woolgathering, I failed to find a reply until I sensed that Miss Amanda's eyebrows had risen high on her forehead. She was standing before Mr. Forrest and drew his arms around her. She enveloped herself in this man as if he were her possession, casually come by, that I—or any other woman—should yearn hopelessly over.

"Oh, sir," I managed, "I wish you both every happiness." And I even dropped a curtsy that was as girlish as I would allow myself.

"And maybe you will do me a favor, Miranda," Mr. Forrest was saying in a voice with an undertone of genial gruffness about it.

"Anything, sir," I murmured, causing Miss Amanda to smile ironically at how utterly—and easily—I was overcome by Mr. Forrest.

"Maybe you'll be able to convince Amanda of the wisdom of a short engagement. She's led me a long enough chase as it is. Do you think you could persuade her that there's no reason for much more waiting?"

"Ah, but there *are* reasons, Gregory!" Miss Amanda cut in, sparing me whatever reply I might have thought of. "Far more reasons than you could possibly fathom!" Her eyes never left me as she spoke those words.

But Mr. Forrest's eyes were upon me, too, and I met them briefly. My glance was meant to convey to him that I would gladly marry her off to him that evening if it were in my power. Her mother was not the only one eager to see her settled. And it was only a moment later when I considered that this was more self-serving than it was a favor to Mr. Forrest. But then I suppose I must have thought that marriage made for miracles. It was still very much my notion that any woman was vastly enhanced by the mysticism of her bridal vows, and certainly I thought that being Mr. Forrest's wife would ennoble his fortunate bride—and correct any flaw of her character. After all, I had kept the great part of my illusions, and it required only Mr. Forrest's tall presence to bring them out in full flower.

In a gesture of considerable manly grace Mr. Forrest moved from behind Miss Amanda and began fumbling in some concealed pocket beneath the wide, glossy black lapel of his coat. Miss Amanda allowed herself some little display of curiosity of this, and of course I was rooted to the spot in the sort of half trance that Mr. Forrest inspired in me. He drew out a smallish flat box bound up with a silk cord. It seemed to be Miss Amanda's third engagement gift of the day. But no, miraculously, it was not for her at all. He sidestepped his fiancée and, wonder of wonders, walked directly to me, holding out the box.

"This is only a small token for you, Miranda," he said in a voice that retained a minor ring of boyish simplicity. "I'd like you to have a little remembrance of our engagement. It's a happy time, and you should share in it."

My heart thundered at these straightforward words that bespoke so thoughtful a heart. Embarrassed though I was at any sort of gift, I felt my eyes filling at the goodness of the giver. I came very close to pure envy of Miss Amanda at that moment.

She sought to shatter it in her usual way. "I hardly think, Gregory, that one's fiancé's giving a gift to one's maid is quite the conventional thing."

"But I thought you despised convention, Amanda." Mr. Forrest did not even turn to Miss Amanda as he silenced her. But I glanced only to see her hand rise to the pearls he had just fastened around her neck. She seemed to find comfort in them and managed a superior smile.

My hand faltered at the box being offered me. And to cover my confusion, I'm afraid I thought of another way to give Miss Amanda a small difficulty. "Oh, sir," I heard myself saying, "I couldn't accept anything without Miss Amanda's permission."

Mr. Gregory looked momentarily as vexed as any man caught between two women. But of course Miss Amanda was then forced to give her blessing, which she did with an impatient toss of the head. And by then I was composed enough to take the box. I should have bolted with it if I'd had my way. But it was clear that I was meant to open it in Mr. Gregory's presence. This I managed to do and narrowly avoided dropping it onto the floor. Inside the box beneath a layer of cotton wool lay coiled a slender, quite simple gold chain of minute links.

It was, naturally, more beautiful to me in its simplicity than the ropes of graduated pearls that gleamed milky-dim at Miss Amanda's throat. But I was wordless, as I often was, and only held up the chain. And then, because my hand trembled, I dropped it into the box again, where it lay in a little golden puddle swathed in the white cotton wool.

How unlike this gift was from the ten-shilling tips casually thrust down by Miss Ward-Benedict, or the pound note left in an envelope behind the departing Mrs. Glaslough. This was a real gift, chosen for me by one who understood that even servants have feelings and that the conventional gesture is often the emptiest.

I managed to stammer my thanks, but only just. And Miss Amanda was so vastly amused at my artlessness after so many days of enduring my stiffness that she kept any further comment to herself.

"Maybe you have something you can wear on it," Mr. Forrest said, perhaps as an alternative to dismissing me.

And it occurred to me that I did. "Oh, sir, perhaps I shall have a hole drilled in my foreign coin and wear it around my neck on the chain. It's the only other gift I was ever given. I should like to keep the two together."

"And what kind of coin is it?"

I reached into my apron pocket, where I carried the copper coin given me on the day I had gone into service. Though I was always on the point of losing it, I had managed to keep it with me, perhaps for luck, perhaps for want of anything else that was really my own. I handed the copper to Mr. Forrest.

He turned it in his hand and seemed surprised. "It's a funny thing to come across this far from home," he said. "An American Indianhead penny."

"Perhaps Miranda has a secret American admirer," Miss Amanda offered from the post she had taken up beside the mantel. But Mr. Forrest seemed not to hear her. "Where did you come by this, Miranda?"

"The Wisewoman gave it to me," I said, without thinking.

"Wisewoman?"

"A fortune-teller," Miss Amanda said, her fingers among her pearls again. "You have no idea how superstitious simple people are in this country, Gregory."

"I doubt Miranda consulted the fortune-teller," he replied. "It's surely customary for the client to pay rather than to be paid."

"She was only a lonely old woman who was being kind," I murmured. And the bond that seemed to strengthen between me and Mr. Forrest gave me heart, for I smiled then and regained a more worldly air.

"And was she kind enough to foresee your future as well?" he asked.

"In a manner of speaking," I answered, "though of course it was veiled in mystical talk, and I doubt I remember much of it."

"I'll bet you remember some of it," Mr. Forrest said, drawing me out. "People do, even when they aren't believers."

"Well, yes, sir, I remember one thing very clearly. The Wisewoman said I would marry twice." I saw Mr. Forrest's surprise at this boldness. But then Miss Amanda crowed with sudden laughter. It was just her nervous sort of quick response when she was thoroughly fed up with being cast to one side even for a moment. "Married *twice*, Miranda? My dear, I shall do very well indeed to get you married *once!*"

Then her laughter pealed again, drowning the moment. She had had enough and waved for me to leave them. And in truth I had lingered longer than I should have done. I was well along the dark hall before I was out of range of her mocking laughter.

Eighteen

Early in December 1911 we returned to the Isle of Wight. And the flurry of events begun in London whipped up into the winds of change that swept away all thoughts of a quiet winter in the country.

I shall always remember the day we returned to the island where I was born, the island I had never thought to leave. To return after a mere month may be a small enough matter to the footloose. But while I was never to miss the hard lights and the hard looks of London, it was unsettling to be thrust back again into the world of the country establishment where I had begun my servitude.

John Thorne had been sent on ahead in the Lanchester. It was piled high with the additional trunks of frocks and gowns and the beginnings of a trousseau that Miss Amanda had acquired in town. Her engagement had loosed a last-minute excess of shopping. It occasioned any number of frantic negotiations with milliners and the sort of superior needlewomen whose specialty is the sewing of monograms with silk thread.

John awaited our party as the steamer arrived across choppy water at the Ryde pier. I remember that Sir Timothy had been made queasy by the passage and sat swathed in rugs. That Lady Eleanor and Miss Amanda had sat flanking him along the covered deck and discussed the plans for an engagement party across their ailing gentleman.

I was free to watch from the bow of the ship as the Isle of Wight grew large on the horizon. It began as a faint shape above the water, insubstantial as a dark cloud. And rose around us until the ferry was embraced by the Ryde harbor and the ship was nudging the iron pier. I saw John Thorne at the front of the waiting crowd. He drew his countryman's cloth cap off, and I saw the brightness of his hair in the dullness of the winterish day, above the somber blacks of the huddle of overcoats. He waved the cap once in the air to salute me. Perhaps in that moment my mind was free of frivolous, preposterous thoughts of Mr. Gregory Forrest, whom we had left temporarily behind in London. Though I wore beneath my collar a new gold chain with an old coin fixed to it by a London jeweler.

I perched on the front seat of the Lanchester beside the taciturn Thorne. And the Whitwells rode behind on the rear seat, as near one another as they ever came, in a jumble of rugs and lap robes. I longed for the drive down to Nettlecombe and Whitwell Hall to last. I was in no hurry to find myself back in the domain run along Mr. Finley's military lines. Nor did I relish the first sound of clashing cooking pots wielded in Mrs. Creeth's heavy hand. It was too like starting at a bare beginning once more, and I wished to be well beyond all that. All in all, I was rather like a child being sent reluctantly back to a severe school. I drew myself up on the seat of the careening auto and struggled to wrap around myself the trappings of my new dignity and the discreet hint of a London manner.

After town, which is never quite daylight and never quite dark, we seemed at the mercy of nature in all its rawness. The Isle looked cozy enough, and as small as a child's toy landscape with its low farmhouses tucked under hills. But the sky was enormous, seething like London's smoke, but fresh with the salt of the sea. It was a watercolor done in shades of blurred gray. The short day darkened quickly. And though we arrived at the gates of the Hall before teatime, it was nearly pitch-black night.

As I was settling Miss Amanda into her room that evening, she drew off her glove in a gesture I was meant to notice. On her hand was an enormous square-cut diamond engagement ring. I was prepared to admire it within limits—something along the line of *It's very nice, I'm sure, Miss.* But she elicited no response whatever. Once she was sure I had seen it, she sent me off to inventory all her trunks and valises to make quite sure that nothing was missing.

In servants' hall I was given a watchful welcome. Mr. Finley was half-inclined to remind me of my duties to the household as well as to the young mistress. But from the first hour I was kept so busy that he very shortly wrote me off. And with an inward groan he turned to consider how Hilda or Hannah might, in a pinch, be made presentable and efficient enough to serve at table.

Perhaps I rather overplayed my role as burdened lady's maid. For Mrs. Creeth herself drew me aside late that night and forced a fortifying cup of tea down me. "Here, now," she said in all kindness, "that young miss'll work you to death. Drink this tea. It's strong enough for a mouse to walk across and will give you a proper warming."

I settled by the dying kitchen fire and rested feet that had run up and down many flights that long day. As I had Miss Amanda tucked into her bed for the night, I lingered half dozing by the hearth and in the end drained the entire pot of Mrs. Creeth's potent tea. She had long since taken herself off to bed with scarcely another word. She was not one to want to hear the latest word of London, a place to her as distant, and quite as ominous, as Bombay.

And what should I have done and what would life have become for me if I had known that at that very moment John Thorne had entered the house by the route he knew so well? That at that very moment he was standing at the foot of Miss Amanda's bed while she held out to him a hand on which gleamed Mr. Forrest's engagement ring?

I was denied that knowledge—or spared it. But just as I was on the point of falling fast asleep in the kitchen settle, I heard the latch on the kitchen door behind me. I started, though not in fear. I thought it might be John.

The fumbling at the door and the sound of boots in awkward stealth suggested another intruder. I rose up just as young Willie Salter made an ungainly entrance into the half-dark room. For a moment I could hardly think who this gawky lad was. Then I remembered him as the son of the widower, George Salter. Willie was the estate agent's son being raised in the Salter cottage on the home farm presided over by his Aunt Winifred.

"Whatever brings you here at this hour, Willie?"

The firelight caught the whites of his eyes as he glanced around the empty room. He was clearly on a mission, and it took some moments for me to know it involved a message for me.

"I've word," he said at last in a voice half soprano and half baritone, "for you from Betty."

I had missed her before then. Indeed, I'd been scanning the house for her from the moment we had arrived. But nothing was said about her in the kitchens. Not even by the babbling Hilda and Hannah, and I hadn't the courage to ask after her. It was clear enough that she was no longer one of the staff. And I feared the worst.

"What have you to tell me, Willie?" I whispered, though there was no one about.

"Betty says she'd write except—except she don't know how. But she wants you to know that she's with us and all is well. That's what she said to tell you: all is well. And to come to the home farm on your first half day."

I was astonished to hear that Betty was in the Salters' house and perhaps under the wing of the silent, no-nonsense Winifred Salter. I remembered her from the night of the Ventnor ball. Her eyes that seemed to see through all vanity. And though I had tried to forget the moment when I'd glimpsed Miss Amanda mocking me at the center of the ballroom in John Thorne's arms, I remembered how Winifred Salter had tried to spare me. One of the few things she had ever said to me had been, "Don't let them make a fool of you." And I was in no danger of forgetting the woman or the words.

Willie Salter's message answered very few of the questions I had about Betty and her future, if she was to have one. But there was nothing I could ask this half-tongue-tied lad. He'd delivered his message and now fidgeted to be off. I told him I would come to Betty at my first opportunity, though I wished for more information to prepare me against my reunion with her.

In the December days that followed, we were a country establishment coming to terms with winter, drawing in against the long nights. The late-dawning mornings crackled with frost in the first crystal light, and the cries of the London street vendors were echoes from a distant world. The smoke rose high and straight above the bare branches of the grove: a wisp of blue from Granny Thorne's cottage and the more distant pillars of gray from the home farm hearths.

Even the Nettlecombe church spire down beyond the gates was suddenly visible in the winter starkness. At sight of it, I turned my mind away from the plaque on the church wall that mourned the death of young Gordon Whitwell. Here, at least, his soul could be quiet.

But I was scarcely out of the house—or in the presence of John Thorne—through that time. He was, if anything, more remote, and perhaps confident of me and my patience. Perhaps he knew that I stole glimpses of him from the windows of the upper house as he settled again in his domain of the garages below, so like the first days I had known of him.

At Whitwell Hall we were all rather like figures in an old painting of country life, more Flemish than English. Going about their tasks in an austere season enlivened by the approach of Miss Amanda's engagement party that even eclipsed the Christmas season. The woodsmen brought boughs of evergreen that lay in the dooryard ready to festoon the house for the festive day. Mrs. Creeth was already growing gaily grim at the prospect of the mince and "marzipany" pies she would have to produce "with precious little help of any sort" and in unheard-of quantity.

In attending to Miss Amanda's relentless needs, I lived a distance from the rest of the house staff. I noted only Mrs. Buckle, who wafted ghostlike around the upper halls as housekeeper. She pretended to be more occupied than she could have been. I got no more than a stiff bow from her even on the occasions when we met face-to-face.

Hilda and Hannah were in greater evidence, though I had never had very much to say to either of them. They provided society for one another. And their country accents were all but gibberish even to me, who had been born not ten miles from them, and in no more promising circumstances. But even in the preparation for great events, one day was very like another in their lives. Hilda still went about calf-eyed with love for the unpredictable part-time footman, Abel, who to her joy was pressed into almost daily service. And Hannah scarcely let a day pass without fumbling some bit of crockery onto the floor, to Mrs. Creeth's loud dismay.

Sir Timothy, exiled from his London club, took up his usual chair in the library and drowsed through the days. Lady Eleanor was bound to her writing table, drawing up lists for the engagement party and writing out the invitations in her lovely, flourishing hand. Hers was an orderly industry, and when I took in a cup of midmorning coffee I once noted a special list of invitations labeled *"Duchesses:* write in third person." She allowed herself no lapse even in a world she moved in with such assurance. And she seemed to keep a prudent distance from Miss Amanda, very likely to preserve the even flow of events that seemed to be working smoothly and to the advantage of all concerned.

I was several days managing even three hours' freedom from Miss Amanda. She seemed as absorbed as her mother in the ritual of the engagement party plans, almost as if she had never been so sulky and reluctant. Once when I came upon her making up elaborate lists of her own—to do, to send for, to invite—she said in a sighing voice, "One must proceed with every show of assurance even when there are so many loose ends to attack one's courage." And when she caught my bewildered and questioning eye, she blinked once and sent me on my way in quite a different tone of voice.

At last I found half an afternoon to visit the home farm. Though when I gained this freedom, I said nothing of where I was going to Miss Amanda. She appeared to have forgot all about Betty's situation. And I did not so much as mention this unfortunate for fear Miss Amanda might make her own inquiries out of idle curiosity. The last thing I wanted was to be sent out in search of information I could not come by discreetly. For all I knew, Betty, who was far advanced in her pregnancy by then, was being held under house arrest by Winifred Salter to spare us all shame. The vision of poor Betty locked in a bare attic capered across my reluctant mind.

But at last I was to know the truth. I set out one wind-whipped afternoon in my most respectable London outfit, shod against the frozen ruts of the country roads. How much I would have preferred a cozy chat with Granny Thorne instead. But I had, in a manner of speaking, been invited to the Salters' by Willie. So I made my way to the home farm, where I had never been, nearly overcome by the unpleasant blend of curiosity and dread.

The dooryard was swept as clean as marble paving. Winifred Salter herself opened the door to my knock. I was struck again by the gracefulness of this rawboned countrywoman. She greeted me with just the degree of familiarity suitable between us, and very much as if I were expected.

Mrs. Buckle and Mrs. Creeth had some cause to envy this woman who was not quite of the serving class and not quite anything else. She was mistress of a commodious house made more comfortable by her own hand. Wool rugs clearly of her making were spread on polished floors, glossed with verbena-scented wax. Lamps with well-trimmed wicks glowed smokelessly in the corners against the early evening. It was a home just humble enough for me to understand and just fine enough to admire.

"You will have come to see Betty," Miss Salter said, then added in a more accommodating tone, "but you are welcome to stay on to tea, though it will be nothing beyond our usual." Her eyes brushed uncritically over me as she nodded toward a chair. Then she was gone, leaving me to observe the pleasant room presided over by this abrupt woman.

But I was not long alone. Betty appeared, filling up a narrow doorway almost as completely as Hilda or Hannah might. She gave out a happy little shriek at sight of me and then advanced ponderously across the room. No artifice of countrified dressmaking nor any number of trailing shawls could disguise Betty's condition. It had gone well past interesting. She swayed as she walked, and her days of darting agilely about had been suspended.

"Oiuu!" she cried, trying to reach around herself to embrace me, "I harf thot you'd give me up! I did an' all! You been gone a donkey's years, and just you look at me! I'm as big as a house!" Even with forewarning, I was poorly prepared for her altered appearance. "I must've had my times muddled," she added obscurely. "I shall do well to make it to March!"

And then the maddening creature seemed ready to ignore her own circumstances and settled as well as she was able into a chair, ready to hear all my London adventures.

"But, Betty, how can you interest yourself in such things in your . . ." I hardly knew how to begin with her.

"Who? Me? I'm orl right, as you see. Miss Salter's been that good to me." And she added in a lower voice, "In her way."

Then I noticed what I had not known to look for before. I saw on Betty's hand a narrow gold wedding band. She followed my eye and grinned as impishly as her old self. "That's right. I'm Mrs. Hubert Sampson!"

"But if you are, why—"

"Oh, orl right," she said, "if you must know everything at once, you must. And I guess I should be grateful that London hasn't made you too grand and la-di-da to bother your head about me.

"It's this way, and I shall tell it all of a rush before Miss Salter calls us in to tea. We've been baking today, her and me." Betty glanced at the door through which Winifred Salter had exited. But it was clear that she was leaving us in privacy until I had been told all and in the way Betty saw fit to tell it.

"It orl started wiv that Ventnor ball when you and Miss Amanda got me up in orl that finery to dazzle Hubert—Mr. Sampson. She took a dim view of all that play-acting, did Miss Salter. Of course, carryin'-on of that sort wouldn't be her way, would it? She's a thought overserious in her thinking, but very sharp wiv it." Betty nodded her head in respect for Miss Salter's character.

"Anyway, she seemed to take an interest in my situation, though she's not a prying woman in the usual way. She come to find out just what we were up to in trying to fascinate Mr. Sampson on my behalf. She figured out I was in the family way, but how, I wouldn't know. Nobody tells her nuffin, and she don't gossip. Still, she keeps her ear to the ground. Oh, I wouldn't try to put nuffin over on *her*. Indeed I wouldn't, even if she hadn't warned me against trying, which she has.

"You weren't orf in London two days before she went to work. Turned up in the kitchens at the Hall, she did, demanding to have a private word wiv Mr. Finley himself. You should have seen the look on Mrs. Creeth's face when Mr. Finley and Miss Salter went off to the stillroom for a quiet talk, just the two of them! The upshot of that was Mr. Finley told me to pack my traps and to be off with Miss Salter and to do just as she told me. He'd have had more to say to me besides, but Miss Salter was standing nearby. I have her to thank that I didn't get the tongue-lashin' of me life from Mr. Finley as well as the sack." Betty's eyes grew round with wonder at these sudden events, and perhaps my eyes were just as wide.

"Well, she marched me over here, and before you could say Bob's-your-uncle, she sent her brother, Mr. George Salter, off to Ventnor to fetch Hubert Sampson. I can tell you, my heart was in me mouth. Still, I was glad enough to put my fate in the hands of others, for I'd played me last card, and no mistake.

"The long and the short of it was this. When Mr. Sampson got here, looking quite out of his depth, Miss Salter went straight to the heart of the matter. She's plainspoken, you know. Mr. Salter, he hung back, but stayed on in case Mr. Sampson might bolt.

"And Miss Salter said straight out to Hubert, 'Well, then, Mr.

Sampson, you will excuse near strangers interesting themselves in your private affairs, neighbors though we have always been, in a manner of speaking. But if you have come to the time of life when you think of marrying, I'm sure you'll find a good wife in Betty here. And dutiful, too!' She give me a look then that was a lesson in itself.

"Hubert colored up something alarming, but there's no gainsaying Miss Salter once she's got something on her mind. She went on to mention that it spoke well of Mr. Sampson's character that he'd been a dutiful son to his mother these many years. But if he didn't take steps, he'd have no one when his mother was dead and him a lonely old bachelor wiv nobody to see to his wants. It shook him to hear matters put so strong. But I do believe he was relieved to hear someone take an interest in his future. His old dragon of a ma certainly don't think of nobody but herself, the old besom!

"Then Miss Salter made it clear that I was in a particular situation myself. She made herself understood wivout spelling things out. But she did say that Hubert could make up for lost time by marrying a ready-made family, in a manner of speaking. I thought this would send him off for sure, but he held his ground. Then Miss Salter asked him if he thought he could do better. And that clenched things.

"We was married in the registry office at Shanklin, wiv Miss Salter and Mr. Salter in attendance. It's orl very hush-hush still. Miss Salter wouldn't hear of me coming up against Hubert's old ma before the baby's born. Too upsettin' all around. So in a way I'm neither maid, wife, nor widow just now. But Hubert calls on me twice a week. And though his ma's half off her head about that, she's coming around. Then when the little stranger makes his appearance, we'll tell her we're married, and we won't make no mention of exactly *when.*"

"But won't she be just as angry to learn you've been going behind her back?" I asked.

"Very likely, but what can she say when the whole district finds out about the wedding and the baby? She can't nip things in the bud when they've already blossomed out, can she? Besides, she's very taken wiv her respectable position in Ventnor, you know. And she'll be so busy brazening it out wiv her friends it'll sap half her strength. And the old trout knows what side her bread's buttered on. She'll have to knuckle under if she expects Hubert to provide for her. He's not *reely* weak in his character, you know, Miranda. He only wants a bit of a shove in the right direction. And Miss Salter give it him."

"And Hubert," I said, "doesn't he mind at all about the baby?"

"Mind? Why, he talks about it—very refined in his speaking, of course—like it was his own. And who knows? Perhaps the next one will be!" Betty beamed at me with all her spirits restored. And I didn't know whether to laugh at the absurdity of it all or weep with relief.

I was spared the decision, for Miss Salter entered the room and gestured us both in to tea.

Willie Salter joined us, and so did his father. George Salter was so tall that his head grazed the low beams at the end of the kitchen where the scrubbed table was laid for a country tea. He had even less conversation than his sister and only mumbled a greeting to me, looking down from his great height. And perhaps his large, wind-burned face colored more deeply in the presence of so many women around his table.

Miss Salter poured out the tea from an earthen pot and handed around plates with thick bread still hot from the oven, and crocks of pale butter. There was a seedcake to follow, just faintly sweet. And the fare was more hearty and satisfying than any amount of cress sandwiches or the iced pastries of a grander table. It was hard to imagine that these silent, even dour country folk had ever acted out such a scene with Mr. Sampson as Betty had just finished describing. Yet I knew that both brother and sister would go out of their way to put things right for those who could not manage their own affairs with any hope of real success. There was little warmth in their manner, but I felt very safe among them, a feeling I had not often known elsewhere.

When it was time for me to leave, Winifred Salter spoke to me over Betty's head, rather as if she were a child. She made it clear to me as Betty's friend that while the girl was in her care she was expected to do her share in the household tasks. But that she was not being used as a servant. She owed me no explanation, but she did me the honor of speaking to me as an equal, with the result that I felt both flattered and rather elderly. And I was urged to come back to visit Betty any time I was free.

As Miss Salter saw me to the door, I sensed that there was something more she would have me know. A moment of hesitation in a woman who never hesitated—something as subtle and as fleeting as that. I almost lingered on the doorstep, for I caught a glimpse of something in her distant-seeing eyes. But either she expected me to read her thoughts or it was not yet time to tell me what was in her mind. So I went on my way, relieved within limits about Betty and half persuaded that Winifred Salter had something else in her heart that might touch more on me than on Betty.

Nineteen

———❧———

In the week of the party, I found a reason to spend another afternoon away from Whitwell Hall. The excuse was a job of work for Granny Thorne. So I was off to her little house, Smuggler's Cottage, around the mere and through the grove. And I went unsuspecting that I was to learn Miss Amanda's engagement party was to be, in a manner of speaking, my own.

The Hall was already filling with houseguests. And I had no more than a glimpse or two of John Thorne that day. He was back and forth in the Lanchester to meet every train. The Hall was in an excited muddle, rather like the feeling beneath my heart whenever Mr. Forrest was expected.

My excuse for a stolen hour or two with Granny Thorne was a new long cloth for a buffet table that needed hemming—the sort of job she savored and did best. The cloth was so long that even folded over and over again it took up a laundry basket. And this made the walk along the path heavy going. The howling, rainswept night when I had first gone to Smuggler's Cottage, urged along by Mr. Finley, was far from my mind that day. The grove had lost most of its mystery to the leafless season, and I feared no madman lurking without cover.

My mind was all on our frenzied preparations for the party. Silver I had never seen was set out on trestle tables, which were in danger of pitching over. Mr. Finley stood through half the night in a long striped overall rouging again the glittering metal, in a state of pique and pleasure that transformed his sour face astonishingly. A thousand Mr. Finleys were reflected in the silver surfaces, each one recording the quiver of his nostril in distorted fashion.

The table in the dining room had been extended far beyond its usual length. And what an expanse of mirror-shiny mahogany it was! Abel was an unlikely figure, standing on top of it with his boots encased in felt bags, setting out the silver plateau in the center and the branched candleholders at precise distances. All this under Mr. Finley's snappish direction, at which poor Abel flinched. From even such memorable scenes as this, I was happy enough to flee the Hall.

I found Granny Thorne only a little pouty at having been left on her own so long. She was up and about again, studiously careful never to touch on the subject of her dead son, Bart Thorne. The scars of that wild autumn night were fading from her mind, though she wore a length of velvet ribbon around her neck. It served to cover the mark left by the wire her son had used in trying to choke the breath from her body. And it was just the sort of embellishment that Granny's idol, Queen Victoria, had permitted herself.

Granny's welcome was as warm as her hearth. And if it is possible to bustle slowly, that is what she did in settling us both before the fire so we would lose no time for chatting from the little that we had. She knew, as usual, as much of the Hall news as if she lived under its roof. But she liked to hear it repeated, and minute by minute the excitement was mounting at the Hall, so that even Granny might learn something new.

I had told her all I knew about the gown Miss Amanda meant to wear, the wondrous silver serving pieces, the turning out of all the bedrooms against the guests' arrivals.

She listened avidly enough, perched like a small, elderly, feathery owl, blinking with pleasure, then finally with impatience. "Well, yes, yes," she said at last, "but enough about the family and all that to-do abovestairs. What do you know of the celebrations for the rest of us? Are we not to drink the happy couple's health, too?"

I must have looked quite blank, for I couldn't imagine the servants with time enough on their hands that evening to celebrate on their own. Nor could I quite picture a festivity held in servants' hall. But of course Granny put me right at once. "Why, come midnight, there'll be a thundering great bonfire on the hill beyond the gate. The Nettlecombe folk are already seeing to that. A firework or two as well, I shouldn't wonder, like what we had for Jubilee Night. Then all the neighborhood hereabouts will troop up to the Hall and lift a glass to the young couple, provided by Sir Timothy. Oh, there'll be time enough for all this." Granny nodded reassuringly. "It's expected!"

"And will you come out for it, Granny?"

"Ah, no. My days for such things are over now," she said, not without some satisfaction. "Not but what I can't still creep about on me stick and get out of nights sometimes when the weather's decent and all's quiet. I shall sit right here at my own hearth and raise a glass of my own wine to Miss Amanda and her young man, and I shall do it just at midnight. It was the same with old Queen Victoria, you know," she added, now nodding with immense satisfaction. "In her dotage she went next to *nowhere.* People came to *her,* which is better yet, isn't it?"

Her eyes flickered to a spot above my head then, but I thought she was only catching a fanciful glimpse of her beloved Queen Victoria. I little knew that time had passed and that John Thorne had come home for his tea. But Granny did not call out a greeting. And this piece of innocent slyness on her part left me sitting there all unknowing.

"Yes," she continued after a moment, "I am better off right here in my own cottage and always was." And then with half a wink, "Even if it isn't quite so spit-and-polish as what Winifred Salter's is. I want for very little here, not but what the afternoons linger on a bit long now and again. But I have my memories, Miranda, as you'll have one day, too."

Her old eyes glowed with watery brightness as she added, "I need but one thing to put my mind at rest." And when I asked her what it was, I could not know her words were meant as much for John's ears as for my own. He must have stood as still as a statue at the door I had not heard open.

"Why, all I shall need to die happy is to see you in this cottage as one of my own family. 'Twill be the best end for me, and the best beginning for you." And perhaps she did not spell out more clearly her hope for John and me marrying because he was there behind me, and it was not her place to do his speaking for him.

At last and not before time, I sensed him there. Would I have sensed the presence of Mr. Gregory Forrest sooner? Perhaps, but when John announced himself with the scrape of a boot, I knew at once that he had heard his grandmother's words.

But it was not a time for confusion. And the old lady and I filled the next half hour in preparing a tea for ourselves and for John. I had been too uncertain of the future ever to think that I might spend the rest of my life at Smuggler's Cottage. As Granny and I went about our tasks in the little hole of a kitchen, it was suddenly more real than any other course. We were two women preparing to feed and cater to our silent man. It was a far more sensible way of life than I was likely to know otherwise. And Granny in her easy manner made even this moment count. She welcomed me into her kitchen, where many a woman would have resented any chit of a young girl who showed promise of taking over and usurping her place.

Granny must have read my thoughts as I was slicing a loaf more generously and less delicately than the gentry or Mr. Finley would have approved. "It's said," Granny noted in her piping voice, half witch, half child, "that there's never room for two women at one hearthside." She rolled an eye at me and tucked a straying wisp of white hair behind one ear. "But that's a load of old rubbish to my way of thinking. There'll be room for you here, and still more room later. I won't live forever, you know. Why, I'm already older than what the dear old Queen was when she went to her reward, though I'm not saying how much!"

"Still and all, Gran, you're saying too much!" John's voice boomed in from the other room, and both Granny and I nearly leaped out of our skins to be overheard. I had rarely heard John's voice lifted. Taking it for a command, we bore in the meal.

Then Granny gave us both another nudge by having me pour out the tea. When I handed John his cup, his hand brushed mine and might have closed over it if it had not given his grandmother more encouragement than he thought she should have. But I was emboldened to give him a straight look. And I wondered again at this stranger who was expected to marry me. It seemed I had rarely seen him at all with any clarity. Our meetings had been misted over by the passions that burned in us both, and just how differing those passions were I was not yet to know.

My mind moved back over the months, and what I recalled must have colored my face. This man sitting in the same rude cottage where he had been born and cosseted by his adoring grandmother was the same man with whom I had writhed on the floor of the carriage house in London. That evil den that reeked with the deathly perfumes of a man thought dead. Gordon Whitwell.

I wrenched my mind from this unbidden memory, only to encounter another one. I saw us sitting, the day of the hunt, on the flat tomb of a young girl in the churchyard. "Come now, Miranda," John had said, "you must bend a bit or you'll be broken by the gale." Words heavily spoken that seemed now as vague as a memory deeply buried by the years. For how can one be both strong and yielding and still survive?

My thoughts blended to their usual confusion as they always did when I forgot to hold myself in an unnatural stiffness. I shifted my mind to the present to find myself sitting at a family tea, very much as if all had been decided and I belonged there without question. If it was a nudge from his grandmother that John needed to marry me, he had it now. This very thought crossed my mind, and what an innocent mind it still was.

There were times, like that one, when I persuaded myself that John Thorne was no more complicated than he seemed, with his large boots planted beneath the plain plank table as he drank his tea a bit noisily. I was not so carried away with the glamour of the great world that I failed to value the easy simplicity of this scene. That I had ever attended a ballet, of all things—and in London—with this rough-hewn man! Both our lives had been pulled out of shape by unlikely forces that neither of us truly understood. His face retained a ruddiness, and he seemed never even to have heard of such a damp, unhealthy, skulking, whey-faced place as London in all his life. Certainly he never mentioned it.

But surely I could not have been quite naïve enough not to glimpse beneath the surface, even in those few easy hours in the cottage that Granny Thorne made so welcoming.

Surely I must have seen some hint of ruthlessness in John's cool eyes, something more than male obstinacy in that chin. And were John's silences not somehow different from the silences of other men? Was his quiet not more stealthy than, say, my own father's stolid wordlessness had always been? Was there not some slight, significant difference between John's way and the ways of all men tongue-tied when they're confronted by a woman—and the need for a woman?

And could I not perceive even a hint in every passing glance from John, a hint that he was seeing the face of Miss Amanda Whitwell's in place of mine? Could I see nothing of this?

I must have. I was already half aware—unwillingly aware. There had been clues. But there had been reasons not to heed them—excuses not to consider them. Are there not always?

The afternoon ended with John walking me back to the Hall through the dark twilight on one of the waning year's shortest days. We walked as if we were already married, together but not touching. He swept aside the occasional brittle branch that barred the path through the grove. And I walked in his shelter.

"You shouldn't be giving old Gran false hope," he muttered at last when we were already deep within the grove.

I walked in silence, not knowing how to defend myself against this charge.

"She's old," he continued at last, "but still strong in her way. She may live a long time yet."

Still I did not speak, and the lights from the Hall were already flickering through the last trees of the grove. A steamy veil rose from the mere, and I knew that if I looked I could see the ghostly gray dome of the folly across the sheet of dark water.

"We'll not be spending the whole of our married life under Gran's roof. She sees nothing of the world beyond her cottage. But you and me—we're not liable to be so tied down. We'll start out with her—it's best that way—handy. But don't give her to think we'll stay alongside her always. There's other opportunities elsewhere "

I stirred then, or rather something stirred within me. I was ready to love and more than half resigned to rejection. But John Thorne was speaking as if something had already been decided between us—or perhaps between us and others. The uncertainty of many weeks seemed to drop from me, and the wind of the evening blew less cold.

This was the way of people like us. A rough countryman in mucky boots does not go down on one knee to propose. And a lady's maid who has but lately had her first glimpse abovestairs does not expect it. Among such as us, things were decided in other ways, and my mind moved a step ahead—a giant step, it seemed—to keep pace with John's words.

"But where shall we go, then?"

"It's a big world," he muttered, "and the century's still young, like us. It's a world . . ." Words forsook him, but somehow I envisioned what he wanted me to see, a world brightly lit, away from the flickering lamps in our corner of it. A world of steam and speed and opportunities for even us. A world more substantial than an underling's dream. I needed no promise more binding than that, nor any compliments that ended with poetry and professions of love. I saw what I was meant to see. And my vision was aided by my need to be loved, even without tender words. I foresaw us together in Granny Thorne's cottage in a sort of honeymoon time. And then I saw us bursting all bonds in some unimaginable way. I saw the turn of a locomotive's wheels, the prow of a ship knifing through curling waves. Doors fell open, and my mind moved easily around the devious demands of Miss Amanda and the shadowy corners of John Thorne's life. I saw us free of all that. Does not every woman see with this particular blindness on the day she learns she will marry?

"There's America," John was saying, as if this were only one choice in half a hundred that suddenly unfolded before us.

We were in the kitchen dooryard then. I felt the cobblestones beneath my feet. But still I was not drawn back to earth, not to this narrow plot of ground. The Hall rose up before us. Light from Miss Amanda's window fell in a rippling patch across the rough paving where we stood.

John fumbled in a pocket of his coat. The brim of his weathered, old-man's hat shaded his young-man's eyes. I saw what he held between thumb and forefinger. It was a gold ring worn nearly to a thread with a single stone set in it. A ruby it was, like a solitary drop of blood gleaming black in the shadowed light.

"It was Gran's and then my mother's. It's yours now."

It gave me courage, this symbol did. Courage to ask, "But when—"

"Soon now," John muttered. "There are reasons—there's no reason —to wait longer."

Though it seemed only large enough for a child's hand, the ring fit my finger perfectly.

Twenty

───────•❦•───────

How little I remember now of the final preparations for the engagement party for Miss Amanda and Mr. Forrest. My mind was divided between my own concerns and my duties. And I was scarcely able to attend to both.

No one in the kitchens had the time to remark on my ring. I could shift it around so that only the thin thread of gold showed faintly on my finger. And perhaps this concealment spared me advice or condemnation. As for Miss Amanda, if she noticed my engagement ring that was so different from her own, she made no sign. Of course she saw! She saw everything. I knew it even then. But she said nothing. I know now that if it had not suited her plans, if it had not *been* her plan, she would have put an end to my engagement. She might have put an end to me.

The night of the party was lit by lightning. I always think of it in just that way. In the overflowing rooms of the Hall, the tall mirrors multiplied the flash of jewels and the tiers of candles. As most of the guests were friends of Lady Eleanor and Sir Timothy, the entire upper house seemed top-heavy with tiaras. Even in this heavy splendor, Miss Amanda shone forth like a young queen. Those who had found fault with her in the past stood muted in admiration. Should I praise the beauty of one who was my double in some strange work of nature or trick of fate?

I am free to do so now. But even then I was astonished by her radiance, which effortlessly eclipsed mine. A radiance that had nothing to do with her silver gown sent from Mr. Worth's establishment in Paris. She had moments of a special brilliance, moments when her violet-eyed, porcelain-complexioned face burned brighter from some dark inner flame.

On that night, which was more a triumph she had conceded to her mother than a moment for herself, she played her role so smoothly and so well that we should all have been put on our guard. She stood between her parents and Mr. Forrest and received her guests—and their compliments—with just the proper degree of composed charm. There was even a hint of shyness in her manner and a diffidence in her gesture foreign to the young woman she was.

I moved under Mr. Finley's snapping finger from task to task, screened from the brilliant assemblage through much of the evening. But I glimpsed enough to feel the reflection of this glory and to know this night as one that would never be quite beyond recall. It reminded me of the ballet I had seen. Even this milling throng, weighted by the heavy grandeur of their winter finery, reminded me of dancers acting out in motion and gesture parts for them written by Miss Amanda.

A trail of Japanese lanterns wavering at the tops of bamboo poles lined the front drive. At midnight these were lit to draw all eyes to the bonfire the villagers set alight down beyond the gates.

The guests assembled before the house or stood sheltering behind the long windows of the warm rooms. Once Mr. Finley and the hired footmen and Abel had handed around the champagne for toasting the couple, the staff, too, was free for a few moments to watch the bonfire and the lanterns and to wait with the anticipation of children the first of the fireworks.

Even Mrs. Buckle threw on a wrap and gathered with the rest of us just where the drive branched off to the kitchen yard. We stood there, damp from our labors, with the winter wind singing in our ears. The flames against the night played across our minds as they must have stirred the primitive peoples who had lived on this island before us.

Hilda and Hannah stood massed together. And of these two, Hilda was discernible only because her eye strayed from the distant brilliance, hoping for a glimpse of Abel. Then, when the first firework roared up above the bonfire to explode in a white flower across the sky, we moaned deep in our throats with just the same sound that came from our betters on the Hall steps.

Our faces were lit with the distant fire. And I saw Mrs. Buckle standing dangerously near Mrs. Creeth, though neither noticed. Even Mr. Finley's upturned face showed awe. And from somewhere, John stepped up beside me, taking my hand with his ring on it. We stood there undeniably together now. The rest around us could notice or ignore, whatever they chose. In that minute or two we seemed free to do and to be whatever we pleased, even in the cramped, judging, joyless circle of our own kind.

There were to be cider and claret cup and toasts to the young couple, and even concertina music in the kitchens later. But I remember little beyond that display of fireworks that built to a breathless crescendo. And above us, nearer than the distant thunder of the explosions, came the delicate clinking sound of the champagne glasses. Perhaps Miss Amanda and Mr. Forrest were standing somewhere up there just as John and I were, with their profiles etched against the same darkness. Exploding fire flowers of rose and white and green blossomed higher and still higher in the night sky until we had almost exhausted our moans of wonder. John's arm moved around my body, and his hand came to rest beneath my breast. And the fire fell from the sky, dying just above the stark branches.

It was in this last flicker of light that something made me turn to find a pair of eyes upon us. As the light winked to darkness, I saw Winifred Salter standing just beyond the circle of servants. She met my gaze, and her eyes remained on me even after I looked away.

I married John Thorne in the first week of the new year, in January 1912.

No one set an impediment in our way. In a scene I could not so much as imagine, John asked Sir Timothy for permission to marry me, with the assurance that both he and I would not allow our married state to interfere with our duties. In this, he went over the head of Mr. Finley, who considered that all such staff decisions must rest with him or pass through his hands.

The butler gibbered with rage for many hours. But there were still guests in the house, lingering on after Christmas and lounging before the ashes of the Yule log in the morning-room grate. The kitchens and servants' hall were thus far too busy to savor outrage overlong. It was the one season of the year without the leisure to talk every matter to death. But Mrs. Creeth muttered darkly in sympathy for Mr. Finley's injured dignity.

They complained at length of the ingratitude of servants as if the two of them were a class apart. But Mrs. Creeth only pursed stern lips when she affected to notice me and would not discuss such an impropriety as marriage in my presence. She seemed not so suspiciously disapproving of John as she had been. Her wrath fell more on me. It was her prejudice that in matters of marriage it is men who are generally the trapped animals and women who ensnare them. In the background Hilda and Hannah made the jokes of the envious and muffled much nervous giggling behind large, reddened hands.

All this while Miss Amanda was calculating from a distance. We hardly spoke in the week before I was married, and I moved with care in her presence, fearing anything that might disturb the tightrope of those days. Nor did she even attempt to draw me out. One result of this mutual silence was that I learned only through the rumors circulating in servants' hall that Mr. Forrest had returned to America, almost directly after the engagement party.

He had gone home to his native land, rumor had it, "packed off by Miss Amanda," with the promise that she would join him in the spring. And they would then be married quietly in New York. "Like a pair of servants on the run!" Mrs. Creeth declared, condemning them—and me—in a single sentence.

Oddly, the house felt twice empty to me with Mr. Forrest not merely gone back to London but on his way to New York. I could have wept with the hollowness in my heart and the thought that I would never see him again. I had to coax my mind back to concerns more properly my own.

In this I was aided by Miss Amanda. She made no reference to my plans for marriage. She did not even pull a long face to show that she knew I was being sly. Though she must have considered such a ploy. But in the final days before my wedding, she gave me all my afternoons off, and so I was able to make such meager preparations as I could think of. One of them was to write to my mother and father, to tell them of my plans. To this letter I received no reply, possibly because marriage had never been in my mother's plan for me.

Perhaps I might have been willing to marry John Thorne over the objections of all the world, my mother's, or even Miss Amanda's, if any had been made. The narrowest engagement ring bearing the smallest stone will transform the heart of any who wears one. And a bride without a trousseau anticipates her great day as keenly as one richly attired. Perhaps more. I moved through those last days to the marriage bed that stood at the end of them. Nothing arose that even gave me a moment's pause except the invitation that came from Winifred Salter.

It was more a summons than an invitation. When Willie Salter told me hastily in the kitchen doorway that his aunt wanted a word with me, I feared at first that something had gone wrong with Betty. So on that free afternoon I cut short a visit to Granny Thorne, who had taken the matter of what I should wear to my wedding upon herself. I was to wear a rather practical costume cast off by Miss Amanda, and it could be made to do for me. In Granny's words, it had "many a long good mile left to it."

Granny grew almost as waspish as Miss Semple, the Ventnor dressmaker, when I would not stand through the afternoon for my fitting. The costume, a dark blue jacket and skirt, fit me perfectly as it was. But I'm afraid that I robbed Granny of an additional hour of pleasure in fussing over it.

I arrived out of breath at the door of the home farm. Winifred Salter opened before I could knock. "Is Betty well?" I asked her in a rush.

"She is quite well," Miss Salter answered, "but I have sent her up to her bed for a rest this afternoon so that you and I might have a word on our own."

I never doubted that Betty was somewhere up in a dormer sound asleep, since she had shown herself obedient to any rule set down by Miss Salter. As I settled in her parlor, I began to suspect that Miss Salter had plans for me as well. There was nothing about her to indicate she meant merely to celebrate my coming marriage, even in the quietest way. And I had no doubt that she knew of it, for little escaped her.

She made one concession to sociability in bringing a pot of tea and a plate of scones right into the parlor. It was clear that we were to be closeted together out of the way of any in her family who might have blundered into her kitchen.

As she poured out our tea, she seemed to measure words long before she spoke, longer even than was her custom. Perhaps she even considered a word or two of small talk to smooth the beginning. But she rejected that notion and at last said, "You are to be married, then, to Thorne."

I nodded, feeling accused in an obscure way. She looked at me directly as she handed me a cup. I could not meet that far-seeing gaze, and I wondered why I should be expected to.

"You are free to make your decision," she said, "freer by far than Betty was." She was not angling for information. Of that I was certain at once. Nor was she implying that I might be marrying out of concealed desperation. She was merely making it clear that she did not compare my circumstances with Betty's.

"It is my choice," I said, "insofar as I have one."

She paused and looked far beyond me before answering. "Yes, a woman can say yes or no, and that is all the choice she has. Or at any rate, that's the case with most women."

We drank our tea in silence then. I had no more conversation than she. I could not even study this long, angular woman without drawing her eye. And so I stared down into my plain white cup, searching for a pattern there that might give the moment shape.

Her saucer clattered down, and she said, "It will not free you—this marriage. You think it will, but it won't."

"No," I said, "I shall have to look after Granny Thorne along with my other duties."

Winifred Salter's hand moved in the air. "Granny Thorne will not be with you long. Even so, she is no burden. The innocent never are."

"And Miss Amanda," I said, perhaps eager to reassure myself, "she will be off to America in the spring, to marry as well."

"You will not be rid of her that easily, mark me!" Miss Salter said. But she read in my look that I would not hear a word against my young lady, whatever I might think of her myself. It broke the servant's code, and Winifred Salter saw that she had played a card she must take back. She was not a devious woman and so was vexed with herself for not choosing her words with greater care.

She fetched up a sigh and said, rather hopelessly, "You will never be first with him—with John Thorne. You know what I mean, don't you?"

But I would not know, and she saw that, too. She wanted to reach across then, I think, and shake sense into me. But it would have been useless.

"I must say what is in my mind. That is why I've asked you here.

It has nothing to do with any but you and my own family. Be good enough to hear me out."

I nodded, seeing she was struggling with herself. "My brother, George Salter, is a good man. I have made a decent home for him here, but he needn't have taken me in. We are plain people, as you see. We want for nothing, and what our neighbors do and what our betters do is not a concern of ours. I would not have meddled in Betty's business if she had not needed it. And I would not speak to you if I did not think . . ." Her voice trailed away as this lengthy speech seemed to sap her strength.

"That I am in just as great need in a different way?" I said.

"Yes. Just that. But your mind is made up. I didn't get to you in time, even if what I had to say could be of any use. I never married, and so I cannot know just how wholehearted a woman is on the eve of her wedding day. I can only see that by looking at you this minute. Still, I can't hold my tongue. I shall say what I have to say, though it does neither one of us a scrap of good. You would do better to marry my brother than to marry John Thorne."

I must have blinked in shock, and it must have seemed rude. I had hardly noticed the estate agent, her brother. Who was he? A tall, awkward man with his sister's long face, though heavily fleshed and burned raw with the weather. He had said hardly a handful of words to me—or to anybody else—since I had been aware of him.

"He's not old," Miss Salter was saying with a sad eagerness that transformed her voice. "Not yet forty, and well situated here. A good estate agent is never out of work, not with gentlemen like Sir Timothy about who know nothing of managing their own properties. I daresay my brother will keep this place and this house for the rest of his life. He's very steady. And I—I will not stand in your way, as you see. There is room for you here."

I could not erase the surprise from my face and could only wonder how many women there were in the world who would offer their menfolk, if only out of the hearing of the man in question.

"I know," she sighed, "you have heard much the same thing from Granny Thorne. And I can see your mind is made up. But I ask you to consider. Never think it is too late to change. It is never too late this side of the church door. But once through it, there is no turning back. I say nothing against your choice. I say nothing against John Thorne. I only tell you what you only think you know—that once you make that choice, you will live with it forever. And you would live a better life if you chose my brother. You would be safer. He would marry you, believe me. I know him."

But she saw the futility of her words. I must have seemed very young and very foolish to this woman, who perhaps had never really been young. She was certainly trying not to be exasperated at my very youthful hardheadedness. And she was as awkward on the subject of marriage as a man, and as incapable as a man even to speak of love.

She stood up then, for we were both ready to put this moment behind us. "Forgive me for this," she said. "It was my duty."

"Yes," I answered, "to your brother."

She shook her head. "No. To you."

Then I was gone, hurrying back to the Hall. Once I was out of sight of the home farm, I broke into a run. I ran until I was out of breath and paining badly from a stitch in my side. I ran unpursued, and yet in some strange panic. For I could not outrun Winifred Salter's words: "You will never be first with him—with John Thorne. You know what I mean, don't you?"

On the day John Thorne and I were married, Miss Amanda broke her silence. Even after all these years I am vexed with myself for remembering more clearly her words in that early morning than the marriage ceremony itself, simple though it was. But perhaps that is fitting, for what was in her heart and mind cast a longer shadow than any words of a clergyman who bound me to John Thorne for such a brief time.

I had taken in her breakfast tray to find her unwilling even to turn her head my way. And I had returned later to find the tray untouched and the tea gone cold. Still, I would have said nothing. But she roused herself when I reached for the tray she had thrust to the far side of the bed.

"Oh, do take that ghastly food away, Miranda. I can't look at it. And leave the curtains drawn. I can imagine how I must look, though I prefer not to."

She looked ill. Her hair was plastered damply to the pillow. Her eyes were circled in lines the color of bruises. There was a faint sour smell in the room, though it was aired daily. As I noticed the smell, Miss Amanda drew the back of her hand across her mouth.

"Shall I speak to her ladyship, Miss Amanda? Perhaps Dr. Post should—"

"Oh, do bend a bit, Miranda!" she cried out. "I am no more ill than I should be, nor is this the first morning. And while I feel wretched, I am in rather good spirits. Yes, quite good spirits, I think. Which you will surely shatter if you persist in impersonating an elderly retainer. Do be my dear little Miranda of your early days here just for a moment to help me face the day."

I could not quite return to the way I had been when first I encountered Miss Amanda in this very room. But at least I did not bear the untouched tray away and nod wordlessly at the door, though I was soon to wish that I had. I stayed beside her bed in the dim room. The sour smell grew less faint in the air.

"You are to marry—Thorne today," she said in a tone as abrupt as Winifred Salter's.

"Yes, Miss."

"And am I not to be allowed to wish you well?"

"Thank you, Miss Amanda."

"I do wish you well, Miranda. It could not suit me better. I should have been glad enough to see you marry sooner, but there were reasons why—it is never wise to rush into anything so terribly permanent. On the other hand, it is equally unwise to wait too long. One always learns too much in the long run. And that only makes decisions more difficult."

"If you say so, Miss," I replied tartly, for I thought she knew no more of what she was talking about than I did.

"And I trust you will take seriously your marriage vows," she was saying, immensely superior now and gathering strength to raise her head from the damp pillow. "A woman follows her husband, you know. To the ends of the earth if it is necessary."

I supposed she was thinking only of herself and Mr. Forrest already off in New York. But of course she wasn't. And she must have noticed that I would not willingly put up with much more talk about marriage vows. She fell silent, and contented herself with studying me. I felt her eyes on my face and composed myself carefully to keep from turning aside. "I wonder if marriage will change you," she mused, "and make us quite different."

"We are quite different now, Miss," I replied.

"Yes, I suppose we are." She saw me bending to take the tray away, and she moved as quickly as a snake. Her hand closed over my wrist. She was suddenly on her knees in the midst of her bed. Her violet eyes were seeking mine again, fiercely now. "Do you go to your wedding night a virgin, Miranda?"

I drew back from her, recoiling from her grasp. I despised her then. We were two women, only that. It was my wedding day, and on this day I should not have to endure insults—from anyone. She could not sense that. My wedding day was her own triumph, her own decision, and nothing to do with me. It did not bind me to John Thorne. It bound John Thorne to her. And so she perceived nothing but her need to know what was not hers to know.

"Do you, Miranda? Men want that, you know. They want you to be a virgin, you know. It is something they can take from you."

I saw the madness in her eyes, but it had been there all along. I had seen the same madness in her brother's. The madness of those who have been denied nothing and who will deny everything.

I heard a voice, my own: "Yes, Miss Amanda, I go to my marriage bed a virgin. Will you?"

She drew back as if I had slapped her, though no one ever had. She considered lashing out at me, and considered again. A smile played across her lips. But I could not read it. She settled back, almost comfortably. At last she spoke. "I lost my virginity," she said. "I gave it willingly to the only man I shall ever love."

I left her then. If she was ill, I did not care. I shuddered to think that I had ever fallen under the spell of her words, even when it was to my advantage to humor her. I left her presence then, and she did not see me again until I was a married woman and no longer a virgin. But in this I had not drawn farther from her, but nearer.

Amanda Speaks

Twenty-One

I am Amanda Whitwell, and I have been intimidated by very little in my nineteen years. I shall certainly not start by being cowed by a blank page. I shall write as I speak. There will be no sudden bursts into the sonnet form. Nor margins filled with the sketches of wild flowers.

For this is not a schoolgirl's journal to be addressed breathlessly to "Dear Diary." My days as a schoolgirl were few and rather unpleasant for all concerned. And while I find myself quite as alone as anyone as misunderstood as I am, I do not write for the eye of anyone now living. Perhaps if I live to be old and ugly and die in a bed from which all passion has fled, this book will be found, the ink quite faded and the cover marred by time. Perhaps future years will vindicate me. Perhaps all the chains that bind young women will have fallen away. Then my book will find its proper reader, yet unborn.

I shall head this, my first entry,

THE NEW YEAR, 1912

for it is to be in this newly born year that I mean to complete the plan for my life.

When we were in London in the autumn, I sent my maid to Asprey's to collect this rather lavish book of blank pages. It was the whim of that moment that I should record my thoughts in a book worthy to receive them—I who have been so careful to keep my thoughts from those who continually pry! And though it would surprise many of those who would invade my privacy, I am not so much the creature of my whims as the mistress of them.

I have said that I am not intimidated by a book waiting to be filled up. But my maid, Miranda, was quite speechless with fright at the thought of having to collect it. I would not be cruel to anyone if circumstances did not continually hem me in and rob me of my good disposition. But I sent Miranda out—quite unnecessarily—into the night and to that most daunting of London establishments, Asprey's. How surprised I was when the poor wretch found her way to Bond Street and back again, clutching this book. By that time she had grown short-tempered with me, as servants often do. I always think it rather pathetic when servants attempt to assert themselves. In the end, it is a game they cannot win. And they are poorly equipped to think such matters through.

Miranda, as I call her—you see I actually named her—had come to me quite unformed. She dropped from nowhere, really, and it was all rather like a joke played by fate. For she looked enough like me to be my twin. It was quite Shakespearean. She could have been made to pass as my double, though at the Ventnor ball I passed as hers, which was rather more fun.

But I cannot think in all truth that the resemblance between us goes very deep. I am called beautiful. And though her face is the image of mine, no one would have bothered to call *her* beautiful. That is an immense difference between us in itself. For beauty is nothing unless it can be made to work on one's behalf—and against others.

And another great difference between us is her boundless innocence. From the very beginning it often took my breath away. While she has been quite clever enough to see through some of my more transparent devices when I wanted her to, she has gone now to her marriage as willingly—and as ignorantly—as I intended.

Perhaps it is because we look so alike, Miranda and I, that I can never think of her as a human being in her own right. Her eyes are the mirrors in which I see myself—and the realization of all my plans. Miranda is my creature, and in time she will know it. Soon, perhaps inconveniently soon if my luck does not hold. Later, if she persists in being as blind as she has begun.

If I were religious, I suppose I might believe she had been sent to me by a Divine Providence to solve my quite complicated problems. Certainly on the very evening when she, newborn into the servants' world, came quaking into my bedroom, I began to think of how I might use her. But the solution grew in my own mind. And I have had no need to call upon a power more supreme. Servants are forever taking advantage of the good dispositions of their betters. It is as amusing as it is useful to reverse this natural order of things. Still, if I prayed, I should think Miranda the answer to all my prayers. Only she was lacking to make my scheme work. And here she is. I am meant to have what I want.

Indeed it was another servant who had given me so much trouble in the first place, and all the real joy I have ever known. John Thorne is his name, and very handsome he is in a brutal sort of way. I cannot think when it was that I first fell in love with him. I must have been a quite flat-chested, insignificant child.

For John is ten years and more my senior—more my dead brother's age than mine. He and my brother, Gordon, whom I scarcely recall, fought together in the Boer War. They were quite close, I believe, rather like those stories by Mr. Rudyard Kipling wherein the gentlemanly officer and the plain, lower-class soldier fight side by side in the shocking heat of some quite impossible climate.

My brother, Gordon, was killed out in South Africa, in one of those places with an unpronounceable Dutch name. Rather symbolic, I suppose, though I rarely think of it. For ours is a dying class. And I should be no better than poor Gordon in his unmarked grave if I did not take steps. We are positively parasites, as I often think when I observe my mother's meaningless posturing of gentility. That she comes by it naturally is little relief, and no solace to me. There *cannot* be another generation like my mother's. Not in this family, at any rate. For I have no intention of continuing to dance in a stiffened gown to Lady Eleanor Whitwell's stately, predictable minuet. It is out of the question because I hear a wilder music in my mind, and I long to throw myself into some shocking pagan dance across a barren hilltop.

Sometimes I suspect my mother thinks me mad. Certainly she is as anxious to pack me off into marriage as if I were on the point of running out of control. How little she knows me! In these final weeks under her roof, I mean to exercise more control than she can imagine. I must be very careful now my goal is in sight.

And if I am a bit ill in the mornings, she either does not notice or dares not notice.

These rather rocky mornings, which will, in time, end, are not as vexing as the need to play mother's game. To be engaged to a rather promising, rather obscure foreigner—even to marry him, as I shall do. All this casts me in the improbable role of the dutiful daughter. Poor Mother! She can hardly believe her good fortune.

She seems to have played every card and to have taken every trick. I have even inherited a version of her beauty, which makes of me a more promising commodity in the marketplace of her mind. Though she would have kept her beauty from me if she could, she now builds on it, thinking it a mother's place to decree a daughter's future.

At present I seem to be a pawn in her game. She believes that she has handpicked Gregory Forrest. Of course he is quite suitable, though I suspect him secretly of being more than a mere pawn in a woman's game. In time I intend to deal with this firmly.

In such bleak early mornings as this one, I can view Gregory quite objectively—the more so now that I have sent him back to New York to await my arrival. He is perhaps more handsome than John Thorne. Yes, I rather think he is. I smile only to myself at this secret unfaithfulness to John. And Gregory is more kind than John. Indeed, who is not? If I were only another sort of girl—or perhaps if it did not please my mother so much—I could quite think myself in love with Gregory Forrest.

I should think my mother is half in love with him herself, though she is never troubled by unsuitable thoughts. Shocking snob that she is, Gregory is a more suitable match for me than a title. Belted earls are not thick upon the ground, of course, and notoriously elderly when they appear. But even if dukes and baronets were in plentiful supply, my mother would not gladly suffer my marriage to one. It would raise me above her. And it would keep me in England. That would suit neither Mother nor me.

She is too uncertain of what I might do next to allow me to move in circles uncomfortably near herself. She would also like to see me well out of the range of the scandal-mongering London newspapers as well.

Nor would I want to remain suffocated by England when wild, anonymous, distant America waits only to fulfill my plans. In England I could never be sure of holding John Thorne forever. Sooner or later we would be discovered and both pilloried upon the class system. I was not meant to be a martyr in any cause, not even my own.

But in a new land like America where a servant's role is scarcely understood and I shall be a foreigner, I shall have John Thorne on my own terms. And I shall have Gregory Forrest as well, to provide for me. To worship me. I'm rather afraid, however, that he will have to worship me from afar after the first. Oh, yes, in America I shall have everything I want. And I want a great deal.

I want John Thorne. I have always wanted him. Nothing, no one else. He is the only thing in my life I have been willing to wait patiently for. Beneath the quilts and coverlets of some long-ago night, I took a childish vow to have him. Unnatural child that I must have been—and clever! Even before I knew what men were for and what their touch could do, I vowed I would have him until I had consumed him. And even then I knew that I would neither stoop to his level nor raise him to mine. Even as a child I had the character not to compromise.

I was far too clever for my mother and that old half-idiot, Buckle. The one frozen in her stance of propriety, the other a stupid old crone who had known nothing of life, even on her own level. I was wise enough to wait in silence for John Thorne. Even then I knew the distance between us because I have always been conscious of the distance between myself and others.

Perhaps the servants—the other servants—came to suspect me in time. They are always the first to know, if only from their own narrow, suspicious viewpoint. I have always had to be more cautious with them than with my mother and poor, blind Father.

But the distance I have kept from servants' hall has been my wisest move. Buckle, who for far too long made free to storm into my room on any pretext, was too stupid to build on this advantage. Hilda and Hannah, of course, do not share a brain between them. Finley is another matter. But I have tried to retain a girlish reticence when he is near. Indeed, I have rather paraded my courtship by Gregory Forrest in Finley's twitching face. There is little more I can do there. Fortunately, I do not have to consult with Mrs. Creeth in drawing up the menus. Nor should I want to, for she has a keen nose for corruption and is quite unsuitably outspoken, I believe. Beneath her disapproving, quite ugly facade, I sense a deep well of intuition that might see through anything. And so, while I have been known to complain, I have not been overcritical regarding food. How tiresome servants are! One day they will all be replaced by machines, and one will need do nothing beyond oiling them.

As it is, one can spend one's life dithering over servants. The need to ingratiate oneself with them is quite maddening. But the brief span of their imaginations works in one's favor. They cannot still quite imagine that John Thorne is my lover. The idea is too outrageous for the peasant mind to grasp. To them, he is of a lower caste even than a footman since he works in the out-of-doors. They suspect me, I'm sure, but they cannot suspect me of sinking so low. Nor can they know of the joy in that descent.

Perhaps that is why I never cease being amused by my friend, Sybil. She pretends not to notice class barriers. She even thinks her misplaced democracy secretly daring when she affects to scorn the station in life that she and I were both born to. Of course Sybil has never had an original thought. This is one reason why I quite like her. She cannot fathom me, try as she may. In her artlessness she has allowed herself freedoms that I have denied myself in pursuit of a freedom beyond her dreams.

I should never go near the stables where Sybil is happiest. To hobnob with the lower classes causes one to lose leverage with them. I have never seemed to be subdued by John Thorne except in the act of love. It was not until last summer that I permitted John to seduce me.

Later, when I told poor Miranda that I had lost my virginity to the only man I shall ever love, she went quite blank with horror. She thought I meant Gregory Forrest, of course. And I rather suspect Miranda of harboring a secret, girlish passion for Gregory. Much good it will do her! Though I naturally mean for Miranda to see a great deal more of Gregory in future. I shall have her in America to serve me and to be a respectable wife for John in case there are prying eyes in that country as well as here. I think I can depend upon Miranda to play her proper role. And if she is a bit smitten with Gregory, that will only serve to keep her in line. Yes, I think I can depend upon everyone to play a proper role.

Even John Thorne. He pretends to a rugged independence that I am very much afraid he has no right to. In the act of seducing the grand young lady of the manor, he was never more the dutiful servant. Half his black moods admit to his enslavement.

When we lay together on the floor of the folly on that night last summer, he must have known how easy I had made it all for him! There was only a moment when I was not in utter control. He hurt me. I had not known there would be pain. Though it soon gave way to more pleasure than a woman is said to have, I mean to remember it as the only moment of pain he, or any man, will ever be allowed to inflict upon me.

His touch will always be rough, of course. He knows no other way. And it does not please me to civilize him. He brings the sweat of the barnyard into my bedchamber. In my world of lavender silks he is more the rough beast, chained but raging with the lust that is answered by the animal within me.

I must think no more of Thorne's body pressing me down and down into the depths of this bed. Today he is marrying my servant, and at my command. Tonight he will take her to a narrower bed, and tear her body against coarser sheets. This is my plan, and I must allow nothing near envy close to it. I have planned another's wedding night more thoroughly than my mother plans my own.

It is my plan that John will join me and my "husband," Gregory Forrest. John will come to us as our chauffeur. Surely it will be quite the thing in a place like New York to have an authentic English chauffeur. He will be the only wedding present I shall ask of my parents. And they will agree. Thinking she has won, my mother will be generous. And when John appears in the livery of Gregory Forrest's New York household, he will have with him a wife as dutiful as himself, and as useful in her way. An English lady's maid—far more respectable than a French one!

How lovely it will be—the long drives through the parks of New York through endless, golden afternoons. I shall be driven through the streets with my eyes firmly fixed on the back of my chauffeur's strong neck. I shall gaze forever at the band of his cap struggling to subdue his curly hair. And once we are in some secluded spot, I shall rap once on the window that divides us. We shall enjoy an interlude then, an endless idyll in some hidden bosky dell, in the high weeds of some wilderness park. All the rest of life will be a golden afternoon.

May John Thorne not grow too quickly old in such service! And all the while, my husband will go about his tiresome business. And John's wife will attend to my more trivial needs. The plan has a lovely shape, and nothing can stop it now. No power on earth.

It is quite dark now, and the hours between tea and dinner drag on terribly. It is at just this time of day, like the hours before dawn, when one's resolve is at low ebb.

I have had to draw the curtains of my room myself, for Miranda, my drab little double, is otherwise engaged. Finley has sent up that bumpkin, Abel, to lay a fire in my hearth. It crackles now in an attempt at merriment. But still the room is cold, and wherever I pace, I am in shadow.

Where are they now? My lover and my maid, who have been married in some suitably simple ceremony? Is she still wearing her wedding finery? I can scarcely remember which of my more sensible cast-off costumes is serving as her wedding dress. I cannot quite see Miranda, though I find myself searching a darkened mirror for a glimpse of her face.

What do people of that sort do to get through their wedding day? Perhaps they are having an early supper in some wretched country tavern. I can almost sense the embarrassed terror of my poor, rigid Miranda as she confronts her bridegroom, and the hours ahead. The coldness at the fingertips; the flutter beneath the heart. Animal passions masked as marital qualms.

And where will they spend their wedding night—in the loft of some crossroads inn? Or will they return to their cottage? And will Granny Thorne spend a restless night in her bed, with ears stopped against the sighs and cries that echo into the night?

I *shall not* torture myself with the thought that Miranda will share the joy I have known. It is, after all, my plan. Besides, she lacks the spark to ignite the fires within John Thorne. I alone inspire the full brutality of his lust. I alone.

Yet I am quite alone at this moment, more alone than I should be. How hard life is! But I shall make them both pay in future for these moments from which I am briefly excluded. Let them enjoy themselves and each other while they may.

But I cannot endure these creeping hours, the taunt of that smugly ticking mantel clock. I longed for evening and darkness without knowing that their wedding night would torture me far more than their wedding day. I wish that he may hurt her terribly! I wish—

I almost said I wish my mother would invade my solitude now. *That* is the measure of my desperation. Any human voice, even hers, would find in me a grateful listener. But my mother, like the servants —like everyone—is never with me when she is needed and never elsewhere the rest of the time. No. No one can see me through this. It is the price I must pay to see my plans fulfilled. And perhaps in time it will have been a small enough price. But it is hard to remember that fact when I am almost too restless to sit at my small table and write these words. Even the pen I hold is ever harder to control, as if it had a life of its own.

Yet there is another life in this room with me. I am not quite alone after all. There is new life, yet to stir. For I am carrying a child. John Thorne's child. Oh, yes, I have been quite faithful to him. There is no doubt about its father.

Even with a will as steely as my own, I could not quite will this child into existence. And so I waited through all this time. It was certain to happen, of course. Thorne is an ardent lover, not a prudent one. I think at last he came to know my purpose, knew it as well as a man ever can. He came to know I wanted a child, his child, in order to bind us together forever, to bring him to his knees finally. And if my—ruthlessness gave him second thoughts, he did not think them in my bed.

This child was needed to set my plan in motion. I could not think of marrying Gregory Forrest until John Thorne's child was there, growing inside me. Without this child, no more than a spark of promise now, I should indeed be selling myself on my mother's terms. I could not consider going to Gregory Forrest's bed if I were not carrying Thorne's child. This audacity is simple justice.

It is the price Gregory must pay for the wife he desires so much more than she desires him. It will set the proper tone for our marriage. For I shall dictate the terms from the beginning. Gregory shall have his proper little bride and need not know until after the wedding ceremony that he has got more than he bargained for. What a test of his chivalry that will be! But I have learned more than a little about dealing with people from a position of concealed strength.

Still, I shall do well to conceal my condition until the middle of April. To put Gregory off much longer flirts with danger. How awkward to waddle down the gangplank in New York already in an embarrassed condition. I could of course throw myself on Gregory's mercy, and that would be a very touching scene, though quite beneath my dignity. But to accelerate my plans and to marry too soon robs the drama of its full flavor. Gregory might in time persuade himself that it is his child. And I cannot give him that satisfaction. It is more than he, or any man, deserves.

The middle of April seems precisely right. All will look well at first. And later—poor Gregory will be considered quite a rake by his New York friends when they learn how scandalously soon his little English bride presents him with an heir.

But Gregory is the least of my considerations. I must have this child to bind John and me together. I must. Otherwise, we might drift apart in time. And that must never be. I have been a bit sick in the mornings, but oh, how clearheaded, how clear-eyed I am the rest of the days! Such plans as mine deserve fruition. I have struck down every barrier now, every impediment that could be set in my way. Yet how terribly, cruelly long this endless evening is.

15 JANUARY 1912

The sickness of the mornings has passed now, perhaps without notice. And I am feeling so fit that I must restrain myself from leaping from my bed at coldest dawn! There is a pinkness in my cheeks that has never been there before. Even dear Mother accuses me gently of taking early-morning walks that heighten my coloring. It has not occurred to her that one of the more pleasant byproducts of pregnancy is a healthy complexion. Compensation in advance for the thickening waistline later on. But I am still willow-slim and dance around my room even before the servants begin their creeping about. On the coldest mornings of the year I throw myself into a ritual dance of triumph. My nightdress unfurls about me like the drapings of Isadora Duncan or Loie Fuller. On and on I dance victoriously on the private stage of my room, with only the dead hearth for footlights.

I am purified by the power that sings in my ears. I might almost dance the role of a vestal virgin and find myself suitable in the part. For I am keeping to my vow of temporary chastity. It is understood that John is not to come to me for a little while yet. So he must make do with poor, dear Miranda a bit longer. How this brief time of abstinence whets my appetite for his great hard body plunging over me and pulsing within me. And how much more it must whet his appetite for me!

But the door is opening now, and I must compose myself in dignity. Miranda is bringing in my breakfast. What a stately progress she makes across the floor that has just witnessed my heathen dance! Her dignity has mounted with each month of her service, for the poor thing refuses to subjugate herself entirely to me. What a pointless pose! But I can be her match in stiff grandeur. I cannot meet her eye, however, since she has become a married woman. I do not fear facing her down, but I should not like to see any alteration in her, any hint that she is transformed by the lovemaking of my lover. One sees too much in the eyes of others. I should live behind a veil all my life if I could manage it. It is too difficult to make eyes lie.

"Your breakfast, Miss Amanda," she says in a voice growing steadily more like an echo of my own.

And I hear myself answering in a tone that feigns sleepiness. I tell her to pour out my tea and to uncover a plate of eggs and another of kidneys. This bounty is scarcely equal to my appetite. I am ravenous. I am hungry for life!

20 JANUARY 1912

Letters this morning, and I suppose I shall have to deal with them. But today I am truly sleepy. No dancing about in this dawn! John Thorne came to me last night. What excuse he gave poor Miranda I cannot imagine and would not ask. It is beneath me to question him, and I shall not have her name mentioned in my bed. It was as it had been in the first warm days of the autumn, when I was still half a young girl and less the woman I have become.

John came to my room just as this new day began, at the stroke of midnight. I had told him to keep away until the narrow novelty of poor Miranda had quite spent itself. I neither chided him for staying away too long nor taunted him with the brevity of his honeymoon. How discreet I was!

I said nothing at all as he stood within the door, waiting for me to discover him. (I knew he was there the moment the knob began to turn. I felt his presence before he had quite entered the house from the terrace far below.) I feel his presence always, as I feel the small sliver of his child in my womb, for both of them are mine and part of me. Even the woman John has lain with these past nights is only another me.

He walked silently to my bed, tearing away his clothes as he approached. I lay as still as a sleeping child until he was upon me. But when he drew back the cover on my bed, he found me naked and waiting, my body arching toward his. I was moist to his first touch, and still eager long after he was spent. He is more completely mine now than before. In marrying Miranda, he became my husband.

21 JANUARY 1912

The postman is working overtime, and still I cannot quite get around to dealing with my letters, yesterday's or today's. I wonder that Gregory Forrest can conduct his business and build his houses or whatever he does and still write so much! But I shall read the latest from Sybil first, for comic relief.

She inquires plaintively about my plans. Poor Sybil half fears I shall reverse myself and be married in an elaborate ceremony in England. Shall I put her restless mind at ease, or shall I let her writhe in suspense awhile?

And now to the letter—almost a packet—from Gregory. He grows restless himself and rather annoyingly insistent. He includes a steamship ticket—no, two tickets. A first-class passage for Miss Whitwell and her maid for an April tenth sailing from Southampton. Yes, I should think the timing is very nearly right. He has followed my lead; may he make a lifetime habit of it! I must reply at once with a show of discreet enthusiasm. How very certain he wants to be of me! And how much he writes. I cannot manage to get through it all without skipping:

> *. . . my darling, you are to have every comfort on the voyage . . . a very superior stateroom on B Deck . . . adjoining cabin for Miranda . . . some additional excitement to entertain you on the crossing as this will be the maiden voyage of the . . . meet you*

at the pier in New York on Wednesday, the seventeenth of April, with all the florists of New York picked clean. . . .

How much the man writes! And if that were not enough, a brochure from the steamship company, the White Star Line, falls from the envelope and is instantly swallowed in the bedclothes.

Yes, yes, a thousand weary times yes, I shall sail on the maiden voyage of the beastly ship, though it shall be more maidenly than I. And I suppose I must read the brochure that extols the virtues of transatlantic travel on the White Star Line, but it has drifted to the foot of my bed, lost in a sea of satin.

1 FEBRUARY 1912

A snowfall in the night that has left the world more ashen than white. A savage wind, too, howling straight off the Channel to pluck at all the windows and make the chimneys whine. To get me through such colorless days, I need John Thorne every night.

But I do not have him every night, and what a vast wasteland my bed too often is. He must yet play his role in the charade and divide his considerable talents between two women. I shall be very glad indeed to have him—and her—more completely under my thumb. Fortunately, his passion persists unimpaired. Perhaps in an earlier lifetime he was one of those pagan potentates with a harem of wives —and in a warmer climate, too. Nice for him.

I should have no real quarrel with these slow-paced winter days. This is the last winter I shall be here. But the situation regarding Miranda is growing awkward. I can find no fault with her, of course. She has had the advantage of the best training. Mine. Still, I must read very carefully as the circumstances become more sensitive. It is time to do more than think of packing and making lists. I have already had the trunks brought down from the box room and have ordered more. Sixteen trunks should see me through the voyage. While I am in the family way, I am not, after all, a family. So there is no point packing more than a minimum. I daresay New York has shops. Certainly the American women one sees in London are over-dressed enough.

But with all this sudden activity, I do not quite know how to handle Miranda. I speak casually of taking her with me. But she seems to regard this rather as a gentle joke—token of my reluctance to leave her behind! Of course she is going with me. The trouble is, she does not yet know that Thorne is going as well. No one does. And I begin to wonder if I am waiting for just the right moment or putting off the inevitable. How easy it was for people in the age of slavery. I should be quite amused to pack Miranda off to New York in leg-irons down in the hold of whatever that ship is· we are sailing on.

"You'll quite like New York, Miranda," I said to her this morning —brightly, if a bit tentative in my tone.

"But, Miss," she replied, "you haven't been there yourself, so how could you know?"

The insolent baggage. How I longed to strike her! A bruise across her cheek would make such a visible difference between us. I shall keep her folding, mending, and packing from dawn until dusk, even if it means taking more than I need.

It is growing quite impossible to talk to Miranda, and just when it would be so amusing to have someone to natter with. Oh, a plague on all servants!

4 FEBRUARY 1912

A sign from heaven that my plan is meant to be!

If not from heaven, then from Father's study. It seems I have not been the only one harboring secrets. Dear, bumbling Father has been planning really a rather generous gift, and he has at last revealed all. He—and Mother, of course—are giving Gregory and me a Rolls-Royce automobile as a wedding present! I daresay John Thorne's endless grumbling about Father's Lanchester has borne this luxurious fruit.

Once I showed myself suitably grateful to Father for his generosity I insinuated the idea that an automobile—a limousine, in fact—of that sort really requires a British chauffeur-cum-mechanic. What a clever line of logic I improvised on the spot! It seems the Rolls-Royce Company concurs. And before this quite unexpected interview with Father drew to a close, I rather think he thought he was the one to offer me Thorne for a chauffeur as a sort of companion gift. Companion indeed!

Poor father had not contemplated the fact that without Thorne, I could hardly take his wife to America as my maid. Once reminded of this, he offered me the pair of them. Rather like being given a pair of Ming vases as it would be a great pity to split them up! Father thinks it quite a satisfactory idea. He also thinks it has originated with him. Could anything be more convenient—and deliciously amusing? Mother remains silent, but I gather that she would prefer hiring new staff to having last-minute difficulties with me. How simply matters arrange themselves once a proper groundwork has been laid. I would recommence dancing madly about my room, except it is littered with yawning steamer trunks. How near victory is!

5 FEBRUARY 1912

I seem to have spent the entire day on the stairs—halfway up, or perhaps halfway down. Father was such a time closeted in his study with Miranda and Thorne that I nearly became frantic with impatience. Finley was in there with them for a time, too. Such a lot of bother, and I'm sure Father must have repeated himself endlessly.

And all the while John had to endure hearing Father's plan to send him to America, when the whole thing was really decided ages ago. And that fool of a butler must be brought into the negotiations to observe protocol. He won't be sorry to see the last of John! Such virility continually on display in the kitchen yard must have made Finley half mad with envy—or perhaps with an emotion far more discreditable.

And Miranda must be consulted—and duly reminded, I trust—that a woman's place is with her husband. The whole idiotic interlude went on so long that I began to think Miranda might be making difficulties. But then I decided not. She is still in that first marital stage—starry-eyed and dutiful to a fault.

I would not leave the stairs until I heard the study door open at last. Then I did not ring for Miranda until it was time to dress me for dinner. One must give servants ample time for thinking things through in their primitive way. And change is so trying for them.

How well I remember Miranda's first trip into the outside world—to London. It quite boggled her poor mind. May an ocean crossing not unhinge her utterly!

Then when I did ring for her—with little enough time to dress me, at that—she came into my room looking like Lady Macbeth. Her face was quite wet with tears, and she tended to sniff uncontrollably. I threw down a hairbrush and decided I really must take a hard line with her.

"Well, Miranda, I do think Father has been generous to us all. Surely living in New York will be a new start in life for you and your husband. After all, America is endlessly praised as the cradle of democracy and an earthly paradise for the working man—and woman, of course. Moreover, I should prefer not to think you are shattered at the thought of continuing to serve me. However much a *burden* to you I might be, I trust you will not find Mr. Forrest a difficult master."

I said more in this vein, though I assume that I did not repeat myself as often as Father does. Still, I seemed to make no impression whatever. Miranda went from sniffs to sobs outright.

"Oh, Miss," she said finally in a strangled voice, "it isn't to do with going to New York at all. I don't mind really." At that point she sounded rather like an earlier version of herself, which was a welcome reversal.

"I'm very glad to hear it," I told her. "But then whatever is the matter?"

Then it all came out in a rush. It seems that the scullery maid who was lately on the staff has come to grief—or worse, really. We had quite a job in the autumn getting the poor little drab married off. Betty was her name. She had disgraced herself and must either find a forbearing husband or throw herself into the mere. We had married her off in haste to a draper in the town, and I gathered that the whole matter had resolved itself. It was not, after all, terribly amusing.

But no, everything had gone wrong. There were complications, and Betty had gone into labor after a perfectly normal pregnancy, only to lose the child. And she died herself soon after. It seems she was at our own home farm, being seen to by the estate agent's sister.

"Never mind," I said to Miranda. "We did our best, and the marriage to the draper, while quite an inventive idea on the face of it, might not have been a great success after such a beginning. I daresay it is all better this way."

But Miranda was not to be consoled and shot me rather a dire look. Half grief-stricken and half resentful of my poor attempts to cheer her up.

What a relief that Miranda was not disturbed at the thought of going to New York. That *would* have been awkward. And this other business of her friend dying has distracted her at quite a convenient time, really.

5 MARCH 1912

There are daffodils now—brave, early ones just down by the terrace steps where the sun catches them. How spring taunts one! And weeks early, too. But in hardly more than a month we embark at Southampton. If one could only ruffle through the pages of the calendar as one does with a novel—rushing onto the best parts.

But I maintain my steady course, even drinking endless coffees after dinner in Father's study, at his feet. His hand drifts down to my head, and we are quite a scene from a Victorian engraving. Mother looks in from the door, unsure about just how to take this tender tableau. For her part, she is offering me bits of old lace to wear on my wedding day and looking almost wan that she will not be there to play her role as mother of the bride. Ah, no, that is not to be. I shall not have her overshadowing me at my own wedding, however lightly I mean to take my marriage vows!

I accept all the lace with good grace, even the yellowed bits, in the full knowledge that I shall be wearing something a good deal less mawkish and more modern on the day in question. Indeed, I have already quietly sent off my own sketches to a London dressmaker—for a rather severe costume with a Russian tunic top to conceal my waist. Heavens, am I beginning to show?

In my bed last night Thorne grew unusually talkative—all in hoarse whispers, naturally. It seems that nothing can hurry the Rolls-Royce Company. They make rather a fetish of perfection. The limousine that Father has decreed is to have special fittings of some sort or other, and the finished product will not be ready to ship until early summer at the earliest. The plan is for Thorne to stay behind and accompany the auto on the ship to New York when it is ready.

I grew vexed at this. But John was allowed to talk me around. After all, it is the ultimate in discretion and quite a worthy crowning touch for my own plans. It will look much better all around if Miranda and I arrive in New York quite on our own. Rather elegantly simple, really, traveling alone with only a maid. Gregory and I will be married then, and he will come to know just what he is in for well before John arrives. However, I shouldn't like poor Gregory to become too wise. It will be enough for him to know that I am to have someone's child. It would not be convenient, of course, for him to know it is the chauffeur's! And John's delayed arrival will only put him at a further remove from implication. I do hope Gregory is not the sort to suspect every man he sees, however unlikely. How little one knows about a future husband. Life is really a game of chance. Still, I am bound to win. I am meant to win.

Yes, a few weeks—even months—of having to do without John is really better all around. In my condition I shall have to leave off violent lovemaking in any case, for a time. I don't like being separated from John, of course. But then I shall have poor Miranda as a fellow sufferer!

1 APRIL 1912

April at last! I have made an early-morning ceremony of tearing the month of March from the calendar. And now here is lovely, promising April, which will set me free.

John thought me half mad. I nudged him from bed before first light —when it was past time for him to be off to his own cottage in any case. Then I insisted that he creep with me to my writing table where I groped for the calendar. Really, everything is in such disarray. I have pushed forward all the packing and kept Miranda at it all day and as far into the night as I dare. And the end result is that I can find almost nothing in its proper place.

We stood there, John and I, in the last of the dark, naked and shivering. I with delight, he with the cold. As I tore the page from the calendar, I placed his hand over mine. Then his great strong hands drifted down to touch me, just where the baby is. He was standing behind me and enfolding me, imprisoning me.

"Am I beginning to show dreadfully?" I whispered, really wanting to know.

And he said the oddest thing in reply. "I could crush the life out of you, just as we stand here. I could crush that thing in your belly as well."

And if I had struggled to release myself from his grasp, I daresay he might have done me an injury. Physically, he is quite strong. But of course I only melted back against him. Then I led him gently, quietly to the rug before the grate, where he might turn his fury into a passion more pleasing to us both.

SUNDAY, 7 APRIL 1912

I might have known! Everything was going so well—too well—and now a really serious last-minute complication just when I was counting the hours.

John Thorne and I have been discovered.

And it is all because I was overtired and growing careless. Still, I refuse to think it my fault. Really, it all happened because Mother and Father *would* give the most tiresome bon voyage party for me on my last Saturday here. If it had not so exhausted me, I would have been more careful.

Such a gaggle of impossible people were invited, half of them bearing useless wedding presents that will either have to be quietly jettisoned or sent on to New York, if I am ever able to get another scrap of work out of Miranda. And all sorts of dreary, arch toasts and speeches after dinner until I was quite pushed beyond my limits with smiling and looking demure.

Sybil traveled down for the party, though it was rather tedious dealing with her when there is so little time left and my thoughts are elsewhere. Still, she fitted in very well with the county types Father had invited. And she is so commandingly large that perhaps I still appear safely diminutive by contrast to her.

After the party, I made it quite clear to Sybil that I had no intention of sitting up exchanging girlish confidences with her in our dressing gowns. I expected John to come to my room. It was, after all, nearly the last moment when we could be together. And surely I deserved some solace after enduring that wretched, endless party. He came to me, of course. I shouldn't wonder if he and Miranda had not passed one another on the path to the cottage. I had not dismissed her an hour before he appeared.

It was, of course, entirely too hectic. I see that now. My room suddenly empty of all the trunks, which have been sent on ahead to Southampton. And the fire dead in the hearth because the entire staff was pressed into the service of the party. And I overtired and very nearly more interested in sleep than in John. And Sybil innocently asleep down the hall, which always makes me feel more like the inmate of a girls' school than a femme fatale. Yes, I can see now that the whole situation was ripe for disaster.

I fear I was even rather absentminded in my lovemaking. Really too tired to be bothered. And then I fell asleep nearly at once. I should have sent John away, of course. After all, I was quite finished with him, and he has been lingering on and on in my room these past nights. Loath to return to his little lady's-maid wife, I rather imagine. But the point is, anyone might have discovered us and at any time. Perhaps it was just as well that it was Miranda.

I awoke on this Sunday morning, knowing at once of the danger. The mantel clock stood at eight o'clock, and the sun was streaming in, striking sparks of brilliant light on the fire irons. And there was John, heavily asleep with his great hairy arm across my breast. And all the bedclothes in a frightful muddle on the floor. We were as vulnerable as two naked savages at the mouth of a cave. I nearly shrieked with fear and impatience.

But I merely pressed a hand over his mouth and shook him with my free hand. He awoke suddenly, and I saw in his eyes, which rarely betray any emotion, that he realized at once the situation. It would have been comic if it had not been so desperate. How was I to get him out of a house already stirring? What odd thoughts panic inspires. I thought first, quite madly, of rushing down the hall to dear, solid Sybil for aid and comfort. Though what sort of help she would have been I cannot think.

Neither John nor I moved in that first horrified, somehow ridiculous moment. My mother's friend, Maude Glaslough, would have known where she was at once. She has spent a lifetime of country house parties in bed with the wrong man. But then she is a married woman, which makes all the difference. Besides, her hostesses always thoughtfully put her in a bedchamber with an alternate escape route. As no one has ever been quite so thoughtful about my needs, I felt quite trapped.

It was not the moment for all this blind panic. It might better have been spent in John's pulling on his clothes, which were strewn all about the room. But that moment passed, and in the next, Miranda opened the only door and strode in with my early-morning tea.

How angry I was at myself for fearing her! And yet all my plans seemed threatened, and it was all too, too unfair. Thorne drew away from me as if I were some loathsome animal. I shall never forget that. We had been lying tangled together. But as John's arm withdrew, I lay completely exposed. I had never shown myself naked to my maid before.

John threw his legs over the far side of the bed and sat there, turned away from both me and Miranda, with his head in his hands. And much good he was to me at that moment!

Still, Miranda did not withdraw, and I could not summon up the wit to dismiss her with a gesture. Or perhaps I feared she would not go.

She stood there still, just within the open doorway, where anyone in the passage behind her might have looked in on this absurd scene. And no one spoke. Perhaps John groaned into his hands. Men seem quite useless in the very situations they create.

I struggled with myself, and with the bedclothes, trying to cover myself. Really, it was too undignified. And still Miranda remained as rigid as a statue at the door. After the first, she did not even rattle the tea things on the tray that balanced in her hand. I shall never let myself be caught so off-guard again, never.

I wished Miranda dead in that moment. I was not, of course, capable of leaping from my bed and bearing down on her like a naked Amazon to wring her neck. But I thought of it. Miranda was put on this earth to serve. If not me, then another. She was meant to appear and to disappear with a wave of the hand or a casual tug on a bellpull.

I refused—I refuse to see her as a woman wronged. She was lucky enough to be married at all; nor would she have been if I had not arranged it. Now she can see how little there is to quarrel over. A husband who cares nothing for her—cares nothing for anything or anyone but me. He sat sagging at the side of the bed, incapable of doing anything. His great naked back cast a long shadow across my bed. I should have thought that generations of peasant husbands in his ancestry would have conspired to bring him to his feet and to stride over to Miranda and to slap her senseless. Women of that class must surely be used to regular beatings from straying husbands.

Perhaps it is as well she knows now. She was bound to find out sooner or later, however blind she chose to be. The time might well have come when I would want her to know. But I shall have to be very severe with her now, I suppose, if I am to get her on that ship to America. I must prove to myself that nothing can stand in my way. It is more than possible that I have been too easy with Miranda up till now. I must really impose my will on her henceforth. The great thing, of course, is not to let her know that I felt more than a passing twinge of fear. Servants are like animals. They sense one's fear and then look for their advantage in it.

I heard my own voice at last. "I should think, all things considered, that we shall be needing another cup for morning tea. Go and fetch it at once, Miranda."

I even managed to meet her gaze, which was exceedingly brave of me. Her eyes had gone quite dark. From violet to near-black. She looked quite changed. Quite thoroughly changed.

Miranda Speaks

Twenty-Two

—◦◦◦∞◦◦◦—

Early on the morning of Wednesday, April 10, 1912, I, Miranda Cooke Thorne, stood on the platform of Waterloo Station in London. Waterloo had been my first glimpse of London—or the world—in the previous autumn. So vast and noisy it was that I had thought then that all London had been put under this single glass shed, webbed with iron.

But I was far from being the same young girl who had gasped and gaped at a train station two seasons before. Though my mind was as benumbed as a lost child's, I was not indifferent to the bustling scene. I welcomed any distraction, any evidence that beyond my small, suffering soul there was still a world of movement, of activity, of change even for its own sake. I tried to be diverted by the kaleidoscope of passengers embarking on a new adventure, dressed in part for the high seas, in part as if they were off for a country-house week in a particularly bracing season. Though I could not see more than a moment ahead in my own life, I imagined that on the first leg of a voyage that began on this solid ground I caught a hint of the open sea. I rather think I hoped the sea would open and swallow me.

There was some veiled promise in that great grimy, echoing chamber, deafening with the shouts of luggage handlers and smelling of grease and smoke. It was a very faint promise, though, and might have been a hint of ends, not beginnings. The start of any journey suggests death, however subtly, but I was still too young to know that. It is true that when the boat train for Southampton clattered backward along the platform and shuddered to a halt, I thought of throwing myself under those unforgiving wheels. Perhaps I wanted to die. Perhaps I had a presentiment that I soon would. Perhaps I didn't care, one way or the other.

I had lost everything that had made up my world. And when one is nineteen, it takes far less than I had suffered to bring down one's life like a house of cards. I had given myself in marriage to a husband who was neither his own man nor mine. I had lain with him through a few short weeks of long nights, knowing perhaps from the very first that our marriage was a mockery, even before I knew what marriage was. He had stirred the beginnings of my passion but had touched me nowhere else. And when I discovered him in the bed of another woman, I was through with lying to myself. All the warnings I had not heeded blared in my head like sirens, driving out the last of my innocence. I daresay that the change that swept over me in that moment was evident.

Miss Amanda Whitwell must have read in my eyes the change she had rung there. In all truth, I could not be crushed by my husband's faithlessness. He had never been more than a stranger to me, even when he held me in his arms in an attempt at gentleness. It is not strangers who betray us. No, she must have seen in my eyes that my quarrel was with her, a quarrel that could never be resolved this side of death.

In all her plans she reckoned without my capacity for hatred. She had lived too easy a life to know that a trapped animal is the most vicious.

Yet I stood on this Platform No. 12, drafty with the uncertain winds of a spring morning, serving her still. I cannot recall now whether I had spoken so much as a full sentence either to her or to John Thorne in that half week since I had found them, naked—and foolish—in her bed. I had thought at the time only of how very naked they were. I think I had never seen anyone unclothed in daylight in all my life. How strangely one's mind works. I thought first of how my mother had always draped a blanket between the kitchen beams on Saturday nights when my father washed himself in a hip bath before the inadequate fire, to screen him from my eyes, and hers. I thought, too, how strange it was to see John Thorne's flesh in the hard morning light, as first he crouched, trapped in the middle of the lavender satins of that bed, and then flung himself away from me, and her. I stared at his naked back then, while she struggled to cover herself. That naked back I had clung to in the nights he had spared to me, clung to, unseeing. I saw now. I saw those broad, muscular shoulders and the curve of his spine. I saw the weakness that dwelt in that powerful body.

I never spoke to him again. Let the other servants and his own grandmother think what they would. What he and I would say to one another later when we were to meet again in America I did not consider. I thrust the last of my belongings into a satchel in the small room up under the roof of Smuggler's Cottage while John Thorne wavered in the doorway behind me, searching, perhaps, for words that would have changed nothing.

I pushed past him then and walked out of that cottage without a backward look. Nor was I any more talkative with the servants in the kitchens of Whitwell Hall. Mr. Finley doubtless had prepared a speech appropriate to my leave-taking. A speech to remind me that in a new country I must be a twice-perfect servant—to serve my young lady in her married state and to represent the best in the British tradition of service, of servitude. I gave him no opportunity for such a speech, meaning to leave his domain as wordlessly as I had entered it. For I could not trust the servants any longer.

I could not know how much *they* knew. I could not even be sure they had not played the obscure roles of silent conspirators as I was drawn into the bonds of marriage with the semblance of a man. A man who was nothing but the obscene plaything of the young mistress of the house they so slavishly served. I could trust no one.

Only Mrs. Creeth came near to breaching my defenses, and in the only way possible. I can think now that she was only a good-hearted, rough-tongued old woman whose darkest suspicions of the sins of others were mere pastimes in her empty life. I can think now that she was more innocent in her way than a young girl. But I would have walked past her out of her kitchen with no more than a nod if she had not barred the way.

On the day we left Whitwell Hall for London, she had prepared a hamper for our journey. Lady Eleanor, Miss Amanda, and I were to travel up to town on the night before the boat train left. Sir Timothy was to stay behind. It was said that the excitement and the parting from his daughter would prove too much for him. But it was also true that he was a difficult traveler and forever in the way. Mrs. Creeth had, nevertheless, prepared a hamper of food—cold duck, junket, cheese, cider—for heartier appetites than those possessed by three women travelers. When she handed me the hamper, our eyes met, as happens between two people who will never meet again.

I expected no speeches from her, and so I was not on my guard. How much less did I expect her to reach out quickly and embrace me in her reddened hands. Those hands that had done so little embracing in a long life. "It is hard to be going off to strange parts," she said huskily in my ear. "And harder still to have left behind your friend in a fresh grave. Ah, yes, I know you was a true friend to Betty. And whether she deserved one or not makes no odds now."

She broke from me then, and my eyes swam with tears. I had not expected anyone ever to recognize my grief when Betty died giving birth to a dead child. I had thought both Betty and I were beneath consideration. Neither of us had ever been expected to play more than small, convenient roles in the lives of others. And God help either of us when we would no longer be useful. God help Betty now in her grave, with only her dead child beside her. And a springtime awakening over the hills above her that she would never see.

I stared at Mrs. Creeth, and just when I might have seen her coarse kindness plainly, my eyes were sightless with tears. I could not walk away from her without a word. "I shall remember Betty as a friend in a friendless world," I said, half whispering. "And I shall remember your kindness, Mrs. Creeth, in this last moment. There is nothing more I will want to remember."

Then I was gone. I dared not even spare a thought to Winifred Salter, across the fields at the home farm. For she had warned me. And we can only flee from warnings not heeded.

I stood on the platform at Waterloo. A wordless, perfect lady's maid. Most of the hand luggage had already been put in the train, sent to the compartment where I would attend Miss Amanda Whitwell on her journey. I was left only with her jewel case, the gift of Mr. Forrest, and a satchel that contained the book from Asprey's that she wrote in occasionally, in immense secrecy.

She stood a little distance from me. Her head turned as she remarked on the flow of people who would be traveling in the First Class of the ship on its maiden voyage. She had seemed for some time, as far as I could tell, more interested in the voyage than its destination. When any particularly distinguished-looking travelers passed along the platform, her conversation with her companions grew more animated. But whenever her glance, which followed her fellow travelers, strayed anywhere near me, she shifted it away at once. Soon she and I would be alone. The thought of that could not be a comfort to her.

She stood with her mother and her faithful friend, Miss Ward-Benedict, who had made another of her sacrificial journeys up to town to see her off. Miss Ward-Benedict had arrived puffing on the platform with a rather unwieldy basket of fruit, which might better have been sent directly to the ship. The three women stood grouped together, the brims of their hats almost overlapping. I think of them now as a photograph made in those times when the great, ponderous hats of the period always seem to overbalance the figures beneath and cast the faces of the wearers into shadow. They drew in the skirts of their spring coats from the last frantic dartings of the luggage carts and the vast entourages of the American people dressed in immense finery for their return to their homeland.

How out of place Lady Eleanor looked in this boisterous, modern setting. Beneath her lavishly feathered hat, her face was like a fragile cameo. She had placed a gloved hand almost timidly on her daughter's arm, where it remained unheeded.

This gesture that spoke so clearly of her love for a daughter who had no means of returning that love only added to Lady Eleanor's beauty. I was sorry at that moment, but not at their parting. The mother would be spared much by her daughter's going. Indeed, I hoped for her sake they would never meet again. Instead, I was sorry that since I was cursed with the looks of another and not myself, that I could not more nearly resemble the mother and not the daughter.

I had dressed Miss Amanda in her traveling costume—the Newport coat and the short whipcord skirt. I had dressed her as one dresses a least-favorite doll—with special care, as an object to be looked at but not approached.

Certain that Miss Amanda would not return my gaze, I lingered over her costume with an eye grown practiced. Her coat was belted, but not as tightly as it might be. She was more softly rounded now and not the willow wand she had been. I knew she was carrying a child. I must have known that much on the day I married the father of that child. She had been ill that morning, and other mornings as well. Had I not seen this before, in Betty? I had not allowed myself to know. On that April morning, though, I knew, without ever having undergone the shock of discovery. I knew now who the father was, as well. It was a grim satisfaction to me, somehow. I had been brought as low by those two people as I could be. I had been plunged down and down into some ice-cold sea until my foot had touched bottom. There was nothing more that they could do to me, even in the madness of their sick passion. Her passion to possess, his to be possessed and brought even lower than he was. I knew them capable of anything but shame; still, I did not suppose they would kill me to silence me. I had no doubt they meant to go on using me. Nor did I think of revenging myself. I hardly knew the meaning of the word. I lived only a moment at a time, nurtured by pain changing steadily to hatred.

I waited impatiently for the chorus of whistles that would summon us to board the train. I wanted only to be gone, even though I must go with the person in the world I hated most. The person who had taught me what hate was. I never thought of escape from her. I had nowhere to go. And that I was a married woman, in the eyes of the law, was another chain that bound me.

Impatience swept over me in waves. I fidgeted like a child. When a mote of soot blew into my eye, I thrust my hand into my coat pocket for a handkerchief that was not there, and drew out instead a leaflet that advertised the famous ship we were to be sailing on. How the leaflet came to be there I cannot recall. I had no knowledge of ships or life at sea or the difference between one vessel and another.

All my life oceangoing ships had been nothing more or less than plumes of gray smoke drifting on the horizon of the Channel. Perhaps I had last seen such a floating feather on the day I entered service at Whitwell Hall. That fateful, fatal day when my father's old wagon had lost its wheel at Dunnose Bridge and I had climbed the flowery hills that command the sea beside the Wisewoman's house. No, I knew nothing of ships, and so I unfolded the advertisement of the ship that awaited us at Southampton. And because these last moments hung heavy upon me, I read every word:

WHITE STAR—AMERICAN LINE
SOUTHAMPTON—NEW YORK SERVICE

THE ROYAL MAIL TRIPLE-SCREW STEAMER

"TITANIC"

WILL BE DESPATCHED FROM

SOUTHAMPTON TO NEW YORK

ON HER MAIDEN VOYAGE

On **WEDNESDAY, April 10th, 1912,** at noon

(Calling at Cherbourg and Queenstown)

Twenty-Three

------◦∞◦------

At fifteen minutes before ten precisely, the White Star Line boat train began to roll out of Waterloo. I had already found the compartment that my young lady and I would occupy on the journey to Southampton. The hand luggage and Miss Ward-Benedict's unwieldy basket of fruit were already secured above, and the jewel case was already planted firmly on my knees for safekeeping.

I sat with my back to the engine, facing the empty window seat meant for Miss Amanda. But it was still vacant as the train moved and the gold tassels began to sway against the dark blue compartment's walls. Hers was the only empty seat. The other occupants cast glances in my direction, some bold, some veiled. They were all Americans and could not quite decide whether I was lady or lady's maid. Whether the jewel case was my possession or only my responsibility.

We had not left Miss Amanda behind. I knew she was putting off the first moment of confrontation with me. It must have seemed to her a point in my favor that we were out in the world then, away from the familiar place from which she drew her power. How she hated even the thought of being at a disadvantage! How she must be dreading a seventy-mile journey spent facing me in this traveling cage. I smiled at her cowardice and at the thought of her lingering somewhere along the passage for as long as she dared.

And with the thought, she drew back the door of the compartment and stepped inside. She looked ready to weep with relief at sight of the occupied seats that meant we would not be alone. No matter how little she cared for the society of strangers, she was glad to see them now. Her shoulders straightened. She composed her face into a mask of insolent calm that I have since come to recognize as the badge of the traveling English. I dipped my head as she picked her way between the feet of our fellow travelers. I did not want them to remark, however silently, on how alike we looked. I wanted there to be nothing between us except what had to be.

At the time I thought that strangers casually thrown together remained strangers. But I reckoned without the sudden familiarity of Americans. My only experience of that nation was Mr. Gregory Forrest. And he seemed far too wonderful to be anything but unique. His compatriots in our compartment spoke in Mr. Forrest's tones, if noticeably louder, and were determined from the first to be friendly. For Americans regard all the world of travelers as a sort of movable feast at which all must be nourished.

I sensed a change in Miss Amanda as her thoughts seemed generally to parallel my own. Her relief that she was not alone with me gave way to a certain dismay that we were both outnumbered by foreigners. Perhaps only then did she contemplate that the world did not turn upon her. She very nearly tried to catch my eye for reassurance before she was swept up into conversation by a youngish lady in the seat beside her.

I could not have been more struck by this lady if I had known that her fate and mine would one day be entwined after I was free of Miss Amanda. She was a very striking woman and robust after a fashion quite different from Miss Ward-Benedict. She was a Miss Rebecca Reed of New York. And I have scarcely encountered anyone since who was more at home in the world. She was a person perhaps not yet thirty who spoke with the experience of twice her years. And she was already speaking in quite assured terms to Miss Amanda before Miss Amanda could quite believe it.

An American voice was still hard for me to follow at first hearing, and so I studied Miss Reed from beneath my hat brim. She was not handsome, but that fact had not impeded her dressmaker or her milliner. She wore a hat dominated by an enormous grosgrain bow striped black and white that escaped the outrageous by a hairbreadth. Her bold manner reminded me of what little I had heard of suffragettes. But she was nowhere near so austere as those grim women were said to be. And the glossiness of her furs bespoke a woman who would not wear sackcloth and ashes—or any uniform—in any cause.

She had already extracted Miss Amanda's name from her and even a bit of her history before I began to attend her conversation, and I noticed my young lady melting by degrees in her direction.

"What fun," Miss Reed was saying, "to be crossing on the *Titanic*. I put off going home weeks and weeks to make the maiden voyage. And of course I'd have booked a First Class passage if it took my bottom dollar for the joy of rubbing elbows with all those *Social Register* types!"

Miss Amanda blanched at both the mention of money and the very thought of rubbed elbows. But I expect Miss Reed was proof against the blanching British, and her conversation rolled on. It seemed that she was by way of being a journalist and supported herself by her pen and her curiosity. I had not known that there was a world of work for women beyond that of the maid and the governess and perhaps the schoolmistress, who suffered the drawbacks of both.

"How lucky for you," Miss Amanda was saying in a voice of failed condescension, "that you are able to make your own way in life. I have always been at the mercy of others and apparently will continue to be, and so I live in rather a limited way."

"Well! A trip on the *Titanic* will broaden your horizons, sure enough!" Miss Reed said amiably. I rather think she mistook Miss Amanda's cold egotism for shyness and sought to put her at her ease. "And even if you're not traveling with any of your menfolk, you'll find quite a number of courtly swains to look out for you on the crossing. It's a custom, you know. An unattached lady is always looked after by one or another of the men passengers. It's perfectly respectable, of course, though you run into a masher occasionally. The main problem is that they're either a little long in the tooth or too fresh out of Princeton. Still, they all come in handy for seeing you into the dining room and onto the dance floor. And they can be invaluable when your trunks get misplaced. I always collect my full share," Miss Reed concluded, tapping her own knee for emphasis and clearly looking forward to the attentions an unattached lady might reasonably expect from a voyage.

Her innocent worldliness was in such contrast to Miss Amanda's small scheming mind that it seemed my young lady had replaced

Miss Ward-Benedict with still another companion who was her self's safe opposite. The stuffy railway compartment seemed swept with a fresh breeze. "I've learned a thing or two about making my way in a cold, cruel world," Miss Reed said, beaming. "I've been through two earthquakes—the big one in San Francisco and one other, a train wreck on the Rock Island Line, and I once wrote up an insurrection in Bulgaria. I've known every disaster except bubonic plague and a husband!"

While this jest seemed to unnerve Miss Amanda, it set off a young lady and gentlemen beside me into fits of suppressed laughter. In a stage whisper clearly audible above the click of the train wheels, Miss Reed confided to Miss Amanda that this young American couple sitting among us were returning from their wedding trip. They were a Mr. and Mrs. Daniel Marvin. Among their claims to fame, Miss Reed related, their wedding ceremony had been cinematographed as a moving picture. It seemed that Mr. Marvin's father was the head of an important American cinematograph company.

Though Mr. and Mrs. Marvin could not have failed to hear their history repeated, they appeared far more preoccupied with each other. Miss Amanda went quite white around the lips at the vulgarity of turning a wedding service into a moving-picture show. Perhaps she wondered, as I did myself, if this was the American way of observing the occasion. One of her hands moved to cover her ring finger, where her large diamond engagement ring was hidden by the leather of the glove.

But Miss Reed moved smoothly on to describe other notable passengers on the sailing soon to begin. "I suppose you noticed John Jacob Astor entering the train," she said to Miss Amanda, who had not. "A tall, languid type of fellow with drooping mustaches and that Airedale dog? Astor's worth a hundred and fifty million dollars, they say.

"And he's another honeymooner, too. The young woman with him is his new bride, though she's younger than his own son, Vincent. Her name's Madeline Force, and they've been in kind of an exile since they were married. She's expecting, from the look of her," Miss Reed added musingly, as innocently interested in this item as in all her other information.

"Astor was divorced, you see, and so he and his bride spent a winter in Egypt and France until the scandal blows over a little. Which it will. J. J.'s mother was *the* Mrs. Astor, you know. Old

Caroline. Ran New York society like Catherine the Great. But she's dead now, and whether young Madeline will fill *those* shoes is anybody's guess. She's starting out under a cloud, in a manner of speaking."

However little the lives of others interested Miss Amanda, she heard Colonel and Mrs. Astor's story out with a dawning look on her face, as if she saw some value to herself in it.

"I pray you, Miss Reed," she said, "to temper your quite amusing stories about the scandals and irregularities among the highborn. I am traveling with my maid. And surely you know how easily shocked persons of that class are about the escapades of the wellborn, which you and I take quite for granted. And how very disapproving servants can be of matters well beyond their understanding. They are all quite wretched moralists."

With this cheap, safe taunt, Miss Amanda sought to turn back the clock many weeks, before she had destroyed what little prospect I had of a happy life by trapping me forever in a sham marriage. Now, with this cruel teasing before witnesses, she meant to return us to that earlier time when the pettiness of mere words seemed the outer limits of her cruelty. She must have suspected that I was past her mere bullying with words now, but perhaps she yearned to distract us both from a game gone deadly serious.

When Miss Reed turned her gaze on me, my face was burning, but I would not avert my head in a cowed gesture. Miss Reed's look seemed to comprehend more than she could possibly have understood, even with all the intuition in the world. With more tact than I would have credited her, she chose to turn Miss Amanda's words into a joke, and her own conversation flowed on again. It was spiky with the famous names of those who would cross on the splendid *Titanic* as if it were the most select hotel. The Wideners and the Fortunes and the Ryersons and the Strauses and Mr. Benjamin Guggenheim and Major Butt and Mrs. Brown and the Thayers and the Countess of Rothes.

Against this roll call of the mighty of a world I did not know, I passed the remainder of our train journey. I sat on, half braced against the next thrusting attack that Miss Amanda Whitwell might level at me from her comfortable covert. And all this while England's soft, rolling countryside and gray church spires receded beyond the window of the boat train.

I doubt now that I mourned the passing of that green and pleasant land. Nor did I so much as wonder if I would ever see my own country again. There was too little in my past life that I would want to conjure up again. And while I was too cast down to be glad about anything—and too fearful of what might happen next—I rejoiced bitterly at putting this distance and more between myself and John Thorne.

In the last moments of that train journey, I made the vow I had been too numb to make before. I vowed that if John Thorne followed me—followed *her*—into our new life, I would never let him touch me again. If she wanted him for herself, then she would have him—completely. And if it was true that the high and mighty of the earth can live down any scandal and pay with money to make the filthy look clean again, then let them do what they would. But I would be no one's easy convenience ever again.

I would play my role as lady's maid and no more than that until the moment when I would rise up against them. I only hoped that I would recognize that moment when its time came around. And with cautious hope I rather thought I would recognize it when it did.

The countryside outside the window gave way to the straggling houses and lines of flapping wash of a suburb. The boat train was slowing now, crossing city streets. We were pulling into Southampton. An air of anticipation circulated through the train as doors began to bang along the corridors and the passengers began to stir. The train crept on, ever slower, past the Terminus Station and beyond. When it shuddered to a stop, we were beside the quay. And above us loomed what seemed the largest creation ever wrought by man.

The great ship rose above us, not like a vessel but more like a vast wall blotting out the day. It stood seventy feet out of the water. Its four funnels rose that high again above the topmost deck. It was festooned with flags, and over the din of the dockside, music drifted.

My heart was in my mouth, and I was able to forget everything except this dwarfing grandeur. The tall prow looked knife-sharp, a great wedge to cleave the sea, swift-seeming even without movement. And on the bow her name was lettered in gold: *Titanic.*

The next hours were lost in the thousand details of embarkation. I was breathless with the unexampled duties I was to perform as lady's maid in this bewildering, astonishing floating city. Its endless corridors. Its grand stairways descending beneath glazed domes. The ship's own servants, who seemed to outnumber its passengers. The champagne and flowers being humped along crowded passageways by stewards smaller than their burdens. The easy laughter of the very rich who have sought and found yet another pleasure to experience in a lifetime full of them. And the exceedingly sharp corners of their steamer trunks rolling perilously near the knees of the unwary. The line of lady's maids, myself among them, at the purser's counter, where ransom after ransom of jewels were to be secured in the ship's safe. The ticker tape that stretched in great fans of colored streamers from deck to quay.

This was the kaleidoscope I had wanted to draw my thoughts far from myself. But of those first hours, still half-landlocked, I remember best Miss Rebecca Reed as we prepared to leave our compartment in the train. Among her hand luggage she carried a satchelful of oddments from which she withdrew a peculiar, not very handsome stuffed toy to show Miss Amanda.

It was a music box in the shape of a pig and too realistic to be droll. When she twisted the object's tail, the mechanism inside played a few notes of the "Maxixe."

As the occupants of the compartment spared a moment to stare at this curiosity, Miss Reed said, "One of the glories of the *Titanic* is that it's unsinkable. Still, for added insurance, I go nowhere without my lucky pig!" She waved it once in the air and then thrust it, still tinkling its tune, back into her reticule. And we all followed her—and it—out of the train and up the gangplank.

The last blasts from the siren sounded just before noon, and the *Titanic* moved from its moorings soon after. By teatime I had decided that if we were not to encounter any rougher seas than those off the anchorage at Spithead, I would be a hardy sailor and never give way to seasickness.

The *Titanic* seemed not even to move. Only to throb gently like a great, gilded whale breathing deep in its throat. I had spent the afternoon settling my young lady in her quarters on B Deck. Her cabin was luxurious, though compact, and defied all my notions of what such quarters should be like. She was to sleep in a four-poster bed and not in a bunk fastened high on a wall. There was a dressing table admirably fitted out. Instead of ship's lanterns, there were electrified sconces along the walls more elegant than those in the ladies' withdrawing room at the hotel in Ventnor. There was even hot water piped directly in, which was a great deal more than could be said for the bedrooms of Whitwell Hall.

My cabin adjoined hers—far too near for my liking, but it was scarcely less comfortable, though it lacked portholes. For it was situated between Miss Amanda's stateroom and the main corridor of that side of the ship. Three or four doors farther along was the Parlor Suite, with its own private promenade deck, occupied by Mr. J. Bruce Ismay, managing director of the White Star Line. This Parlor Suite's opposite number on the starboard side of B Deck was occupied by Colonel and Mrs. Astor.

At either end of our corridor were sights of astonishing splendor. Forward, the passageway gave onto what seemed a vast reception hall and the grand staircase, which was the central crossroads of the ship. It was dominated from above by a great clock set in under the glass dome from which daylight fell deeply into the heart of the ship. The clock rarely failed to catch my eye whenever I hurried past beneath it. It was set between two bronze figures depicting Glory and Honor crowning Time. This great work alone looked far too heavy to include in any conveyance expected to float.

At the other end of the corridor was the *à la carte* French restaurant, where I suffered the first embarrassment of a servant who has never served at sea. While she was in it, I had not been allowed to linger in my young lady's stateroom unpacking her trunks. It was close quarters for two women who could never again engage in even the pretense of civility. And so she thought of a number of errands to send me on. If she thought I would allow myself to be as baffled by this vast ship as I had once been in even more vast London, she reckoned without my determination to find my own way. But I did go wrong almost at once when she sent me out to book her table in the ship's dining saloon.

Following a number of men dressed as waiters toward the subdued clinking of cutlery, I made for the restaurant at the end of our corridor. When I stepped up to the velvet rope hung across the entry, I caught my breath at the magnificence of this place. It was, I suppose, a rendering of the most luxurious Paris restaurant imaginable. French furniture of a bygone century stood grouped in an ocean of white napery against pale walnut paneling. Beyond the silk-draped bays of one side extended the Café Parisien, which was a stretch of enclosed deck set up less formally with wicker furniture and potted palms that swayed only slightly.

Almost at once a foreigner I know now to have been Monsieur Gatti stepped up to inquire how he might be of service. He must have known at once whom he was dealing with. I was dressed far too plainly to be a First Class passenger and a bit too correctly to have been from steerage, if a steerage passenger could have passed all the barriers from that remote sector of the ship.

When I asked if I might book my young lady's table for the voyage, he very kindly explained in a picturesque accent that he was the *maître* of this restaurant, which was his domain, and had nothing whatever to do with the White Star Line. This was an alternative for those who preferred French cuisine to English cookery and who did not care to take their meals at the regular sittings in the main dining saloon situated on D Deck far below us. He was good enough to direct me to this main dining room, which proved to be even more awesomely vast than his domain.

And beyond or beneath this dining saloon were a Turkish bath and a swimming bath and a gymnasium and a children's nursery and ballrooms and lounges and smoking rooms and writing rooms. More luxuries and comforts to be indulged in on the choppy seas than ever I had imagined on dry land. All this splendor in layer on layer into the depths of the sea itself. And even lifts to take one up and down, lifts that the Americans oddly called elevators.

I dressed my young lady for tea in a gown with a large bouquet of silk flowers at the waist. I stood behind her to attend to her hair as she sat at the dressing table. Our eyes never met in the looking glass. She got through the time by reading out the names on the passenger list, determined, I imagine, to become as knowledgeable about them as Miss Reed was. And to fill up the silences with words requiring no response.

Her eye drifted down to her waist when she thought I didn't notice. I rather think she would have made the crossing largely in her own stateroom, safe from prying eyes and the need to be civil to strangers, if she had been traveling with a more amiable maid.

But I did not detain her longer than was absolutely necessary and stood back to signal that she was quite ready to join her fellow passengers. I should have thrown her to the wolves if there had been any about. As it was, my hands stung from having so much as touched her. I thought her as diseased in body as in mind. She had infected everything she touched, and it seemed impossible to be beyond her grasp.

She did not ask me for a last-minute opinion of her appearance, as once had been her custom. She would have swept grandly from the cabin if there had been room enough for this gesture. However, she was determined to make some impression on me, I suppose. For she turned at the door and wrenched Mr. Forrest's diamond engagement ring from her finger.

"Here," she said, holding it out to me. "Take this down to the purser and put it in the safe with the rest of my jewelry. I do not choose to be an engaged woman during the crossing." Then she was gone, and the enormous, lovely, meaningless diamond lay winking in the palm of my hand.

There was a saloon on the deck below ours set aside as a lounge and dining room for maids and valets. A sort of floating servants' hall. But I chose not to join my fellow servants just yet. I went directly from the safe where I left Mr. Forrest's ring to the open promenade of A Deck above.

I had tied a long scarf over my head to brave the sea winds. And I stood for a moment, poorly sheltered by one of the great, smoke-spewing funnels as the raw evening wind caught at my breath and the ends of my scarf.

I crossed to starboard, drawn, I suppose, by the coastline sliding past. Perhaps I was not yet ready for the emptiness of the open sea, though I had dreamed of it, unreasonably, all my life. The deck smelled of tar and new paint, the breeze of salt. But I thought I caught a scent of land as well, of England in April, the smell of damp turned earth, of the forest floor, and of lilac.

It could not have been. I was only being fanciful. But we were very near shore then, with the sun falling into the sea ahead, and the rocks and trees still close, throwing long shadows.

Two gentlemen stood along the railing, occupying themselves chiefly in keeping their pipes going in the stiff breeze. I heard one say, "We have passed Selsey Bill and have dropped off the pilot at Nab Lightship."

The names meant nothing to me. Yet I sharpened my gaze at the cliffs and rises and little fans of sandy beach near enough almost to touch. I seemed to know where we were. It was almost as if we were making no journey at all, as if we had never left. For yes, those lines of terraced houses descending to a beach and a pleasure pier must be Shanklin, not five miles from where I was born at Whitely Bank. Not five miles, perhaps, from where my mother and my father might be sitting to their meager, wordless tea.

This was the Isle of Wight we were sweeping past as if it were only a sort of backdrop painted for a play. How strange it looked from this vantage point. And yes, past Shanklin Chine there was the eminence of Dunnose rising from the Undercliff. There the very place where my father's wagon had lost its wheel at the bridge. If I could have a little time, perhaps I would spot the Wisewoman's cottage from among the many glowing evening-white that seemed more closely clustered than they were. And if all the wheeling, begging seabirds ceased their cries, perhaps I could hear again her prophecy, just as she had spoken it, riddlelike. *"Your future lies,"* she had told me, *"beyond a mountain of ice where you will die and live again. I see you in a world so strange and distant that the images seems like the trickery of a gypsy's false promises, even to me. . . ."*

But no, there was no time to search for her enchanted cottage or to divide the Gordian knot of her words. The ship knifed on with uncanny speed, coiling the water in a straight furrow. And there, ahead, one last pier, like a rigid black web hugging the sea. Here was Ventnor, its pier black and charred against the blaze of the setting sun. We were off Ventnor now, and small boats bobbed in the bay, and white handkerchiefs saluted us.

Somewhere up the steps of Ventnor town was the shop of Mr. Hubert Sampson, the draper. Neither quite a bachelor now nor yet really a widower, ascending the narrow steps above his shop, perhaps, to take his tea with his monstrous mother. And somewhere a street or two away, the photographer's shop where Betty and I had had our photograph made on our first half day out. And there the hotel with all its windows fired by the sun where Betty and I had had our tea. The same hotel where—

But I would look no more. How thin the threads from which I wove these meager memories. I would not go back now, even if I were given the wings of the diving gulls that followed the ship and bound it still to solid earth. I studied the curling foam seventy feet beneath me, the green-black water laced in white, and heard one of the pipe-smoking gentlemen say, "And there's St. Catherine's Head just there, and the last of England. We'll make Cherbourg by nightfall and Queenstown by tomorrow midday. Then a straight shot to New York."

Perhaps it was this overheard reminder of our destination that moved me then. Something nagged at the back of my mind. Something I had left undone. I could not think what task it was. But already I was drawing the glove off my left hand, laying bare fingers that the sea wind bit at. I pulled at the worn ring with the ruby pinpoint set in it. I twisted it until it came free and slipped it off my finger. Never mind that it had once been Granny Thorne's and then her daughter's. John Thorne had put it on my hand, and it had no business being there. He had never given me a wedding band. Perhaps he had not thought of it, or thought it necessary. Perhaps *she* had forgotten to tell him to give me one.

I held the ring between forefinger and thumb for a moment. I dropped it then, over the side, into the sea.

Twenty-Four

A ship is like a planet following a course foreordained. Even the largest of all ships and the fastest, the *Titanic,* was like a small world in the great universe of the Atlantic. And if a ship is a world, a journey on it is a little lifetime. Faces appearing in the servants' saloon or among the wealthy taking their morning bouillon beneath the lounge tapestries became immediately familiar. Persons twice encountered were like figures known since childhood.

But one encountered Miss Rebecca Reed of New York more often than anyone else. She seemed everywhere at once, darting about in search of friends new and old, with perhaps the motive that she should write up an account of this marvel-filled maiden voyage. I cannot think how often I must have passed her as I went about my duties; I devised a great many of them to keep me away from my young lady's stateroom. And while Miss Reed was civil—and informative—to all, her eye was particularly drawn to the famous and the colorful among her fellow passengers.

On the first night out, when we entered Cherbourg Roads to pick up the passengers from France, Miss Reed was nearest the gangplank to pipe aboard these additions to the passenger list.

From the gossip in the servants' saloon and the wealth of information overheard from Miss Reed, I soon felt more at home on the high seas than ever I had anywhere on dry land.

Miss Reed nearly crowed with delight when she saw among the

Cherbourg arrivals a Mrs. J. J. Brown of Leadville and Denver, Colorado, and Newport, Rhode Island, U.S.A. Indeed, all the throng on deck stood back to observe the arrival of this Mrs. Molly Brown as she came up the gangplank, grasping the rope with a gloved hand set about with diamond rings that blazed like carriage lamps. I stood staring myself at the edge of the crowd, as unobtrusive as possible in my dark frieze skirt when I might better have been about my duties. But Mrs. Brown was such an arresting figure no one could have kept from having a look. She was no longer young but as sprightly and arch in her manner as a girl half her age. And she was dressed in a costume that made even her fellow Americans drably sober by contrast.

Mrs. Brown was assured of a boisterous welcome from all in this traveling club. But she received an especially warm greeting from Colonel Astor, who stepped from the crowd to embrace her. For it seems that when his New York society friends had forsaken his ballroom and his opera box after the scandal of his divorce and remarriage. Mrs. Brown had remained loyal and tolerant. And had even spent much of the winter in Egypt with the Colonel and his young bride.

Scarcely was Mrs. Brown aboard than the crowd stirred again as Sir Cosmo and Lady Duff Gordon stepped from gangplank to deck. I was beginning to learn that the Americans were more moved by the English peerage than any Englishman is. And I puzzled then, as I have puzzled since, over the strangeness of the American nation in turning their backs on British rule. For a people who had turned their backs, they spent a great deal of time peering admiringly over their shoulders.

Lady Duff Gordon was as beautiful as Mrs. Brown was startling. She rejoiced in the glory not only of her own position but in the notoriety of her sister, Elinor Glyn, whose novels Lady Eleanor Whitwell thought so unsuitable for a young girl's reading. The Duff Gordons were traveling incognito as "Mr. and Mrs. Morgan," a ruse that deceived nobody and was perhaps not meant to.

With the arrival of the passengers from France, the *Titanic,* for all its speed, drifted into easy routine. A bugle sounded to announce every sumptuous meal, and the ladies changed their clothes easily as often as if they were spending a long weekend in such a royal country retreat as Sandringham. After each meal the lovely paneled lounge below on D Deck was thronged with friends gathered to drink their coffee in the upholstered niches, recessed within the carved white paneling that resembled ice sculpture.

The younger travelers inclined to the Café Parisien to draw up the wicker chairs in companionable circles beside the trellised walls. In the afternoons the ladies were drawn to the novelty of the swimming baths, which were afterward given over to the gentlemen in the early evening hours.

The gentlemen also repaired to the gymnasium for regimens of exercise prescribed by the instructor there, Mr. McCawley. And for lessons in squash far below in the courts, they were attended to by Mr. Wright.

Our docking at Queenstown just past noon on the second day caused scarcely a ripple of interest, though it was our last landfall before the open sea. For here the embarking passengers were mainly poor Irish immigrants shunted directly into steerage. Poor though they were, they could not have been poorer than I, or they would not have been able to afford the passage.

The ship drove on, riding the water as if it were a ballroom floor or perhaps a sheet of glass or a skim of ice. The passengers of First Class were buoyed up as much by the continual melodies of Mr. Hartley's orchestra as by the watertight compartments beneath their feet. I hear those melodies yet in evenings grown quiet. The themes that a vanished world moved so gracefully to. The selections from *The Merry Widow* and *The Chocolate Soldier*. And less graceful but more popular than all the rest, "Alexander's Ragtime Band."

Lofty and low, we were all drawn together in this false, lovely, beautifully shaped shipboard world. The exclusive circles of friends traveling together widened to embrace yet other circles. Invitations handsomely engraved went out for dinners given in Monsieur Gatti's restaurant.

Even I was treated with great civility by the British servants and baby nurses in our own saloon, and with hearty friendliness by the American servants. Miss Fleming, Mrs. Thayer's maid, both conducted herself and treated me as if we were persons in our own right and not mere appendages of our employers. I was soon on pleasant terms with Miss Annie Robinson, the stewardess who saw to the needs of the passengers in our corridor. And there was Mademoiselle Victorine, too, the French maid of the American Mrs. Ryerson, wife of the steel magnate. Victorine was the glass of fashion in the servants' saloon, and the soul of propriety. I recalled with a smile Mrs. Creeth's long-ago mutterings about the dubious characters of "Frog" maids.

To record and direct this briskly paced sea life, there was even a daily newspaper that ran to twelve pages, titled *The Atlantic Daily Bulletin.*

In all this world of careful fashion and careless frivolity, Miss Amanda's beauty and her appearance of breeding did not go unremarked. Miss Reed had been quite right about the conventions governing a lady traveling alone. From the first night Miss Amanda was surrounded by swains of all ages eager to shelter her from the rigors of a rigorless journey. She had me dress her with the greatest attention. She was determined to be a carefree young girl again, now that it was too late.

The only words spoken in her stateroom were her commands delivered to me with an imperiousness she hoped to maintain. I spent much of my time collecting her pearls, the gift of Mr. Forrest; her diamond bracelets; the pendants; and the jeweled clips and shoe buckles at the purser's office. And then returning them again, later each evening. I was sent to collect every item except her engagement ring.

Her swains included young Mr. Jack Thayer of Philadelphia. He was a handsome, nearly beardless boy of no more than seventeen, whose father was the vice-president of the Pennsylvania Railroad. And the list of her conquests reached in more worldly directions, to Major Archibald Butt, who was the American President Taft's military aide.

But my young lady had settled on a different sort of "protector" from the first evening. He was nowhere near as courtly or as respectable as young Mr. Thayer or Major Butt. But he was very much more to Miss Amanda's taste. He was a Mr. Clem Sawyer of San Francisco. While he spent much of his time at the card table and in the preserve of the gentlemen's smoking room, Miss Amanda had not escaped his notice. Nor he hers, for he was by far the handsomest man on the *Titanic.*

Even before the last of the gulls that followed us from Queenstown had turned back, Mr. Sawyer had formed an alliance with my young lady. On the Friday night they dined in the *à la carte* restaurant. I sat up till quite two o'clock to undress her. On the Saturday night it was later still.

I have reason to remember that night particularly. The sea air and the long day had combined to make me very tired. Fearing I might nod off before Miss Amanda's return, I found a dozen tasks to keep me alert. And I opened the portholes in her stateroom for the brisk air. The weather was growing colder every hour. I would not have her return to find me sleeping and thus to give cause for criticism on some safely minor matter. She was searching for just such an issue with all her might.

I was occupying myself with the mending of a frock that had split at the waist when someone knocked on the cabin door. It was Miss Reed. She was dressed in a black dinner gown of extreme, elegant cut. And her face was animated with agitation. I asked her to step inside, though my young lady had not yet returned.

"How well I know!" Miss Reed said, striding in and throwing herself into a chair. She dug about in a small reticule set with arabesques of black jet for a cigarette, which proved to be as black as her costume. She fitted it into a gold holder. The room was at once filled with the dubious perfumes of Turkish tobacco. "I know I'm a terrible busybody," she said, perhaps to me. Then she occupied herself with brushing ash from the bodice of her gown. "Your name is Miranda, isn't it?"

"Yes, Miss." I did not wonder at her knowing, though I was marked in the passenger list only as Miss Whitwell's maid. Miss Reed knew everyone and everything.

"Are you a married lady?"

I hesitated, and it did not escape her notice. "Yes, Miss. I am married."

"Well, I suppose that should put me at my ease a little," she replied, but still I hadn't an idea what she was getting at. "I guess I better just plunge in. Molly Brown would. The fact is, Miranda, that your Amanda Whitwell shows every sign of disgracing herself. And it's serious business, believe me. The kind of people crossing on this ship pretend to immense tolerance and sophistication and that kind of thing. The plain fact is they forget nothing and tell everything. And they're as stiff-necked as a Quaker meeting, with the forgiving spirit left out.

"Amanda Whitwell is bound for New York to marry Gregory

Forrest, who is, whether you know it or not, one of the best catches of the decade. There are people on this ship who will know Amanda in New York. But they'll refuse to know her if she makes a fool of herself with Clem Sawyer. Good grief! The little idiot is on her way to New York to be married, and she's acting like a jaded woman of forty with two husbands and three fortunes in her past!

"And everyone on this ship knows Sawyer. He's stinking rich with new money—probably not his own. But the point is, he's a menace with women. As a rule, his taste runs more to chorus girls and worse. Anyone can put up with that sort of thing in a man. But with a young lady of background and with promise of . . ." Miss Reed seemed nearly overcome by concern at this turn of events. But she could not still herself. "I suppose I can say this since you're a married woman. Sawyer won't stop short of taking Amanda to bed."

Nor would she want him to stop short, I thought, and drew myself up stiffly in case Miss Reed perceived this unspoken thought in my face. She misread it entirely, as she had misread Miss Amanda.

"Oh, I know, I know. English servants are wonderfully discreet. 'See no evil, speak no evil, hear no evil'—that sort of thing. I don't doubt you would protect your young lady from hearing any innuendo if you could. And I suppose she's led a sheltered life up to now and has gotten temporarily carried away with that good-looking devil."

I nearly smiled bitterly at that, but Miss Reed continued in a rush. "But damn it, Miranda, I wonder if you can't have a word with Amanda. I know how close Englishwomen are to their maids. Why, you even look alike! Couldn't you just give her a kind of warning? The poor thing doesn't know the danger she's in, and I doubt she'd be warned by a stranger. I think a word from you might be just the right touch."

I believe I would have let myself go entirely then. I believe I would have told the breezy, kindly Miss Reed things that would have shocked her far more than a shipboard romance with a Mr. Clem Sawyer.

I was half free then in this strange world, sailing farther and farther as we spoke from the strictures that had bound me all my life. And I could think of little I had left to lose by speaking my mind. What little was left—of gainful employment and the shreds of self-respect

I still clung to—might be taken from me at any time by the fiend who was my mad double, Miss Amanda Whitwell.

Perhaps what saved that moment—and spared Miss Reed—was that I did not know where to start. Should I tell this American lady, who was in her heart more innocent than she knew, that Miss Whitwell was pregnant by my husband, a lowly man-of-all-work without a mind of his own? Should I tell her that it was my opinion that Miss Whitwell had arranged my marriage only when she knew she was pregnant, to prove her power over my husband? To prove her power over Mr. Forrest, the husband she meant to have for her own? To prove her power even over me, when she had proved that well enough already? Should I tell Miss Reed that Amanda Whitwell was maddened by self-love? That no man, not even Mr. Clem Sawyer, could have the least influence over her because she was ruined already? Because she saw others only as they could serve her. And that her eye roved everywhere to serve her lust, which went far beyond the needs of her body?

My mind even drifted to the book from Asprey's in which Amanda Whitwell had very likely recorded her dark deeds and darker—far darker—thoughts. The book lay on her writing table not six inches from Miss Reed's elbow, and it would make for illuminating reading. Miss Amanda had made a point of leaving it in plain view. I am convinced that she meant me to read it when she was not near. What she dared not say to me, however little she feared me, she longed for me to know. She hated that John Thorne had even played at being my husband for those few short weeks. I daresay she had written in that book passages meant to prove that he could be inflamed by her and her alone. She saw me only as a husk of herself, outwardly similar, but empty of all her power, and she would never be done proving that. But I had not read her book in a servant's sneaking way. I did not need to.

Should I fling that book into Miss Reed's lap or read out passages from it?

No. I could not do that to either of us. It was unthinkable.

I felt bent beneath the burden of all this that I could not say. And if I had told the plain truth, Miss Reed would have thought me crazed. I could say nothing. My silence protected Amanda Whitwell. She had won again. I stood unspeaking, like any tongue-tied servant. Miss Reed only sighed at my silence.

Still, she was not a lady to give up easily in what she thought a good cause. She started to speak. At that moment Miss Amanda entered the room. I turned quickly toward her, guilty in my thoughts. She surmised that something had been going on behind her back, a thing she could never abide. Her face looked blurred from the effects of champagne. There was a raw, reddish patch across her cheek of the sort left by the scrape of a man's beard. She staggered with perhaps more than the sway of the ship and turned a bright, mechanical smile on Miss Reed, who soon beat a hasty retreat. Our visitor covered her exit with effusive good nights. I was left alone in the stateroom with Miss Amanda.

"What did she want?" she demanded in a slurred voice before the door had quite closed behind Miss Reed.

"I couldn't say, Miss."

"Oh, couldn't you? It seems that you have very little to say for yourself these days. However convenient you happen to be to me, Miranda, I advise you not to take liberties with my good disposition. I am bound to tell you that you are becoming a bore. A beastly bore, and a terrible prig into the bargain."

"I expect you are tired, Miss," I said in an empty voice.

"Yes. I am very tired indeed, mostly of you." She tore at Mr. Forrest's pearls, which were looped around and around her neck, till I thought she would break them. But I did not try to help her. Perhaps I dared not approach her. Her eyes never left me, and I saw so much madness in them that I could scarcely force myself to hold my ground.

"Shall I speak to the stewardess about drawing your bath, Miss?"

"You shall speak to *me*," she barked as she jerked loose the clasp on her diamond bracelet and threw it into the corner, where I would have to grovel to retrieve it. "You shall speak to me, and quite truthfully, about what that Rebecca Reed was doing in my stateroom."

"She had called, Miss, but found that you were out."

"And yet when I returned, she left at once. Do you not think that curious behavior, even for an American?"

"I couldn't say, Miss."

She dropped her voice then. She must have begun to hear it echoing about the stateroom like a fishwife's. And I caught a hint of her old cajoling tone when she continued. "Be good enough, Miranda, to tell me in simple language what Miss Reed's business was here, and do not make me ask you again."

After a lengthening pause, I said, "She had come in friendship, Miss. She is concerned that your association with a certain gentleman on the ship has left you open to unfavorable comment among the other passengers."

Her eyes brightened then, for she was spoiling for a fight. "The certain gentleman being Mr. Sawyer, I trust."

"Yes, Miss, so I believe."

She hooted with false laughter. "How pathetic! How very spinsterish and pathetic of her! What wouldn't Rebecca Reed do for one idle glance from a man like Clem Sawyer? Oh, how very high-minded people are who have no opportunity to be anything else! You two must have got on splendidly."

"Yes, Miss. She is kind to me."

"Kind and prying, I daresay. People who will stoop to servants will stoop to anything."

"Yes, Miss. That's very true."

"Well, then, you must tell me precisely what you told her when she was kind and prying enough to concern herself with my reputation and well-being."

"It was not my place to tell her anything, Miss."

"How right you are to remember that. Yet, my dear Miranda, what would you have told her if you had not been such a mealymouthed, sniveling little servant?"

"I would have told her, Miss, that if anyone needed protection, it would be Mr. Sawyer."

Her eyes went black, and the red patch on her cheek glowed fiery against her white skin. She took a half step toward me, and all I could see was her distorted face. Her hand flashed in the air, and she struck me with all her might. I reeled against the table, sending her diary crashing to the floor. And I felt the hot, salty blood stream from the place where my tooth had cut my lip.

"You insolent, pious little bitch," she whispered. But her words came from a great distance. The immense chasm that had always existed between us opened up at last and revealed its depths. I was still the servant I had been in the previous moment. But Amanda Whitwell had finally lost control of herself. It was a poor prospect for her future. For now she had come past being able to manipulate others without showing her hand. The mark of that hand stung on my cheek. In even this we seemed similar, for the red place rubbed on her cheek by the passionate Mr. Clem Sawyer had marked her, too.

"Do not speak to me for the remainder of the voyage. I shall hear not another word from you or I shall find something to deprive you of that I have not taken already. And never fear—when I look for something, I find it. I do not wish to hear your voice until we have docked in New York and must make a favorable impression on Mr. Forrest. And no, you need not ring the stewardess for my bath. I shall not be sleeping in my stateroom tonight. Indeed, I am just going."

She turned and jerked open the cabin door. There in the entryway outside stood Mr. Clem Sawyer. He was a study in black and white, a tall, lithe figure in evening clothes, silhouetted against the corridor lamps. He had grown tired of waiting for Miss Amanda, and it showed in his lounging posture.

As he stepped forward to claim her, he glanced idly into the room, and I met his gaze. He had the hollow-cheeked handsomeness of an earlier period. And his face was divided by the spiral of smoke rising from a cigarette that dangled from his mouth. He noted the thin line of blood that ran to my chin. His look seemed to say that servants were often in need of just such correction. He slipped his arm around Miss Amanda's thickened waist, and the door closed behind them.

Twenty-Five

Sunday, April 14, 1912, was a brisk, brilliant day on the gray, shadowless sea. I awoke at my regular hour and entered my young lady's stateroom, out of habit more than anything else. It was empty, of course. I stood beside her undisturbed bed, which had been neatly turned down the night before. And my mind wandered along unwholesome lines.

I wondered if this was not, perhaps, only the second time in her life that she had spent an entire night with a man. I was in no danger of forgetting the first time that she had. Perhaps to torture myself, perhaps to make me hate her more, I forced myself to relive the previous Sunday morning when I had found John Thorne with her and the pitiless morning light laying them bare. That scene—only seven mornings before. I might have been washed by a great wave of disgust for the man who was my legal husband. But he was already remote from my mind, and receding.

I had left him behind, and I was not prepared yet to face the inescapable fact that I was bound to him by law. I had never been truly oppressed by any law except that which Amanda Whitwell dictated. We were still another night's journey away from the world we had known and she had controlled. I wondered idly what John Thorne was doing at that moment, back in that country where he had carried servitude to such lengths. What was he doing without his pair of women—the one to be obeyed and the other to obey? But I found that I could no longer see him clearly. Not his face: the cragged strength of that mask. I could see in my mind's eye only his naked back as he sat slumped on Miss Amanda's bed. Clem Sawyer, a more worldly man, must have other ways of greeting the dawn. I turned away from the untouched bed, and I turned my mind from these thoughts.

A more accommodating servant might have ruffled the bed. She might have hollowed the pillow, drawn the blankets half onto the floor, mussed the sheets. She might have lain in it a moment herself to keep scandal from spreading among the stewardesses. But I had no reason to cover my young lady's traces. I was married to a corrupt, corrupted servant, to my sorrow. He would serve both sister and brother and perhaps both alike, for they had convinced him that he was the more acceptable to them as an animal than as a man.

But he was far away, and Miss Amanda was on her own now, whether that truth was dawning on her or not. I was not so much as to speak to her, and that decree freed me more than it freed her.

I smiled at the thought of her waking in the bed of a strange man who had awakened beside so many strangers. I smiled, too, at how vexed she would be that I would not be there to bring in her morning tea and to ease her into another easeful day.

Instead, I picked up the book from Asprey's from off the floor and put it away on the lowest shelf of the bedside table, as one puts aside a book not worth reading. I collected the pearls that had been flung over a chair back and found the suede drawstring bag where they were kept. Following a glimmer of fire to the corner beneath a porthole, I retrieved her diamond bracelet. Then I screwed the porthole shut. We were in northern waters now, and the breeze off the placid sea was biting. I had just heard a steward in the passageway speak of the ocean's "flat calm." But it was as cold as—how would Mrs. Creeth put it? As cold as charity.

I laid out my young lady's clothes for the day—tweeds, I decided, and shoes suitable for strolling on the deck, and a veil for anchoring her hat. I did not suppose she meant to attend church services. I left then to return the jewelry to Mr. McElroy at the purser's office.

I felt strange and footloose with freedom on that Sunday morning, and hardly knew what to do with such an emotion. As I was taking a turn on the open deck, bundled to the eyes in a thick scarf, I met the Countess of Rothes's maid. We stood chatting a moment in the scant shelter of the davits that held the lifeboats in place. She told me that servants were allowed to attend morning services, though they were held in the First Class dining saloon.

I went at once to change into a sober outfit and a hat suitable for churchgoing. Then I screwed up my courage to enter the lovely great dining saloon, and looked quickly about for an inconspicuous corner amid all its Jacobean carving.

I needn't have felt shy. Of the eight or so maids traveling with their employers, several were there, and even a few of the gentlemen's gentlemen. Even Victorine, who must surely have been a French Catholic, was there in a smart hat, perhaps for the pleasure of sitting in this grand, temporary church, where all the sideboards groaned with silver. Second and Third Class passengers were admitted as well, until there was quite a large, varied congregation.

In place of an organ, the ship's orchestra played, which was lovely. We did not kneel, for gilt chairs had to make do as pews. The entrance of the ship's captain, Captain Edward Smith, created a stir. He had come to conduct the service.

The captain looked at least as impressive as a clergyman. A well-set-up elderly man with a handsomely barbered nautical beard and luxuriant white mustaches. The double row of brass buttons against his dark uniform gleamed like altar-candle flames, and he led us with quiet authority through the service and the Prayer for Those at Sea.

Just past midday, I returned to my young lady's stateroom to find that she had returned, changed, and gone away again. I laid out a tea gown for her late afternoon, and rather wondered if she was not making herself scarce because of me. Mr. Sawyer was surely more a creature of the night than of a Sunday flooded with sunlight. I wondered what Miss Amanda was finding to do with herself.

But she was waiting for me that evening to dress her for dinner. This was inescapable. And it was the moment for her to test her own decree that she should not hear my insolent voice. It had not occurred to her perhaps that there would be unnatural silence when before I had said, "Yes, Miss" and "No, Miss" in response to her every observation.

She was sitting at her dressing table in a silk kimono. "I shall not wear the black tonight," she said, fixing on her own image in the mirror. She paused, waited, and continued. "Black seems to be all the rage among the American women, and it suits very few of them."

Another pause, as I stood silently waiting for an instruction.

"The pink, I think," she said at last. "Girlish, but not virginal. I can only hope you have bothered to mend it where it was badly made at the waist."

I drew out the long pink gown, and she put out a hand for it. Then she rather lost ground by searching the waistband, where she could not find my invisible needlework.

"And I really cannot decide about the right jewelry," she remarked, draping the gown over the arm of her chair. "Not the pearls, I think. They are not nearly as fine as Mrs. Widener's. And I suppose once I am in New York I shall have to wear them endlessly as they were a gift of Gregory's. But on the other hand, they're not as vulgar as Mrs. Widener's. Go and get them."

I left for the purser's safe and returned to find that she had contrived to get herself into the pink gown on her own, though it was hanging every which way. She had even pulled a pair of silver slippers out of the bottom drawer of a steamer trunk and had plunged her feet into them.

She was adjusting the straps of her gown, smoothing them over her shoulders with a mathematical precision. She was determined, I suppose, to show that she could give herself more careful attention than I was able to provide her. And in this she was quite right. No one could have given herself closer attention than my young lady. "I have decided I don't require jewelry," she said to her looking glass. "Take the pearls back."

And once I had returned from this errand, she had managed to make good her escape. The long fur wrap that had been a gift from her mother was gone from its padded hanger, though the hanger still jiggled. She had eluded me, and in consequence was gone well before the dinner hour. The bugle from the dining room did not sound for quite another half hour.

We were trapped, she and I, in the middle of the ocean on a vast ship that had become too small. I wondered how we would last out this voyage in quarters growing ever closer. For we had gone beyond the point of no return with each other.

I need not have wondered how we would manage. I was never to be in that stateroom with her again.

———

That night, there was hymn singing in the Second Class dining saloon. It was a very pleasant evening indeed. Victorine was there, and she and I shared a hymnal. She did not even try to follow the unfamiliar words of English Protestant hymns. But she tapped her foot continually in a sprightlier rhythm, particularly when the rest of us sang a hymn that still plays in my heart:

> *Eternal Father, strong to save*
> *Whose arm hath bound the restless wave,*
> *Who bidd'st the mighty ocean deep*
> *Its own appointed limits keep*
> *O hear us when we cry to Thee*
> *For those in peril on the sea.*

Afterward Victorine and I took a turn on the uncovered Boat Deck. I was more comfortable there after dark than in the glare of day. I could not quite rid myself of the idea that servants should not be mingling with the mighty on such a promenade.

Victorine took another view. She must have thought me quite a country mouse. I daresay she would have invested me with some of her worldliness if she could. She was quite as aware of herself as of her position as maid to the distinguished Mrs. Arthur Ryerson. Victorine's eyebrows arched in the manner of Frenchwomen as she made some observation, and she would lay a gloved hand on my sleeve as she spoke. She spoke a great deal in her picturesque accent and knew much about our fellow passengers.

She was discretion itself, though, in her references to Mr. and Mr. Ryerson and their three children. She was even discreet about their children's governess, who was aboard, though maids and governesses always seemed to be natural enemies. I was discreet to the point of stony silence on the subject of my Miss Whitwell, and I expect this silence was not lost on Victorine.

There were several strollers on the open deck that evening, and they were all subjects for Victorine's commentary. "There, just ahead," she said, "those two are Monsieur and Madame Harris. He is the Broadway producer—very famous, but not social. She has broken her arm, poor thing. See how she carries it in a sling." Victorine pressed my own arm for emphasis as we swept past the Harrises. "And there are Monsieur and Madame Marvin. They are the honeymooners whose wedding was placed on film. Very modern, is it not?"

The black water seemed to glow beyond our promenade, and I was drawn to the railing between the lifeboats. The sea was as calm as the mere at Whitwell Hall—as still as a painting without a subject. There was the sensation of great speed as the ship cut through the night. Yet the only real evidence of movement came from the smoke streaming backward out of the funnels that seemed to rise miles above us. "And I wonder where that Mademoiselle Reed is keeping herself this evening?" Victorine said. "Inside, out of the cold, perhaps. And she travels with that small musical pig! The little toy that plays the 'Maxixe.' Is it not droll?" She laughed and sang a snippet of the pig's song in a music-box voice. But somehow I could not attend her. The immense emptiness of the Atlantic seemed to draw all my thoughts far from the brilliantly lit ship. Somehow it called to me. But I shook myself free of its silent voice. Our teeth were chattering with the cold. It was better to maintain a brisk pace.

Farther along, a couple stood very close together beside the railing. There was a pinpoint of light from the end of his cigarette. She was swathed in a long fur coat, beneath which gleamed a pair of silver slippers.

I walked quickly past them, though they were turned to one another and would not have noticed. Victorine had had to make a little skip to keep pace with me. "Was that not your Mademoiselle Whitwell?" she inquired, her eyebrows high.

I nodded, and she said, "Ah, she is a one, with that Mr. Clem Sawyer. . . ." But her voice trailed away while she tried to interpret my silence.

Miss Amanda had snared her Mr. Sawyer for still another evening, another night. It would be a point of pride—perhaps a point of honor with her. She would not sleep again in her own stateroom on this voyage if she could help it. She would betray Mr. Forrest again and to the limit. She would betray him in advance, and I would be her unwilling accomplice. She would go on betraying him. It took no imagination to see the future as she saw it. She would go on betraying Mr. Forrest long after he knew it.

I could not think of it any more. Her future was too bound up with mine, and I could see no way out of it. Instead, I fell back on the sort of thought that sees a maid through nearly anything. I thought that my young lady should have been wearing her other wrap—the plum-colored velvet one edged in fur, instead of that long fur more suitable for daytime. She had made the choice herself, and it had not been the right one.

Yes, it was far more comforting to think as a maid and not as myself. For there was something in me that would no longer serve. There was something in me struggling to be born. Perhaps a self that was quite as much a stranger to the maid I was as to Miss Amanda Whitwell. A self that lurked in mystery behind the mask that she and I shared.

We had had enough of the open deck, Victorine and I. The night was arctic-cold. Just before we pulled open the heavy doors in search of warmth, I looked up once at the brilliant stars. And there above us in the crow's nest was a sailor standing watch in his lofty lookout. The ship was quieting for the night, and the sailor's perch so high among the stars seemed very cold, very lonely, very reassuring.

On the grand stairway beneath the great bronze clock, we passed an elderly lady and gentlemen. "Eight hundred miles from New York," he said to her. I trembled with the cold that clung to me, and at the thought of that new life drawing steadily nearer.

It was nearly eleven o'clock when I returned to my little airless cabin next to Miss Amanda's stateroom. I had lingered only a moment outside her door to listen for a sound. Her room was silent. There was nothing to hear except the faint whir of the ship's engines below and the steady creaking in the new walls.

Without my young lady to settle for the night, I indulged myself in preparing for bed in my own cabin. Here was another moment when I was free of her. An ordinary, empty moment that I must fill up for myself. I bathed as well as I was able in the small basin. I brushed out my hair with more than usual attention, avoiding the mirror. I had spent little of my life staring at my own reflection. I had instead spent too much of it in the presence of another, who seemed to spend all her time searching the mirror.

I drew on a flannel nightgown. It was a castoff of Miss Amanda's, for the rosebud pattern on it had faded. There was an edging of lace at the throat, and I was comfortable in it because it seemed more mine than hers.

But it was too early to sleep. I had got into the habit of sitting up until all hours waiting to see to my young lady, and the habit tugged at me. I went instead into her stateroom and automatically looked about in search of something that needed attention. The jewelry was safely away, and once I had closed a steamer trunk that was gaping open, I could think of nothing to do.

I stood in the midst of the room almost as if I were waiting for something to happen. And almost at once something did. I thought I heard a noise at the door. In the empty room it startled me considerably, for of course I was unsuitably dressed. But no, the sound, whatever it was, came from farther off. The room seemed to shift position, putting me off balance. I staggered, and when I planted a bare foot down to brace myself, the floor was not where it had been. After the faint sound, the ship had veered. The lavender water in the dressing-table bottles swayed and rippled. It was a very odd sensation. I thought at first of an earth tremor before I recalled how far we were from land.

Then the second thing happened, more puzzling than the first. I thought I had been struck deaf. The ship was suddenly still, utterly still. I could not think what it meant. I had never heard the faint, steady rattling of the hangers on their rod in the steamer trunk until they abruptly ceased their rattling. I had got so used to the hum of the ship's engines that I could not quite realize they had stopped.

But there was soon the sound of hurrying feet in the passageway outside. I opened the door a narrow crack to see a steward and then another hurrying by. I heard one say, "Ice," and thought he was rushing some order to a stateroom. The Americans always insisted on ice in their drinks.

I stood at the door until the engines below ground into life again. But it was a curious half life, and labored. We were not proceeding with the usual speed. Still, we were proceeding. I would have gone to my bed then but for the hurrying footsteps outside and the distant sound of doors opening and closing.

I sat down in the chair beside Miss Amanda's bed, neither alarmed nor quite comfortable. The steady vibration of the ship that played on the brass headboard of the bed was comforting. I may even have dozed for a moment, but in the next there came a flurried sound outside and a sharp rap on the door.

When I opened to this knock, Victorine was standing there in rather a wild state. She was wearing a dressing gown, but her hair was still up, though it was fast escaping from its combs.

"Oh, Miranda, I have only slipped away a moment. My lady—Madame Ryerson is in such a state! She does not know what to do. I must go back at once, but I come to see what you think!"

I did not know what to think, but Victorine gave me little time. "The steward, he comes to Monsieur and Madame Ryerson's door. I have already retired into my quarters, but I hear through the wall. He says there is a great iceberg outside and we have stopped so we do not run it down! Mrs. Ryerson is in a great confusion. She comes to me and says, 'Victorine, shall I wake Mr. Ryerson, or shall I not?'"

"Is it serious?" I asked her.

"Oh, no, the ship is one that cannot sink, but still it is very exciting, and everyone is pouring out onto the decks. It is said there is ice heaped on everything!"

Then she was gone, all her usual composure consumed by her excitement. I might have followed her if I had been dressed. Instead, I stood there undecided. It must have been midnight by then. I had turned to go to my own cabin when I staggered again. The engines may have stopped once more. I could not tell, for there were more voices in the corridor outside. But something else very strange had occurred. The stateroom was slightly tipped in the direction of the outer wall, toward the port side. I had to walk up an incline to reach the door.

I had thought to feel more secure in my own cabin. But there a glass had fallen from a shelf and lay shattered on the floor. More to protect my feet from the shards than anything else, I drew on my stockings and my shoes. Then, because it was clear that the noise of voices outside was not going to cease, I decided to dress myself entirely. With all this hubbub, Miss Amanda might take fright and return in haste to her own stateroom if she could manage it undiscovered.

I was just reaching for my plain dark frock when the stewardess, Miss Robinson, burst into my room. Looking past her, I saw she had already thrown open the door to Miss Amanda's stateroom. "You are to put on your life preserver at once," she said and pointed a finger to the hammocklike arrangement where it was stored. I had not so much as touched it, and so Miss Robinson fitted the large cork vest onto me, jerking the straps at the top and at the waist. "But I should have put on my dress," I said.

"No, no, never mind about that. Where is Miss Whitwell?"

"I couldn't say."

Miss Robinson's face was very flushed. "If she is in the Palm Court or the Café, she will be sent down for her life preserver. Put it on her as I have done yours. Just a tug here and another down there, and it will fit. This is only a formality, as you might say, but don't take no for an answer from Miss Whitwell. It is Captain Smith's orders."

Then she turned to go, for she was in charge of eight or nine staterooms. I was somewhat encouraged by the "formality" of the life preserver when I noticed she was not wearing one.

She stopped in the doorway and looked back. "Have you a warm coat to put on over the preserver?"

I made a move to the gray wool coat that served me in all weathers. It was in reach on a hook. But she said, "No, no. It is fitted and won't go over your life belt. Doesn't your young lady have a loose-fitting evening cape or something of the sort—something warm?"

"Yes," I replied, "but I could not wear her—"

"She may thank you for it later," Miss Robinson said in a low voice. "And while you are awaiting her return, you might go to Mr. McElroy and get out Miss Whitwell's jewelry if it is in his care." Then she was gone, and I was left with something to do.

I made my way out into the corridor, now thronged with people either wearing their cork vests or struggling with them. There was something of a fancy-dress ball about the scene. Several people who had perhaps drunk too much were laughing uproariously. Others looked rather shamed at wearing the ungainly costume. I quite forgot the spectacle I might be making of myself with my hair streaming down my back and my faded old nightgown billowing beneath the life preserver. There were ladies in the passageway with nightcaps on their heads and dressing gowns that would not close over their life jackets. And there were gentlemen in odd assortments of pajamas, hunting boots, and tweed caps.

There were others who had strolled directly from the Palm Court lounges and had not yet been persuaded to cover their dinner clothes with anything that would have spoiled the lines of their attire.

On the stairway down to C Deck where the purser's office was, I caught a glimpse of Mrs. Molly Brown. She was wearing an exquisite costume of black with enormous lapels striped in black and white silk. But she looked perfectly equal to donning a life jacket if the need arose. Another lady was saying to her, "I *will* not get out into one of those open boats on a night like this, not for an absurd boat drill! Why, what can they be thinking of?"

And Mrs. Brown replied, "Oh, well, honey, a little fresh air and exercise wouldn't hurt you any."

There was rather a mob scene around the purser's counter. Mr. McElroy looked on the point of bolting from his post. I could not know it then, but he was badly needed up on the Boat Deck to see to the loading of the lifeboats. At that moment, however, he had his hands full with two conflicting tasks. One was to dissuade the ladies from collecting their jewelry, which was taking up precious time. The other was to hand the jewelry over to them as quickly as possible to be rid of them.

More demanding women than I had won this skirmish. When it came my turn, he handed over Miss Amanda's jewelry in an unhandy mound, with the pearls looping from their drawstring bag. I bore it all away, terrified that I might drop something. Anything dropped would be forever lost under the pounding feet of the passengers, who were growing more and more confused, and milling in every direction.

I managed to climb the stairs back to B Deck, where the crowds nearly swept me on and upward. Then I made my way against the tide of people surging along the B Deck corridor. Just as I reached our door, I saw the entire Ryerson family, who were quartered farther along our passageway. Mr. Ryerson was awake indeed, fully dressed, and leading the entourage of wife, a son of perhaps twelve or thirteen, two other children, their governess, and at the rear, Victorine. She alone was without a life preserver.

She dropped behind and clutched my arm, saying, "Your young lady—where is she?"

"I couldn't—she isn't in her stateroom," I said, meeting Victorine's gaze.

"She is in the stateroom of another?"

"I—yes, I suppose she must be."

Victorine gave me a look of both concern and immense worldiness. "Do you know—where that stateroom is?"

I shook my head.

"Then let us hope she finds herself protected by a gentleman who knows the meaning of chivalry."

"Are we in real danger?" I asked her.

"Maybe yes, maybe no," she replied. "We are told to be tranquil, and yet it is said the mailbags are floating in the hold. It is said that the stokers have forsaken the furnaces and are swarming upward." Her eyes flew heavenward. "We are in the hands of God." And then she was gone before the Ryersons could miss her.

Miss Amanda's stateroom was almost as I had left it. Miss Robinson must have pulled down the life preserver—it lay across the bed in a heap. This argued against Miss Amanda's having returned in my absence. It suggested, too, that she was not in any public place, or she would have been sent down to get it. I knew in my heart where she was. She would have made it her business to be in Mr. Sawyer's bed by now.

I stood staring at the heap of cork and straps, the image of the one wrapped around me. I wondered how such flimsy, ungainly things could stand between anyone and death. The lamps still blazed in the room, and the electric heater was still warm. It would have seemed a far safer refuge than the teeming corridors except that it stood at a crazier angle than before. Yet the whole unsinkable ship was standing at this frightening angle. I knew if I dared scramble to one of the portholes, I would be able to look directly down into the sea. And so I lingered on, hoping to make a sanctuary of the stateroom. And perhaps I waited because these were the last moments of my servitude. Perhaps I stood there unmoving, struggling to stand upright, because some part of me still waited to attend my young lady, some part of me that called from the past.

But what had once been the major part of me—my whole existence—was ebbing now, though in the next hour I was to learn how hard it died. I stood with the jewelry of my young lady in my hands, a clump of meaningless glitter that could not count for as much as the flimsiest life preserver ever made. But I did not stand there long.

A stewardess I had never seen before appeared suddenly in the doorway. "What? Not gone already? Everybody up on deck. Ladies to the lifeboats on the port side!"

I could discover nothing in her tone beyond the briskness of her command. Yet she would not leave until I showed signs of moving. "Ladies to the port side!" she repeated, more impatient than before.

"And maids?" I asked.

"All ladies!"

The panic that was growing in me lurched suddenly. I felt it beneath my heart. I stepped to the dressing table and opened my hands. Miss Amanda's jewelry fell in a scatter across the tabletop. Then, just as I was, without thought of a warm wrap, I bolted out of the door and darted into my quarters, no conscious thought in my mind. Lying on the edge of the basin was the stateroom key. I had been wearing it during the day on an elastic band around my wrist. I slipped it on over my wrist now, and hurried out into the hallway.

First the stewardess ahead of me and then I were caught up in a surging band of passengers from steerage being led the long distance from their quarters below by another member of the crew. I fell in among them. There was no easy laughter or banter among this group. Their faces were strained. A woman swathed in a plaid shawl large enough to cradle her baby in was weeping outright. But I was well along toward the end of the brightly lit corridor before I noticed the most ominous thing about this group. The men's boots were gushing water, and the women's skirts were wet nearly to the knees.

We were led up to A Deck on the sumptuous stairway they had never seen. Then up the additional flight to the Boat Deck. The higher we climbed, the more deafening was the noise. The shrieking, mind-shattering sound of escaping steam. The ship itself was screaming, threatening to drown every human voice.

When I had staggered through the door to the deck, the frozen air struck me a blow. My eyes teared, but I struggled to make sense of the scene. Only such a little time before, Victorine and I had taken our stroll on this very deck. Now I could scarcely see the deck for the people moving as in a strangely giddy pantomime, and robbed of their voices by the shriek of steam.

There was the sound of thunder cracking as a rocket shot straight up, arched in the black sky like an enormous, fiery-white question mark. It threw a new sort of light on the deck. Forward toward the bow were the davits for four lifeboats. Behind, far along the ship, were the davits for another four. It had been in the midst of the open space between that I had last seen Miss Amanda and Mr. Sawyer. But they were not there now. It was the only space along the deck at all clear of people, for it was not near a lifeboat.

One, perhaps two, of the forward lifeboats were gone. The figures around those that remained were standing in groups of two or three. There were families, too, but they were parting, were being parted.

Again as in a pantomime, I saw through the throng the Ryerson family. In this light Mrs. Ryerson's face was ghastly white but determined. Her hands reached out in the effort to gather in all her children, who looked more excited than fearful.

Mr. Ryerson had removed his life preserver and was urging it on a protesting Victorine. No, no, no, she was mouthing, her head shaking as she tried to thrust the life preserver back at her employer. She pointed to the lifeboat as if this were to be protection enough. But he was having none of this, and at last he wrapped the life preserver hastily around her as if she were a troublesome child, and he the servant.

I drew closer to the lifeboats, though I had no thought of trying to get in one. They glowed white, and their wooden hulls would be like walnut shells on the ocean so far below. How could anyone exchange the *Titanic*'s riveted steel for those wooden husks? A woman shrieked louder than the escaping steam. Colonel Astor stepped forward and handed Mrs. Astor into the boat. She wore beneath the cork vest a dress that suggested an afternoon's motoring tour of the countryside.

I moved still closer to the lifeboat. No one was crowding in—not yet. The women were hanging back. And once I was closer I saw why. The tilt of the ship caused the lifeboats to stand out and away from the side, suspended from above by the ropes, called lines at sea. There was a gap, and a sheer drop between ship and boat. But the women were being handed across it from man to man. The children and babies were being passed well over the heads of the rest.

I saw the young Mrs. Marvin, who had traveled down in the boat train in our compartment. She clung to her new husband, and his head inclined to hers as he sought to loosen her grip on his sleeve. I saw his lips move, convincing her, reassuring her. He pointed backward across the width of the ship. I gathered he was saying that the boats for the men lay that way. At last she allowed herself to be persuaded. She turned her face away from her husband's as if she could not bear a longer parting if this must be. She was handed then into the lifeboat by a man who still contrived to keep one foot perilously planted on the deck and the other on the edge of the lifeboat. As he eased Mrs. Marvin into a place among the other women, I saw it was Mr. McElroy, the purser.

Fewer and fewer women remained in the knot of passengers on deck. Mrs. Ryerson had ordered the governess into the boat with the two smaller children. The hands of a crewman were on her shoulders, and Mr. Ryerson was pleading with her to go. But her own hands were planted firmly on her young son's shoulders. She would clearly not leave him behind. I was not at all sure she would leave her husband, either.

She turned abruptly then at something her husband said and pushed her son ahead of her toward the boat. He was ready to make the leap across when a ship's officer threw out an arm to bar the way.

The boy was not to go. Mrs. Ryerson drew back, clasped her son to her, and turned her face away from the open boat where her other children waited. Mr. Ryerson turned from pleading with his wife to pleading with the officer, and at last the boy and his mother were allowed to go. But in a voice that carried over the sound of the steam, the officer boomed, "No more boys!"

Victorine remained on deck, bustling about as if to seem too busy to enter the fragile lifeboat. I heard a familiar American voice just behind me. It was Miss Reed's. She was being hurried along by a pair of gentlemen, one in full evening dress and the other in ship's uniform. She clutched something to her bosom and was saying in an audible voice. "No, no, if this is only a precaution, I don't choose to take it! I'd sooner take my chances with the ship. No! Under no circumstances! Take your hands off me!"

They led her protesting right to the deck's edge, but there she balked in earnest. Somehow her hat had been knocked hopelessly askew, and she could not have seen much from beneath its wide brim. A crewman standing beside her reached out suddenly. He tore the object from her hands and hurled it among the lifeboat passengers.

Miss Reed gave a final howl, more of outrage than fear, and dived into the boat. It was only then that I realized they had thrown her pig into the boat before her, the pig that played the "Maxixe."

My ears adjusted to the sound of voices, even through the shriek of the steam. Or perhaps the ship was dying, and its own voice was subsiding.

"See you in the morning, my dear—at breakfast," I heard a man say.

"Are there sailors enough to man that boat?" called another.

And then: "Room for a few more ladies in this one. Where is another lady?"

I drew back at that, when I might better have put myself forward. But I could not go. It still seemed out of the question. I had lost track of the time I had spent on the open deck and was suddenly aware that I was chilled through and through. I could only turn and bolt back to the warmth of the glowing ship. It was pitched forward by now, as well as listing to port. I noticed this as soon as I tried to run down the staircase, which was half empty.

My hand, blue with the cold, clutched the banister. I was soon going hand over hand as the cant of the ship seemed to force me backward as I tried to descend.

But where was I going? Was I rushing insanely back to my own cabin, or was I going to search for Miss Amanda? My mind was numbed by the cold and by fear. I had not believed the men who had seemed to tell their wives that this was only a boat drill. Yet how could I leave this great place that still glowed warm and bright?

I continued, hand over hand, until I reached the foyer of B Deck. I raced along the corridor. My feet seemed to carry me, slightly uphill, past the entrance to my own cabin.

I knew then what I was doing if I knew nothing else. I could not remember that I hated Amanda Whitwell. It occurred to me that she would die, perhaps that we both would die. But if I lived and she did not, I could not have her the burden on my conscience that she had been on my life. Nor could I revenge myself on her in this terrifying way. I could not be as cruel as she and go on living. And perhaps keeping her alive would spare me the awesome need to make my own life with my own hands. I don't know what else my panic inspired. My mind was in a great tumultuous muddle. And on I ran, determined to find Amanda Whitwell.

But where was she? I had nearly reached the end of the corridor when a steward loomed up from nowhere. "Here now, wot's this? You didn't ought to be down here!" He caught my arm and shook me as a terrier shakes a kitten. "I've got me hands full keepin' the gate closed across the passage farther abaft to keep them steerage passengers out. Proper pack of animals, they are!"

My mind reeled at the thought that now the steerage passengers were being turned back. I had a vivid image of the earlier ones soaked with seawater long before now.

"Tell me if you know where Mr. Sawyer's stateroom is," I said to him.

"No, Miss, I couldn't say." He turned me back in the direction from which I'd come.

"But I must know!" I said, ready to fly at this brute of a man twice my size. I even raised my hands, clenched into fists, with the stateroom key bobbing senselessly on my narrow wrist. I would batter this Goliath to the ground. But he was proof against this little display.

"Wot you must know, Miss, is you'd be better in a lifeboat than wot you'd be hangin' about here. I tell you I'd be in a boat meself if it was my place to go."

"Oh, please, if you know where Mr. Sawyer's cabin is, tell me!" I threw myself on him then, and it had a strange effect. I had done the one thing that would draw his mind from his duty. He knew more than I. He knew he was about to die, and this was the last time in his life that he would hold a woman in his arms.

In the moment when I had thrust myself against him and could see nothing but the polished buttons on his uniform, I sensed this. I looked up at this stranger. He gazed down at me, and his exhausted eyes were seeing some other woman, far, far away.

He spoke then in a husky whisper. "Well, Miss, I'll tell you the truth. But then you must go. Promise me you will." I nodded, but he said nothing. His hand moved down my arm and clasped mine. Our fingers laced together. He led me a step or two to a stairwell beyond a narrow door, used only by the crew.

We stood in the angling doorway at the top of a flight of metal steps, and he said, "I'm the steward for Mr. Sawyer's stateroom, Miss. Know him of old—crossed with him before, I have, on the *Oceanic*. He don't travel with a valet. 'Twould cramp his style, if you take my meaning. He was down on C Deck below, Miss."

"Was?" I said "Did he—"

"Look down, Miss."

I looked down the ill-lit stairs. At the bottom, black water lapped a stairstep. How deep it was I couldn't tell.

"Mr. Sawyer's stateroom's forward," the steward said quietly. "He wouldn't respond to my knock. I thought of breakin' down the door. But I didn't want it on me head—destroyin' company property. That was earlier, Miss, before we knew—properly knew, I mean."

"Then his stateroom—"

"That's right, Miss. It's underwater. Has been this past quarter hour. When I went back, the forward part of the passageway was like a bloody underground river."

It couldn't be. I could not believe that the greater part of the ship was dead already. That we on these upper decks were edging toward that same death. I could not believe what I saw vividly in my mind's eye. Miss Amanda lying trapped against the ceiling of a room, a deathtrap swirling to the top with freezing water. I saw her naked body in the blackness turning in the snares of floating sheets. I saw her hair, hair like mine, turned to a seaweed's tendrils. I saw her lungs burst for want of air. And all the while I stood a few feet away, dry-shod still. It could not be. And I knew it was true.

"You must go now, Miss," the steward murmured, so gently that I barely heard him. "You promised you would."

Perhaps he took me for a woman in love with Mr. Sawyer. Perhaps he knew more—knew everything. I turned and ran downhill, down the white corridor, my mind curiously cleared by the sort of shock destined to be followed by another. I knew what I must do now. I must live. Whoever I was, whatever I had been, wherever I was going —I must live.

Yet there was faint hope of that now.

Twenty-Six

Over the pounding of my own feet I heard another pounding. I was still a dozen doors from my own quarters. But I stopped, and staggered on the dipping corridor floor. I heard the pounding of fists against a door and screams behind it, the screams of a familiar voice. I thought first of what could not be. I thought it was my young mistress trapped in this stateroom.

I grasped the handle of the locked door. The screams echoed almost against my ear. "My God! Let me out! I am a dead woman in this place! Hear me! Save me!"

"Victorine!" I screamed back.

"Yes, yes, it is Victorine. Open the door! Why have I been locked in this place?"

I looked back in the direction from which I'd come. The steward was gone, lost forever in the maze of corridors where I had never penetrated, and no one would again.

The key to Miss Amanda's stateroom was still on my wrist. I wrenched the elastic band off and tried the key in the lock. It slid in, but it would not turn. The screams continued. "Hush, Victorine! It's Miranda."

She fetched up a sob. "A miracle," she said, almost quietly. "Make haste, or I will try to get through the porthole and throw myself into the sea. I cannot be caged!"

I threw my weight against the center of the door. With no effect whatever. There was no center panel in it weaker than the frame. It was solid, immovable. I drew myself back against the corridor's opposite wall, hiked the skirts of my nightdress up, and charged the door. I kicked at the last moment with more more might than I had, the heel of my shoe aimed against the mechanism of the lock itself. It popped like gunfire. The door fell open, battering Victorine backward.

She recovered herself, slumped against the slanting wall, and leaped toward me. I could not think why she was there at all when she should have been in a lifeboat by now. And I was struck dumb by her appearance.

She wore the life belt Mr. Ryerson had forced on her. All her hair had fallen about her shoulders, made huge by the cork belt. And on her disordered hair was plunged a diamond tiara. Her hands raised to claw me in desperation or relief were covered with rings. Bracelets sparking white and red and green and sapphire blue coverd her forearms. Though I did not believe I had more than minutes to live, I stood and stared.

"My God, my God!" Victorine gasped, rushing out into the hall and nearly rushing back inside again. "I could not make myself go into the lifeboat. I come back instead to Mrs. Ryerson's stateroom to save her jewels. She go off with nothing, of course, only thinking of her children and Monsieur. So I come back, and then some—some fool come along and lock all the stateroom doors! Why they do such a thing? My God, you save my life. Come on. We must go! I go in that lifeboat now, by God, if I find it!"

She grasped my wrist and we plunged down the corridor. She would have rushed me past the doorway to Miss Amanda's stateroom and my cabin. But my mind was growing more keen in the face of her panic.

I wrenched away. "Go on!" I said. "I must get something warm to wear." She staggered on down the corridor, on and down in the direction of the sinking bow.

The door was locked. Someone had come along and locked all the doors with maniac efficiency. I found the key on my wrist one last time. It was for this, then, that I had brought it. I turned the key and banged the door back. If I had found Miss Amanda in there then, I would have wept with relief. I would have saved her if I could, if I could have saved us both.

But the stateroom was empty. I stood in its miniature magnificence one last time. Nothing was changed except that the steamer trunk had pitched forward over on its lock. I could not lift it; yet I did. And I threw it open to find the evening wrap she had not worn. It was wadded in a jumble of her other things. The beading on her gowns, the soft satin, the brocades, the lace in tiers, all in a fearful tangle now, heady with her scent. It was as if she were in the room with me. As if I might feel the sharp edge of her voice or of her hand.

I found the fur-trimmed wrap. How flimsy it looked. But I dragged it out from the muddle by the silk cord that tied it at the neck. I threw it on over my life belt. It had been made for fashion, not for warmth. I tied the silken cord in a tight knot at my neck. It would leave my arms free. I turned to go then. I had not left enough time to live as it was.

The lamps flickered once, but burned bright again, catching the treasure left on the dressing table. I moved toward the brightness, clearheaded no longer, and stared down at the jewelry. The diamond bracelets lay there, vivid and self-important. My hand went out and brushed them aside. A brooch wobbled and rolled of its own accord down the back of the table. The strand of pearls, the gift of Mr. Forrest, lay half out of their sack. I snatched them up and wound them around and around my neck, stuffing the end of the loop down into my life preserver. But I was not done. My hand worked through the jewelry. A pendant two hundred years old meant nothing to me. Nor did a cluster of rubies set in a platinum star. My hands worked through this worthlessness, searching with wills of their own. At last it was there, the thing they searched for at the peril of my life. It lay quite alone, a circle of gold set with an enormous diamond. The engagement ring that Mr. Forrest had given his intended.

I jammed it onto the finger that had once worn the ring John Thorne gave to me. The ring that was already at the bottom of another part of the sea. This ring and the pearls—these must be saved, for they were Mr. Forrest's gifts.

The lamps dimmed, dimmed red, the color of a dying flame, of autumn. I fled. My hair whipped madly about my face. The skirts of my nightdress stretched and tore against my stride. I slipped, half fell, touched the downward slant of the corridor floor with one hand for balance, and rushed on.

I ran toward music. Yes, I could hear it plainly. There was no sound of escaping steam now. Perhaps there was no escape of any sort. But there was music. I heard the ship's orchestra playing. Lively ragtime music. It pulled me on toward the grand staircase.

The dimming lights still faintly illuminated the steps, pitched backward like a collapsing terraced garden. They seemed to lead nowhere. I leaped at them, fell almost at once, and crawled up to the landing. A man lay there in evening dress, only his white tie pulled a little out of shape. His eyes were closed, and he lay sunk in deep, wheezing sleep. Beside his outstretched hand an empty gin bottle lay. I crept past him and on up the half flight to A Deck.

There was another flight to climb to the open deck, but I was aware of voices over the music, and figures milling on the covered promenade on this level. I staggered out through a door that had fallen back. A knot of people there were clustered beside the great square of openness that gave out on calm, brilliant sea. Their backs were all turned to me, but I could make out their outlines in the murky light. There were women 'among the men.

Their silhouettes were fantastic for being so ordinary. The outline of a fashionable hat here and there, wrapped around by a motoring veil anchored by a glittering hatpin. The shapes of life belts bulked in the dark shadows in the exact contours of lavish fur jackets.

But there were cries among them, and a thunder of cries farther off. Perhaps from the high stern of the ship, perhaps from the boats already in the water.

The cries nearest me rose in a crescendo. There was a boat directly above, being loaded from the open deck. All the crowd down on this covered promenade waited for it to be lowered. But would it stop for them?

The cries, the hoarse shouts of the men burst out again, and the crowd before me parted long enough for me to see what they saw. There, beyond the railing, hung a woman upside down. Her head dangled down from above. Her face was blurred into a frozen scream. She had been trying to enter the boat from the deck above and had fallen into the space between. Some invisible hand or hands from above had caught her by the foot. And now the crowd on A Deck grasped for her, reaching out into the void in an attempt to draw her in to safety.

A man flung his cigar backward, planted his foot on the railing, and with an enormous reach—like the wingspan of an eagle—he gathered the woman in. They lay her out on the deck. Her fixed eyes blazed with fear, and I thought she must be dead of the shock. But she stirred in the moment the helping hands left her. She was up in a crouch, like an animal at bay. Then she was on her feet. She darted without a backward look at her rescuers toward a ladder. She pounded up it, determined to enter the boat again.

But there was no time to follow her. Almost at once, the lifeboat began descending in fits and starts upon its fall. It was being lowered at alarming speed. First the bow dipped downward, and then its stern. It was teeming with people. Among them I caught a glimpse of a child in her little sailor straw hat. The wing of feathers on a woman's hat. And yes, the twinkle of a diamond tiara. Victorine was in the boat. She had saved herself.

But the boat was perhaps seven feet or more from our level, swinging out perilously over the sea. And it was making no stop. It lowered past our horrified gaze before anyone could react. It had dipped below us, and still I hung back from the crowd.

"You must jump, Hattie," a man said just in front of me. But the woman drew back, nearer him.

"I can't!" she moaned. "It's too far—these skirts—I'd be in the water. The fall alone would kill me."

Another man, all in black, broke from the shadows and darted through the crowd. He leaped like a monkey onto the rail, both hands and both feet drawn together on the narrow bar. Then he soared out into space, flinging himself down and down onto the heads of those in the lifeboat.

I turned in terror and ran back into the ship and across the foyer to the starboard deck. Whatever was to be found there could not be more horrifying.

A woman stood directly before me. She rested a hand in the posture of calm upon the railing. I had never seen her before. She bore herself with immense dignity and distinction. The lady was looking down at the water. I stepped up beside her, drawn to her tranquillity. Below us, a lifeboat was just settling into the water. The oil-stained sea seemed to cushion it gently. Amid the tight cluster of hats and shawls and blanketed heads that looked like cobblestones from this height, a sailor was standing, an oar barely visible in his hand. He was looking back up at the lady beside me. He did not see me in the shadow of a girder. No one seemed to. It was as if I were dead already.

The seaman called up to her. "There'll be another boat put down for you!"

At that the lady looked upward, and I followed her gaze. The davits above us on the Boat Deck were all empty. The stars shone vividly in the spaces where before lifeboats had overhung. She looked at me then, this stranger, shook her head gently, and turned back into the ship, drawing a wrap more closely around her shoulders.

I stood alone then on the starboard side. I could not see very far along the ship in either direction. But I could tell that where the bow had been was a slick of oily water, and the stern behind was standing high out of the sea. A hum came from that direction, a hum of voices crying out—shouts, prayers, messages flung out to the boats—all blended into a rhythmic insect sound. I was not alone, and yet I had never been so alone in all my life.

Out across the flat water fanned perhaps a half-dozen lifeboats, white slivers like folded-paper boats on a garden pond. One boat carried a light, and the others seemed to be drawing instinctively to it, and farther from the *Titanic*.

The ship shuddered, and the last of the distant hissing ceased. Over the chorus of hundreds of far-off voices, I heard music again. Faintly, for the musicians were playing nothing as lively as ragtime now. It was a mournful, stately melody, distorted by the other sounds, no proof against the size of the sea. The music broke as I listened, notes scattered to the wind set up by the rushing ship. It began to slide. It shook, but not violently. There were explosions deep within it. Boilers giving way, perhaps. Or the collapse of kitchen crockery. Or the great crystal chandeliers thundering down on parquet floors. Or all the tables and the silver of the dining saloon slipping all together across the rose carpet to splinter against a paneled wall.

The ship was sliding into the sea as steadily as it had cut through its crest so short a time before. The water rose to meet me. There was no terrifying height now. If I stood rooted to this spot another whole minute, I would step directly into the sea. It would close quietly over me. I would never have to hear those dreadful sounds of destruction again. My ears would be stopped against them, and my eyes blinded against this vision of world's end.

A figure plunged from the open deck above my head. It did not exactly fall plummeting down. It seemed to be leaping clear of the ship with a certain hasty grace. And then another figure followed, like two slender boys plunging into a quiet pool on a hot summer afternoon. I watched them drop the short span into the rising water. They had calculated the drop. They had sought to leap clear of the ship. Looking directly down, I saw it was awash with floating debris. Deck chairs, oars, a snaky tangle of lines, a length of canvas, a fragment of trellis.

I would not look to see if the two boys surfaced, or if the sea and the suction had drawn them down. I threw a leg over the railing. I hungered to be gone. I thirsted for the icy sea that would stun me into a forgetful nothingness. I could think only that it was wrong to be drawn unprotesting down with the dead weight of this great ruined ship. I balanced on the railing and stared at a strange, roiling waterfall that surged beside the ship's hull. I was not six feet above it. But I threw myself outward, trying my best to overleap the hillock of rushing water. I leaped outward into the maelstrom.

The water's first blow knocked me senseless and stopped my breath. I sank beneath the rushing surface and swirled in an eddy, my arms and legs thrown outward. Down and down I was drawn, like a starfish caught in a whirlpool. The cold paralyzed me. I could not have drawn the icewater into my lungs even if I had tried. I did not hold my breath; the cold held it for me. And I was as blind as any sea creature of the lower depths.

My hands worked against numbing water. I kicked my feet free of their paralysis. Suddenly my head broke the surface. The cork vest had bobbed upward, and I was drawn with it. The velvet cape that was to be proof against the frozen night fanned out in the water about me. Its thick fur border was reduced to a narrow slick line now.

I saw a swimmer's head many yards before me. Beyond him was the unspeakable sight of the ship, still making its slide into the blackness. Its lights extinguished in winking rows as it went. Then, far above, one of the great funnels buckled and fell into the water. A ribbon of sparks unfurled to join the stars, and I was thrust backward by the shock wave set off by the funnel that slapped the water like the flat of a hand. It settled just where I had seen the other swimmer's head.

I envied him his oblivion. There was no more feeling in my hands and feet. They were useless to me, as well as painless. I could not swim farther from the ship. But perhaps the thrust of the fallen funnel had pushed me clear of the suction that dragged others down with it.

But I had to move. I could not die by inches in this way—freezing in the act of drowning, dead twice over. The cape that floated in a circle around me seemed to hamper even the thought of movement. I reached up to pull the silk cord that bound the cape around my neck. But my fingers were useless on the wet knot. They brushed my neck like the fluttering tail of a fish. Still, I had to move.

Something in me called me back to the ship, to the nearest solid mass in all this black, deadly emptiness. I turned from the temptation and threw myself in another direction.

I could feel the pain shooting down my arms as far as the elbows, and so I knew they could not be quite useless. And the cork vest just managed to keep my chin out of the water. I breathed now—and as if each breath were the last. I choked on the air that numbed my lungs. And I swam, I flailed, I struggled through the water.

For how long? An hour—two? No, I could not have been in the water longer than five minutes. No one could. I was blinded by the saltwater after the first minute. My legs and arms moved with only the memory of command. My soaked hair drew my face down and down and down again, and I could not fight much longer. The knot of silk at my neck combined with the loops of pearls to close my throat. The life preserver seemed to lose its buoyancy. I sank then and drifted like a dead woman just beneath the surface.

I could have slept then, slept easily and forever, except that I was overcome by an urge still stronger. The need to thrust myself up for one final draft of air to ease my exploding lungs. I drew out of the water, and my skull seemed to splinter against some hard, unyielding object. It might have been a floating timber, but it was suspended above the sea's surface. My hands lunged upward in reaction and grasped the solid wood of a board horizontally set just above the lapping waves. Yes, I could almost feel it as my fingers clutched it and struggled for a better hold. I could even think of pulling my whole weight up a little, and the weight of my soaked clothing.

It was an airless place, under that narrow plank, stuffy and freezing at once. I tried to see, but there was blank darkness and nothing more. The sound of the water echoed hollowly. I was in some enclosure. There was the rumbling sound of men's boots and men's voices. They were somewhere just above me and the thing to which I clung. I was neither alone nor dead. But where was I?

My hand moved along the smooth edge of the wooden plank to the place where it joined a sort of curving wooden wall. The solidness of this place baffled me, forced my mind to work. The heel of my hand worked down the curving wall to the waterline, and then down beneath it. There below the surface of the water I felt its lower edge. I ducked my head again beneath the surface and followed around the wooden lip that floated half in and half out of the sea.

The cork vest buoyed me suddenly upward, and I was in the open sea once more. Lurid lights played across the phosophorescent waters. And there were the sounds of more voices, not hollow now, though some echoed across great distances.

I had surfaced beneath an overturned lifeboat. The plank where I had clung had been a rough seat stretched across the boat's midsection. And now I was clinging to the outer hull, a hull ringed around beneath the waterline with a border of cork. The boat swayed sickeningly in the water. And just above where my face had suddenly appeared where the boots of a dozen men—perhaps more—standing on the overturned boat's curving underside. And there were others nearby in the water, struggling toward the place I had achieved. Some cried out, "Save one life! Save one life!" Others floated in silence, corpses, perhaps, held up by their life belts. I had no power to cry out. I held on by my fingertips to the boat's edge, my head so near that those standing above me, swaying back and forth on bending knees to keep the shell on an even keel, could not see me at first. Others lay across the curve of the boat, their boots in the water. One such slid away in the first moment and disappeared unprotesting beneath a little swell of sea.

I clung there, though I knew I could not live long in the water. But I was not to be discovered just yet. The men standing on the boat moaned low in their throats, a sudden sound, in unison. They all stood facing forward, and a shadowy light played over their features. They were blackened with coal dust; it ran in rivulets down their faces. I took them for stokers who had escaped somehow from the prison of the ship's furnace room and coal hole and had made their way to this nearly useless overturned boat. They moaned again, and if they had not needed their arms to maintain their balance, they would surely have covered their faces with their hands.

I managed to turn in the water, to see what they were seeing. And once I saw, I tried to scream, but no sound came. It was a sight to make anyone abandon all hope. The great ship I had forgotten, had thought was at the bottom of the sea, was only now dying.

It stood nearly perpendicular out of the water. And against the sky its stern rolled slightly as the *Titanic* made a final plunge like a knife into flesh. Its stern was clustered, clotted with people. They swarmed together, slid, fell down decks that were suddenly sheer walls. And there were hundreds of them, spilling from the high cliff the ship had become. Hundreds upon hundreds. More people than I thought the ship had carried. I saw them all die. They fell writhing together. They fell in pairs, so close they must have been clasping hands. They were dashed to death amid the debris. They were drawn down into the great drain the ship created. They were all swept away in the same moment by some terrible unseen hand.

The ship's great propeller was outlined in black against the brighter night. The rearmost funnel refused to snap free, and the ship was gone. A great sigh spread across the water, and a vast whirlpool described a single revolution. Yards away, the overturned lifeboat felt the pull. The men above me staggered, but the boat remained afloat.

There were more cries from the sea, hopeless laments now. I blinked away the water from my lashes and saw in the distance other lifeboats, far more secure than this one, still standing off, keeping their distance from the wretches cast adrift. Those nearest where I clung continued to make their painful way toward us.

A man's head suddenly surfaced at the end of the boat. He threw up an arm and shouted. One of the men above me risked turning his head. "Get away, get away!" he roared. "You'll swamp us, you fool!"

But the man in the water was no threat. I saw his hand fall away, and I saw nothing more of him.

I clung there, lifeless from my neck down. My hand crept up along the overlapping planks that formed the ship's hull. But I could do no more. My hand reached out and closed over the toe of a stoker's boot.

He jerked his foot away, and the boat wobbled crazily. "Goddammit!" he cried out. "Get off, get off, you bleeding leech. I'll deal with you!"

I looked up the immense distance of his height. He was wielding an oar. At the risk of his own balance, he swung it in an arc like a pendulum to sweep me away. I turned to deflect the blow, but I would not loose my slight grip on the boat. The oar caught me full in the face, seeming to crush my cheekbone. I floated free then, not quite dead enough not to know what had happened. I saw the pinwheels of pale lightning in my brain, but I could do nothing. I could not even evade another blow from the oar, or survive it.

I heard another voice. "Christ!" it said. "It's a woman!"

"Can't be," came another voice. Did they all have oars to beat me away from their refuge?

An oar lay flat on the water. It slipped beneath me, or I floated over it. I grasped it, rolled my body on it. It could not beat me. I would gather it up into a death grip so it could not hurt me again.

It drew me through the water and out of it. I was being pulled onto the boat, while all the men on it seemed to be standing on its farther edge to balance my dead weight. I felt the rough rippling of the overlapping planks. And I was colder than I had been as the night air found the length of my body. At last I was lying across the keel, where I had been put, my weight distributed equally on either side.

"That's right," came a voice, "you've all but capsized us. And for what? To bring on another corpse!"

No, I tried to cry, *no, I am not dead. Don't roll me off!* But I could only moan far down in my throat. I could only moan, but it was enough, and I was left where I lay.

I lay amid the feet of the men. A forest of thick, booted legs that straddled the keel. The pain began to return to me. It needled the backs of my legs where my nightdress was plastered. My nose throbbed and gushed with blood. My cheek was shattered, and I felt the swelling drawing the skin around it. My hand drooped before me over the curve of the boat and into the sea. I would not have had the strength to draw it back if it hadn't been for the flash of brilliance beneath the water. It was the glitter of the diamond ring. I had forgot it was on my hand, but I could draw my hand in then and curl it beneath me. I dared make no other move.

They had taken on more survivors from the water after me. They had found a better use for the oar than its first use on me. Perhaps their panicked hearts were moved by the cries that seemed to rise up from the sea farther than the eye could look.

But the cries from the water had all ceased now. It would have been absolutely still if the men above me had not begun to chant. I could not follow the words at first, though the rhythm of them was clear and seemed to aid their balance as they swayed above me, bracing against every swell of the sea. The words, though, were caught and blown away except for a scrap, a phrase: ". . . through the valley of the shadow of death . . . fear no evil . . ."

They were praying. They were praying in the stumbling tones of men who had not prayed since they were boys, and struggled to find their way back to that innocence, that hope.

I could not join in with them; I could not listen longer. My mind slipped away from me.

I awoke to shouts, and remembered nothing in the first moment. We were lower in the water, dangerously low. For how long the air had been leaking from beneath us I didn't know. The world had gone from black to gray. It was just dawn. I was able to raise my head to see the line of the horizon. A gray sea, growing choppy, beneath a gray sky.

I had paid the full price of lying thrown across the sharp spine of the boat. I had stiffened and could do nothing but raise my head. As the morning sea grew more choppy, I could only keep my face from dipping repeatedly under with each wave's slap against the boat. The effort to keep my head out of the water and the occasional failure to do so half revived me.

"Damn your eyes!" a voice thundered above me. "Can't you see what we're up against? Pull on those oars, you sons-a-bitches. We're swamping, I tell you. Come and take us orf. You've room enough in that boat, goddamn you to eternal hell!"

The gray sky brightened, but if a manned lifeboat was drawing anywhere near us, I could not see it. I saw nothing but gray sky and sea. I felt nothing but the salt stinging on my face, biting deeply into its wounds.

I seemed to drift away then. And came back to myself for only a moment. But it was the most memorable moment of my life. Hands grasped at my body. They tugged at my legs. I felt myself drawn over the keel of the boat. My shoes were in the water again. *No, no, not the water.* But other hands caught me under my arms. I was turning, being turned. But not in the water. Out of it. I was being pulled and thrust into another boat. A boat that rocked sensibly, right side up.

There was a patch of sky directly above and then the shadow of a woman's hat so near it would not come into focus. "Make a little room here," a voice said, a woman's voice hoarse with the cold.

"Lay her back across my knees," said another, strongly flavored with an American accent.

I fell as if onto an upholstered settle. I fell across a line of women huddled in the midst of a lifeboat, stiffly erect with row on row of others before and behind them.

My head lolled back, and I heard a sharp intake of breath that could not have been mine. "Oh, dear Lord, don't look at her face!" someone said.

"She can't be alive."

"She is, she must be," said another. "Take her hands. Rub them."

I felt my hands being taken up and briskly massaged. Then the hand with Mr. Forrest's ring upon it was suddenly held up higher.

"Look!" said a woman's voice. "Just see! That ring. Those pearls. It's Amanda Whitwell."

Amanda Speaks

Twenty-Seven

I lay there, still not quite knowing.

I lay across the knees of the women in the boat. There was a hint of warmth in the huddle of their bodies. But it was not welcome. The freezing cold had kept the pain away, particularly from my face. But the pain was creeping back now. One of my eyes was swollen shut. The other would not quite close.

At first the lifeboat lurched repeatedly. The women around me flinched and braced themselves against the impact as one after another of the men who had been standing on the overturned boat leaped into this one. How they found room I could not see. Perhaps they simply hurled themselves into the midst of this new set of castaways and hoped for the best. Finally the boat stopped its frightening, sudden pitching as the last man made his leap. We were packed together more closely than before, half wet, half dry, chilled to the bone and beyond.

With an eye that struggled to see, I could just make out the row of women above me. Their life belts glowed livid in what remained of the night. Their voices, the hard slap of a roughening sea, the shouts from elsewhere as if all the boats were converging—these sounds came and went. I was deeply unconscious at times and half aware in the intervals between. Each time I came near waking, the day was brighter. At last the world seemed suffused with rosy light. A collective sigh lifted from the boat to greet the sunrise.

And I lay there, still not quite knowing.

They were forcing something on me. The rim of a bottle touched my lip where it was split. I opened my mouth to cry out in pain and swallowed whiskey instead. It was no more than a tablespoon's worth, but it burned dreadfully as it found its way down my clenched throat. But it made me more alert than before, behind the misshapen mask of my face. My head lolled, and I was aware of the solid line of backs hedging me in. I grew restless, and hands tightened around me. But I could not have rolled off into the bottom of the boat. The knees on which I lay were pressed too close against the figures in front of us. I lay in what seemed a trough of human forms, with the sea at my head and feet. I was like a body borne by hired mourners across a watery graveyard.

I must have caught a glimpse of something outside—above the boat. My mind dimmed, and I thought we were in the bay off Ventnor. It seemed we were back just off the Isle of Wight, with the abrupt cliffs that rise from the beach standing over us. But these cliffs were as white as snow, as ice. They loomed all around us in the dawn, smooth and shadowless. Great palaces and cathedrals and Alps of ice. They gathered light from the sun that could not melt them.

The talk, the cries, the babble of voices—all these meaningless sounds defeated me. I could only lie cradled in pain and wait. Wait until I could understand the riddle. The puzzle of words I had heard when first I was handed into this boat.

But the voices rose meaninglessly into a chorus of calls. Someone stood up in the row behind, rocking the boat, and waved something with all her might. It was like a flag on fire. She waved it back and forth, signaling. I thought it must be her hat that she had set fire to. Bits of charred ribbon and veiling scattered over the boat and away.

It was quite day by then. I could feel the warmth of the sun. And why not? It was—I struggled to think of the season of the year and could not. Our boat veered, tipped. Hands clutched at me. Voices rose, hollowly now. The sunlight vanished, and we seemed to have drawn alongside one of the mountains of ice.

But no. This sheer wall was less bright than ice. There was the sound of timber grinding against iron. Straight above us was a great ship, standing high in the water, haloed in black smoke from its own funnels. I saw the pattern of the rivets that climbed its side, and the faint arcs of rust around its portholes farther up. An old ship rested in the water after its exertions. We lay in its shadow, its protection. Far up the hull—too far up—was a great door. In it stood sailors, working with ropes, looking down at us. Muscular men in dry uniforms moved in the routine of rescue. The survivors in our boat who still had tears wept them.

The lifeboat rocked again, alarmingly. But it was nestled like a tug against the great ship that had loomed out of the dawn. I could not wonder at its being there. I could not know of the frantic messages that had sparked across the Atlantic through the night now past. I could not calculate the odds against any ship finding this scatter of lifeboats—drifting, swamped, manned by women.

I could only wonder at the ladder that unrolled down the ship's side. It seemed to me that I saw it quite clearly—ropes with wooden steps between. Jacob's ladder from the Bible, it seemed to me. One by one, the passengers ascended the ladder, clinging against the great height of the hull between twisting ropes. Women and men—they looked alike to my dimmed vision in their bulky life belts. And how slowly they went! An empty mailbag was lowered. After a moment, a small boy in a child's sailor hat with streamers was raised in the bag.

I did not wonder how I would be taken up that ladder. Perhaps it was only for the First Class passengers, not servants. I rested from this thought. Later, hours—no, minutes—later, the lifeboat seemed to bob more lightly on the water. The row of human backs that had hedged me in was gone. Boots splashed the water in the bottom of the boat. I was being held up. The cape fell around me, heavily wet still. Hands ran ropes beneath my arms, around my body, under the clinging cape and the life preserver.

I hung suspended over the sea and began to rise. My bruised shoulders knocked against the ship's hull as I was drawn up its side by hands above. Sea and sky spread limitlessly in every direction: gold and gray, rose and green. The icebergs, for that is what those great shadowless structures were, littered the sea. They drifted, perhaps, but they seemed firmly rooted, more fixed than any work of man's. My head drooped. I saw the stains of my own blood in a wide dark river soaked into the front of my life preserver. Below my dangling feet, perhaps ten yards below, the lifeboat that I had left assumed its shape. Its narrow pointed prow danced on the water. An oar lay across it. The remaining passengers huddled in the boat's center, all their heads thrown back, watching me raised to rescue.

Hands reached for me and drew me into the ship. Now I thought of Jonah, safe in his whale. They laid me gently on a floor unbelievably flat and solid. I felt sickened by its steadiness, and my heart continued to pitch. The loop of the pearls escaped from within my life belt. It rattled against the hard deck. My head rested back, and a pair of hands came forth to release my throat from the silk knot of the cape.

"She's very far gone," a voice said quite clearly. I yearned to be more completely gone. I lay on that warm, hard, dry deck in Miss Amanda's cape, her pearls, the ring Mr. Forrest had pledged his future with. I lay there even in my young lady's cast-off nightgown, now torn and stained beyond recognition. Still, I would not know. I would not know that in this first flurry of confusion a mistake had been made. A mistake that might take root and flourish. In this night-turned-day that had clouded the survivors' minds, I was mistaken for Miss Amanda Whitwell. My mind turned to embrace this fact.

Had this not happened before—this confusion? Of course it had. I struggled to remember the occasions. But now it could not be my face that was seen and misread. My own mother would not recognize me. With the eye that had any vision in it at all, I could see my own cheek, swollen to grotesque size. I had been mistaken for Amanda Whitwell on far less evidence than our similar faces. My face was now a bruised pulp. Hers—hers was at the bottom of the sea. The jewelry I had swept up because it had been Mr. Forrest's choice—that jewelry alone had marked me as her. But it was an error that I could put right at once.

Yes, that was what I struggled to say. That was what I was trying to tell the figures that stooped over me on a deck thundering with hurrying feet. I tried to speak, to explain. But my jaw had dropped down, like the jaw of one dead. It would not work properly. It would receive none of the weak commands sent from my mind. I must explain, yet I could not. *No,* I said to whoever was there, *I am not Amanda Whitwell. I am Miranda Cooke. No, Miranda Thorne.* But no sound came. Perhaps even then I did not will it enough.

They dared not move me; they could not leave me where I was. I heard the hurried uncertainty in their footsteps. The shuffling, the kneeling over me. At last I was carried away in a blanket made into a litter with four men at the corners. Doors were thrown back. There was more warmth as they carried me farther into this nameless ship. Through a large saloon, heavy with the sound of women weeping, I smelled broth and steaming coffee. A child cried out over and over in a foreign tongue. Then I was borne off down a long passageway, where people stood anxiously in doorways and turned their faces from mine.

I was taken into a stateroom. Light flooded in from portholes. There was a bed—a proper bed, not a bunk—and the scent of fresh linen. It was not the sort of place where I should be quartered. I tried to tell them that.

The bed was as soft as eiderdown. In this room full of voices a familiar one spoke out from the others. It seemed to be Betty's. But no, Betty was dead, too. Dead and buried—properly—in the earth. And this was not Betty's accent or anything like it. I could not think who it was, though I heard the voice so plainly. I even felt warm breath on my aching face as someone bent low, scrutinizing me.

"My God, my God! It *is* Mademoiselle Whitwell. She has saved herself! It is a miracle!"

It was Victorine. I meant to call out to her, and I gathered my forces. But someone had thrust her aside. A doctor, perhaps. He knelt over me, and his hands touched my face in a practiced way, bringing no pain. He issued commands over his shoulder and stepped aside.

Another voice spoke then. I was growing used to the sounds of these familiar strangers who spoke their lines illogically, as in a play that needs rehearsing. I heard Miss Rebecca Reed's voice. There was no mistaking it.

"Amanda?" she said, very near me.

I did not struggle to speak then. I lay there and would not fight. Miss Reed's hand touched me. It avoided my face but ran lightly down my body. They had taken the cape away and the life belt with it. I wore only the nightdress, stiffening now with the salt from the water.

"It is a miracle!" Victorine cried again.

"Yes," Miss Reed replied, "but it may take another. She's not saved yet."

Victorine whimpered in the background.

And Miss Reed continued, as if I were not there, "She has more grit than I gave her credit for. There wasn't another woman in the water who made it. Where is her maid?"

Victorine swallowed her sobs and burst out, "I look all over this ship. I ask everyone. I don't mind who I ask—stokers, fine ladies, anybody. I look in all the cabins and in the galley where there are people being warmed behind the ovens." Victorine's voice wobbled and broke. "I even look under the blankets of the dead. She is not there. She is not anywhere. I look, I look, and still I look, but there is no Miranda."

"When did you see her last?" Miss Reed asked.

"It was—I had been locked in Madame Ryerson's stateroom. Miranda got me out. But no, she turn back and say she must get something warm to wear. And then—"

"That was where she made her mistake," Miss Reed said grimly.

"Perhaps there will be another lifeboat," Victorine offered in a hopeless voice.

"They are all in now, and accounted for, except those that swamped," Miss Reed answered. "Everybody left alive has been rescued." Her tone softened. She must have seen that Victorine and I had been friends. "I'm afraid we must face up to things in the cold light of day. Those who could be saved have been saved. We can only pray for the others, and wonder why we were chosen to live."

"Then Miranda is dead," Victorine said.

They did not weep for Miranda. Had I myself not seen hundreds die? There were not tears enough for all. Miss Reed's hand seemed to rest on me. I drifted into a sort of sleep then, away from this nightmare. I dreamed nothing. But I heard Victorine's voice over and over until it became my own: "Miranda is dead."

Twenty-Eight

The ship that had saved us was the *Carpathia*. It was old, easygoing, reminding no one of the *Titanic*. It had been making its unhurried way from New York to the Mediterranean along a southern route that had never known an iceberg. When the *Titanic* sent out its frantic messages on that fatal night, the *Carpathia* alone had answered the call. It had steamed north, startling its elderly passengers with a sudden burst of steam that rattled their beds. Soon it found itself treading the ice fields that the *Titanic* had failed to heed.

At dawn it had reached its nameless destination. The saloons were piled high with blankets. The galley was fragrant with hot nourishment. Retired doctors had been tumbled from their staterooms to attend the survivors. The crew was standing by in readiness, and the passengers were even then preparing to give their cabins to those the sea might surrender.

Yet the *Carpathia*'s passengers and crew could hardly believe it all. They were said to have stared in horror as the first woman from the lifeboats around them in the water made her fainting way up the rope ladder. They had to be told over and over again that the unsinkable ship had sunk, that the unthinkable must be believed and acted upon.

The sight of the survivors stunned them. Women dressed in the height of fashion rose directly from the sea. Infants, blue with cold, lay cradled in the arms of nurses struck dumb with horror. Mrs.

Molly Brown appeared on the deck, her hands a mass of broken blisters where she had pulled on the oars through the night, pulled away from the *Titanic,* which had threatened to draw all the lifeboats —all the life—down with it. Mrs. Astor in her smart dress and smarter hat stared back in disbelief at the sea that had taken her husband. A lady's maid appeared in a diamond tiara. The lady herself, Mrs. Ryerson, reached out again and again to embrace her three children, to still their questions about their father.

Seven hundred such survivors stumbled or were lifted into the safety of the *Carpathia.* And those found dead in the open boats were laid out with as much dignity as could be summoned.

In the full light of morning, when the sun was a great globe well out of the red water, the *Carpathia* weighed anchor. Its flag flew at half mast, and it turned in the sea in search of a passage through the cliffs of ice. It turned back to New York, carrying those chosen to survive the *Titanic,* carrying the news that the world would find so hard to comprehend. For the rest of that Monday, women stood on the open deck in borrowed clothes, scanning the sea for the sight of only one more survivor, someone—husband, father, brother—someone too beloved to be lost.

But the *Carpathia* only lingered at the spot where the unsinkable ship had vanished. It lingered in a wash of deck chairs and debris and empty life jackets. It crept across the grave of the fifteen hundred lost, and then it steamed away.

Eight hundred miles to the west on the afternoon of that day, Gregory Forrest sat at a drafting table beneath a skylight. His shirt sleeves were turned back, and his long, square fingers were ink-stained. He was putting the last touches onto a rendering of a building of his own design. It was a block of flats offering more sunlight and sanitation to those who would live in it than the cramped tenements it would replace. He pushed the eyeshade up off his forehead and passed the heel of his hand across his strained eyes.

At that moment a boy hired to carry messages for the architectural firm burst into the workroom. In his hand was a newspaper, its black headlines seeming to leap off the page.

In the evening of that same day, two thousand miles and more to the east, a wireless message, streaking from ship to ship, was overheard. Blurred by distance and repetition, the message told a conflicting tale to those listening along the perimeters of England:

The *Titanic* had hit an iceberg. . . .

The *Titanic* would be delayed. . . .

A dozen ships claimed the honor of rushing to its side. . . .

They converged to tow it into port. . . .

All its twenty-two-hundred passengers and crew were safe. . . .

The *Titanic* had lowered its lifeboats. . . .

The *Titanic* was sending up rockets and flares. . . .

The women were being put off in the lifeboats. . . .

There was even the outrageous hint that the *Titanic*'s watertight compartments had ruptured. That it was at the bottom of the sea.

Messages fanned out across England. Crowds gathered in the streets of Southampton, in all the seagoing towns. A boy on a bicycle was sent out from Ventnor to carry word to Whitwell Hall in advance of the evening editions of the London newspapers. He hammered on the door to the kitchens just as Mrs. Creeth delivered the dinner's first course to Mr. Finley. He was on the point of bearing it up to the dining room on a slightly dented Georgian silver tray.

The world on either side of the Atlantic was alerted and began the vigil that would end only when the *Carpathia* steamed into New York harbor three days later. The world held its breath.

But I knew little of that at the time. The world had shrunk to a single stateroom on the *Carpathia*, given over to four of the *Titanic*'s survivors. I lay in one of its beds, unable to speak. And then unwilling.

I lay there from Monday dawn until Thursday night as one who has died and waits to learn of an afterlife. I lay there in the twilight world of the concussion victim. My head rang in the rhythms of rolling waves of seawater. There were times when the pain ebbed a little that I thought I was still on the *Titanic*, that I should bestir myself and go about my duties.

But there were times of absolute clarity, too. A doctor loomed over me, his knee braced on the edge of the bed. With bare hands and main force he thrust a shoulder I did not know was dislocated back into place. My body arched in pain, but I did not cry out. And then my right arm lay useless in a sling across my breast.

My cheek, which I had thought shattered, was cleaned, daubed, cushioned with bandages. My lips were coated with a salve. A bandage wound around and around my forehead. I heard a doctor say that my injuries would need careful attention later but that they looked worse than they were. That the real danger was the concussion.

"Will she come back to herself?" a lady's voice asked him.

"It is impossible to say," he answered. "Time will do what it can. She will not be the same as before."

I wanted to agree. I knew that if I opened my eyes, I could see, could look directly into the doctor's face. But I dared not.

Time passed, and my world shrank further. Its outer limits were the four corners of my bed. I dared not venture beyond in my thoughts. In an evening when the stateroom was bright with lamplight, a hand supported the nape of my neck. A spoon lightly touched my lips. Someone was urging soup on me. It startled me out of sleep, and I opened my eyes to see a lovely woman with a tragic face trying to feed me. She met my gaze and looked away. My eyes were blackened, half swollen shut. They could betray nothing, but the lady could not bear to meet such a lifeless stare. It was Mrs. Astor. The new widow of the richest man in America was trying to feed me broth. I knew somehow that we shared this room, along with other women thrust together by these incredible circumstances. I had heard the sounds of their weeping together.

When she saw that I could not swallow, she rose and carried the bowl away from my narrow line of vision. As she stood, I saw Mrs. Astor was expecting a child. The only dress she had saved hardly concealed her condition. It rang a distant bell in my mind. I thought of an unborn child. I thought of the bottom of the sea. I thought of a child drowning within a drowning body.

We spent fitful nights. Mrs. Astor slept on a cot wedged in between the door and the foot of my bed. She and two others—three of the wealthiest women in America—newly widowed, lay wakeful together. And I, the helpless impostor in their midst, feigned sleep.

I slept with the sound of the sea rushing in my head. After the first exhaustion I must have willed myself to sleep. No one urged me to speak. Perhaps they were afraid I might rave, adding the cries of the crazed to their mourning. I dared not speak. I could find my voice, perhaps, if I tried very hard. But could I find the voice of Amanda Whitwell?

It was evening when we entered New York harbor, the evening of

April eighteenth. Tugboats hooted outside the portholes. There was the sense of immense electricity in the air, as if the New World were lit with impossible brilliance. The ship's engines ceased for quarantine. The steady swing and creaking stopped, and my head ached wretchedly. I would have been sick if I had eaten anything. I had survived the sea, and now I dreaded the land.

We sailed slowly up the bay of New York, still as a millpond. The hooting of the tugs became a throbbing medley of sound. The women in the stateroom stood by the portholes and wept at sight of the Statue of Liberty.

We were edging toward the pier. The stern swept out into the great river beside the nighttime city. The engines went dead. The tugboats lined us into land. And beyond there was the sound of masses of people calling out, crying for the first word, calling out the names of the living and the dead.

I could not go on like this. I must tell someone. I managed to move the hand that was not in the sling. I edged it beyond the bed. The diamond flashed, but the room was empty for a moment.

I slept, withdrawing. This was neither life nor death, and I sought a better oblivion. When I awoke, there were stretcher bearers in the room, waiting to go about their work. They stood uncertain at the foot of my bed where Mrs. Astor's cot had been. Beside me, someone had taken my hand. He had thrown his hat on the floor. His necktie was pulled loose from his collar. My hand and its ring were lost in his grasp. I turned toward him as toward the light. My eyes could not focus clearly on anything so near. Still, I saw his fingers were ink-stained. I could not keep from seeing more. His head bent over my hand. His hair was a lustrous black. My heart turned over, and I passed across a great barrier. It was Mr. Gregory Forrest, come to claim Miss Amanda Whitwell.

I awoke in a hospital bed, having dreamed of the clanging bell of an ambulance plunging through distant streets. The room was a bower of flowers. A screen stood between my bed and the window. Through it filtered cloudless sunshine. I was in another bed, another room, another climate.

Doctors consulted in low-pitched voices in the hall outside. The dressings on my face had been changed. My nose lived in a little enclosure of its own. New bandages throbbed at my temples. Stitches had been taken in my lip. I felt their rough, alien presence with the tip of my tongue. My lips, I thought, were sealed. I slept again, comforted by that fancy.

He was often there beside my bed in days that dimmed and brightened in no particular order. He sat silently and did not urge me to speak, even when waking surprised me into opening my eyes. I grew accustomed to seeing him there. The outline of his strong profile against sunlight and then against the dark. I came to expect him to be there beside me, as if I had the right to expect anything.

Once I awoke to see an elderly woman in his place. Her hand covered my own, and she spoke a word or two that I did not understand. I gazed at her, seeing that she was a stranger and thus safe. She smiled back, shyly. Her hand went out to touch my brow, but it was swathed in bandages, and her hand moved uncertainly in the air. She seemed to speak to me as to a child, her own child, though I understood nothing because I did not understand German. I only vaguely knew that this was Gregory Forrest's mother.

I heard a doctor's voice, nearer, in the room. He was saying, "She should be clearing now. There is no reason why she should not begin to speak soon and to understand."

But there were reasons—one enormous reason. I was not who they thought me to be. Bandages and wounds only obscured a face that might have misled them, anyway. But I could not tell them, for then they would know that the woman they were nursing back to health was in reality dead on the ocean's floor. That I was only her despised servant, accustomed only to being ordered about and reviled, married off like a slave at the whim of my mistress. A servant with only the wounds that shielded me truly my own. A servant sunk in a silence that lied on my behalf.

Then he spoke, Mr. Forrest spoke, asking the doctor, "Is it possible that she will never be—well?"

"Time is the great healer," the doctor replied, easing around an answer. "There is no reason to foresee permanent damage to either mind or body. But she may not be quite as she was before."

Did all the doctors mouth the same sentiments? Had I not heard this before, on the *Carpathia?* But still I clung to those words as if they were Holy Writ, as if there were a direction in them for me to follow: ". . . not quite as she was before." I slept again, ready to follow the pathway that seemed to open out before me.

I had already decided on my course then, though only the deep recesses of my mind were capable of decision.

He was sitting by my bed again in an early dawn. He had been there every day, I remembered, keeping a morning watch before he went off to his work. I had loved him for so long that none of this seemed strange. But before, I had seen him only across immense distances. I remembered him sitting at the table at Whitwell Hall in his immaculate black. The little quirk of puzzlement just discernible in his brow at the crosscurrents of talk. For then he had been the foreigner in the strange land. I remembered meeting him in the great hallway when I had blundered in my maid's uniform upon him. I remembered his asking me my name, and I remembered the footfall of Lady Eleanor on the stairs that had sent me scurrying for cover down the servants' steps. I remembered then the throb beneath my heart that only he inspired.

"Amanda?" he said, and I dared not stir in the hospital bed, though my heart sang out in response.

"Yes?" I said through broken lips. "Yes."

Twenty-Nine

When it was time for me to leave St. Vincent's Hospital, I was removed to Gregory Forrest's family home in Brooklyn. There I lay in a room more comforting than I had ever known before. It lacked the studied grandeur of Whitwell Hall, but it was as spacious as a house in the country, though all day long and far into the night Bushwick Avenue below was loud with carters' traffic. There was a pattern of trellised roses on the wallpaper, faded a little, that was more homelike than lavender silks. And there was a bay window set into the far corner, catching the light for an enormous fern that turned all its fronds to the sun.

There was also a little maid-of-all-work named Ursula, who frightened me more than anything, anyone else in this house. Could not one servant know another through some unfailing instinct? She had a mop of flaxen-colored hair that escaped from a little white cap when she remembered to wear the cap at all. And she had no intention of bearing away trays of food uneaten when she had climbed a flight to bring them to the invalid.

"Eat now," she said, sternly coaxing, "or I swear I'll put a bib on you and feed you like a baby!" Then she drew all her features together in a saucy expression. And I ate, half convinced that the servant I had been would never be recognized by the maid who served me now with such breezy independence.

Once I dared speak at all, I asked her to bring me a mirror. The long cheval glass in its tall mahogany frame on brass feet was far across the room. And it had been turned discreetly away from me.

Ursula hesitated. She had been given her instructions to keep me from mirrors. But she did not allow herself to go about burdened by instructions. "Mrs. Forrest said you wasn't supposed to see yourself." I lay there, waiting her out. She pinched her small pointed chin and considered. "But Lord have mercy, you look so much better than you did. . . . Maybe just a peek. But if you start yellin' and carryin' on, I'll break the thing over your head!"

I must have looked very startled and ladylike at that. Ursula grinned and crept with exaggerated care across the carpet and withdrew a hand mirror from the dresser drawer.

She was on the point of handing it to me, but held it back, teasing this strange child propped up against a dozen goosedown pillows. "Now, remember," she said, "just a peek. And while you're lookin', bear in mind you didn't even look human when you got here. Lord, when they carried you in and I caught a glimpse of you, I threw my apron over my head!"

I put my uninjured hand out with some of the impatience of Miss Amanda Whitwell. In the next moment I was staring into the mirror. Ursula hovered at the foot of the bed, pity and worry warring in her.

I stared into a face that was neither mine nor Amanda Whitwell's. It was the face of a battered stranger. I took more comfort in what I saw than Ursula could know. She need not have dreaded my crying out. I examined myself as one looks impassively at the face of a stranger. I lingered over details. The bandage around my forehead had been removed. My black hair, brushed out but tangled by the pillows, showed no evidence of the properly severe style in which I had once dressed it. The flesh about my eyes, still swollen where I had been struck by the oar, was shading from black to a greenish cast. Gashes were beginning to heal, though my cheek and my eyebrows were still crisscrossed with lines that had recently been angry.

I lingered over a scarred eyebrow, and once again a distant bell rang in my mind. Ursula seemed to hold her breath as I was transfixed. But my mind had returned to another time and place. I stared at a thin line of scar tissue that broke the arch of my eyebrow. At last I was able to dredge up a distant detail. Miss Amanda Whitwell's eyebrow had been divided in just such a way. She had been thrown from a horse when she was a child. The accident had left a single tiny imperfection. She had taken pride in telling of this incident, which had ended her brief period as a horsewoman. Any one of several such marks on my own eyebrow might have seemed precisely like it.

By then I had come past the time for telling the truth. I was becoming in the isolation of my bed—Amanda Whitwell. Not an Amanda Whitwell who had ever lived, but one who had learned to scheme from her. And so I had gone beyond the time of looking for signs that the perilous course I had undertaken to follow would work. Still, I took comfort from the scarred eyebrow, though I was not yet ready to meet the gaze from my eyes.

My nose had emerged from its splints, but it was still bandaged—and painful. The line of my lip was still starred with stitches of coarse black surgical thread. I examined it with less vanity than Ursula suspected me of. I thought only that the swelling now and the faint scar later would soften the line of a lip that had grown hard before its time. I remembered the thinness of my pursed mouth in the presence of Amanda Whitwell. And how much more rigid that line was drawn after I had discovered her early one Sunday morning with—

I drew back from the thought and was determined to look into my own eyes, to meet my own gaze if I dared. I looked then into violet eyes, shaded by pain and the vagueness brought on by concussion. But I felt a stir of faint hope. Those, too, could pass as the eyes of Amanda Whitwell. They would work for me and not against me. Amanda seemed to be alive within the mirror, behind the eyes. They were the most certain thing about her. She seemed to look at me, and I could not read any uncertainty in her expression. I could read nothing.

A letter was lying one morning on the table beside the bed. I had tried not to think beyond this room before. I had concentrated only upon playing my part and living with successful stealth through each day as it came. I had dreaded the future, but the letter was a reminder that I would be held responsible for the past as well. It lay there for an hour, unopened, while I shrank from it. The postage, I could see, was British. The spidery, perfect calligraphy was Lady Eleanor Whitwell's hand.

At last I took it up, anchored it with the useless hand that extended from the sling, and tore it open with the other. The heavy paper within unfolded of itself on the bed. I caught the scent of verbena that always hung so lightly in Lady Eleanor's boudoir.

And still I put off taking it up and reading it. Before, all the messages back and forth between Gregory Forrest and the Whitwells had been by Marconigram. I was to be spared any distraction. But now—now I must take up another thread of a life that was not mine.

My darling daughter,

Your father and I thank God that you have been spared to live when so many others have not. Our anguish in those days of uncertainty before we knew are behind us now, and I shall not recount that fearful time. I only pray that you are now all but restored to health, and I place all my trust in Gregoɪy. If you cannot be here with us, I take great comfort in knowing that you are with those who will soon be your own family.

How thoroughly does such a great tragedy drive out all other considerations. I have often thought in these past weeks how many opportunities that you and I, my dear and only child, have lost in the past to be truly mother and daughter. But I shall not lose myself in times now past, and I urge you not to.

I can only hope that when you are a married woman, however far away, you and I will find a way to grow closer, if only in our thoughts. But I shall ask for nothing more beyond the precious gift that those who love you have been given—that you live. I could not have borne your loss. To have lost your brother in a far-off war has cast a shadow across my life, and perhaps it has made me less a mother to you than I should have been. To have lost both my children would be more, by far, than I could bear.

In the midst of our rejoicing at your survival, the household has been saddened by the loss of your maid and good companion, Miranda. As soon as responsible word reached us, your father informed John Thorne of the death of his wife.

In view of her faithful attendance to your needs, it has occurred to me that some memorial should be made. I have therefore put into train the preparation of a small plaque to be affixed to the church wall, just inside the vestry. The vicar has been good enough to see to the carrying out of this plan. We pray for Miranda's soul and hope that her memory will remain alive in your heart.

I shall write no more just now, for I do not wish to tire you,

*dear Amanda. Be assured that through your life I can find a way
to live my own.*

Your loving mother

Ursula, who never knocked, discovered me with the letter beside me
and my swollen eyes even more swollen with tears. I wept not as the
daughter of such a loving mother, but as one who had never known
such love. I was not Amanda Whitwell in that moment when I
seemed so convincing in her part. I wept far more than Amanda
would have. I wept, too, for the Miranda who was dead now, dead
and remembered with kindness. Dead in ways far beyond my control
or contriving.

But I had not quite wept all my tears before my mind began to
work in the scheming way that all who live a lie depend upon. I
thought of my injured arm, and knew that it delayed my writing back
to Lady—to my mother in a handwriting that was not her daughter's.
Later, perhaps, the results of the injury would seem to alter the
handwriting of a daughter who had, perhaps, never written a line to
her mother before in any case.

Ursula was unnerved by my tears. She had seen no such display
of emotion from the invalid before. She ran to find Mrs. Forrest, who
came to linger tentatively at the door until I asked her to sit beside
me. I could not put her off. I could no longer keep those willing to
love me at arm's length. Perhaps her German heart feared English
coldness.

"You are—moved, perhaps, from a word from your home?"

I nodded and tried to smile.

"I understand such a thing." She nodded, and her eyes grew bright
with encouragement and the hint of tears. Gregory had her eyes.

"I came from Augsburg, in the old country, when I was no more
than a girl. Oh, how long ago it seems! I came with my blond hair
in braids wound around and around my head and my eyes wide to
see wonders. And since, I haf shed my share of tears over letters from
home, though this has been my happy home for more years than you
haf lived. It is a happy sadness. It is your mother who sends you
word?"

I nodded again.

"And there are others besides your dear mother and papa? A
grandmother, perhaps?"

"No," I said as I struggled to turn deception to a kind of truth. "There is a very old woman, though, with a heart full of love. She lives in a small cottage on—our grounds. She has been like a— grandmother to me. She's known many hardships, but her heart is young. She combs strong tea into her hair to banish the white, and she lives surrounded by portraits of the royal family. She has made her memories happy, as I hope to make mine."

Mrs. Forrest patted the back of my hand, and I turned it to hold hers. This pledge of faith warmed her, and she began to talk, to reminisce. She told tales of her brewer husband and his rise to prosperity. How his hopes and plans were crowned now in his son. She told me about these men she loved, and I listened with an attention that she could see went beyond politeness. I heard more of Gregory Forrest than Amanda Whitwell ever had, even more than if she had listened.

In the evenings Gregory sat beside my bed. And in those evenings the Amanda he had loved began to interweave with the Amanda before him. He had fallen in love with an image he adored, and it was fortunate for me that she had kept him remote from her essential self. I could not match her brighter facets. I could not stun him with my wit or raise a satirical eyebrow while I dangled him on a string. I could only play on Amanda Whitwell's silent moods, her sulks when she sent him away. I could only hope to fill those secretive silences with another Amanda, more loving and more kind.

The immensity of the task and all its risk swept over me as I lay there behind a facade of bandaged flesh. The true Amanda would have forbidden him the room until she looked quite herself again. But I came to thank my wounds for buying me a scrap of time.

I could have spoken to him, and at length, well before my face returned to a normality that was to be only subtly changed. We were both inflamed by the eagerness of lovers parted and reunited. But I contented myself with being an eager listener for the most part. I was not yet confident that I had found the right voice—her voice. How often it had rung in my mind even when I was about my other duties at Whitwell Hall. How closely I had come to speak in her vocabulary, and yet I was not equal—I would never be equal to her ringing tone of command. I would have to work very hard to achieve even an echo of it. And I would not try to match her easy, contemptuous laughter, her little cruelties that hinted glibly at greater ones. I would not bring that back to life even if it cost me everything. Even if it cost me Gregory.

I could never be—how had the doctors put it?—quite as I had been. I prayed that Gregory Forrest would not see the differences, not read them for what they were. I prayed that he would rejoice quietly that those things he had only endured in Amanda had been stripped away. My desperation gave me a cautious vanity. I sought to be an Amanda that had never been. There were moments, even early on, when I thought that goal worthy enough to compensate for any deceit. I knew that I could be a better wife to Gregory Forrest than Amanda would have been, or chosen to be. But would I be betrayed? Would I betray myself? My mind wandered until it faltered through this dark thicket of possibilities and pitfalls.

On the evening after his mother had sat with me, I was forced to speak. There were still a thousand things I did not know. The weight of them was bearing down on me.

I spoke to him as soon as he was beside me. I tried not to grip his hand very hard as I screwed up my courage. "Gregory, I feel very foolish and very forgetful." Yes, that was spoken in one of Miss Amanda's more languid tones, though it lacked her utter boredom. "Your mother has been good enough to sit with me—"

"And talked you into a trance about her son's boyhood?" he interjected.

"Well, she did just touch upon the subject in passing." I drew in my cheeks, still a little painful, in Amanda's arch manner, and he squeezed my hand.

"And what do you want to know that Mother didn't get around to telling you?"

"It's serious, Gregory, and I feel more than stupid for not knowing." I hesitated and pressed on. "Your mother speaks of her life with your father, and I don't know if he is—living."

Gregory pressed my hand again. "No, my dearest. My father isn't living. If he were, you'd have heard his big voice echoing throughout the house. And no hospital rules could have kept him from bursting in here to meet his future daughter-in-law. He died very suddenly not long after I met you."

I seemed to stand at the edge of a limitless quicksand swamp. "Oh, Gregory, I must have known, mustn't I?"

"No, my dear, you wouldn't have known. It happened at one of those times when you had—well, you'd banished me. I had gone to the Continent, and there a letter caught up with me. When we were together again, I didn't want to trouble you."

I lay there then, refusing to think in the patterns of another. "There is nothing now that I do not want to know, Gregory. Nothing that concerns you can fail to concern me. I have been very—tiresome in the past. Tiresome and childish." I cursed Amanda Whitwell then, who had spent every hour in Gregory Forrest's presence, in his arms, plotting to satisfy her lust for another man, who was not a patch on this one.

I listened from then on. I listened on her behalf and on my own, to make up for a great deal in her life and mine. I listened as he told me of his work, his family, his life. He introduced me, a foreigner, to his country, which lay beyond the windows of that room. He told me of his boyhood friend, Sammy Bettendorf, who had died needlessly with all his family in the burning of their firetrap tenement. He told me what had given him the goals that directed his life. He was a young man fueled by his plans, and I heard them all, scarcely able to hope that I could play my role at his side. I would have been caught up in his selfless ambitions even if I had not loved him. I had known few people in my short life who looked beyond the moment. And too many of those saw their only goals in using others to benefit themselves.

He opened his heart to me through an evening that stretched almost until dawn. And then he drew me up short. "But you've heard all this before, Amanda. You've listened through my grand plans and my castles in the air and all my schemes to rebuild New York as a place fit for all people to live in safety and—dignity."

"I could hear it many more times, Gregory. And I live to see it happen."

"And you no longer think—let's see, how did you put it once—that I 'reek of idealism'?"

"I could never have said such a thing!" I replied with considerable spirit. And absolute honesty.

That night ended as I knew it would. I had feared this inevitable moment, and longed for it. Gregory was beside me on the bed. His arms moved gently but surely, confidently around me, and held me. I felt the controlled passion of his sheltering embrace.

The hand that bore his engagement ring rested on his shoulder, muscular beneath his coat. He held me, not yet attempting to cover my bruised face with kisses that might give me pain. But I felt the pain. My lies had been only too successful. I sank out of my depth, tormented by doubts. I felt both too uncertain and too experienced. Another man—another sort of man—had held me, in a bed narrower than this. I screamed behind unspeaking lips, screamed in terror at what I had already set in motion. There was every likelihood of failure. And success could come only through more deceit than even that other Amanda had ever needed to sustain. Was any love worth this eternity of lies?

I knew it was. I knew it was worth anything. And if I should be unmasked later, and surely I would be, it would be worth it. I had never demanded anything of life before. But I was not now what I had been.

I searched his face as he drew near to mine. I examined it as if I were of his station in life, as if I had a right. I who had been trained never to meet the gaze of my betters memorized his eyes, which looked so deeply, yet not questioningly, into mine. The strong line of his barbered jaw. The lips that would seek mine soon. I forced myself to lie easily in his embrace, and I held him as tightly as one hand could manage. "You are all I want," he said. And all the world beyond us fell away.

Thirty

Gregory Forrest and I were married in June 1912. My only attendant was Miss Rebecca Reed. She had left her card at the Forrest home in Bushwick some time before, and I had been thrown into the worst panic I had known since the night I found myself alone in the waters of the Atlantic. I would not see her, and she had to make the lengthy trip back to Manhattan with only coffee and apologies offered by Gregory's mother. I lurked in my room above, stunned by indecision. Here was a person—a keen-eyed woman who supported herself by writing newspaper articles—who had seen me on the *Titanic* as who and what I was. She had seen Amanda Whitwell, too. She had known us both well enough to take notice of our similarities. And perhaps our differences.

On the *Carpathia,* had she been sure that it was Amanda who lay disfigured in that stateroom and not I? I struggled to remember what she had said when she and Victorine had looked down at me in that bed. But I could remember nothing. I was too frightened to think, much less remember. Though I was up and about by then, I dared not pace the floor for fear I would be heard in the parlor below.

My arm was out of the sling, and so on the following day I wrote Rebecca Reed a note in a wavering hand, pleading the remnants of bad health and asking her back for tea. Much as I wanted to, I could not hide from all the world. As I sealed the envelope, I wondered if I had sealed my fate as well.

Mrs. Forrest was delighted at this evidence of my recovery. She even ordered a car for herself with a great show of secrecy and returned with a large parcel from Abraham & Straus. It contained a tea gown for me with all possible accessories. Stockings, slippers, undergarments frothing with lace. She hung back like a shy young girl as I held up the gown before me and stood before the glass. How easily I had deluded this good woman, and how conscious-stricken it made me. I turned to her, hoping the gratitude in my face would conceal the guilt. But in the next moment I could only return to wondering if Rebecca Reed would be so easily misled.

I dressed my hair precisely as I had dressed Amanda Whitwell's, though my injured arm grew numb long before I had quite finished. The lingering marks on my face decreed a discreet dusting of powder. And I spent the final moments before my guest's arrival primping myself before the mirror, moving through a ritual by rote that I had before practiced on another. Ursula opened the front door below, and in that last moment I reached for the rope of pearls that had lain like a survivor in a dresser drawer.

I stood on the darkened stairs of the house I had never explored, the house where the man I was determined to marry had grown up. My hand gripped a banister of black walnut, and I fixed my gaze on the hall below, where a palm that lived in a copper pot stood before a tall gold mirror. The mirror rose in an arch, festooned with gilt flowers, near the ceiling. I had spent so much time searching the message of mirrors that I refused to catch a final glimpse of myself. I descended to the hall and walked closer to the conversation in the parlor.

When I appeared in the doorway, Miss Reed rose at once in her abrupt way. She might have borne down on me if Mrs. Forrest had not already burdened her with coffee and a plate of cakes. I forced myself to greet her by her first name in a voice far from my own as I stepped out of the shadowy hall.

I moved across the room in the posture of a lady. Every instinct drew me in other directions. My hands longed to clasp themselves before me. My back and my shoulders ached to straighten. My head began naturally to incline itself to await the instructions of my betters. And all this would be a fatal error. I had worried that my face and my speech would undo me. Now I feared that my carriage would betray me first. How thoroughly I had learned the manner and the mannerisms of a servant. Now I must jettison all that in efforts that must be right the first time through.

Miss Reed—Rebecca—searched my face with the quick intensity of her character and profession. "My dear Amanda, you're very nearly perfection again! How lucky for you—and for us all." I was just able to meet her look, and I forced my eyes to wander upward to her hat, as if I were appraising it. Perhaps that glance would return her thoughts to herself.

I tried to reassure myself that this woman had been no more than a casual brief acquaintance of Amanda Whitwell. That she had herself undergone the shock of shipwreck—that, like most people, she might easily be more preoccupied with her own adventures than with another's. I urged her to tell Mrs. Forrest the story of her musical pig. It was the sole account from all the great horror that might be told over the coffee cups merely to amuse.

With very little further encouragement, she launched into the story of her mascot, the stuffed pig. Mrs. Forrest looked utterly confused by such a tale, and so Rebecca Reed made rather a longer story of it. And I smiled and nodded throughout, employing a sort of universal language.

She was a natural storyteller. I sat, easing by degrees into the chair. I even remembered to toy idly with the long strand of pearls as I had seen ladies do in drawing rooms. It struck me that perhaps Amanda Whitwell had been as far from being a real lady as I. Her purpose had always been to draw every eye in the room, to cause others to notice and to defer to her. Perhaps a lady's true role lay elsewhere. Perhaps it lay in turning attention and conversation away from oneself in the interests of sociability. Perhaps to be truly well-bred consisted of uncentering oneself. The pearls moved over my fingers as Rebecca Reed directed more and more of her monologue to the woman who was to become my mother-in-law. If only I could let the rest of the world do the talking, perhaps it would save the moment, and my life. But the rest of the afternoon proved the impossibility of that.

Even early on, I did not give way to false confidence. I was more threatened by the presence of this near-stranger than I was with Gregory. With him I could hope for the love that alters a man's perceptions, even if it does not render him blind. But a woman is far more likely to see through another woman than is any man. Keeping myself in check, I noticed that Rebecca's gaze, shifting at times in my direction, would linger on me. Her eyes followed the line of my gown. She caught repeated glimpses, or so it seemed, from the corner of her eye without ever dropping the thread of her story.

At last, when I thought she meant to rise and go, she turned to me and set her coffee cup aside. "You know, Amanda, journalists are outrageously thick-skinned types. We have the reputation of nosing around disasters like a pack of vultures, and I suppose we live up to our reputations. We have to if we mean to make a living. What I'm trying to say is this: would it be too painful for you to give me an interview about your experiences on the *Titanic?* I know, I know, you really shouldn't have to relive the whole terrible business." She waved her hand in the air as if to dismiss herself before I should. "But you see, the New York newspapers are still gobbling up every inch of copy they buy, steal, or invent about the whole thing. And the London papers are doing the same, in a stodgier way.

"All sorts of people—survivors, I mean—are still giving interviews just to tell the most awful whoppers that nobody could possibly believe. And there are going to be Senate hearings, too. After all, it's as tragic a scandal as we've ever known. Fifteen hundred people dead on a ship that never held a boat drill and didn't carry nearly enough lifeboats. That plus the fact that the *Titanic* was barreling along through an ice field and ignoring iceberg warnings right and left.

"Frankly, I'd like very much to write up a sort of brief account from your viewpoint. As you might well imagine even without reading the papers, every woman who got off the *Titanic* swears she left in the last lifeboat."

Rebecca Reed ran down then, while we both had time to recall that I left the ship even after the last lifeboat. Was I what newspaper people called a "scoop"? She had seemed to talk me into submission. The fact was that my mind had been darting about while she spoke, and in conflicting directions. I drew back from the idea of telling anything about my experiences. They were not mine to tell. And they provided every opportunity to trip myself up. There had been a conspiracy of silence in the Forrest household that had been meant to erase the memory of the disaster from my mind. I had traded on that. I had not reckoned with the rest of the world, so assertively represented by Rebecca Reed.

I knew I must grant her an interview. And not merely to be rid of her. She was kind and straightforward. But while she was nothing like a vulture, she had the tenacity of a leech. I thought cautiously of how an interview might lend credence to my story. It occurred to me suddenly that for the rest of my life, however I might live it, I would be identified as a survivor of this famous disaster. Perhaps a word now would forestall many later. And perhaps Rebecca Reed was a great deal more trustworthy a reporter than many another might be. It seemed possible that a number of journalists had already been turned away from the Forrests' door. A glance at Mrs. Forrest tended to confirm just that.

When she saw I was willing to be drawn out on the subject, Gregory's mother rose and excused herself. And while she was the least stern of women, she admonished Rebecca Reed rather emphatically that I was not to be upset or "questioned to death."

When Mrs. Forrest had left us, Rebecca drew her chair closer to mine. *If she knows,* I thought, *this will be her opportunity to accuse me.* But no, she was merely warming to her journalist's task and flipping open a notebook taken out of her handbag with lightning speed.

She was not going to accuse me; she did not even particularly look as if she meant to hang me with my own words. Yet my heart stopped and my tongue thickened. I must pitch now into a morass of believable lies. I could not tell my own story, and the story she wanted to hear ended in death. How I longed at that moment to rise up and scream at this woman, I AM NOT AMANDA WHITWELL. *If you know it, don't torture me further. And if you hadn't known it until now, keep my guilty secret, for I have no other life to live but hers. . . .*

And yet I sat so silently, the pearls moving over my fingers. I must have seemed to be forcing myself to remember moments that were only painful and not damning.

"There are things," I said in a thoughtful, distant voice, "that I don't recall at all. The shock, perhaps. And it had been such an ordinary evening. I dined, of course. And in the dining saloon, not the *à la carte* restaurant."

"Then I rather think I must have taken coffee in the Palm Court and after that a turn on the deck. Yes, I'm quite sure about that. It was a terribly cold night, and I wore—my long fur coat." *Yes, yes, that was quite true. She had been on the deck that night. I saw her there; anyone might have seen her. But of course, she wasn't alone. . . .*

"Not alone, surely," Rebecca said, lifting her pencil from the page, yet not quite looking me in the eye.

"No, I took a turn or two around the deck with Mr. Sawyer." *That was true enough, but had they dined together, taken their coffee together in the Palm Court? Had Rebecca seen them?*

But Rebecca only said, "And then?" and prepared to write again.

"And then I went to my stateroom"—*yes, she had gone to a stateroom* —"and went to bed rather early. The brisk air had made me sleepy."

Rebecca Reed's pencil hovered above the page. Discretion and the dictates of journalism battled within her.

"Rebecca," I said, "it had come to my attention that some of our fellow passengers misunderstood the attentions I was receiving from Mr. Sawyer. I believe I may well have deserved those raised eyebrows. I flirted outrageously." *Was "flirt" the right word? It must have been. Miss Reed's eyes were wide and looked appreciative of this candor.* "As shipboard romances go, it was no more than an innocent flirtation, but it did occur to me that perhaps Mr. Sawyer's reputation as a —lady-killer had preceded him. I sent him away quite early on that Sunday night, and he was far too suave a man to do anything but go quietly."

There. I could not have avoided mentioning Clem Sawyer. He hung heavily in Miss Reed's mind. Her pencil still hovered as she digested information that was more interesting to her womanly side than useful for her account. And I was nearly overcome by my own audacity, and by the irony that I was still being more careful of Miss Amanda's reputation than she had ever been of it herself. I had quenched the subject of Mr. Sawyer.

"And I suppose," she said, "that he conducted himself like the rest of the gentlemen and stood back while the women were saved."

"I never saw him after our stroll on the deck in the early evening," I replied, "but it would have been very like him to conduct himself with honor in the face of danger."

And still the interview was far from over. It stretched before me like a minefield.

"You were awakened by the sound of the ship striking the iceberg?"

"No, my—maid awakened me. She—she hadn't liked to disturb me at first." I thought of Victorine. Of what happened to Victorine.

"Oh!" cried Miss Reed, forestalling the painful topic of Miranda's death. "I'm so glad to know you don't claim to have heard the first impact of ship against the iceberg! Half the people interviewed said it sounded like a thunderclap and that they knew in a moment the ship was sinking. Such balderdash! It was quite a small sound. I scarcely heard it myself." But she was not to be drawn out with the telling of the story from her viewpoint. She fell silent, and her pencil poised again on a fresh page.

"I sent Miranda to the purser for my jewelry. Only the things Mr. —Gregory had given me. After all, there was no point in burdening her with everything. And neither of us thought there was any real danger. I didn't even bother to dress, and I went back to bed."

"And to sleep?" she asked.

"Yes. There was a good deal of noise from outside. Still, I had been roused from first sleep and dropped off again at once. It seems very foolish now.

"I awoke again some while later. The stateroom stood at an alarming angle. I threw on my life preserver and then a cape over that and thought to go out and see what was happening. But when I got to the door, I found it had been locked from the outside."

"Yes, many of the staterooms had been locked up by the crew, but of course they should have checked inside first. Even the crew members seemed unable to realize the danger. They could think only that people might be robbed in their absence. You weren't the only one locked up."

"Oh, who else was?" I asked. Carefully. Casually.

"Victorine, actually. Mrs. Ryerson's maid." Miss Reed cleared her throat. "It seems that your maid, Miranda, broke the door down and set her free at the last moment."

A shadow fell across my face. I cast it there to mask the relief at seeming not to know already what I had just been told. The shadow spoke of my emptiness at losing Miranda, and so it was not entirely false. And I spoke again.

"I was able to break down my own door with a chair, but of course it cost me precious time. And I saw the adjoining cabin, Miranda's, which was empty. The crew had not bothered to lock up the servants' quarters, thinking, I suppose, there was nothing of value in them. I never saw Miranda again. She must have thought me safely off the ship by then."

I stopped, wondering how I could manage to sustain this awful mingling of half-truth and falsehood. Miss Reed busied herself with her notes. She was sparing me now, allowing me to grieve over my maid. Giving me credit for feeling the burden of having brought her on a voyage that killed her. But Rebecca shortly put another question.

"Surely there was still time to get yourself into a lifeboat?" *Had there been time? Was I now about to fall through a hole in my own story? Surely no one could be sure of precise timing, but still . . .*

"I went up to one of the decks where they were loading the boats. It was a—terrific muddle. I was frightened, and I'm afraid I gave way to an unreasonable instinct. I rushed back to my stateroom to get— a book of blank pages. I kept a diary of sorts in a lovely book I'd had bound at Asprey's. I can't think now why I would have been so consumed by the need to have it. Perhaps it was the kind of memento one needs at such a time—rather like your pig."

Miss Reed was forced to agree, but my mind lingered on the book from Asprey's that no Amanda would ever write in again, and no reader would ever see. But I could see it vividly in that moment, just where I had put it aside in her stateroom. It had surfaced now, its contents still secret, to play one more small role in my deception.

"Yes," Miss Reed was saying, "people did go back for the most extraordinary things. And of course you weren't able to keep the book with you. You must feel somewhat robbed of your past without it."

"I suppose I do."

We paused then, each of us caught up in different ironies, but she urged me to continue. And then I could recount my own salvation as it had happened. Standing on the deck until the last moment, when the sea curled at my feet. The endless minutes in the water and the endless night in the boats. I could only hope that the truth of this last portion would carry the falsehood of the first. I had given my performance, and now the curtain was ringing down on it. I had done my best and my worst.

The account, neatly edited and with no mention of Mr. Sawyer, appeared in the following day's edition of *The New York Times,* bearing Rebecca Reed's byline. Gregory read it and said he would save the newspaper cutting for our grandchildren. I managed a wan smile at that. Though when he suggested I might like a copy sent to Sir Timothy and Lady Eleanor, I shook my head quickly.

Once she had gathered her material, Rebecca rose to go. We stood alone at the door, for in America servants rarely see anyone out. "I hope," she said as uncertainly as a schoolgirl, "that we can be friends.

I feel I didn't know you—before, and that I had quite the wrong impression of you. But I expect that's often the way with first meetings." All her crisp professional manner had deserted her. She hesitated a moment longer.

I wondered if I should reach out and take her hand. Where was the precise line between easy sophistication and undue familiarity? I had lived so far behind that line that I was at a loss. "Everything will be very strange here," I said, "in a new country. I shall depend on my friends."

She turned to go. Mrs. Forrest had thoughtfully sent for a car to take her back. It purred at the curb. "You're feeling—well now?" she asked. How carefully she asked, more carefully than she needed to. I nodded, and as if she had said too much, she went quickly down the steps to the waiting car.

I stood for a long time behind the closed door in the dark hallway. I could not decide if I had passed a tremendous test or if I had failed. I could not be sure if it had been a test at all. My mind wrung the afternoon of all its possible meanings. Surely it had gone well—better than I deserved. But in that last moment I remembered again Rebecca Reed bending over me on the *Carpathia*. The exploratory hand that had moved over me.

Could it mean—yes, perhaps. Perhaps she knew that Amanda Whitwell had been expecting a child. And then on the ship—and now Amanda was not. Could she think I might have lost the child in the sea? No. Surely not. Perhaps she suspected the truth. Perhaps she knew I was an insignificant maid pathetically got up to impersonate a lady. Or did she, after all, only see that lady?

I was never to know. The mercy of a stranger may well be the most valuable of all gifts, and the least understood. Perhaps I posed such a great problem to Rebecca Reed's determined open-mindedness that she could not solve me. Perhaps her mind was so firmly fixed on the story she wrote that she mistook my fiction for fact. She had heard far less plausible stories from far more prominent survivors.

Perhaps I was frightening myself over a shadow. *The guilty flee where no man pursueth,* I thought, conjuring up the line out of thin air. And I climbed the steps to a room that could no longer be my refuge.

I stood again before the mirror in my bedroom on the night before I was to marry Gregory Forrest. The floor around me was littered with the tissue paper and open boxes in which my trousseau had been sent. How all the richness of this new wardrobe had tortured me! It had arrived from all the smartest shops in London, sent over the sea by Lady Eleanor Whitwell. She had replaced her daughter's original trousseau down to the last detail.

How carefully she had matched and duplicated what now lay buried in the *Titanic's* hold. She must have journeyed up to London to make these selections herself. She had written to me—to Amanda: "through your life I can find a way to live my own." And this had been one of the ways. What pleasure the extravagance must have given her. This had been her celebration of her daughter's survival.

Now an impostor would wear those clothes, an impostor who had in the past garbed herself only in Amanda Whitwell's castoffs. The inappropriate gifts sent from elderly aunts. The hat that had never been quite the thing. Last year's skirt. A shirtwaist with a bit of Swiss embroidery pulled loose, not worth bothering about. Shoes run down at the heel and no longer smart enough to merit repair. I had always lined her cast-off shoes with a bit of paper, for her feet were a size larger than my own. I bent now to layer paper into the butter-soft blue calfskin shoes that I would wear when I wed the husband meant for her.

While the traditions that celebrate brides seemed to have nothing to do with me, I thought of a scrap of verse as I folded the tissue paper: *"Something borrowed, something blue . . . and a penny for her shoe. . . ."*

The quiet, cluttered room where I lurked among the opulence of these "borrowed" clothes seemed filled with a distant voice. I froze like a thief in the act of slipping the shoes on my feet, fearing it was Amanda's voice that rang in my mind. But no, it was another, an older one.

It was the Wisewoman's voice, as clear-spoken as if I were still the girl who had blundered on her house in the folded hills of the Isle of Wight. I saw again her mystery-filled cottage on the day when she had told—foretold—my fortune. Though I had not truly forgotten it, the prophecy sang out again, more certain now that it was being fulfilled. Just as the Wisewoman had decreed, I had died and come to life again beyond a mountain of ice, an iceberg that drifted in patterns that only seemed random.

And she had given me—a penny. An American Indianhead penny. I had understood nothing of the gift, for she had told me to take it back, back where it had come from. She had known my fate would lead me here.

Suddenly I had to find it. Find it and, yes, the gold chain on which it hung. The sudden memory of the chain that Gregory had given me on the day he had given Amanda the pearls returned, staggering me. The chain that might betray and reveal me. My hand moved to my neck where once the chain had lain hidden beneath the high collar of my servant's shirtwaist.

But the chain was gone. I could not remember when I had last been aware of it. Because it had been a gift from Gregory, I had made it a part of myself. And I had no idea of when it had left me. It must, I thought, have been lost in the sea, lost with so much else.

My temples pounded. I could hardly catch my breath. And yet surely I had nothing to fear from a gold chain and a near-worthless penny that were gone now. I must simply find another penny now, another one to honor the bridal traditions.

I searched a small drawer at the top of the dresser where a few coins lay scattered. I worked through them, and my hands grew frantic. I was working through them now as madly as I had searched through Amanda Whitwell's jewelry on the sinking ship. And miraculously, among the unfamiliar American nickels and dimes and the newer pennies, I found an Indianhead.

I held it up to the light, examining the faint, worn image of a copper man. It was not the same penny, but it would have to serve. I slipped it into my shoe, where it was lost in the layered paper. I jammed the shoe back onto my foot, and still my hands shook.

Returning to the mirror, I still tortured myself. With my hair brushed out and tumbling around my shoulders, I could see nothing and no one but Miranda. I wore a long white nightdress severe enough to have been one of my own—of Miranda's.

But it was Amanda's voice I heard. It was all around me in the room. Often enough when I needed to conjure her up, she was reluctant, elusive. But now, in such a moment as this, when I wished to drive the very thought of her away, she seemed to taunt me. I could see her face everywhere except where I most wanted to see it —in the mirror. Even the whiteness of my nightdress seemed to sneer. I was to be a bride who had no right to wear white.

On the last night of her life when I had dressed her, she had called for her pink evening gown. "Pink, I think," she had said—was still saying in this room she never reached. "Girlish but not virginal."

Not virginal.

I heard a soft knock and, in the mirror I saw the door open behind me. Gregory stepped inside the room. I turned and rushed into his arms. I hurried to shelter myself from the ghost that haunted me, to stop my ears against her deathly voice. To hide my face from hers, from his.

He held me until I stopped trembling. I felt the length of his body and longed to believe no other man had held me closer. "Better now?" he said at last, still sheltering me from fears he would not inquire into.

"Much better."

"And better still tomorrow."

I could only nod at that. Tomorrow would mean—

"And you won't mind being compliant tomorrow night?"

Again, a word from some other life surfaced too suddenly. I looked up to him. "Compliant?"

"Once—oh, a long time ago—you told me that men expected women to be decorative by day and compliant by night. I think you tended to resent it at the time."

"Then," I said, trying not to cling to his strong leanness too fiercely, "then, not now."

We were married, Gregory and I, in Grace Church, Brooklyn, that City of Churches. Grace Church stands at the top of little Grace Court, just where it wanders down to the bay like a country lane. Even the church itself would be more at home standing in a field on the Isle of Wight. It was very like the Nettlecombe church at the foot of the drive beyond the park of Whitwell Hall. That church with the plaque that commemorates Gordon Whitwell's death in the South African war and the plaque that recalls Miranda's death at sea.

There were only the four of us: Gregory and I, Mrs. Forrest, and Rebecca Reed, clustered before the vicar in the small, cool cavern of the church. I stood before the altar of God and pledged my life to Gregory Forrest. I stood in a severe costume, the skirt of which was cut more amply than my waist because it had been copied from one made for another bride. I stood in her shoes, hoping the tissue paper would not crinkle.

When the vicar asked if there was anyone in this company who knew of any impediment to our union, my heart stopped. Yet no stranger stepped from the shadows to sever the knot now being tied, to kill the serpent of my deceit within its egg. I heard Gregory's voice far above me: "With this ring I thee wed." My hand was in his, and he had placed there a gold band beside the diamond engagement ring.

I married Gregory Forrest that afternoon somewhere between spring and summer. The walls of that small, squat church did not split wide and dash me to death. The tall colored windows did not collapse to tear me with shards. But with the word and the deed of this simple ceremony, I had become a criminal. I had married the only man in the world I could ever love. Yet I was married already, and to quite a different man.

Thirty-One

———— ⌒∞⌒ ————

Mr. and Mrs. Gregory Forrest
are at home to their friends
at eight o'clock
on the twenty-eighth of June
Nineteen hundred and twelve
Supper and dancing to follow

Number Two, Montague Terrace
Brooklyn, New York
R.S.V.P.

Gregory and I were at home in the house on Montague Terrace from the first day of our marriage. There were a few days and more nights when I could regard myself as the wife of Gregory Forrest, with all the rights and joys that contract accorded. There were precious spans of time when I could half dismiss the harsh fact that the contract was invalid, that I was a criminal. A bigamist.

We lived, like all honeymooners, to love and to forget for a little time all the darkened world beyond the glow of our love. And like all the newly wed, we were strangers whose greatest joy lay in banishing the strangeness. We did not question each other. That would have been to question love itself.

All this bright intensity conspired to make me neither Amanda nor

Miranda, but a young woman brought suddenly to life by a husband's passion.

It was a lovely house, standing at the foot of Montague Street in a row of town houses immensely old by New York standards. The row was a solid palisade of red brick merchants' mansions, which Gregory said derived from the "Federal period." But our house stood out among all its neighbors, for he had applied an architect's skill and a husband's love to make ours more modern and more welcoming.

The facade had been resurfaced in limestone—silver-gray stone that shaded to verdigris in the evening hours when New York is tinted by the moody light of a more poetic city. Gregory had replaced the old, many-paned windows that had been miserly with the light with long, unmullioned windows that drew the sun deeply into the rooms. At the rear he had pierced the outer walls to the floor and replaced them with French doors glazed in long, uninterrupted panes.

Boxy rooms became expansive. Narrow doorways, some sealed with layered wallpapers, became broad arches. The grain of wooden flooring came suddenly to light, and the walls were washed with silver-leaf and palest green. And darker corners were illuminated by Tiffany lamps with glass shades petaled like lily pads and willow trees in the same silver and green hues. It was a house that invited joy and banished shadows. And it spoke of the present, not the past.

When we took up our residence there, the mortar in the flagstone terrace across the garden side was still wet. This piazza was set about with great urns of terra-cotta pottery alive with peonies, those very American flowers that flourish in the brief perfect week before spring gives way to tropical summer.

The terrace stood above a back garden that rose in a little hillock to screen the roofs of the dockside warehouses below. We looked directly out onto New York harbor. It was a mural brought to life by the busy shipping of the bay and the snapping flags of Governor's Island, which lay off our shore across the shallow Buttermilk Channel. In the distance beyond the island, the Statue of Liberty raised her torch, the most brilliant star in the star-filled summer nights. In those nights great steamships, all illuminated, began their voyages back to the world from which I had come.

Our bedroom, too, looked out on this ever-changing view through windows as generous as the rest. I stood before one of them on our wedding night, vowing myself to silence at the end of a day when my vows had led from deception to criminality. The hand that bore its new wedding ring grew cold as it seemed to recall with a memory of its own that other ring it had once worn. The ring I had cast into the English Channel when the *Titanic* had passed the Isle where I was born. And it was the hand that had signed two church registries, two licenses of marriage, within this single year.

Gregory stepped up behind me. I clung to his hands that encircled my waist. I rested my head against his broad shoulder, and my hair cascaded down the brocaded sleeve of his dressing gown. I meant to melt in the passion he stirred within me. I was almost ready to give myself to this man, whom once I could glimpse only as a far-off god. This forbidden passion welled up in me, a feeling utterly new that would soon sweep me away, out of all my selves.

I was in his arms and would soon be in his bed with nothing but my lies between us. His face found the hollow of my neck. I had brushed my hair to a dark brightness and had scented it lightly with verbena because that had been the very signature of Lady Eleanor. I longed for a hint of her loveliness—her loveliness and no other's. His lips found the hollow of my neck screened by my hair. He kissed me more gently than I had ever been kissed before. There were such things as kisses that did not bite and maul. Kisses that claimed me more gently and with far greater authority.

He drew the nightdress down from my shoulders. It lay about my feet. His hand slipped beneath my knees; he lifted me from that silky puddle of the nightdress and carried me to his bed.

But I could not surrender before I spoke. In a lifetime of lies I must speak one truth, and now. I lay there naked in his arms. I must speak while I still could.

"I don't come to you as a bride should come to her husband. I am not—"

His lips stopped my whispered confession. And then he said, "You come to me just as you are. You have come back almost from the dead, from a great distance. From nowhere. Our life begins now with that miracle. Nothing else before has ever happened."

We gave a party to begin our married life in that beautiful house. I feared the scrutiny of Gregory's friends. Yet I had begun to learn to live with fear. It was not friends of my husband whom I feared the most, nor even very much the suspicions my husband might come to have.

There was someone I feared with all my heart, and I could not even say his name in secret. I could not speak it even beneath my breath.

Mrs. Forrest had lent me Ursula to help out until I had time to engage my own staff. She and I—and an army of caterers—made the elaborate preparations for the party. Ursula and I worked side by side in the kitchen. It was not such an outrageous circumstance for an American household. I banished from my mind the horror it would inspire in the breasts of Mr. Finley and Mrs. Creeth. And I was not unpracticed in the preparations for a party. It was serving as its hostess that caused me to lie anxiously awake at night long after Gregory had gone to sleep.

But it was a lovely party. I stood beside him at the door, and we greeted the arrivals without the intervention of a butler. I fell back on the shyness of a new bride, and of a foreigner. I smiled and nodded and took hands and accepted the inevitable compliments that were the due of Gregory Forrest's bride.

I stood in a gown from Worth's London workrooms, and the pearls that had followed me from one life to another. I stood there dressed as a creature from the farthest limits of a serving girl's—any girl's—fantasies. And I willed myself to believe that all of life would be so perfect. I even managed to content myself with such an evening as this if there might be a terrible price to pay for it.

Like any new bride, I saw the universal signs of envy in the eyes of girls who had set their caps for Gregory Forrest. And I parried the thrusts of the curious who would gladly have had me relive the last hours of the *Titanic* as a sort of evening's entertainment.

To the rippling rhythms of the piano I danced through the evening in our room that overlooked the bay, and my dancing was not noticeably worse than the skill of most of my admiring partners.

I marveled, like any newcomer to these shores, at the sudden overwhelming friendliness of Americans. They were determined to make me welcome. And while they might well know more of England than I did myself, their knowledge came from books and plays and holidays. If I had possessed the meanest Cockney accent, they would have thought it charming. And because they had been told my father was a knight, they confused me with royalty and treated me with hearty deference. They left me with the fleeting impression that

I could do no wrong. And in that they were very wrong themselves. Yet every woman deserves one such night, whatever else her life consists of, whatever price she must pay on the following day.

The house still bore the unmistakable signs of a successful party the next afternoon. The scent of half a hundred perfumes lingered along with fugitive cigar smoke. A champagne glass overlooked by the caterers had to be fished out from beneath a chair. There were flowers to be salvaged and flowers to be weeded out of the silver urns. And a rug to be tugged straight, where it had been rolled aslant back over our temporary dance floor.

Ursula had her hands full, creating order again in the kitchen below. And so I was alone and very much myself, performing the duties of a parlormaid in parlors of my own. The front doorbell rang. Without hazarding a glimpse from a front window, I fled up to my room to return myself to the semblance of a leisured lady. I was flying up the stairs and tearing off my apron and the kerchief knotted over my hair as Ursula approached the front door.

Once in my room, I stepped quickly out of my cotton dress and reached for the gown Mrs. Forrest had given me. My hair was intact, to a degree, beneath the kerchief. And I daresay I took more hasty pains to return myself to the pose of a lady than any real lady would. Perhaps just such a lady as I was trying to be had come to pay a call. Perhaps in New York ladies did not merely leave their cards and go away. Rebecca Reed certainly would not. And if it was Rebecca, she was the last person in New York who should see me looking like a servant.

At length, Ursula appeared in my room, just as I was easing into a pair of slippers. "There's a man here to see you, Mrs. Forrest. Says he knows you and says he has something to deliver. I sent him around to the tradesmen's entrance in the back, but I don't know if I should have or not. If he's delivering something, that's the place for him to be, but he wasn't wearing a uniform or nothin' like that."

No, he wouldn't be, I thought. "His name?"

Ursula colored vividly. That was one of the things she was forever forgetting to ask.

I knew by then. I must even have known that he would not give his name, not short of seeing the woman he had come to see.

"Should I—"

"No. Just show him into the front hall. I'll be down in a moment."

In that moment I rushed to the front of the house, where the windows of empty rooms looked down on the street. My throat closed as I saw what stood before our door, already attracting a crowd of small boys. It was a Rolls-Royce limousine, immensely long and high, with all its brightwork mirroring the sunshine. I even saw the outstretched arms of the silver nymph unfurling her nickel drapings above the radiator cap, the symbol of the company. If it had been a hearse sent to bear my dead body away, I could not have felt more lost. I wished it were a hearse, come for me.

I stood at the head of the stairs as long as I dared. Long enough to know that he was standing in the hallway below. I saw the flaxen lights in his hair, alive in the dim light. I fancied I saw his square-toed boots grinding into the carpet, and his heavy arms slung down at his sides. I saw only the breadth of his shoulders beneath the straining serge of the old dark suit he had worn to be married in. He had never been a man for indoor spaces, except for bedrooms veiled by night.

I began to walk down the stairs in a gown now suddenly and ludicrously too fine. I walked blind with fear and empty of any idea. I did not know who I was or what he expected. I knew only who he was. John Thorne. The only man to whom I was legally bound. My husband.

He turned and his eye followed upward, from the tip of my slippered toe up the draped silk of my hobbled skirt. To the sash at my waist. At last to my eyes. I could not turn and run back up the stairs. I wanted the house to be empty of all listening ears, and I wanted it to fill suddenly with rescuers. I could not retreat. I could not think. I was almost on a level with his eyes now. A step or two farther down, and I would be standing in his shadow.

He moved toward me, and I put up a hand, glancing toward the back stairs that led down to the kitchen. It was as imperious a gesture as Miss Amanda's. Perhaps it *was* hers. Perhaps it would convince him if he needed convincing. We stood there like statues until we heard the faint sounds of Ursula among the pots and pans far below.

I nodded to the front drawing room, and he stepped back to let me lead him there. Would he have stepped back for Miranda? I had not quite gone beyond the entrance to the room before his rough hands seized my waist. I whirled on him before he had time to turn me. Hiding fear with outrage, I muttered, "No!" and flung his hands away. We were destined to play out this scene in voices strangely muted. Neither of us wanted a witness.

I told him to sit, which he was loath to do. I took up a position beside the mantel. Above the cold fireplace was an enormous mirror. I hoped its reflected glare would dim me in his eyes. I hoped for some miraculous reprieve.

When he spoke, his voice startled me. I had forgotten the country burr in its sound. It was as if I had never left—his place and his side. It was as if the great change I had worked to make was, after all, only a game that must inevitably end. A charade.

I had forgotten his voice. My ear was attuned now to American speech, and I was trying to speak in this new way to erase my past. And I had forgotten the heavy animal strength in his body, the weather-whipped face, the hands that had . . .

He was like a visitor from another planet in this room. I wished him back there. I wished . . .

"So have you nothing for me, then?" It was a soft growl beneath the burr. Threatening, perhaps, only because I thought so.

"What is it you want?" I tried to read the pale harshness of his eyes, and could see nothing there. Yet he watched me—her—like hunter's prey, new light showing in those unexpressive eyes.

"Well, if there's no prospect of more privacy than what we've got now, a kiss, perhaps."

"I think not." Was he rising to a crouch? Would he spring on me? I knew what he had had from her. And how could Amanda Whitwell, who had been so free of herself before, stand on her dignity now?

He was turning a cap in his hands. I only just then noticed. The same countryman's tweed cap he had always worn when he drove the Lanchester for Sir Timothy. It was banded in leather, stained with his sweat. The cap seemed to speak more eloquently than either of us.

"I've brought the Rolls—Sir T.'s gift to the happy bridal pair."

"I saw it from the window."

" 'Twill show the Yanks a thing or two about what a proper automobile's about."

The words did not match a faintly thoughtful, mournful tone in his voice. He looked down at the cap in his hand, more the servant than I had remembered. Not the sullen renegade that had made him so unpopular in the kitchens of Whitwell Hall. Not the hawkishly handsome brute who had ripped the nightdress from my body on my first night at Whitwell Hall. He was out of his depth now, but not so far out as I.

"Whatever we had planned," I began, "must be considered again. Things that seemed possible when—"

"She was alive," he interrupted. And I remained quiet, not knowing how I had meant to finish. "Things look different nearer to," he said, and he ceased looking at me altogether. He had looked his fill. He stared into the Oriental pattern of the hearth rug at my feet. "You're—content here, then?"

"Yes. More content than I had thought to be."

"And want for nothing more?"

"No. Nothing."

He gripped his cap as if he would turn it inside out. "And yet a long, hard time I've had coming here," he said.

"Not so hard a time as I," I retorted, with the spirit of both Amanda and Miranda combining.

"No," he said. "Two weeks on an old tub from Liverpool for me. But you fared far worse. There in the first days we thought—we feared you were both dead."

"And if Miranda had lived and I had died . . ."

His gaze stopped me. The pale grayness of his eyes seemed smoky. They did not pierce; they seemed only to reflect. "Miranda did live," he said. "Amanda died."

The stillness of the afternoon dropped like a shroud. There was still the chatter of the small boys in the street. Ursula's clatter in the kitchen. Yet the silence deafened me. I fought the faintness I longed to give in to. There was no escape that easy.

"You knew," I said finally.

"I know now. I didn't know before. When Sir T. took me into his study and told me my wife was dead in the sea, I believed him. Had no reason not to. I've taken my betters at their word. You have reason to know that. I've taken them at their word even when their word wasn't as good as Sir T.'s. I've known my place. I'm in this room now on the far side of the world because I've followed the ghost of a dead woman who'd bewitched me into believing I only lived in order to give her what she wanted because she deserved it. But you're that woman now. And you want nothing from me."

"I want more from you than ever she did," I said.

"Yes, but it will not be so easy to grant."

We both pondered that. I should not be able to talk him out of whatever he had decided. I was not one of his betters who might command him and he obey out of habit. He who had always lived in their thrall knew an impostor when he saw one. It would do me no good to turn on him now like a cornered vixen.

"It's easy to see how they think—they think you're her."

"And yet you weren't fooled."

"No," he said, looking away, seeming almost to spare me, seeming not to take notice of my stylish hair, my expensive gown.

"What gives me away? Not that it can still matter."

"There's not the calculation in your eye."

"Oh, but there is. I've done nothing but scheme and plot and lie. I almost dare not open my mouth for fear I'll tell the truth, or that the truth will tell itself."

"Ah, but it's from need. *She* calculated and connived because it was her nature. I don't speak ill of the dead. It was her nature. She was mad, and you're not."

"And yet you mourn her loss," I said, nearly capable of offering him comfort.

"No, lass. I mourn yours."

The stillness descended again. We could not, after all, fill it up, even when silence would no longer serve to protect me. He mourned me, and I stood before him, yearning to live. John Thorne mourned me, and I could not grasp his meaning.

"I am your wife," I said, forcing myself to say it. "You have your rights. And I have gone through the masquerade of marrying another man, whom I love. I had never known real love before, and neither had he, but that is no justification." I could not see John Thorne's eyes, but still I spoke, as if I were a witness for my own prosecution. "I have married him, but it is not legal. You are the only person in my life who knows the truth. You must do with it what you will. If you take from me now what I have, at least I will have the memory of it. I will not even hate you, if I can help it."

He sat slumped in the chair. The strength seemed to drain from him. He looked immensely weary. An animal who had tracked down his quarry and was too winded from the chase to try it to death. No, that was not right. He looked more a man, slumped there, than he had ever looked before.

"You had as much right to marry Forrest as I had to marry you."

"And what do we make of those two wrongs?" I believe even now that I would have agreed to anything he said. I was wearier than he.

"Perhaps we make a pact."

"The last woman you entered into a pact with—"

"Is dead," he said, too loud. We waited to hear the sounds in the kitchen. We were conspirators. Our eyes followed distant noises with the same dread of discovery. We were closer in that moment than ever we had been in the mockery of our marriage bed. We were not hunter and hunted, accuser and accused. We were both lost souls, and if we did not cling to each other, still the barriers between us were down.

"I would claim you if I could," he said, just above a hoarse whisper. "But I claimed you before only to let you be used, and so I won't claim you now."

I stood motionless, not yet able to feel the warmth in this faint ray of hope.

"I took you to bed and loved your body because it was like hers —hers, without the clawing thirst that no man alive could quench. Would you believe me if I told you that in those few weeks we lived as man and wife, I began to think for myself? I began to know you were the better woman, and better for me? But it was too late."

I made myself remember those nights in the cramped bedroom of Smuggler's Cottage. I remembered that silent writhing and the brutality of his thrusting body. Was that the only way of love he knew because he had spent too much of himself on her? Was all that rough rutting really ardor and not merely lust? Had he been wordless not because he did not love but because he did not know the words?

"If you had a—genuine feeling for me, it will not make things easier for us now," I said.

"Ah, the paths you and I have set out on were never meant to be easy, were they?"

I waited. The afternoon light slanted lower in the room. My hus—Gregory would soon be home. But still, John and I must play out our hands. There was no other way.

When I looked up again, he was standing. His cap hung from his hand, but he did not twirl it like some bumpkin underling. "I'll leave you to him. You deserve a fresh start—a real chance at a life for yourself. I'll make no demands on you. You're dead to those who knew us both. My own granny mourns you, but she's mourned many and kept her faith.

"And you'll be to your husband what—*she* couldn't have been. You'll have his child one day, and not mine." His eyes flickered down to my waist, narrow within the cinched sash. He had seen that narrowness in his first glance, as I stood on the stairs.

"You will give me that?"

"I've given you little else, except cause to flee from me. Yes. I give you that."

"But still, we are married."

"No," he said. "I'm a widower, and the few who know me know that."

"You will go back—back to the Isle?"

He looked up in real surprise. "Back to the Isle, to England? What's there for me? What ever was? No, I'll see a bit of this country, where it's said a man can make his own way. I'll go out West and farm or hunt or hire out by the day." I saw the far distances in his eyes. "By the day," he repeated, "not the night."

He was turning to go now, dissolving the last link between us. The fear that had dogged my every moment began to fade. I was left with an emotion that was neither joy nor despair. And I could not let him go without saying what was in my heart.

"Because of today," I said, "I shall never think of you with bitterness. I shall remember you—fondly for the rest of my life."

He stopped, his back to me. His head dipped low. He was not a man capable of tears, I thought. And yet I shall never be quite sure.

I walked behind him to the door. He might not have turned back a last time. He slung his cap on his head. "The Rolls," I said—it loomed at the curb, stretching nearly the width of the house. He reached in his pocket for the keys to it.

"No," I said. "You keep it—take it."

He turned then. The ghost of a smile played at his mouth. His eyes crinkled. Had I ever seen him smile before? "You've come a long way, lass, if you're handing out Rolls-Royces to strange men who come to your door."

I was beyond savoring the only jest John Thorne and I ever shared. "No," he said, "I'll make my way in this new country on feet of my own. It's a hulking great thing anyhow, that Rolls, and not much use on rough roads, I daresay."

He dropped the keys into my hand and walked away. Our fingers never touched, though I would have taken his hand in a final clasp. I watched him stride to the corner and turn up Montague Street. The evening sun was bright on his back. He squared his shoulders as he went. It was a gesture I could understand. He walked in a new posture, in a new land. We had that in common.

I watched him out of sight, and the tears coursed down my cheeks. Tears of joy and loss and redemption, and whatever tears are made of.

Thirty-Two

———◦◦◦———

Number Two,
Montague Terrace
Brooklyn, New York, U.S.A.
November 4, 1913

My dearest Mother and Father,

If my letters have been reticent over the past months, they were only to keep you from worrying and perhaps to give me the pleasure of breaking happy news with some attempt at flair. On the evening of the night before last, you became grandparents.

A little grandson, with all his fingers and toes intact, one who can manage a sleepy smile at his mother. When he is awake, his eyes are revealed to be a startling shade of blue. Gregory believes they will shade to violet in time, to honor his mother, and I rather expect brown for his father. But what his coloring will be remains to be seen. He is bright red just now, and quite bald. And he enjoys the best of appetites.

We have not decided on a name. My friend, Rebecca Reed, suggests "Orchard," because he is a "little Forrest." I only manage to smile wanly at this, and plead temporary weakness. And I rather imagine that Gregory and I will settle on Theodore—Ted. An American Presidential name for the first member of the Whitwell line to be an American by birth.

He entered the world at Long Island College Hospital and rather precipitously. I trust he will continue to be as forthright throughout a long and successful life. Gregory and I were attending a party on Fifth Avenue when our son began to make his appearance felt. And so we drove directly to the hospital, skimming at breakneck speed over the Brooklyn Bridge. I reported to the ward in rather an elaborate dinner gown and what Gregory calls "the ancestral pearls." The effect on the nurses was a bit more sensational than one might wish. And the Rolls outside in the hospital drive was allowed to linger because it was thought to be an ambulance. The drama of our arrival nearly eclipsed the greater drama of our little boy's arrival a very few hours later.

His proud father is now interrupting his busy schedule (which is pronounced skedule on this side of the Atlantic) to call at agencies in search of a nanny. Once she is engaged, I shall begin to think of going home. I rather think a certain Miss MacIntosh—somewhat elderly, highly recommended, and Scottish to the bone—is in the front running for the nanny post. But Gregory is determined to interview every available applicant in New York to make certain that he has discovered the best. Fatherhood in America is taken very seriously indeed, but nowhere more so than in our family. And the conventional view of fathers-to-be pacing up and down in hospital waiting rooms is borne out in fact.

The sunniest room at the front of the house has been done over as the nursery. Gregory has cut a door between it and the hall bedroom beside it for the use of whatever Miss MacIntosh is awarded the position. And so Baby will have quite a proper suite. It is even now being done up in a light-blue enamel, the color scheme having been left until the correct choice between pink and blue could be made.

We are, all three, very happy, as you must know. And we will all be happier still when we are at home. It is a house that has only lacked the ring, or perhaps the wail, of a child's voice to make it quite perfect.

I am sorry, Father, that your health does not permit an ocean voyage, for I would very much like to see you with your grandson on your knee. But Gregory charges me to tell you both that we shall have a trip home to England and to Whitwell Hall as

soon as Baby is old enough to be a good traveler. And in days
and months as full as those to come promise to be, the time will
pass very quickly.

To share this news with you, dear Mother and Father, adds
greatly to the joy I feel today.

Your devoted
Amanda

In the year and a half since I had become Mrs. Gregory Forrest, the
mask of my duplicity had begun to grow almost comfortably into my
face. By a husband's love I was transformed far beyond my desperate
attempts to transform myself.

His world would have been quite as strange to the real Amanda as
it was to me. It was a world of unfurling blueprints that turned up
in every corner of our house. And there was the clean smell of new
lumber and fresh paint about Gregory when he returned from the
newest building site. He was inflamed, and often exhausted, by his
work. And I shared it with him as much as I could. I even ordered
a pair of jodhpurs from Abercrombie and Fitch and a plaid woolen
jacket more fit for the Canadian wilderness so that I could tramp
about the next proposed building site while my husband fashioned
in his mind and mine the new structure he would raise there. Our
hopes together went into the bricks and lintels, into the steel frame-
works that rose against the sky.

I cannot believe the real Amanda would have found much joy in
all that. I cannot believe she would have flourished in the warmth
and the heat of his love as I did. I cannot believe she would have been
content to step aside, as I often had the need to do, and let him get
on with his work. For a man must work. It is the other side of his
love for a woman.

She would not have been amused, though she might have laughed
at him. Nor would she have been reformed, for no power on earth
could have achieved that. And her child would not have been his, as
mine was.

Still, I felt the silent thrusts of guilt. And that guilt was the impulse
behind the letters I wrote with faithful regularity to Lady Eleanor and
Sir Timothy. I composed them laboriously, often with a dictionary
on my knee. I sat through whole days writing and rewriting them,
reaching for scraps of memory to make up into the whole cloth of a

changed and yet plausible daughter's personality. The letters were meant to convey enough of the spirit of that real daughter as I could conjure up.

It was strange and eerie how often I felt the need to dredge Amanda Whitwell up from her watery grave. If she had not been truly dead, if she had walked suddenly into the house on Montague Terrace, my life would have come to an end. It was a nightmare that robbed me of much sleep. Yet, ironically, I often needed to bring her back. A hint of her wit, her languor, her spirit, essentials of herself that I could turn in a direction of my own.

I wanted Lady Eleanor to have a daughter almost as much as I wanted to be Gregory Forrest's true wife. I wanted her to know and to experience the love she deserved. If my letters proved to be more loving than any that her real daughter would have written, surely Lady Eleanor was too happy to have them to wonder.

Yet those letters only deepened my deception. I often found myself writing lies quite apart from the signature. A show of eagerness to return to England for a visit was chief among them. No matter how much they longed to see their grandson, I dreaded the day that they would, and I was prepared to forestall it. For that would mean I would have to play my role on my own native ground. And the audience would not be limited to Lady Eleanor and Sir Timothy. There would be the servants to confront as well.

I dreamed night after night of returning to Whitwell Hall. As in all nightmares, fantasy twisted into a terrible kind of truth. In my dreams I was clad in a magnificent gown. I sat in the dining room of Whitwell Hall on just such an autumn evening as I had first seen it. I sat there more bejeweled than I could possibly be, like a beribboned, bewigged figure in an eighteenth-century watercolor, playing at deception behind a narrow black eye mask.

I sat at that table being served by those with whom I had once served. Great silver salvers appeared at my side, borne first into the room by Hannah, then Hilda, then Mrs. Creeth herself. I dreamed of walking through endless corridors, more mirrored than Whitwell Hall, in a stiff brocaded gown with a farthingale skirt. And in the hallway I would come on Betty in her mobcap busy with a feather duster, brushing the cobwebs from a branching candelabrum. In my dream I moved in silent skirts toward her, though I knew it was forbidden, fatal. And when she turned toward me, where her face had been was only a grinning skull, stained with churchyard earth.

My nightmares ranged through every corner of the Hall and over every acre of the parkland. I was often beside the milky mere, where the madman had lurked. I saw him rise again and again from the white water, death-dealing and dead. I stumbled through the grove, where every branch lashed my face and caught at my dress. I glimpsed again and again the cottage in the clearing where I had been another married woman. And I stood teetering at the tops of all the corridors and flights of stairs that are the true landscape of dreams.

Every nightmare ended in the same way, whatever its other horrors. I was unmasked. The delicate black mask that grew smaller on my face was ripped away, first in the midst of a grand dinner, then on a dance floor crowded with laughing guests. No matter how hard Gregory sought to protect me, to fend off those plucking hands, I was unmasked. It was usually Mr. Finley who saw through me and found it his duty to send me forcibly back to servants' hall. I tumbled down endless flights of stone steps to sprawl on the floor of the kitchens in a welter of ribbons and brocades I had no right to, and all the jewels bedecking me lost their light and died. I lay at the end of every nightmare on the cold stones of the kitchen floor, beneath the feet of the lowliest servants. And when I awoke, the bay of New York was gray with dawn and my pillow was drenched.

But a greater nightmare than any of my own forestalled the inevitable return to Whitwell Hall. I did not have to think of very many excuses to postpone the visit. For the distant thunder of war began to boom beyond the horizon in the early months of 1914.

And in August of that year, when our small son, Teddy, was astonishing us with his ability to pull himself upright, to sway there a moment before sitting down abruptly—in that precious moment the Great War thundered out of the Balkans and erupted over Europe.

At first we in America observed the war at an immense remove. Even England fought far from its shores with an assurance in the outmoded cavalry tradition that had served it in an earlier age. In time, the more modern German military machine began to rumble in every direction, toward France, toward Russia, and a generation of young men began to die.

I followed the progress of that foreign war with its unfamiliar place names in all the newspapers of New York. And because President Wilson had promised to keep us out of war, I used what I read mainly in my letters to Whitwell Hall. It became an excuse, increasingly less feeble, not to travel. After all, England was at war, though Lady Eleanor's letters touched more lightly on it than my own. Abel, the part-time footman, had been called up, she noted once in passing. There were food shortages that the inhabitants of the Isle scarcely noticed in the midst of their burgeoning gardens. Yet the war was reason enough to keep from returning to England. I did not precisely long for the hideous conflict to last. I longed only for the safety it ironically afforded me.

And in May 1915 the irony compounded when America lurched suddenly nearer the war. The occasion was the sinking of the British ocean liner *Lusitania,* torpedoed in Irish waters with a fearful loss of life that brought back my worst memories. And the wartime months mounted into years.

America began to prepare and then to mobilize for the war we were told we would not enter. A militant note entered the mounting patriotism of a people who had never known war in their own time. Young boys hardly five or six years older than our Teddy were entered into the fashionable Knickerbocker Greys, and spent their after-school hours drilling in the Seventh Regiment Armory on Park Avenue with the butts of dummy guns dragging on the floor behind their small forms.

The harbor of New York grew steadily more congested with ships painted a dull gray. I closed the curtains of our long windows commanding this view earlier in the evenings. For the war was casting a longer and longer shadow. I saw it, like so many millions of wives, cast across my husband's face. I saw the set of his jaw as he read the evening papers, following the blurred battlefield maps with a square, ink-stained finger. He was preoccupied now, and proof against most of my attempts to draw him away from that distant threat, to draw him nearer.

My eyes found again and again the sprinkling of gray at his temples, and I longed to think he was past the age for soldiering. But I could not be sure. And to all the uncertainties that had made up my life, I added this menacing new one.

At last, the pledges of neutrality that President Wilson had been able to maintain with Germany collapsed. On the blustery last day of January in 1917 the noose was tightened about England's neck when Germany announced unrestricted submarine warfare in British waters. We were emphatically cut off from England, but the situation was too grim by then for me to find any personal ease in it. In April of that year the President called for a declaration of war, and the Congress voted it into effect. And on the fifth anniversary of our wedding day, my husband was commissioned Captain Gregory Forrest in the Army Engineers.

Like any wife, I felt my world shudder to a halt. At the darkest edges of my imagination I saw him already dead in some foreign trench even before I saw him in his uniform. I cursed the reading I had done, the following of the war in the safe pages of the morning papers. They had taught me too much and fanned my fears. I longed to know less. In reaction, I performed the usual mental gymnastics, balancing the unspeakable possibility of losing Gregory forever against the more present horror of being apart from him at all. I yearned to strike bargains with fate.

I would invade my son's nursery and enfold him in my arms, incurring the disapproval of Miss MacIntosh, upon whose territory I had trod. I held my son close, in fear of giving up his father, and I scanned his face in search of his father's. I feared the responsibilities of raising a son through a war that seemed to stretch endlessly, of raising him alone. And across all this dark void I sought to stretch a smile of false strength.

It was not until early autumn that Gregory was sent overseas. In that long summer I had resigned myself to doing without him as long as he was stationed in the United States. But now, inevitably, he had been summoned to that new way station to Europe, Camp Kilmer, and he would soon be in a zone of war that I could only envision as an outpost in a continual line of fire.

During his last leave, the house could barely contain him. His military boots, polished to glass, stood like sentinels in our room. His Sam Browne belt lay coiled like a snake in a chair I avoided. All the brusque, mystical world of warring men invaded our rooms, so that even in those few days together we were not alone. And when his handsomeness in uniform inflamed my passions, I cursed myself. I cursed the war. And I might even have cursed Gregory if he had not tried to hide his eagerness to be gone.

For yes, that is the way with men. They can come close to weeping like women at parting, but there is something else in them, something invisible to our eyes. They will throw themselves into battle. They are small boys again, brandishing sticks above their heads and hungry for the fray. And when to this is added their need to protect their homes and their way of life, they must be gone, to leave us standing cold with fear in rooms of racking silence.

On the night before Gregory was to go overseas, we stood together in the shadows of the nursery until Teddy had drifted off to sleep with a small lead soldier gripped in his fist. I longed to pull it away from him, but I dared not rouse him. And so I stood very near his father, trying not to cling. In the faint glow of the night light, we gazed down at our son's dark curls against the pillow, the tip of his ear just visible above the tucked-up blanket. What would I not have sacrificed to extend that moment to eternity?

We had a late supper that night, on trays before the living-room hearth. The curtains were drawn against the sound of autumn leaves sweeping across the terrace. And the only light came from the fire that reflected in a copper bowl of chrysanthemums on the low table. A bottle of champagne stood cooling in a silver bucket nearby.

We sat before the fire, and I lay against Gregory, within his encircling arms. The quiet and the nearness should have been enough. Yet I longed to fill the silence with all the words that I wouldn't be able to say in the time to come. An endless vista of crumpled letters, delayed, spaced by distance and the uncertainty of war stretched ahead. But we said little at first. Perhaps we would have said less if it had not been for the noisy ticking of a clock somewhere in the house counting the seconds as time withdrew from us.

I knew then what I must say, must tell on this eve of our leave-taking. I could not let myself think that I might lose him forever, that this was my last chance. But even so, I knew I could not let him go without telling him the truth. Surely it had been all the lies of the world that had brought civilization to this brink. My brave smiles in seeing my husband off to war were falsehood enough. I must clear my conscience of an older deceit, and a greater one.

I lay against him, and his chin rested in my hair. We both sat gazing into the fire; I need not look him in the eye. It should be easier this way. It should be easier to tell him, if it was possible at all.

He sensed that I was about to speak, and his arms moved closer around me. Then I could say nothing. I could only close my hands over his. My—the engagement ring winked in the firelight.

At last he said quietly, "What I—what we have to do now will be a small enough price to pay for five years of the kind of happiness we've had."

I could only nod. I could barely do that. My eyes were brimming, and I would not be a weeping wife.

"These years have been as happy for you as they've been for me?"

"They have been the whole of my life," I said.

"And there'll be many more years, and safer ones after the war."

I nodded at that, too, because I was expected to, not because I could see beyond the great wall of the war. "Gregory, when I say that our time together has been the whole of my life, I mean it very literally. Before we were married, before, in England, I was a stranger to you." *No, no. That wasn't the way to begin. What was?*

"Two people are always strangers before they're married." His hands tightened in a playful squeeze. "Friends rarely marry."

I sighed then, and slipped almost effortlessly down into a great dark place. "But few are ever such strangers to one another as you and I were, Gregory."

The far-off clock seemed to resume its ticking, while the rest of the house appeared willing to impose a safe silence. Gregory waited, and his hands tensed beneath mine. Or perhaps mine grew wooden to keep from gripping his.

"We had scarcely even met before—before I came to America."

And the silence again, while he waited to hear me out. My head pitched forward. My shoulders drew in as I shuddered with every kind of fear. "Oh, Gregory, the young woman you fell in love with died in the sea. I'm not Amanda. I am only her—"

His hands had turned beneath mine, and our fingers were laced together. He drew me back beside him. "You are everything I wanted in her," he said, "and more."

The fire crackled, and a log fell, throwing a fan of sparks against the screen. They flickered there and went white, then black.

"You've known," I said, but he seemed not to hear.

"A young man is capable of falling in love any number of times," he was saying. "Once I fell in love with a beautiful young vixen in a London drawing room who well knew how to make a young man suffer.

"Later I fell in love all over again with a young woman who was lying very battered and very frightened in a hospital bed. Oh, I won't say I saw through her at once."

He loosed his hand from mine and slipped it into a pocket of his coat. "The day I brought you home from the hospital a nurse gave me your possessions, and among them this." He drew out of his pocket a slender gold chain. It gleamed in the firelight, swaying there before my eyes. And from it, gleaming more dully, a worn Indian-head penny.

I wanted to reach for the familiar chain and the Wisewoman's coin. Could they be real when I had relegated them in my thoughts to the bottom of the sea? But I had no need for them now, nor any need to hide them, to hide anything.

"But I loved her from the beginning," Gregory was saying, "that girl in the hospital bed, at first maybe because she needed it. Now I have other reasons. Each day I find new ones."

The tears were streaming down my face, and I hardly knew what they were for. I fell into a sudden mourning for all the time I had spent—had misspent—in playing a role that had failed. Yet the tears were of relief, too, for the role had become real, and in that it was no failure.

"And still you never told me," I managed to say. "How often I searched your face and considered your words, and yet you never told me."

"Should I have?" Gregory asked. "Should I have taken a riding crop to you to beat the truth out of you? It was your story—to tell or to keep. And if the past was painful for you, I wanted you to deal with it in your own way. Finally, I rarely thought of it, though I think I knew all along that this evening would come."

"But, Gregory, there's more. I was not free to marry you. There's more you don't know."

His arms cradled me, more certain than I had ever known them.

"Don't I?" he said. "Are you going to tell me tonight that we have no marriage—that it doesn't exist? With our child asleep upstairs and all the world howling and brandishing swords outside the walls we've raised together, are you going to tell me we aren't married?"

His voice had fallen to a husky whisper. "No, no," I whispered back. "I could not tell you that. It wouldn't be true."

Thirty-Three

―――⤬―――

Precisely three-quarters of a year after the evening that Gregory went off to war, I gave birth to our second child. A fair-skinned, flashing-eyed little daughter whom I named Eleanor. She was born in June 1918, but her father could not learn of her arrival until the letter found him somewhere in France in mid-July. He did not hold her in his arms and swing her high over his head until she was six months old. And it was the most glorious Christmas of our lives, the Christmas after the war.

I had stood at the nursery window the month before, with Teddy, now a sturdy five-year-old, beside me and the new baby in my arms. We stood there at attention like soldiers on that November day when the Armistice was signed. Even our small street was a turmoil of parading people. The flags that suddenly sprouted from the window of every house snapped in the air. And in the bay the fireboats threw plumes of water and sounded their sirens far into a night when everyone either wept or sang, but no one slept.

The world was new-washed with freedom, with peace, with prom-ise. And when my husband came home to me, I could not question the miracle. I could only hold him in wonder at his wholeness, look-ing beyond the lines the war had etched in his face. The boots he marched home in had lost their mirrored finish. I stood again in the window high above the street to watch while Gregory consigned cracked, flaking boots to the trash can, along with the Sam Browne belt and the faded, often-mended greatcoat and uniforms.

In a world that had paid a terrible price, we turned then, the four of us, toward the future.

It was the summer of 1920, and a world entirely altered, before we made the much-postponed trip back to England.

In the depth of the war days, letters to and from Europe had all but stopped going through. This long silence served to slow the pace of our exchange once peace had come. Lady Eleanor's letters still glittered with their former elegance, but there was a faded, forgetful quality in them, too. She was growing older, and as fewer things mattered to her, she hankered more to know the grandchildren she had never seen. After Sir Timothy's death in the first winter of peacetime, there was a new sadness in Lady Eleanor's messages, a plaintiveness that I knew must be answered by a visit as soon as travel was allowed.

I had had too much to dread during the war to fear this final chapter in a life that had not been truly my own. Time had dimmed my fears, as I hoped it had dimmed the eyes of those who had known me as another girl, long ago—long dead. Well before we sailed, I looked toward that journey as one last test of my credibility as the woman who had once been Amanda Whitwell. But before we embarked on the sea voyage, which I dreaded for itself, I was resigned to confessing the truth one final time, to the one person left who deserved my honesty.

We embarked in the early summer from the port of New York on the White Star Liner *Olympic*. She was the sister ship of the *Titanic*, twice armored against icebergs by a double hull and destined to live out a long, dignified, and largely uneventful career on the Atlantic run.

I had not set foot aboard a ship since the long-ago night when I had been carried on a litter from the *Carpathia*. I did so now armored like the ship against both my memories and the reunion that lay at the end of the voyage.

I had forgotten much about shipboard life, and the sudden reminders shook me more than I would show. The abrupt shudder as the great bass siren thundered. The creaking sway of the long corridors that followed toward the bow, dipping in a long valley amidships. The haunting scrape and percussion of the ship's orchestra that played newer tunes behind the potted trees in a Palm Court sadly like its companion at the bottom of the sea.

But the mother of two small, active children has little time to indulge the ghosts of her memories aboard ship. We were a working architect and his family making a once-in-a-lifetime crossing together. Long before we booked our passage, we conducted lively debates about whether to cross in Second Class or First. Whether to include Miss MacIntosh in our party or to deal with the children ourselves. In the end, Gregory's decision prevailed, and we booked a pair of First Class cabins, though they were a long way from being the sort of suite once occupied by Colonel and Mrs. Astor. And Miss MacIntosh was included, mainly to keep the children from overwhelming whatever staff we would find at Whitwell Hall.

We disembarked at Southampton on the fourth day of July. Which was to young Teddy's loud dismay only another summer's day in England and not the festival bright with fireworks that it is in America. We traveled up to London in what must have been the same boat train that Amanda and I had ridden in on the last day I had spent in my native land.

Our party occupied a compartment entirely, while Teddy trod back and forth across our feet, alternately drawn to the English countryside flashing past and bored by it. I could only remember an earlier journey and a compartment filled with the *Titanic* passengers. Of young Mr. and Mrs. Marvin, whose honeymoon voyage was to be the entirety of their married life. Of the sharp-voiced, sharp-eyed Rebecca Reed, who had befriended both Amandas. And if an impersonal railway compartment could haunt me so forcefully, I grew cold at the thought of the house that stood at the end of it.

We lingered in London only long enough to change trains in Waterloo Station. And we were soon off again on the afternoon express to Portsmouth Pier, where the steamer to Ryde awaited. There, across the choppy inlet of the Channel, lay the Isle of Wight, darkened by mist and distance, the island where Mary Cooke had been born.

We transferred from the boat to the little narrow-gauge railway train that still ran out on its rickety pier, seeming to meet the boat halfway. And while Teddy was intrigued by a miniature train suspended dizzily over water and by the trainman's gold-braided cap and frock coat and green flag, both children had reached the outer limits of their energy and their patience with traveling. They went to sleep at once as the train picked its way across the valleys and through the deep cuttings, pausing at one seaside resort after another.

I forced myself to gaze out the windows on that last leg of a long journey. I had forgotten how small, how drawn-in this landscape was. There had been a time when this had been all the world to me. Now it was a constricted place. It had me by the throat. I could not remark on its familiar features: the Frisian cattle grazing the hillsides, the thatched villages tucked under hills like turned furrows, the graveyards like gray stone forests beside the solitary churches.

I would not let my mind drift beyond a certain patchwork of fields and pastures where I thought the village where I had been born must be. There the parents of Mary Cooke might still live their near-wordless, brutal existence. Nor could I look in the other direction, where the Channel continued to reappear beyond the high elevations of the cliff to see if I could catch a glimpse of a lonely cottage like the Wisewoman's.

All this while, Gregory sat beside me, his eyes on me, his hand over mine, offering me in silence his strength. For though he had said nothing, I knew that he meant to support me in whatever course I found to take when I was to be at Whitwell Hall again, as the daughter of the house.

We were met at the Shanklin station by a beardless boy in a chauffeur's cap too large for his cropped head. Though I did not think of it then, he was a member of the generation who had been left to muddle on after the deaths of their older brothers in the war. He seemed to be all the chauffeur now employed at Whitwell Hall. He was a driver from a commercial firm hired only for the homecoming of the daughter. Handing his American travelers into a battered car rather like an oversize taxicab, he smoked an unending chain of cigarettes as he drove, with one hand, out of the town and into the countryside.

I sat facing the rigid figure of Miss MacIntosh, staring past her at the young driver's stringy neck beneath the cap balanced over it. Here was the first ghost laid, for no rugged chauffeur, heavy in country tweeds, steered a family limousine. The relief in this erased bit of the past must have shown in my face, as I could not tear my gaze from the lolling, obviously insolent young driver. I turned at last to find Gregory's eyes on me, knowing that he followed my every thought, all the way back to another time.

It was evening when we passed through the gates and drove up the avenue of black Italian pines. I could dismiss then the frightened young girl who had once trundled up this dark way between her parents in a broken wagon. My eyes and my thoughts swept ahead of us to Whitwell Hall at the end of the drive. Dim lamplight flickered at a pair of upper windows in an otherwise darkened house. Counting up and across, I knew they were the windows of Lady Eleanor's own sitting room.

We stood at last beneath the portico. The knocker was newly polished, but the paint on the great door had cracked and blurred. We made a tableau there in our jumble of luggage, with our two small children staggering in fatigue, clinging on either side of the motionless Miss MacIntosh. "Mac!" Teddy cried. "Are we there now?" And Miss MacIntosh nodded precisely once.

We seemed to wait endlessly for the door to open, though we were expected, anticipated. I thought of flight then, but only as one does who is confronted by the inevitable. I spent the time instead seeing us as we must have appeared. A very foreign family, dressed in a practical but un-English manner. My husband seemed to loom unreasonably large, as American men do in England. My children were not the rigid statuettes that English children are, but then they were American. My thoughts moved in every direction before settling upon myself, for I knew whom I would see—who would see me when the door finally opened. My last thought was a crumb of manufactured confidence. The fashions had changed radically in eight years. The lines of my dark traveling suit composed an unfamiliar silhouette. Skirts that had once failed to clear the ankle were now climbing up near the calf. I had chosen the close-crowned, wide-brimmed three-cornered hat because it obscured my face. And there was a ruff of lace frothing up above my collar to follow the latest style and to give me the look of a mature woman. Time's shifting fancies had offered me such protective coloring as they could. I only regretted briefly the passing of the motoring veil that would have covered me more effectively when at last the door slowly opened.

An elderly man stood there in a familiar coat grown loose on his frame. He was—what had *she* once said? *Quite as gray as an old rat.* It was Mr. Finley—Finley, now past his middle years, past combing false color into his hair in tribute to youth. His eyes had grown watery, imprecise. His movements were slow and rheumatic. A trip from the kitchens to the front door had been a long, perhaps painful odyssey, yet he was not quite broken by time. There was the whisper of old authority in shoulders that would no longer square themselves. And a hint of assurance that must speak of his now being the only man of the house.

"Miss Amanda," he said. "It's Miss Amanda come home to us."

Lady Eleanor used a cane now. The beauty she had always possessed had grown nearly transparent. It continued to echo earlier times: the delicate purity of an eighteenth-century cameo, the sinuous line of an Art Nouveau sculpture. To all these advantages were added now the tracery of age. A vein showed blue and feathery at her temple. The choker of pearls at her neck recalled her Edwardian heyday and concealed such ravages as time had put there since.

I had schooled myself over and over to call her Mother. Yet in that first moment, in the sitting room upstairs that she left only occasionally now, we could only embrace. And I buried the face that might betray me too soon against her shoulder as we held each other very close. I must be for her what she most wanted me to be.

But soon she had put me aside for a first look at the children. They stood suddenly awake and awed to silence at sight of her grandeur. The lady like an illustration from a fairy story stood above them, a study in silver and pale blue, leaning on her silver-mounted cane. She drank them with her eyes and sat down at once to have small Eleanor, her namesake, in her lap and Teddy by her side. Their father and I might have crept away in the twilight then, and we would not have been sorely missed.

It is not true that the elderly live only in their memories. I was braced against Lady Eleanor's, ready to remember convincingly anything that surfaced from the past in her conversation, until the time for truth-telling was right. But she did not often draw either of us back to the days of the other Amanda, nor further back to her recollections of her son, Gordon. The war and time and, above all, my children stood between us and then. She was content to sit long hours in the near-empty house with me at her side. Often the only sound was the clinking of the tea things. I drank from cups I had never used, but their pattern was familiar, for I had washed them in the kitchens often enough.

And so those deep-summer days proceeded, and I grew almost easy there. Even in the bed each night that had once been Amanda Whitwell's. And if her mother had ever known whom Amanda had shared that bed with through stolen nights, she had willed herself to forget. I awoke each morning to a world vivid with birdsong, in the room where once I had brought in an early-morning tea tray, starchily, in my uniform. In the room where I had once found my—where I had once found John Thorne naked beside Amanda Whitwell. Little about that room had changed, though the lavender hangings were paler now. And I had changed enough to sleep peacefully through the brief nights there, with my husband at my side.

The passing days emboldened me. I searched out at the back of a cupboard a sturdy skirt and jacket, now hopelessly out of date, that had been Amanda's. And it became my uniform as I dared explore more and more of the grounds in the early-morning hours before Lady Eleanor was ready for company. I even found a pair of Amanda's watertight brogues and lined them with tissue paper for walks on the soggy lawns.

The house and grounds were shadows of themselves. The war had taken its toll, and the death duties—later—would take the rest. I walked the grounds more freely than I had dreamed possible, for I knew this place would never be mine, that I would not acquire earth and stone in the same way that I had acquired a life—not this earth and stone. When it was left to me, I knew that I would sell it. So I looked at it with the intensity of one who knew she would never see it again.

Where once the gardeners had bordered the lawns with beds of flowers were now the blackened remains of compost heaps. They were relics of the war, when flowers and lawn alike had given way to vegetable gardens. And later, when the postwar world had seemed to eliminate the whole race of gardeners, a sort of natural wilderness had begun to reclaim the manicured perfection of the past. Grass that would never be trimmed back to the quarter-inch now ranged everywhere, healing wounds.

I even walked down that strange byway where the double rows of rhododendron led on to the curious circle of stone beasts that had once stood in their heraldic ring like vast chessmen for the Stonehenge ancients. But now they were mostly toppled and left to lie in bits on the weed-patch green, looking older even than they had been devised to look.

I followed the path through the grove, now nearly grown across. But I only stood at the edge of the clearing where Smuggler's Cottage still stood, settling steadily into the earth. I would not go nearer to the place where that serving girl had once been mocked by false marriage. Nor would anyone have greeted me in the doorless entry, for Granny Thorne was dead. And it was said, by Finley himself, that her grandson had gone off to America and could not be told of her death, for he had seemed to vanish from the face of the earth.

On those November-like days that inevitably appear in the midst of an English July, I explored the odd corners of the Hall itself, though I was slow to mount the narrow steps that led to the attics, and slower still to set foot in the kitchens.

But I was drawn at last over what seemed miles of carpeting in need of patching to the attic where Betty had once lived those few months of her brief life. And in this emptiest, loneliest outpost of the house, I met the past face-to-face.

For the garrets where Betty and I had slept were the least changed. There was little enough to alter. I had difficulty finding just the angled rooftop room that had been Betty's. When I did, I stood in the doorway expecting to see the ghost of her writhing on her narrow bed, stripped now to its rope underpinnings. I was half-resigned to find her sunk again in the sickness that had signaled her fatal pregnancy.

But I was never more thoroughly alone anywhere than I was in the dimness of that small place where no one had entered for many years. Only the skeleton of the bed was still there, and the small deal chest of drawers that had been too ample for Betty's few possessions. The curtain over the one window had rotted from its rings and lay in rags on the floor.

I meant to turn from this bleak desolation in the first moment. But something led me to the battered chest of drawers. The mirror above it was too milky to do more than record my shadow as I opened a drawer with hands oddly eager.

It seemed to be empty, but my hand discovered a bit of cardboard, and I drew it out and held it up to what light there was. It was a photograph, its gray image turned to yellow. I could make out two figures whose faces would almost have touched had it not been for their absurd top-heavy hats. Two servant girls grouped together on a narrow bench to fit their images into the lens of a village photographer. They might have been any two nameless drudges celebrating a half day off amid the meager delights of a seaside town. A look of bright, bleak eagerness played about their faces. Who they had been would be a mystery to the next stranger to find their photograph. But they were no strangers to me. For that distant day returned to me, the day when Betty and I had set off on our half day in pursuit of an afternoon of freedom for ourselves and a chance at Mr. Sampson for her.

I searched for more in those merging faces, but they seemed to fade as I scanned them, consigning themselves to the past. And it was in those moments before I returned the photographs to the drawer that I shed my only tears in memory of what was past. I stood there humbled by the life I had been able to have and for the life Betty had lost.

Whether Lady Eleanor was able to come downstairs to dine or not, dinner was laid in the fine dining room for Gregory and me each evening. I sat in a serviceable, spare dinner gown, cut along the most modern lines, with my husband in the same room where I had first caught a glimpse of him.

We were served by Finley, who maintained the averted eyes of an earlier era as he went about his duties. My hand trembled on the first night when he appeared at my side with a silver dish from which I was to serve myself. But Gregory's expression at the far end of the table gave me to know that Finley would see no more than it was his place to see, and that he would perceive only the young lady he had served when she was a headstrong girl. I was not to be unmasked by Finley, despite my nightmares.

And this led at length to my doing what Amanda Whitwell would never have thought to do, nor would she have had reason to. I paid a visit to the kitchens. I could not stay away, though I put off going. I was haunted both by the past and by the emptiness of the upper house, which was clearly served by a smaller staff of servants than once it had. I must know who was there, belowstairs, and who was not, and I must see them with my own eyes. Though I prayed they would see nothing in mine.

I was determined to go, but how slowly I walked down those stone steps in the narrow passageway where the odors of cooking clung as they always had.

Perhaps I expected to find what I had found in the first evening of my service at Whitwell Hall. I would not have been greatly surprised to find Mrs. Buckle and Mrs. Creeth locked in their eternal conflict. But the kitchens were a quieter place now. Mr. Finley, it seemed, spent more and more of his time in his small office off servants' hall. He rested there, though he pretended otherwise, between duties.

I found the kitchen in the charge of two vast, matronly figures. They were dressed in identical decent black beneath their aprons, and their cuffs were turned back over enormous arms.

It took a moment while I stood there undiscovered before I saw that they were Hilda and Hannah. They had not grown old, of course, but they were strangely subdued, and invested with a fugitive sort of dignity.

At last one sensed me there and whirled around with a little shriek. "Oh," she gasped, "'tis Miss Amanda—Mrs. Forrest as I should say!" She dropped a curtsy then, which nearly broke my composure.

The other turned and dropped a curtsy, too, though which was Hilda and which was Hannah I could not tell or remember, which would have been very like the Miss Amanda of old.

They were not tongue-tied long, and flattered by a visit from the young lady of the house. Their eyes devoured my clothes, and they saw, as people will, what they expected to see. Soon they were talking servants' and village gossip to me, interrupting one another continually. Very little of it meant much to me. Though they had never left their posts, the past was remote to them, too, or seemed so at first.

In dribs and drabs, though, the occasional familiar name emerged. Mrs. Creeth had been "done in" by the rigors of a wartime household and had been pensioned off to a cottage in Nettlecombe "that had a lovely bit of garden but the walls streamed with damp and the drains smelt something chronic!" She lived just a turning away from her old enemy, Mrs. Buckle, but the pair of them had made it up in their dotage and were now great comforts to each other.

It emerged more slowly that Abel, the footman, had been killed at Mons, and I could not ask more about him. For I could not remember or distinguish which of them had loved him. The sober black uniforms that they both wore might have signified that now they mourned him equally.

I turned to go then, but I was not to be let off without admiring the kitchens. And in truth they were spotless and hung with copper pans that glowed like suns with Brasso and the grease from their ample elbows. They had left off the skittish ways of their youth and had settled to lifetimes of sober work, pulling together in the same harness. And if one was maiden still and the other a widow, it little mattered to them now.

When I bade them good-bye feeling less an impostor before them than I had felt anywhere else, perhaps it was Hilda who said, "Oh, Miss, it was ever such a turrible thing about poor Miranda. We were that knocked about by it! The sea takin' her and all. Why, it seems no longer than yesterday when we got the word and couldn't hardly credit it. I says at the time to Mr. Finley, screwin' up my courage, like, 'Why, Mr. Finley,' I says, 'it might have been any of us swallowed up like that by the sea, and very cruel it is, too!'

"But you know Mr. Finley, Miss." She dropped her voice and glanced in the direction of his office, where we could hear the steady deep breathing of his sleep. "He says we was in no such danger whatever, as nobody would have picked us out as lady's maids, and it was no more than divine proof that we should know our place and stick to it, which of course we've done. Still, it give us the shivers, Miranda's passing did.

"And Lady Eleanor, she put up ever such a lovely tablet on the church wall, all devoted to Miranda's memory. Wonderful bit of carving it is, too. You ought really to see it, Miss."

It was perhaps the only thing either of them might be capable of saying that would have shaken me. But one of them was intent on the jewelry on my hands, and the other seemed to be calculating the probable cost of my silk stockings. And so they noticed nothing else. "No," I said, "I don't think I should be able to look at the plaque in the church. It would only sadden me."

They nodded knowingly and dabbed the ends of their aprons at the tears that came easily to their eyes. "She's happy now, I daresay," one of them sighed, "Miranda is."

And I could only nod, agreeing to that, and make my escape. But not before they both dropped final curtsies.

In the last week of our visit Lady Eleanor and I were sitting out in the bentwood chairs on the terrace. As the time for parting drew on, she pushed herself beyond her limits to savor our company and to make each fleeting day count against the empty ones to come. We were on the terrace beyond the long morning-room windows so that she could watch the children playing on the lawn. Teddy had uncovered the remnants of a croquet set in the potting shed and had set it up in a random pattern on the grass for the pleasure of bossing his small sister through the game.

I sat there drinking in the pale sun, and Lady Eleanor sat beside me, protected from its rays by an old-fashioned hat with a brim of stiffened chiffon. Her white hands, spotted with age, gripped the arms of her chair again and again as her spirit seemed to struggle out of her body to join the children at their play. While her thoughts seemed far away, perhaps seeing another brother and sister of an earlier time, her eyes never left the two before us.

This was the time. I could not put it off longer. I could not leave my confession to the hurried agony of the final leave-taking. I must tell her the truth, and whether or not she knew it already was not the issue. I must tear away the last veil of deceit so that I would not run the risk of seeming a liar in her eyes, if she knew. And if there was no perfect time for such a task, there would be no better time than now.

I had planned—rehearsed—nothing, and so there was no proper way to begin. I was not even assured of gaining her attention. I dared not begin such a confession by calling her Mother. Yet "Lady Eleanor" was too abrupt; it plunged us both too quickly into the truth. I could not begin at all, and yet I must.

"There is something I must tell you before we leave."

She seemed not to hear me, though her hand twitched in slight impatience.

"I cannot go away without—"

"Oh, just look at little Eleanor!" she cut in. "Just see how she has managed to get a ball right through one of the hoops and is fairly crowing with glee!"

I could not quite give up. I must try once more. "You must hear me out," I said to Lady Eleanor gently. "You must—"

"Hush," she said, and her hand reached across to grip mine. "Hush, my dearest Amanda, for don't you see? I am quite intent upon my grandchildren."